LUCK OF THE DRAW

Creed couldn't stand it any longer. He slid his chair away from the table, put his hand on the butt of his Colt's, and said, "You cheated, McGrath."

"What did you say?" demanded McGrath, also sliding away from the table.

"You cheated," said Creed. "I saw you deal that last card from the bottom of the deck . . ."

McGrath acted as if he was going to pull his gun.

Creed did pull his and would have killed McGrath if not for Ritter slapping him with a backhand, spoiling his aim. The ball nicked McGrath's left earlobe, and the flame from the revolver's blast singed his beard.

Ritter struck Creed again, shouting, "Hold on there!" He grabbed at Creed's gun hand, seized it, and forced Creed to aim at the deck. "I have the winning hand," said Ritter. "See for yourself." Four sevens stared hard at Creed.

"I'm going to kill that son of a bitch!" whined McGrath. . . .

Berkley Books by Bryce Harte

The CREED series

CREED
WANTED
POWDER KEG
CREED'S WAR

CREED

CREED'S WAR

BRYCE HARTE

BERKLEY BOOKS, NEW YORK

To my distant cousins,
Dr. Ray Howard Houchin and Ed Moody,
and all the other descendants of those first Houchins
to settle in Virginia in the early seventeenth century

CREED'S WAR

A Berkley Book / published by arrangement with
the author

PRINTING HISTORY
Berkley edition / November 1991

ISBN: 0-425-13030-4

A BERKLEY BOOK © TM 757,375
Berkley Books are published by The Berkley Publishing Group,
200 Madison Avenue, New York, New York 10016.
The name "BERKLEY" and the "B" logo are trademarks
belonging to Berkley Publishing Corporation.

PRINTED IN THE UNITED STATES OF AMERICA

10 9 8 7 6 5 4 3 2 1

REAL HISTORY

Every ship and riverboat mentioned herein was afloat at the time of this story, and as in all of Slate Creed's adventures, every geographical detail is as exact as can be determined down to the twists and turns in Mammoth Cave.

New Orleans is still a marvelous city, and its history is filled with characters more colorful than most novelists could ever imagine. Charlotte Beaujeu is a composite of several ladies whose social life would be considered questionable in a different age. Percy McGrath was typical of gamblers of the day.

John Murrell and his personal servant Lije did haunt the Natchez Trace for years, but nothing is known about their last days. Also, the other bandits and killers of the Trace are historical figures.

Arlington Scott Houchin was one of the author's great-grandfathers, and all of the Houchins and their history depicted herein is as true as the author can make it.

As an aside to the Houchin history, the author relates how he wrote this story of Slate Creed and Scott Houchin and his Thoroughbred colt Pride, then afterward, while doing some research on his family genealogy, discovered the following sentence in the actual will of William Davis Houchin:

"I further will & desire that . . . my son Arlington S. Houchin have what is called Caney Valley . . . which I estimate at $225.00 & that *he shall have the 2 colts that he has raised as his own property* & his oxen which he paid his own money for."

Special Thanks

The author wishes to express special thanks to
George W. Armstrong, Chris Foster,
and Kathy Wesley of Natchez, Mississippi;
and Betty Peger, Ricky Carroll, and Dorothy Brooks
of Brownsville, Kentucky, for their invaluable contributions
to the historical research for this book.

PROLOGUE

When morning came, Creed rose early, ate in the hotel dining room, then rode over to Dr. January's to fetch Bill Simons. When he arrived, he was surprised to see the horses of Jake Flewellyn and the Reeves brothers tied up in front. He met the men on the porch as they came out of the house with Simons, who wasn't moving too fast.

"What the hell are you doing back here?" asked Creed a bit testily. "I thought I told you boys to go home."

"We did," said Jake. "Just like you said. And we delivered your letter to Miss Texada, too. She read it, then sent us back here to give you her answer." Jake reached inside his coat, pulled out a folded piece of paper, and offered it to Creed.

"Her answer?" queried Creed. He took the letter, opened it, and read:

My dearest darling Clete,

I hope this letter finds you well and hardy. I am fine, but Granny is not well. She grows weaker every day. I pray she lives to see Christmas and the New Year. She asks about you all the time, and I do not know what to tell her except that you are well and that you are about the business of clearing your good name. This makes her happy, and every time I tell her she says she has a great surprise for you once you have cleared your name. I do not know what she means by that, but I fear it is only the chattering of an old woman.

I have read your letter, and I miss you, too. And I love you, too. I wish you could come to me right this minute and hold me in your arms, but I know this cannot be until you have cleared your name.

Jake has told me that they tried to catch Jim Kindred

1

before he could get back to Hallettsville but that they failed to catch him. He rode into town this morning and went straight to Markham and told him that he knows that you are in Victoria. Markham has been ordered to take some of his men to Victoria to relieve the Yankee colonel there. He is preparing to leave this very minute, and I expect him to do so within the hour. That is why I am asking Jake to take this letter to you immediately— to warn you about Markham.

I want to see you so much, Clete darling, and I want you to hold me in your arms and love me the way you do. But I know this cannot be yet because of the danger you are in with Markham and the Army. As much as I loathe writing this next part, I must tell you to stay away from here and from me until you can come home without worry of being punished for the crime you did not commit. The Army has placed a bounty on you, and the Detchen brothers have been bragging that they intend to collect it if you ever come back here because the Army does not care whether you are captured dead or alive. If anything should happen to you on my account, my darling, I would never be able to live with myself or in this world without you.

So as much as I love you and miss you, I must ask you not to come home again until you are a free man. I will be all right, and I promise you I will remain faithful to you until that wonderful, glorious, beautiful day comes. Until then, my darling, I am

Your ever loving,
Texada

Creed folded the letter again, put it in his coat pocket, and looked at his four friends through misty eyes. "Well, boys, I suppose we better be riding out of here before Markham shows up," he said.

"Where to, Creed?" asked Flewellyn.

"That's a good question, Jake," said Creed. "A very good question."

1

Creed stood at the rail of the steamer *Crescent City*, which was berthed at the end of the long pier at Indianola. He looked out over Matagorda Bay. The water was peaceful, pleasing to the eye. Sea gulls floated over the harbor on a light breeze. Creed heaved a sigh and let his head droop for a second before he turned to scan the port city. Within the hour, the ship was scheduled to set out for New Orleans, and he was wondering if he was doing the right thing in leaving Texas at this time.

Three days earlier Creed had been in Victoria, saying farewell to his friends Jake Flewellyn, Bill Simons, and Kent and Clark Reeves. "I'll ride down to Indianola," said Creed, "and take passage on a steamer for New Orleans. Then I'll take a riverboat up to Memphis. Blackburn said he wanted to make one more raid into Tennessee before coming home. He and the others sparked some girls up around Nashville when we were posted in that area during the war, and he said he wanted to visit them once more before settling down."

"I recollect some of them girls," said Flewellyn. "Real friendly types, they were." He squinted at Creed, smiled, and said, "Seems to me you was shining up to some gal up near Bowling Green when we was posted there in '61."

Creed looked a little sheepish and said, "Yeah, I guess I was." A vision of the girl came to mind, and he felt warm inside. "Mattie Whittaker," he said. "She had the greenest eyes. You know, if it hadn't been for a streak of luck at a roulette table in New Orleans, I think I might have gone back up to Tennessee with Blackburn and the others."

"But you didn't," said Simons. "You came home like the rest of us."

"No, I didn't go north with Blackburn and the others," said Creed with a shrug. "Not then, but I'm going north now."

3

"You shouldn't be going alone, Creed," said Flewellyn.

"You boys shouldn't be riding with me," said Creed. "As long as I'm wanted by the Army, I'm just trouble for you boys."

"No, you ain't," said Clark Reeves. "Ain't that right, Kent?"

"Yeah, that's right," said Kent Reeves. "We should ride with you to keep you out of trouble."

Creed laughed and said, "But I'm not riding all that far. I'm going to catch a ship out of Indianola for New Orleans and then take a boat up to Memphis."

"Well, we can ride with you as far as Indianola," said Clark. "Can't we, Kent?"

"That's right," said Kent. "We can ride as far as Indianola with you."

"All right," said Creed, "you two can ride that far with me, but not Jake and Bill. You two go straight back to the ranch and take that letter to Texada for me."

"You can count on it," said Flewellyn.

"I told her where I was going and where she could write me if she had a mind to write. I'll be writing to her through you, Jake. I'll send the mail to the Oakland post office. You be sure to check up there for a letter every week or so, you hear?"

"Sure, Creed," said Flewellyn. He looked around for a second, then back at Creed. "You'd best be going now. Markham and that column of Yankees ought to be coming down the road any time now."

"Yeah, I guess I'd best be going," said Creed. He nodded at Simons. "Bill . . ."

"Go on now," said Simons. "Find Blackburn and them others and make them tell the truth, then get your tail back here where it belongs."

"I'll do 'er," said Creed in his best down-home voice. He looked to Flewellyn. "Jake . . ."

"Just git, boy," said Flewellyn.

"Right," said Creed.

He and the Reeves brothers rode to Indianola that day, reaching the port town at dusk. It was too late to book passage on the steamer leaving the next day for New Orleans, so Creed had to settle for taking the *Crescent City* two days later. Clark and Kent stayed over in Indianola to see him off that morning. They helped him get his horse aboard the ship and placed in a stall in the hold, then they returned to the dock to say their good-byes.

When that was done, the Reeves brothers rode off for home, and Creed went aboard to wait for the *Crescent City* to sail.

"Hey, mister!" said a small boy coming toward Creed.

Creed twisted his head to see the towheaded youngster. He guessed from the size of the lad that he was only seven or eight years old, but there was something in the boy's eyes that said he was a lot more mature than his real age.

"You want me, son?" asked Creed.

"Yes, sir," said the boy. "Is that your horse in the hold? The gray one?"

"Yes, that's my horse," said Creed, suddenly worried that something might be wrong with Nimbus.

"I thought so. I saw you loading him with two other men a while ago. He sure is a beauty, mister. What's his name?"

"Nimbus."

"Nimbus? What kind of name is that?"

Creed chuckled, looked up at the sky, and said, "You see that cloud up there, the one with the gray bottom on it?" He pointed with the index finger of his left hand.

"Yes, sir."

"Do you see how the white part sort of looks like a crown or a halo on the gray part?"

"Yes, sir."

"That's called a nimbus," said Creed. "My granddaddy once said that ghosts appear out of clouds that are something like that, and I thought that was pretty scary until the day my Nimbus was born."

"How's that?" asked the boy.

"Well, the day he was born it was cold and drizzly and there was fog everywhere. We knew his mama was about to foal, but she was out in the pasture, and we couldn't find her in the fog. We heard her whinny real hard, and we knew she must be giving birth about then. Then she was quiet, and we lost track of her again. My little brother saw her standing in a hollow. There was fog all around her, but it was low to the ground. As we got close to her, we heard something in the grass. We stopped and listened, and in a few seconds, there he was. Her colt. He popped up out of that fog just like my granddaddy said a ghost comes out of a nimbus, and that's why I named him Nimbus."

"That's a keen story, mister."

"What's your name, son?" asked Creed.

"Charles, sir, but I like to be called Charlie. My mother doesn't like it. She calls me Charles, but my friends call me Charlie. You can call me Charlie, if you like."

Creed held out a friendly hand and said, "Glad to know you, Charlie. My name is Creed, Slate Creed."

Charlie shook Creed's hand and said, "Glad to meet you, Mr. Creed. Are you just going to New Orleans? Or are you going on from there like we are?"

"I'm headed for Tennessee."

"We're going to Michigan, I think. Wherever that is."

"Michigan, huh?"

"Yes, sir. My mother just married a Yankee named Mr. Carrier, and he says he's got a farm up in Michigan, and we're going to live there."

"Michigan is a long way away," said Creed.

"That's what my mother said," said Charlie dejectedly. He looked down the pier, squinted, and said, "Say, Mr. Creed. Ain't those the two men who helped you load your horse on board?"

Creed stared down the dock and saw the Reeves brothers running his way. Now what? he wondered.

Before he could consider any possibilities, the *Crescent City*'s whistle blew, announcing its departure. The longshoremen on the dock cast off the lines, and the deck crew began pulling the heavy hawsers aboard the ship. Black smoke billowed from the steamer's single stack, and the whistle whined again.

"Creed! Creed!" the Reeves brothers were yelling as they waved their arms to get his attention.

Thinking they were close enough to hear him, Creed cupped his hands around his mouth and replied, "What is it?"

The brothers reached the end of the pier. "It's Kindred!" yelled Clark.

"And the Detchens!" yelled Kent.

Kindred? The Detchens? wondered Creed. Where? He looked up the pier and saw the trio coming toward him on horseback. They were armed. Damn!

The ship drifted away from the pier. Its mighty side wheels groaned into motion. Water began to foam up on each side of the ship.

Creed watched the Detchens and Kindred ride up to the Reeves brothers, who turned to face them. He saw the riders' mouths move but couldn't hear what they were saying; their faces were angry. Clark and Kent answered them with shrugs of innocence. One of the Detchens pointed a shotgun at the Reeveses. Kent and Clark raised their hands to show that they were unarmed. The other Detchen looked at the ship and saw Creed. He pointed, and his twin and Kindred shifted their view in Creed's direction. Kindred shook his fist at Creed and shouted something that Creed couldn't hear. The Detchens turned on the Reeves brothers and shot them both. Clark and Kent stumbled backward and collapsed on the dock.

Hearing the shots on the pier, the longshoremen took cover, and the passengers aboard the *Crescent City* shrieked in horror.

"No!" screamed Creed. "You bastards!" He reached for his Colt's, but it wasn't there. It was in his cabin. He ran to get it.

Kindred raised his rifle and fired at Creed. The bullet struck the side of the ship just above the water. He took aim again, but Creed disappeared through a passageway.

The other passengers now took cover wherever they could.

Creed rushed inside his cabin, saw his Henry rifle, grabbed it, and checked to see if it was loaded. It was. He headed back on deck.

The *Crescent City* was well out into the harbor. The pier was fading rapidly behind.

Creed spotted Kindred and the Detchens on the dock. He noticed that they were wearing badges. Lawmen? he wondered. How could this be? It made no difference. He took aim at one of them and fired. A Detchen toppled from his saddle. He fired again but only hit a pile in front of the other Detchen, who had jumped down to tend to his brother. Another shot, but it fell short of Kindred, who had taken cover behind the pile in front of him. Two more shots were just as ineffective. He decided it was senseless to shoot anymore. He dropped to one knee and wept.

2

Little Charlie was the first person to approach Creed after the shooting. He edged up to him and put a comforting hand on Creed's shoulder.

Creed looked at the boy through moist eyes and saw sympathy. He felt better, at least assured that he wasn't suffering alone. The love in little Charlie's eyes made his own tears burn less as they ran down his cheeks. He put aside his rifle, grabbed the youngster, and hugged him because he needed to touch another human being.

"They were my friends, Charlie," cried Creed softly. "They were my friends, and those bastards shot them down in cold blood. They murdered them, Charlie."

"Charles! Charles!" shrieked a woman. "Come away from there, Charles!"

Creed heard the shrill cry and assumed the woman was Charlie's mother. He let the boy go and looked up at the lady, half-hoping she would be as sympathetic as her son.

She wasn't. Her haggard face was framed in a Sunday best bonnet. Her blue eyes were filled with fear, anger, and hatred. She reached out a rough, reddened hand, grabbed Charlie's arm, and pulled him away from Creed.

Creed heard footsteps behind him. They belonged to more than one man, but he didn't care. He was still hurting inside.

"Just stay where you are, mister," said a hard, husky male voice behind Creed. The beat of a belaying pin being slapped on an open hand emphasized the command.

Creed obeyed, and out of the corner of his eye, he saw a meaty hand grab hold of the barrel of his Henry and take it away.

"All right now," said the man behind him. "On your feet."

Creed stood up slowly, turned, and faced three men. The largest of them was the ship's first officer. The other two were deckhands. All three had belaying pins and were holding them in a threatening manner. Creed didn't like their attitude, but he was smart enough to know that he would be quite unwise to do anything to antagonize them.

"The captain will want to see you, mister," said the first officer. He stepped aside and pointed toward the ladder that led to the bridge. "This way." He stepped off briskly.

Creed started walking but at a slower pace. This didn't suit the deck apes. They nudged him in the back with their clubs. Creed picked up the pace and followed the officer to the bridge.

Captain Zipprian was an old sea dog who had only recently returned to the Gulf Coast after spending the war in the North Atlantic trade. He had made the run over the bar and through Paso Cavallo on dozens of occasions, but he knew his success was due to his careful attention to piloting his craft through the treacherous channel, which he was doing when Creed was brought before him. The first officer knew not to disturb Zipprian until the ship was on the open sea, so they waited.

Once the *Crescent City* was clear of the pass, Zipprian looked at Creed as if he'd only just then arrived on the bridge. He took Creed's rifle from the first officer and examined it, sniffing the barrel to verify that it had been fired recently. He nodded as if satisfied, then began the interview.

"What is your name, son?" asked the captain.

"Slate Creed, sir."

"Well, Mr. Creed, I understand you fired this weapon on my ship." He held up the Henry. "Is this true?"

"Yes, sir, it is," said Creed, looking Zipprian straight in the eye.

"Mr. Parrish says you were firing at some lawmen on the dock. Is that true?"

"I don't know that they were lawmen," said Creed.

"Mr. Parrish, didn't you say they had badges?" asked Zipprian.

"Yes, sir," said the first officer. "I saw them through the glass, Captain. They were lawmen all right."

"What do you have to say now, Mr. Creed?" asked the captain.

"Captain, the men I was shooting at are old enemies of mine. They killed my brother and my best friend this past summer, and I just saw them shoot down two of my best friends in cold blood."

"Mr. Parrish?"

"There were two men lying on the dock before I saw Mr. Creed shoot at the lawmen, Captain," said Parrish. "They could have been dead, but I can't say for certain, sir."

"They were unarmed," said Creed, "and the Detchens murdered them in cold blood."

"The Detchens?" queried Zipprian.

"Two of the bastards who just murdered my two friends on the dock," said Creed. "The other one was Jim Kindred, a no-account who was wanted by the law the last time I saw him down in Mexico."

"That may be so, Mr. Creed," said Zipprian, "but as far as I know, the men you were shooting at were lawmen, and that is against the law where I come from."

"Captain, he shot one of them," said Parrish.

Zipprian's bushy white eyebrows rolled up his forehead at this news. "Shot one, you say?"

"Yes, sir."

"This puts things in a different light, Mr. Creed. I was intending to let you have the run of the ship until we reached New Orleans, at which time I intended to consult the authorities there to see if there might be a warrant for you. However, I can't do that now. Not since you've shot a man. A lawman at that. No, sir. Now I must place you in confinement until we reach New Orleans, at which time I will advise the authorities there of what has transpired this day and turn you over to them. Mr. Parrish, take the prisoner away and put him in the ship's brig."

"Captain, they murdered my two friends in cold blood," said Creed angrily. "What did you expect me to do? What would you have done in my place?"

Zipprian was impressed by Creed's argument. "Good point, Mr. Creed. Did anyone else aboard ship see them shoot your friends on the dock?"

"I don't know," said Creed, wracking his memory. "I was talking to a small boy when everything started."

"A boy?"

"Yes. His name is Charlie."

"I know the lad, sir," said Parrish.

"Bring him to me, Mr. Parrish," said Zipprian. "After you've put Mr. Creed in the brig."

3

Little Charlie was scared out of his white canvas trousers when Mr. Parrish ordered him and his parents to the bridge to be interrogated by Captain Zipprian. He hadn't understood everything that Parrish had said to his mother and stepfather, but it had sounded like trouble for sure.

Once they reached the bridge, Parrish introduced them to Zipprian, who tried to appear affable yet authoritative.

"Is me little Charles in some sort of trouble?" asked Mrs. Carrier in her Irish brogue.

"No, ma'am," said Zipprian, smiling to assure her that her son hadn't done anything wrong.

"It's about the shooting, isn't it?" she queried.

"Yes, ma'am, it is," said the captain. "Mr. Creed says your boy was with him when it started. Is that so?"

"Mr. Creed? Is that the man who did the shooting of the fellows on the pier?" she asked.

"Yes, ma'am," said Zipprian, noting that she said "fellows" instead of employing the singular as Creed had.

"Well, I don't know that Charles was with him at the time of the shooting," said Mrs. Carrier. "Were you with the man, Charles, when the shooting started?"

"They started it," said Charlie.

His mother slapped him upside the head and said, "Answer me question, Charles. Were you with him when the shooting started?"

"Mrs. Carrier, there's no need to punish the lad," said Zipprian sternly. He sympathized with the boy.

"He's my son, and I'll be doing with him as I please, if you don't mind, Captain Zipprian."

Zipprian glared at her, then said, "Perhaps I should question the boy directly."

11

"Yeah, let him do it, dear," said Mr. Carrier. "He's the captain of the ship, and he's the law here."

"The law?" queried Mrs. Carrier. Suddenly, she had more respect for the captain.

"Yes, ma'am, that's right," said Zipprian. "Now if you don't mind, I'd like to ask the boy a few questions."

"All right, if you have to," said Mrs. Carrier. She grabbed Charlie by an ear and said, "And you better answer him with the truth, Charles."

"Sure, Ma," said Charlie, pulling himself free of her.

"All right now, Charles," said Zipprian.

"Charlie. My name is Charlie," he said defiantly. "Only my mother calls me Charles."

"Spirited lad, aren't you, Charlie?" said Zipprian with a grin that said he liked the boy's spunk. "That's good. Now, Charlie, tell me what happened when the shooting started."

"Before or after the men on the dock shot Mr. Creed's friends?" asked Charlie.

"From the start," said the captain. "Wherever you want. Just tell me what happened."

"All right, I'll do 'er," said Charlie. "I was talking to Mr. Creed about his horse when his two friends came back down the pier yelling at him about something."

"What were they yelling?" asked Zipprian.

"His name, I guess. The ship started moving about then, and there was too much noise to hear everything clear."

"All right, I can understand that," said Zipprian. "So what about his friends on the pier?"

"They were yelling something about some other men. I didn't catch their names, but Mr. Creed was real upset about them, whoever they were. Then those men on horseback came riding down the pier. Mr. Creed's friends started talking to them, then one of them saw Mr. Creed on the ship. The other two looked at him, then two of them turned on Mr. Creed's friends and shot them dead right there on the pier."

"Are you sure about that, Charlie?" asked Zipprian.

"I saw them do it, Captain. Mr. Creed's friends even had their hands up when they were shot."

Zipprian stroked his whisker-free chin with a thumb and

forefinger, then said, "What happened next, Charlie?"

"That's when one of them shot at Mr. Creed, and he ran to get his gun."

"One of them shot at him first?" asked Zipprian.

"Yes, sir. Then he got his gun and shot back at them. Got one of them, too." Charlie was proud of this last fact. "I hope he killed the bastard, too."

"Charles!" gasped his mother just before she slapped his face. "I won't have you talking like that."

Charlie rubbed his cheek and glared at his mother. He didn't like being slapped, but she was his mother and he guessed that gave her the right.

"Mrs. Carrier," said Zipprian, "did you see any of what happened on deck?"

"No, sir, not until Mr. Creed was shooting at them lawmen on the pier."

Zipprian nodded, then asked Mr. Carrier the same question.

"I didn't see anything either, Captain," said Mr. Carrier.

"Well, thank you, folks," said Zipprian. "That will be all for now."

"What have you done with Mr. Creed?" asked Charlie.

"We're holding him in the brig for now," said Zipprian.

"Brig? What's that?" asked Charlie.

"That's the ship's jail, son," said the captain.

"Jail?" queried Charlie. "What for? He didn't do nothing except shoot one of those bastards who killed his friends."

Mrs. Carrier slapped him again and said, "Charles, I told you to watch that mouth of yours. Now I'm telling you to mind your own business. If the captain wants to put Mr. Creed in his jail, that's his right. He's the law on this ship."

Zipprian felt sorry for the boy and said, "Don't worry about Mr. Creed, Charlie. If everything you've just told me is true, we'll let him out of the brig soon. Now you and your folks can go. Thank you, Charlie."

The Carriers left the bridge, and as soon as they had, the captain said, "Mr. Parrish, I want you to speak with every man who was on deck at the time of the shooting and ask him what he can remember about the incident, then report back to me as soon as possible."

"Does that include the passengers, Captain?" asked Parrish.

"I'll talk to them myself," said Zipprian.

"Yes, sir," said Parrish. "Do you think the boy was telling the truth?"

"What reason would he have to lie?" asked Zipprian. It wouldn't be the last time that he would ask this same question about the same boy.

4

Neither Mr. Parrish nor the captain could find anyone aboard the *Crescent City* who could completely corroborate Charlie's version of the shooting incident. Therefore, Captain Zipprian decided to play it safe and keep Creed in the brig until the ship reached New Orleans, where everything could be sorted out properly with the aid of the authorities there.

At dawn the first day out of Indianola, the *Crescent City*'s forward lookout spotted a schooner that appeared to be adrift. He notified the officer of the watch, and the captain was awakened with the news. Zipprian spied out the sailing vessel, the *Mary K*, through his telescope and saw a distress flag flying from its main mast. He maneuvered the *Crescent City* to within hailing distance of the smaller craft.

"Ahoy, there! Are you in trouble?" yelled Zipprian through his megaphone.

The captain of the *Mary K* shouted back, "Lost our rudder. We've been adrift for four weeks. We're in bad shape. Can you tow us into Galveston?"

"Can do," replied Zipprian. He gave all the right orders to his crew. Lines were cast back and forth until the two ships were joined by an umbilical cord of hemp. Then the *Crescent City* took the *Mary K* in tow and proceeded to Galveston, which was the nearest port.

Locked up below decks in a brig cell that was situated in a corner of the hold, Creed was barely aware of the excitement until the *Crescent City* steamed into Galveston harbor and the ship's rolling ceased. While everyone else was busy looking at Galveston or getting the schooner tied up to a pier, little Charlie clandestinely visited Creed in his cramped quarters and told him everything that was happening above decks. Creed sat Indian-style on his pallet on the deck as Charlie

15

related the news; then their conversation turned to Creed's plight.

"I told them what happened, Mr. Creed," said Charlie, "but I guess they didn't believe me."

"I appreciate what you did, Charlie," said Creed. "I'm sure the captain believed you. He told me he did, but even so, he said that he was keeping me here just in case you might be mistaken about a point or two."

"He said those men were lawmen, Mr. Creed. Were they?"

"They weren't the last time I saw them," said Creed, "but I guess anything is possible. I know Kindred was a deputy sheriff in Lavaca County when I came home from the war, but he broke the law and got himself arrested. I can't see how he could have become a deputy sheriff again after that."

"But what about those other two?"

"That's a good one, too, Charlie. Those Detchen brothers are two of the meanest polecats that ever drew the breath of life. I can't see how they could become lawmen either."

"Well, one of them ain't nothing no more," said Charlie. "It looked to me like you sent him straight to Hell, where he belongs."

Creed tilted his head at Charlie and said, "You think you should be talking like that, son?"

"Like what?" asked Charlie, taking offense.

Creed chuckled and said, "Never mind, Charlie. Forget I said anything."

"What about you now, Mr. Creed? We're pulling into Galveston. Do you think the captain will turn you over to the law here?"

"I reckon so, Charlie. Galveston is as good a place as any, I guess." He looked around at his cell, which was sectioned off on two sides by bulkheads and on the other two by wooden bars, one of which held the door and the other a slot for the passing of plates of food. In the corner was the slops bucket. "Yep, Galveston is as good a place as any."

"What will they do to you, Mr. Creed?"

"That's hard to say, Charlie. They might not do anything or they might hang me. Who knows?"

Charlie blanched and said, "Hang you?"

Creed laughed and said, "Don't worry about it too much, Charlie. I don't think they'll hang me in Galveston." Back in

Hallettsville, sure, he thought, but not in Galveston. "Don't worry about it, Charlie. I'll be all right. Now you better go before someone starts missing you or someone comes below and finds you down here."

Almost as if he'd been given a stage cue, Mr. Parrish came down the ladder to the hold. Charlie scrambled to hide behind some crates as Parrish approached the brig.

"What's going on up there?" asked Creed innocently to draw the first officer's attention to him.

"We're pulling into Galveston," said Parrish.

"Galveston? I didn't know Galveston would be a stop on this trip."

"We weren't supposed to lay in here," said Parrish, "but we took a schooner in tow this morning and the captain brought it here. People on board were in bad shape. The captain thought it would be best to bring them here instead of towing them all the way to New Orleans."

"Oh, so I suppose the captain will be turning me over to the law here instead of in New Orleans," said Creed.

"Actually, no," said Parrish. "That's what I came to tell you. The captain doesn't want to lose any more time here in Galveston. He figures if he turns you over to the law here, that he'll have to lay over tonight and maybe tomorrow, too, trying to get everything straight about what happened in Indianola yesterday. He'd rather just go on to New Orleans, where he'll have enough time to explain things at his leisure."

This was good news to Creed, but he didn't want Parrish to see his joy. "That's too bad," he said, feigning disappointment. "I was hoping to get out of here and back on dry land as soon as possible."

"Sorry, Creed. You have to stay down here until we dock in New Orleans."

"And when will that be?" asked Creed.

"Two days from now, if we're lucky. Three at the most. Anyway, we'll be home for Christmas."

"That's right," said Creed. "Home for Christmas. Well, thanks for telling me, Mr. Parrish."

Parrish waved and left.

Before Creed could get depressed about Christmas and not being home for the holiday again this year, Charlie came out of hiding. "How come you're disappointed about not being turned over to the law in Galveston, Mr. Creed?" he asked.

Creed smiled and said, "Oh, I'm not disappointed about that, Charlie. I'm glad the captain's taking me to New Orleans."

"You are?"

"Sure. New Orleans is in Louisiana. The law there isn't going to give a hoot about what happened in Indianola, Texas."

Charlie took a turn at smiling and said, "Yeah, I guess you're right, Mr. Creed, but are you sure about that?"

"Sure as I can be," said Creed. "Now you run along before someone else comes down here."

Charlie left Creed to his bittersweet thoughts, all of which were of home: Texas, Hallettsville, Glengarry, Double Star Ranch, and Texada, the girl he loved. The pain of separation was so great at that moment that he wanted to die. Instead, he curled up on his pallet on the deck and tried to sleep, hoping he would dream of happier times.

5

The *Crescent City* remained in Galveston longer than Captain Zipprian had wanted to stay, and this worried little Charlie. He thought the ship's master might have changed his mind about turning Creed over to the law in Galveston, but he learned soon enough that he was wrong.

The neighing of a frightened horse rippled the colors of Creed's dream, fogging them until they were no more than fuzzy shades of gray. Then the imagery of slumber passed into conscious awareness, and his nap ended.

The horse neighed again.

Creed's eyes opened. His first thought upon awakening was that something was happening to Nimbus, but that wasn't it at all. He rolled over and looked in the direction of the sound. From his brig cell, he could see that Nimbus was in his stall, standing tall, alert, and attentive to the same noise that had first interjected itself into Creed's sleep, then interrupted it.

Creed stood up and watched as the livestock ramp on which he had brought Nimbus down into the hold was lowered through the hatch. As soon as it was in place, a handsome youth wearing buckskins and a brown felt slouch hat led a horse down the ramp and put him in the stall next to the one that held Nimbus. The two animals whinnied at each other, then made snorting sounds that didn't sound too friendly. The newcomer reared up as if he wanted to jump over the wall between him and Nimbus, but his handler kept him in tow.

"Easy, Pride!" said the youth. "Easy, boy!" He stroked the horse's neck and held the stallion's jaw close to his mouth as he continued to talk to the animal in a soothing voice. "I know you want to get at him, but that's not for you. No, sir. You're supposed to be a lover, not a fighter. You got to learn that now, Pride. You're a lover, not a fighter. I didn't come all the way down here to Texas just to have you fight with this gray stallion. No, sir. You're going home to stud, Pride. You hear? To stud. Pa's got a whole mess of mares just waiting for you, boy, and you're going home to take care of every one of them, you hear?" The lad continued stroking the horse.

The stallion settled down for the moment and gave Creed the opportunity to study him. He was a beauty, a Thoroughbred from the looks of him. Creed remembered seeing a few like him when he was riding in Kentucky with Morgan during the war. He admired them for what they were: racehorses and nothing else. He had seen them run a few times at Metairie Park while he was in New Orleans after the war, and from that experience, he could see how some men developed a fever for them. Thoroughbreds were truly magnificent horseflesh.

Mr. Parrish came down the ramp and approached the youth. "Is the gray giving you any trouble?" he asked.

Pride started, but his master calmed him again with a few strokes and soft words before he answered the first officer. "Oh, no, sir," said the lad. "The gray's just a little stirred up about another stallion coming into his pasture. That's all."

"Pasture?" queried Parrish, snorting a laugh. "I've never heard of a ship's hold being called a pasture before."

"Well, I know it's not a pasture," said the youth with a smile, "but it's the gray's territory. He was here first, and now Pride has come along as a sort of interloper. You know, an intruder."

"I see what you mean," said Parrish. "You know a lot about horses, I take it."

The youth blushed and said, "Not as much as some, but enough to keep from being sold a nag."

"Well, that's good," said Parrish. He turned to leave.

"Sir, does the gray belong to someone on board this boat?" asked the youth.

"First off, this is a ship, son," said Parrish, "not a boat. But to answer your question . . ." He pointed a finger toward Creed and said, "The gray belongs to him."

The lad turned, saw Creed behind the wooden bars of the brig cell, gulped, and then asked, "Is he in jail?"

"It's called a brig on a ship, son," said Parrish, "but it amounts to the same thing. Jail or brig. They're meant to hold them what can't keep the law, although the captain's not so sure this one has broken any laws yet."

"What's he in there for?"

"Why don't you go ask him yourself? He won't hurt you, and I'm sure he'd like to talk to someone." When the youth hesitated, Parrish added, "Go ahead. He won't hurt you."

"Sure," said Creed. "Come on over here. I'd like to ask you about your horse."

"Go on," said Parrish. "I've got to go back on deck. We'll be getting up steam and shoving off soon." He left.

Creed noticed that the young man looked his way but made no move toward him. He offered encouragement. "My name is Slate Creed." He held out his hand toward the youth. "My horse's name is Nimbus. What's yours?"

"Mine or the horse?"

"Both," said Creed with a smile.

"Mine's Scott," he said, taking Creed's hand in friendship. "Scott Houchin. Actually, it's Arlington Scott Houchin. From the Green River country up in Edmondson County, Kentucky. I hate my first name, so I go by Scott. And my horse's name is Pride."

"Pride," said Creed. "That's what I thought I heard you call him, Scott, but I wasn't sure. Good name for a proud stallion like that. Pride. Yes, sir. Good name."

"What are you doing in here, Mr. Creed? If you don't mind me asking."

Creed heaved a sigh and said, "No, Scott, I don't mind. I shot a man."

Scott's eyes widened, and he took a half step backward. "You killed a man?"

"He and his brother had just killed two of my best friends. I tried to kill his brother, too, but the ship was too far out in the harbor by then."

"I don't understand. You didn't kill him on this ship?"

Creed smiled and said, "Maybe I'd better tell you how it all happened." And he did. When he was finished relating the tale of the shooting, he said, "So how do you and a Thoroughbred stallion happen to be on this ship heading for New Orleans?"

"Well, sir, that's a long story," said Scott.

"Well, go ahead and tell it to me," said Creed with a smile. "I'm not exactly going anywhere."

"No, I guess you ain't," said Scott. "Well, it started during the war. . . ."

6

The Houchins were among the first settlers of European ancestry to make their homes in Edmondson County, Kentucky. Of course, it wasn't called Edmondson County when the eighteenth century became the nineteenth. Part of it was Hart County, part Warren, and part Grayson. The three sections were brought together in 1825 to make Edmondson County. The first Houchins threw up log cabins along the Green River and ran a ferry for folks traveling the road from Louisville to Nashville by way of Bowling Green. In time, they spread out over the whole county.

Scott Houchin's branch of the family carved their homestead out of the wilderness on a hill south and a little west of a bend in the Green River known as the Turnhole. Scott was the oldest of three sons born to William Davis Houchin and his second wife, Edith, Edie to those who knew her. Scott's older half-brother, William Davis Houchin, Jr., was one of the thousands of Kentuckians who enlisted on the Union side during the war, joining a local militia unit when he turned sixteen in '62. Scott wanted to go to war, too, but his father needed him at home to help with the farming. Besides, Scott was only thirteen when hostilities broke out in '61, and although he was old enough to fight late in the war, he stayed home.

During the first year of the conflict, Davis, as the senior Houchin was known, came into possession of a Thoroughbred mare. A planter from Nashville was returning to his home from Bardstown, where he had taken the horse to be bred, and was traveling by way of Mammoth Cave, crossing the Green River at the ferry of the same name. A heavy rain had caused the river to flood, making it near to impassable. The ferryman refused to cross until the water receded, but the planter insisted that he and his horses be taken across the Green immediately. When the ferryman continued to balk, the planter commandeered the

22

ferry at the point of a gun. Needless to say, the lines couldn't withstand the force of the raging current, snapping and leaving the planter, his animals, and the raft at the mercy of the torrent. The craft broke up when it struck a giant oak, which stood on the river's edge when the water was flowing normally. The planter drowned, of course; but his horses—the pregnant mare and the gelding he was riding—managed to reach dry ground a few miles downstream, soil that belonged to Davis Houchin.

Scott caught the two horses and brought them to the Houchin corral. Scott's sister, twelve-year-old Clarenda, found the planter's body impaled on a broken tree branch downriver two days later, when the flood subsided. Davis searched the planter's clothes and found an oilcloth pouch that contained several hundred dollars in negotiable bank notes and a packet of papers pertaining to the mare. The mare's registered name was Buck's Honey, and she'd been bred to a stud named Kentucky Knight.

Davis took the planter's body into Brownsville, to the undertaker, and he sent a letter to the deceased's address in Nashville, hoping to inform his next of kin of his demise. The planter was buried in Brownsville in the meantime.

A year went by and no one answered Davis's letter. In that time, the mare foaled, bearing a healthy colt. The equine mother had all the right instincts, doing all that was natural for her to do during and after the birth. When the foal finally managed to prop himself up on all four unsteady legs, the mare whinnied her approval, and Edith remarked, "That Honey sure is proud of him, ain't she, Pa?" Davis agreed, and then it struck him that Edith had come up with the perfect name for the colt. "That's it, Ma," he said. "We'll call him Pride."

Davis figured the gelding and the mare and her offspring were now legally his property, if for no other reason than that they were payment for caring for them all this time. No matter, though, because no kin to the planter ever came to claim the horses or even the planter's body. To cover his own tail, Davis went to court and obtained the proper papers that made the animals his chattel.

The war ground on, and Davis watched the colt grow into a magnificent specimen of horseflesh. He knew that it would only be a matter of time before he could take Pride to Bowling Green and start him training to be a racehorse, and if the colt worked out a winner, then the next step would be the tracks at Nashville or Louisville or maybe even New Orleans.

Things didn't quite work out as Davis planned, however.

Kentucky, like her sister slavery states that had remained in the Union, suffered at the hands of bandits who called themselves guerrillas. Some proclaimed themselves to be loyal to the Union, while others waved the Stars and Bars as their banner. In truth, most were simply renegades out for plunder, and they cared little whether their victims were Unionists, Confederates, or Neutrals.

A band of the vermin heard about Davis Houchin's bred mare and colt and plotted to steal the horses. They chose Christmas Eve to do the misdeed.

The bandits slipped onto the Houchin farm in the dead of night without being seen or heard. Not even the hunting dogs sensed their presence; at least they didn't until Honey felt her yearling colt was in danger and tried to protect Pride from the intruders. The mare reared up, neighed, and crashed the gate to her stall. Then the hounds set up a howling that was heard clear to Silent Grove.

"What's that all about now?" grumped Davis in that rich, down-home twang that distinguishes Kentucky hill folk from other Southerners as well as other Kentuckians. He rolled slowly from his warm bed into the cold night.

Davis Houchin was in his sixtieth year of life and no longer moved as fast as he once did. He flexed his rheumatic fingers, then rubbed the sleep from his rhinitic blue eyes, the redness caused by too much strong drink on too many occasions. He raised his left hand slowly and brushed back the white thatch from his forehead, only to have it fall back where it had been in the first place.

"Pa! Pa!" called Scott, coming on the run. "Someone's in the barn!"

"The barn?" queried Davis. He sat on the side of the bed with his forearms resting on his thighs. His bony elbows and knees poked through the worn sleeves and legs of his sweat-stained long johns.

"Yes, sir! The barn."

"Get the shotguns, Scott," said Davis evenly, the sleep clearing from his eyes instantly.

Scott did as he was told.

Edith turned up the flame on the lamp in their bedroom.

Clarenda came out of her bedroom carrying baby sister Parizada. The two youngest boys, seven-year-old John Wesley and four-year-old Ben, came out of the boys' room rubbing their eyes and yawning.

"Is it Christmas already?" asked John Wesley.

"Edie, tend the younguns," said Davis as he slipped into his trousers and pulled on his boots. He snapped his suspenders over his shoulders and headed for the kitchen.

"What's wrong, Mama?" asked John Wesley.

"Nothing, son," said Edith as she gathered her children to her like a mother hen would gather her chicks.

"Where's Papa going?" asked Clarenda.

Davis stopped at the bedroom door, looked back over his shoulder, and said calmly, "Turn down the lamp, Edie. No need in letting who's ever out there know we're up and coming for them."

Just as she had when she was the housekeeper for the Houchins and the nurse for Davis's first wife, Edith obeyed.

Scott met his father in the kitchen. He had donned his pants and boots. He handed the double-barreled Remington to Davis and kept the sawed-off American Arms shotgun for himself.

"I'll go out the back," said Davis. "Scott, you stay in here and look after your mother."

Scott didn't say anything, but his expression protested the order.

Davis's eyes became paternal, caring, when he looked at Scott and realized that his son was nearly a man now. "All right, come along, but keep low, son," he said softly. "This ain't a coon hunt we're going on."

Scott nodded with grim determination.

Davis opened the door; it creaked. He was certain that the trespassers had heard it. He knelt down in the doorway to listen for any sound from the barn, but the dogs were barking too loudly for him to hear anything else. He figured the intruders hadn't heard it after all.

The sky was clear, starry, and moonless. The night air was cold and crisp. Davis and Scott could see their breath as they crept outside, then ran for the corral fence, reached it safely, and knelt down behind it. Davis was surprised that they had gone undetected so far.

"Now don't shoot unless I do," whispered Davis. "We don't know who or what's in there yet. Could be coons. Could be men."

Just then the barn door flew open, and out came one shadow of a man riding the gelding and leading Pride. Another silhouette followed, riding Davis's horse and leading Honey.

"Pa, they're stealing Pride and Honey!"

"Hold on there!" shouted Davis, rising up and aiming his shotgun in the direction of the thieves.

"Let's get out of here!" shouted the second robber.

Both thieves kicked their mounts and tried to speed off.

Davis fired.

The man on Davis's horse screamed as his back arched from the impact of the lead slug. In the next instant, he slumped forward and fell from the animal's bare back.

Scott took aim at the lead rider but held his fire.

"Shoot him, Scott!" snapped his father.

Scott still didn't shoot.

"Dammit, boy!" Davis cut loose the other barrel of his gun, but the shot fell harmlessly short of its target. Davis listened in frustration as the robber rode off, then he turned to his son, his eyes filled with anger. "Dammit! Why didn't you shoot him?"

Scott leaned backward, expecting his father to slap him no matter what he answered. "I was afraid I'd hit Pride, Pa," he said cautiously.

That wasn't a thought that had crossed Davis's mind. He had feared that his son didn't have the stomach for killing, and that was a shame he couldn't bear.

"Hit Pride?" queried Davis, stammering, caught off-guard by Scott's response.

"Yes, sir," said Scott slowly. "I mean, no, sir. I didn't want to hit Pride, I mean."

Davis strained to comprehend, finally did understand, then nodded and said, "Right good thinking, son." He patted the youth on the shoulder and said, "Come on. Let's see who that is that I shot. Keep your gun on him just in case he ain't hurt that bad and he's got a gun of his own."

They walked over to the wounded man writhing in pain at the side of the road. He had a revolver in his hand and started to raise it at Davis.

"Drop it, mister!" said Scott, taking aim at the fellow.

But before Scott or the thief could do anything, Davis kicked the pistol from the man's hand and said, "We'll have none of that, mister."

"You shot me bad," whined the robber.

Davis knelt down beside the man, rolled him over roughly, then rolled him back again. "Yep," he said, "sure did. Killed you, I did. You're bleeding like a butchered hog, friend. What's your name so we can put it on a marker for you?"

"Don't let me die!" whined the thief.

"Can't help it," said Davis. "You best make your peace now because you ain't getting a second chance."

The man coughed up blood.

"See there?" said Davis. "Got you in the lungs, I did. Even a surgeon couldn't help you now, friend. I done killed you good. So tell us your name, and we'll see that your kinfolk hear of your death, and we'll bury you here or in Brownsville till they come and dig you up and take you home to put you in your own ground. Better tell us quick like. You ain't got long."

"Name is Keady. George Keady. From Bloomfield."

"Have you been a horse thief very long, Mr. Keady?" asked Davis rather matter-of-factly.

"I'm not a horse thief," he said, wincing.

"You're not?" queried Davis. "Then what do you call a man who steals horses? A parson?"

"No, sir," said Keady meekly.

"I thought not," said Davis rather haughtily. "All right, Mr. Keady, how about your friend? What's his name?"

Keady coughed up more blood, then said, "Jim White." He winced and added, "From Russellville. Logan County."

"You done the right thing, friend," said Davis. "I'll tell the parson who speaks over you that you did the right thing before you died, and he'll relay it to the Lord for you. Maybe that'll get you out of Hell sooner. Just maybe. Of course, that'll be up to the Lord."

Keady's eyes fogged over, then went blank. He was dead.

"Come on, son," said Davis. "It's cold out here. Let's go back into the house. Tomorrow's Christmas. The Lord's birthday. Day after, we'll start out to find this Jim White and our horses."

When morning came, Davis's chestnut mare was standing in front of the barn, but the gelding, Honey, and Pride were nowhere in sight. Scott put his father's horse in the corral, and the Houchins celebrated Christmas as if nothing had happened. The next day, just as Davis had said they would, he and Scott went looking for their horses.

Russellville did have a Jim White, but he wasn't around and hadn't been for some time—or so they were told. Word had it that he was riding with a guerrilla outfit: Anderson's, Gano's, maybe Quantrill's. No one knew for sure. Since Anderson and Quantrill operated mostly in Missouri and Gano raided in Kentucky and Tennessee, Davis assumed White was riding with Gano. That was all well and good, but finding Gano's raiders wasn't going to be easy. Davis decided to take a different tack. "We'll look for Pride and Honey," he told Scott, "instead of White. It's pretty hard to hide a couple of horses like them, especially the way they were marked by Nature and the way we marked them."

They started by asking around Bowling Green. No one had seen White or the horses that the Houchins described, but they were told that a man who had stolen horses to sell would most likely take them to Louisville, Nashville, or Memphis, maybe even Cincinnati, a big city where they wouldn't be noticed so much. Davis thought that was a most likely proposition, but he wondered if he could afford to be away from the farm for the length of time it would take him to travel to all of those places. He looked at his son, saw a budding man, and made a decision. Scott would have to share the chore with him.

Davis decided to go to Louisville and Cincinnati because they were farther away than Nashville and Memphis, and Scott was less likely to have trouble in the two smaller towns. They left home in the middle of January, and they were home again by spring plowing time in March. Neither of them had had any luck in locating the stolen horses, but both had been wise enough to ask those folks that they met to send them word if they should come across Pride and Honey.

The summer wore on, and no news came. Davis wondered if his single big chance to advance in the social and economic strata had eluded him, but not so Scott. His concern was for his horses. Breds or not, they belonged to him or so he felt emotionally.

After the fall harvest—when the tobacco was hanging in the sheds to dry, Edith had put up all her preserves for the winter, the root cellar was filled, and the hog and steer had been butchered, salted, and stored in barrels—Scott got to wondering if Jim White

had ever returned to Russellville. He discussed the possibility
with his father. Davis thought White's return to be unlikely,
but Scott said there was the chance of it. Davis had to agree
to that, but he was against riding over to Logan County to find
out for certain. Scott asked if he could go alone. Davis knew
that he would be foolish to try and stop Scott, so he gave his
son his blessing, his horse, his shotgun, ten dollars in silver, and
a word of caution: "Don't trust anyone, son, and let the Lord be
your guide in everything." Scott accepted all of his father's gifts
with equanimity, cherishing each of them as if they were gold,
including the parental advice.

No one remembered Scott from his visit of the previous winter,
and he didn't try to shake up their memories by asking around
Russellville about White. Instead, he was able to get a job as a
clerk at George Norton's general store and also find lodging in
the rear of the building.

Norton's store was the ideal place for Scott to learn about the
town, the county, and the people who resided there. It being fall
with winter rapidly approaching, most of the men of the town and
many from surrounding farms would spend several hours each
day sitting around the Franklin stove, talking about the progress
of the war, the Negro question, the elections, and so on. Just as
often, they would speak of receiving mail from other parts of
the state and the country. Scott overheard these conversations
and was able to learn the whereabouts of Jim White. Much to
his displeasure, White was riding with Quantrill in Missouri.
Scott made up his mind that he would have to go to Missouri,
find Quantrill's guerrillas, and thus find White. He was on the
verge of taking leave of his employer when Fate intervened and
dealt him a high card. Quantrill had given up the war in Missouri
and had fled to Kentucky. Scott wouldn't have to quit work and
ride off now; all he had to do was wait.

Jim White didn't return to Russellville just yet, but a friend
of his did. George Shepherd had been a guerrilla in Missouri,
and he knew White well. Shepherd married a fellow guerrilla's
widow, bought some land, and settled in Logan County. He
came into the store and asked if White had come home yet.
After receiving the cold shoulder, Shepherd revealed that he had
served with White in Missouri and that the last time he had seen
his comrade was a few months earlier after the defeat that had
sent Quantrill packing to Kentucky. One band of the guerrillas,

including White, had gone south to Texas, while another group had followed Quantrill to Kentucky. Others, like Shepherd, had quit the war and moved on.

Scott ingratiated himself with Shepherd, playing on the former guerrilla's penchant for talking about himself and his adventures in the war. Shepherd spoke of battles, raids, and skirmishes, all in the name of freedom, and he bragged about the number of Yankees—regulars and militia—that he had killed in the line of duty. Using guile, Scott asked Shepherd about the weapons the guerrillas had used, how they obtained supplies, where they would camp and hide from the Yankees, and how they found remounts when their horses were killed in battle or were spent from their long marches. Shepherd answered every question in great detail, but to Scott's disappointment, he failed to mention White stealing any Thoroughbred horses. Then he asked Shepherd if they were ever allowed furloughs, and Shepherd laughed and said they were. At that point, he related the one story Scott had been waiting to hear for months.

"Last winter Jim White and I decided we'd had our fill of killing Yankees for a while," said Shepherd, "and with Christmas coming, we decided to take our leave of Missouri and come over here to Kentucky to spend the holiday. We met up with a few fellows from the Order."

"The Order?" asked Scott.

"Sure, you know," said Shepherd. "The Order." He looked about them to make sure no one else was listening, and once he was assured they were alone, he said, "You know, Scott. The Order of American Knights."

"Oh, sure," said Scott, vaguely recalling something he'd heard about the organization and remembering it wasn't good.

"Well, like I was saying," said Shepherd, "Jim and me met with a few fellows from the Order, and one of them told us about a fellow up to Edmondson County who had a Thoroughbred mare and a first-class colt that were begging for new owners. Fellow's name was Keady. He said we could steal them horses, sell them real quick, and have us a neat little bundle to divvy up. I didn't want no part of it because I was tired of riding right then, but Keady talked Jim into going along with him. Told him the owner was a Yankee. Glad I didn't go along because Keady caught a load of buckshot and was killed and Jim said he barely got away with his life. He got away with the horses, though. Fine-looking mare and what a colt! I'll tell you, there was a horse who was going to run like the wind. You could tell he was blooded with just a one-eyed glance.

"Well, sir, Jim brought those horses up to Bloomfield, where we'd met Keady and I was staying. He didn't feel like telling Keady's kin what had happened to him, so we headed out for Missouri again, taking that mare and her colt with us as far as Bishop, where we sold the mare to a planter named Kalfus who was also a doctor in Louisville. We took the colt with us back to Missouri by way of Indiana and Illinois, thinking no one would suspect us of being guerrillas if we came back that way.

"When we reached St. Louis, Jim wanted to visit a cathouse, and while we were there, he got a little drunk and got a little rough with one of the girls. That brought the bouncers. Jim pulled a knife on them, and that started the fight. He cut one before we made a hasty retreat out a second-story window. He jumped on the back of the colt instead of his own horse, and we rode off with me doing everything I could to keep up with him. That colt could run.

"Well, we got away, but Jim had himself a real problem now. He had that colt, but that Thoroughbred wasn't born to be ridden into no battle with bullets flying all around him. Jim knew he needed another horse, but he was fresh out of money. Not willing to try to steal another, he sold the colt to a Texan who was waiting for the war to end so he could go home and take up his cattle business again. He was staying at the Planters House on Fourth Street in St. Louis. His name was Jewell, and he was hoping to return to a place called Columbus as soon as possible."

7

"Well, sir," said Scott as he fiddled with a straw from the horses' hay, "as soon as I found out where Honey and Pride were at, I quit my job and went home to tell Pa about what I'd found out. Pa and I went up to Louisville and laid claim to Honey, and after a little squabble in court, she was returned to us all proper and legal. That was just about the time that General Lee surrendered to Grant.

"As for Pride, Pa wrote a letter to this Mr. Jewell in St. Louis that I'd heard about, but we never got any answer. He sent another one to the hotel in St. Louis where Mr. Jewell was supposed to be staying. He asked about Mr. Jewell, and we got an answer on that one. His complete name was Samuel B. Jewell, and he left a forwarding address of Columbus, Texas."

"I know it," said Creed. "Columbus is the county town for Colorado County, which is just to the northeast of where I hail from in Lavaca County." He thought about Texas and home for a second, and a twinge of nostalgia rippled through him. He sighed, then returned his attention to Scott. "So did your father write to Mr. Jewell in Columbus?"

"Yes, sir, he did," said Scott, "and Mr. Jewell answered saying that he'd had a Thoroughbred stallion that he had purchased from a Mr. White in St. Louis that winter, but that the stallion had died of bilious fever during the boat trip to Texas. Pa said he didn't like calling a man a liar unless he had real proof, but he said he'd never heard of a horse contracting bilious fever before. He said he couldn't blame Mr. Jewell for wanting to keep Pride, but he belonged to us and that was that. We would get him back."

"So how did you do it?" asked Creed.

"Pa tried getting a lawyer back home to do something," said Scott, "but that didn't work. So Pa said we'd have to go after Pride ourselves. My brother Billy returned from the war, so Pa

32

sent him and me down to Texas to find out if Mr. Jewell was telling us true or not. We found Pride on Mr. Jewell's ranch near Columbus. We went to him and asked him to give Pride back to us, but he told us we were in Texas and our Kentucky claims didn't mean nothing down there. Billy wanted to take Pride, but Mr. Jewell told us if we tried anything, he'd see to it that we didn't ever get back to Kentucky again. Well, Billy didn't take too kindly to that sort of talk, and he was all set to square up with Mr. Jewell right then and there. I thought sure he would, too, but all of a sudden he said, 'Come on, Scott. There's more than one way to skin a polecat.' We went into town to the sheriff, but he wouldn't do nothing about helping us. So we got us a local lawyer, and he took Mr. Jewell to court to make him give Pride back to us. It didn't look like the judge was going to do it until our lawyer said Billy had fought for the Union and that Mr. Jewell had gone to Missouri because he was trying to avoid the war. Right then and there, the judge ordered the sheriff to get Pride from Mr. Jewell and give him back to us."

"It's good to hear that Colorado County has an honest judge," said Creed with a snicker.

"Well, at least he was a Federal judge," said Scott.

"So your brother is with you?" queried Creed.

"Oh, no, sir. Billy and me, we took Pride to Galveston so we could book passage on a ship for New Orleans, and then we planned to take him up the Mississippi on a riverboat, but Billy decided he didn't want to go home just yet. He said there wasn't nothing to home for him, and he wanted to have himself a look around the country a bit before settling down. He said he'd be coming home by spring. I'm to tell Pa and Ma that."

"So you got lucky and caught this ship," said Creed.

"Oh, no, sir," said Scott. "Pride and me, we set out for New Orleans four weeks ago on the schooner *Mary K*."

"Four weeks ago?"

"Yes, sir. The *Mary K* is that schooner this boat come across drifting out on the ocean."

"You were on that schooner?"

"Yes, sir, we were," said Scott.

"And you were adrift for four weeks?"

"Yes, sir."

Creed thought about it for a second, then said, "Mr. Parrish, the man who was just down here. He said the people on that schooner were in rough shape. Did you run out of provisions or something?"

"Yes, sir, we did. We ran out of food and water in the first two weeks, but fortunately it rained a couple of times, and we were able to refill the water barrels that way. We tried catching fish, but we didn't have much luck at that. A few folks wanted to kill Pride and carve him up into steaks, but the captain wouldn't let them do it." Scott opened his coat to reveal the butt of a pistol. "Good thing he didn't let them have their way," he said, "or I might have been forced to use this." He patted the gun.

Creed smiled and said, "Good for you, Scott. I feel the same way about Nimbus. I think I'd shoot anyone who tried to hurt him. As a matter of fact, I did shoot one Yankee who stuck him with a saber. Of course, I would have shot that Yank anyway, but he did cut Nimbus."

"Nimbus. That sure is a strange name for a horse," said Scott. "What's it mean, Mr. Creed?"

Creed laughed and said, "You know, there's a youngun on this boat who said the same thing to me just yesterday." He thought about that for a moment, then became sad. "He asked me that just minutes before my two friends were murdered on the pier," he said softly.

Scott wasn't sure of what to say now. All he could think of was to ask about how Nimbus got his name.

Slowly, Creed related that story, and by the time he was finished with the tale, he and Scott were fast friends.

8

During the next two days the *Crescent City* navigated the one hundred miles of the Mississippi River between the Gulf of Mexico and New Orleans, and Captain Zipprian docked his ship at the Morgan Steamship Lines company docks between the Morgan Railroad Ferry landing and the Third District Ferry at the head of Elysian Fields Street.

During the remainder of the cruise, Scott Houchin and little Charlie had kept Creed informed about the ship's movements and other news that might concern him, including any scuttlebutt that might be circulating among the crew. From what they could garner, the captain still intended to hand him over to the law once they landed in Louisiana. This was as much as Creed had expected, but he didn't think that the law would be waiting for him when they reached New Orleans. It was little Charlie that brought him this bad news.

"I heard them talking on the pier, Mr. Creed," said Charlie. "The captain and the dock master. He told Captain Zipprian that the Army had been around yesterday asking when the *Crescent City* would be docking because there was a man on board they wanted to arrest right away. Said he was an escaped prisoner who was supposed to be hanged."

"That would be me, Charlie," said Creed.

"You're an escaped prisoner?" queried Charlie.

"There's more to it than that, Charlie. Let's just say that some Yankees want me dead for a crime I didn't commit, and I escaped to prove I'm innocent. I mean, I'm trying to find the men who really committed the crime so I can clear my real name. Do you understand, Charlie?"

"I think so," said Charlie, scratching his head.

Creed's mind was already in gear on a plan. "Charlie, I can't let the Army take me off this ship. I've got to

35

get out of here before they come for me. Do you understand?"

"Yes, sir, I do."

"I need your help, Charlie."

"I'll do anything, Mr. Creed," the boy said eagerly. "You just
name it."

"For starters, do you know where we're docked?"

"Well, New Orleans, of course," said Charlie.

Creed smiled and said, "I know, Charlie, but at which pier?"

"You mean they got names?"

"Yes, Charlie, they do."

"Sorry, Mr. Creed, I don't know the name of this one, but I
can go ask."

"Good boy! You do that and then go get Scott Houchin for
me right away."

"Yes, sir," said Charlie. He started to dart off.

"And, Charlie!" called Creed, stopping the boy. "Don't tell him
anything except that I want to see him and that it's urgent."

"Yes, sir." And he raced up the ladder and out of sight.

Creed looked around his cramped quarters for anything that
might help him escape. He couldn't see anything. He tried
to force the bars, but they were as strong as iron. Now
what? He looked at the horses, Nimbus and Pride. Neither
of them had particularly cared for the sea voyage, but they
had calmed down once the *Crescent City* moved into flat
water. Both of them were now happily eating their hay
and oats. Creed couldn't leave Nimbus behind, that much
was certain. But how to get the stallion out of the hold and
onto the dock? And what about his gear in the cabin that
he never got to use? He couldn't leave it behind; his money
was there.

Creed loathed being dependent on anyone else. It made him
feel weak and insignificant. But there were times when he had
no choice—like now—and he had to face them as bravely as
those times when he was in full control of his own fate. He
said a silent prayer, asking the Almighty to help Charlie and
Scott to come through for him.

Almost as if they'd been cued, Scott and Charlie came down
the ladder and raced over to Creed's cell.

"I brung him like you wanted, Mr. Creed," said Charlie quite
proudly, "and I found out that we're tied up to the Morgan docks

in front of the French Market and something called *Plah-suh Darms*, whatever that is."

"In American," said Creed, "we'd call it the Battery. *Place D'Armes* is French for 'a place of arms or weapons.' It's where the French used to muster the troops for drills when they owned New Orleans."

Charlie nodded his understanding.

"You wanted to see me, Mr. Creed?" asked Scott.

"Yes, Scott, I did. I need your help to get out of here."

"Gee, Mr. Creed, I don't know about that," said Scott quite reluctantly.

"Aw, come on, Scott," said Charlie. "We got to help Mr. Creed get out of here before the Yankees come for him."

"The Yankees?" queried Scott.

"That's right, Scott," said Creed. "They want to hang me for a crime I didn't commit, and they're coming here to take me away if I don't get out of here first."

"Well, what was it you were supposed to have done, Mr. Creed?" asked Scott.

"Some men I rode with during the war raided an Army supply wagon train after the war was over, and they killed a few Yankees while they were doing it. They were caught several months later, and to save their own hides, they said I led the raid. Now I wasn't there because I was gambling and doing things with a lewd woman here in New Orleans around the time the raid happened in Mississippi. The Yankees didn't believe me, so they gave me something like a trial, but they didn't let me do anything to prove my innocence. They wanted me to be guilty from the start. I escaped from them, and now I'm trying to find the men who pointed the finger at me, so I can bring them in and make them tell the truth and clear my real name and live like a free man again."

"Your real name?" queried Scott.

"Yeah, you said that to me, too," said Charlie. "Are you telling us that your name ain't really Mr. Creed?"

Creed heard his grandfather Dougald's voice saying, "If you want folks to trust you, you got to trust them first." He looked at one boy, then the other and said, "My real name is Cletus Slater. I changed it to Slate Creed to remind me that my family's honor is at stake here, as well as my own. Do you understand that, boys?"

"Yes, sir," said Charlie.

"Well, I'll tell you, Mr. Creed," said Scott, "I was raised to respect the law."

Creed looked young Houchin dead in the eye and said, "So was I, Scott."

Scott shrugged and said, "Well, sir, Pa told me not to trust anyone and to put my faith in the Lord, and so far, I ain't gone wrong following his advice. After I first met you, I went to praying about you, Mr. Creed, because I like you, and I asked the Lord for some sort of sign that you were all right with Him. Well, sir, I ain't had that sign yet, but I remembered something else I once heard Pa say. He said, 'A man who sets well with the Lord ain't afraid to tell the truth.' Well, sir, I figure if you had something to hide, you would have told me some fancy tale like . . ." He scratched his head, then said, "Well, I don't know like what, but I do know that you'd have made up something a lot fancier than what you just said. Well, I'm sure you're telling the truth, and that means you must set well with the Lord. So what can I do to help you, Mr. Creed?"

"Thanks, Scott," said Creed. "That means a lot coming from you. You, too, Charlie." He reached through the bars and patted Charlie on the head. "Scott, I'd like you to saddle up Nimbus for me, and then I need you to get the crew to lower that livestock ramp down here right away."

"That sounds easy enough," said Scott.

"Charlie, do you know which cabin was supposed to be mine?"

"Yes, sir."

"Good. I'd like you to go up there and get my things for me. My six-guns are supposed to be in my saddlebags. Make sure they're in there, then bring them to me." He dug into the coin pocket of his trousers and pulled out a key. "The door should be locked, so you'll need this." He handed the key to Charlie. "Go now and hurry back, but don't let anyone see you go into my cabin or when you're bringing my things back here. Understand?"

"What if your things ain't there?" asked Charlie.

"Then hurry back and let me know, so I can think of what else to do pretty fast."

Charlie winked and said, "You can count on me, Mr. Creed."

"Good boy!" said Creed with a wink and a smile. "Now git!"

Charlie ran off for the ladder and was gone.

"How are you planning on getting out of here, Mr. Creed?" asked Scott. "You aren't planning to shoot somebody else, are you?"

"No, Scott, I'm not planning to shoot anyone, but I may have to scare a few people out of my way. Now how about getting Nimbus saddled for me?"

"Yes, sir."

9

Little Charlie slipped in and out of Creed's cabin unnoticed, gathered up his belongings, and brought Creed's saddlebags to him, while Scott was saddling up Nimbus.

"Your guns are in there, too," said Charlie. "They sure are heavy, aren't they?"

"Not when you're shooting at some bad hombre who's shooting back at you, they aren't," said Creed with a wink, remembering how, when he was Charlie's age, he'd admired a man with a gun.

Creed checked his revolvers to make sure both were loaded, then strapped on his gunbelt, sticking one Colt's in the holster and the other inside the waistband of his pants, behind the holstered piece. He squatted as if he were hunkering down in the saddle. The butt of the second pistol gouged at his gut. He stood and shifted the gun's position, then squatted again. It felt better, not perfect, but better. It would have to do.

"All saddled up," said Scott as he joined Creed and Charlie.

"Good," said Creed. "Now go get the crew to lower that livestock ramp down here."

"Yes, sir," said Scott, "but how do I do that?"

"You mean how do you do that without lying, right?"

Scott nodded and said, "Yes, sir."

Creed understood and said, "I don't want you to lie either, Scott." He thought for a second, then said, "You're anxious to get Pride off this ship, aren't you?"

"Yes, sir."

"Then tell them that," said Creed.

Scott smiled and said, "And that won't be a lie. I'll do it, and I'll be right back." He headed for the ladder, climbed it, and was gone.

Creed looked at the other boy and said, "In the meantime, Charlie, you go round up Mr. Parrish, the first officer, and tell him I want to see him right away."

Charlie's face twisted into a questioning frown, and he said, "What if he won't come, Mr. Creed?"

Creed's eyebrows twisted together as he said, "You like to make sure things are going to work right, don't you, Charlie?"

"Well, I sure don't want them to go wrong now," said the boy rather sternly for one so young and so small.

"That's real good thinking, son. Well, if he won't come when you tell him that, then kick him in the shins and make him chase you down here."

Charlie frowned and said, "What if he catches me before I can get down here again?"

Creed laughed and said, "You kick him hard enough, Charlie, and he won't be able to catch you."

Charlie smiled and said, "I get it." And he ran off toward the ladder.

While Charlie was climbing out of the hold, the deckhands began lowering the livestock ramp through the overhead hatch. As soon as it was in place, Creed heard Scott thank the men, then come below.

"Now what do I do?" asked Scott.

"Now you make yourself scarce, Scott," said Creed. He held out his hand to the lad and said, "I'm glad I met you, Scott Houchin. Thanks for your help."

"I'm glad I met you, too, Mr. Creed," said Scott, shaking Creed's hand. "I hope we meet again."

"Something tells me we will, Scott," said Creed, "and next time I hope I can return this favor."

Scott smiled and said, "I hope I ain't behind bars then."

"You just keep following your pa's advice, and you won't have to worry about that, Scott."

"Yes, sir." He nodded, then left the hold by way of the ladder instead of the ramp.

In the next minute, Charlie came running down the ramp with Mr. Parrish hobbling after him. Creed crouched down and waited.

"Come back here, you little brat!" yelled Parrish.

Charlie made a beeline for Creed's cell in the corner. "I had to kick him real hard," he said nearly out of breath.

Parrish saw Charlie in the corner and came after him. "Now I've got you, you little brat," he said.

Creed stood, drew the Colt's from inside his waistband, and said, "Just hold on, Mr. Parrish."

Parrish started to snarl at Creed, then he heard the double click of the Colt's being cocked. He looked down at Creed's hand and saw the gun in the dim light.

Creed raised the Colt's to shoulder height and aimed it at the first mate. "Mr. Parrish, I believe you have the key to the padlock on this door," said Creed, fingering the heavy lock with his free hand. "I'd be obliged if you'd open it for me."

"So you lied to the captain after all," said Parrish, not moving a muscle.

"No, Mr. Parrish, I didn't lie to anyone," said Creed. "It's just that I can't afford to be handed over to any Yankees just yet."

"Yankees?" queried Parrish. "What Yankees?"

Charlie put in his two cents, saying, "The ones the captain and the dock master was talking about wanting Mr. Creed."

"I don't know nothing about any Yankees," said Parrish. "Why do they want you?"

"I don't have time to explain, Mr. Parrish," said Creed. "Suffice it to say that it would serve no purpose for me to fall into their hands at this time."

"Aw, give me those keys," said Charlie, reaching for the ring of keys hooked to Parrish's trousers by a short chain.

Parrish slapped away Charlie's hand, then said, "You should have told the captain about the Yankees, Mr. Creed. We're not all Confederates on this ship, but we are all Southerners. It would have made a difference."

"Will you quit palavering?" grumped Charlie. "Those Yankees might be coming right this minute."

"The boy's right," said Parrish. He unlocked the door.

"Charlie, run up on deck and see what's going on," said Creed. Then to Parrish, he said, "Give me those keys and get inside here."

"You don't have to lock me up," said Parrish. "I want to help you get away."

Creed lowered the Colt's to hip level and said, "Mr. Parrish, I don't have time to figure out if you're telling me true or not, so just do like I said."

Parrish shook his head as he unhooked the key ring. "You're making a mistake not taking my help," he said. He offered the keys to Creed but let them fall to the deck before Creed could take them.

Creed's initial reaction was to try to catch the keys, but he stopped when he saw Parrish reach for the gun. Creed let the sailor grab his wrists. Instead of struggling to free himself, Creed pulled his hands backward and apart, forcing Parrish's arms apart and causing Parrish to lean forward off balance. This was the opening Creed wanted. He slammed his knee into Parrish's groin, then watched the bigger man crumple to his knees before him. The mate was hurt and hurt bad.

Charlie came running back down the ramp. "There's Yankee soldiers on the dock, Mr. Creed."

Creed looked at the stunned first officer and said, "Sorry, Mr. Parrish, but you asked for this." He released the hammer of the Colt's down to the safety position, then cracked Parrish over the head with the barrel, opening a nasty cut in his scalp and knocking him unconscious. Certain that Parrish would be no further trouble, Creed looked at Charlie and asked, "How many Yankees are there on the dock?"

"About ten, I reckon," said Charlie.

"On horseback or are they infantry?"

"They're all afoot."

Creed thought fast and said, "Charlie, which way is the ship facing? Toward the city or toward the river?"

"Toward the city."

"All right then. I want you to run to the back of the ship and start yelling that I'm getting away. Say I've jumped into the river or something. Keep on yelling it until those Yankees come running to you. Understand, Charlie?"

Charlie smiled broadly, winked, and said, "You bet I do, Mr. Creed. You can count on me."

Creed tousled the boy's hair and said, "I know that, Charlie." Then he held out his hand and said, "I'm glad I met you, Charlie. Thanks for your help. I hope we meet again someday."

Charlie puffed himself up to receive the manly gesture and said, "You're welcome, Mr. Creed, and I hope I meet you again someday, too."

"We will, Charlie. Now git."

Charlie ran up the ramp, then along the deck toward the stern of the ship.

Creed walked halfway up the ramp, peeked out of the hold, and saw Captain Zipprian on the pier talking to a Yankee officer and another man. Near them stood the squad of soldiers that Charlie had mentioned. Then he heard Charlie shout from the stern, and he ducked below again. Charlie continued to shout just as Creed had told him to do, while Creed took Nimbus from his stall and mounted up. He waited until he heard the pounding of several feet running on deck, then he kicked Nimbus and rode up the livestock ramp as fast as possible. Once on deck he kicked the Appaloosa again, and in two quick steps more they leaped over the gunwale to the pier below, a distance of five feet straight down from the railing to the dock.

"There he goes!" shouted Zipprian, pointing out Creed for the soldiers.

"Shoot him!" commanded the officer.

The squad of men positioned themselves to obey him. They aimed their Springfields in Creed's direction, totally disregarding the dozens of other people in their line of fire. Individually, they fired.

As soon as the horse's hooves struck the wooden pier, Creed turned Nimbus toward the city. Without looking back, he kicked the Appaloosa into a gallop, and they sped off as the soldiers' bullets fell harmlessly around them.

10

The last time Creed had been in New Orleans he was delivering a herd of cattle to the Crescent City Livestock Landing and Slaughterhouse Company situated on the right bank of the Mississippi, below the city's center. Only four months had passed since then. Four months prior to that, he had gone to New Orleans to surrender to the Union Army and to obtain a parole for serving in the Confederate Army. Both visits seemed like eons ago, so much had happened to Creed during that time. But that was the past. For the present, Creed was in the midst of a new adventure.

Longshoremen and stevedores heard the rifle fire, followed by the heavy clippity-clop of a horse's hooves on the wooden dock. They stopped their work and turned to see Creed race down the Morgan Steamship Lines pier toward the French Market and Jackson Square, formerly the *Place D'Armes*. Shoppers and strollers in the plaza shifted their attention to the horseman speeding by them atop the magnificent gray Appaloosa stallion, and their eyes followed him as he entered Magazine Street. Some gentlemen shouted and shook their fists or canes at Creed, protesting his dash through the crowds of pedestrians, but Creed ignored them; their necks weren't in jeopardy here.

Creed turned onto Toulouse Street, looked back over his shoulder, and saw that he was in the clear. He slowed Nimbus to a trot, rode two more blocks, then rounded the corner onto Royale Street. His destination was the home of Charlotte Beaujeu. The three-story brick house rose majestically next door to M. DuMorney's casino on the block between Canal and Customhouse streets. Creed rode up to the wrought-iron gate of the carriage drive between the house and the casino, dismounted, lifted the latch, led Nimbus inside, closed the gate

behind them, and then walked the Appaloosa to the carriage barn
in the rear. He opened the barn door, took Nimbus inside, and
placed him in a stall.

Creed knew that he was taking precarious liberties here, considering his acquaintance with Mlle. Beaujeu was limited to two
evenings of gambling at M. DuMorney's casino and two nights
of fiery lovemaking in her boudoir during his first trip to New
Orleans that year. He hadn't stopped to see her on his last visit,
because he had been desirous of returning to Lavaca County as
soon as possible in order to begin avenging the murders of his
brother, Denton Slater, and his best friend Jess Tate. He hoped
that Charlotte would understand this oversight and would accept
him into her home once again, if for no other reason than to give
him refuge from the Yankees that he knew must be pursuing him.
He considered the mademoiselle as he approached the rear of her
house.

Charlotte Beaujeu was a descendant of the French admiral who
had commanded the small fleet that carried Monsieur Robert
Cavalier de La Salle's colonists to America in the seventeenth
century and deposited them on the coast of Texas instead of
their intended destination at the mouth of the Mississippi. Being
seafaring people, Charlotte's antecedents made many voyages
to Louisiana before her great-grandfather, Georges Beaujeu,
took up residence in New Orleans during the conflict that
was called the Seven Years War in Europe and the French
and Indian War in America. Georges brought with him his
Haitian bride, Emilie, the mulatto daughter of a sugar planter
and a house slave. Armand, the quadroon son of Georges and
Emilie, married Manuella Delgado, the daughter of a Mexican
comerciante, during the Spanish rule of Louisiana, and Benito,
the fair-skinned youngest son of this union, wed Madeleine
Porter, the daughter of a Mississippi planter.

Charlotte was the first child born to the marriage of Benito
and Madeleine, and Denise was the second. Madeleine was a
happy bride and a nearly perfect mother until the birth of her
third child, a boy that Benito named Robert. Madeleine looked
only once at her newborn son, then disclaimed him as her own
because he had the facial features and chocolate coloring of his
great-grandmother, Emilie. Realizing that Benito was descended
from Africans on his father's side and Indians on his mother's

side, Madeleine left her husband and children and returned to her father's plantation in Mississippi. Benito tried to convince her to return, but she refused, suing him for divorce instead. Brokenhearted, Benito returned to New Orleans and put his affairs in order, including putting his children in the care of his parsimonious maiden sister, Marguerite; then he took his own life with a dueling pistol.

Marguerite raised Charlotte, Denise, and Robert on the meager income from the trust that their father had left for them, depriving them of many of the simplest of life's material pleasures. She educated the children herself, raising them to be proud of their French and Spanish heritage, while trying to deny their African and Indian ancestries.

When the Yankees captured New Orleans, Robert enlisted in the Federal Army and died of dysentery during the siege of Vicksburg in '63. Typhoid took Denise and Marguerite on the same day during the epidemic of '64.

Prior to those sad events, Charlotte left her aunt's home and began associating with a gambler named Percy McGrath, who set her up in a house on Burgundy Street. McGrath lavished gifts on her and asked nothing from her in return—not even a tryst in bed now and then—except that she play hostess whenever he set up a private poker game at the house.

Gradually, Charlotte became a part of the gambling community of New Orleans, although the only game she played—and that was strictly on rare occasions—was lotto. When McGrath would leave town to ply his trade on the riverboats, she would permit private games in the house as long as the participants were honest gentlemen gambling for the sport. At the first sign of cheating, she would put an end to the game and excuse the players from the premises with a double-barreled shotgun. She provided the gamblers with the best wines, liquors, cigars, and food, and the grateful gentlemen would pay in kind. She branched out into a special kind of prostitution by providing the gamblers with female companionship when they wished to take a break from their game. Her reputation as a hostess grew until her association with McGrath became a detriment to her. He left on one of his river excursions, and when he returned, he discovered that she had moved to the house on Royale Street. McGrath shrugged, found another girl for the house on Burgundy, and let Charlotte go about her business.

Creed met Charlotte at DuMorney's casino, while he was playing roulette. His luck with the wheel hadn't been too good; he was barely breaking even. Then Charlotte entered the smoky betting parlor. The whole room seemed to come to a standstill as every head turned toward her. She was absolutely beautiful: black hair, sapphire eyes, olive complexion, rosy cheeked and ruby lipped without the aid of cosmetics, buxom where it counted, and possessing an air of charm that captivated every man who had the good fortune to come within earshot of her angelic voice. DuMorney's floor bosses rushed to attend her, but she brushed them aside with a flick of her parasol as she made her way toward the lotto game. Those gamblers who knew her tipped their hats, bowed, and greeted her as if she were the queen of England. All the other men, the ones who didn't know her, with the single exception of Creed, merely stood speechless with their jaws hanging.

Charlotte was accustomed to this sort of reaction from the patrons of DuMorney's or any other casino that she visited, but when she saw Creed standing casually beside the roulette table studying her with an appreciative eye but with a face that was absolutely unreadable, she was taken aback, miffed by the countenance of this handsome stranger in a tattered Confederate Army officer's uniform, who couldn't be any older than she, yet seemed older in wisdom and worldliness. She walked straight up to him and stared at the amber flecks in his green eyes.

Creed stared back passively.

"With a face like that," said Charlotte, "you should be playing poker, mister."

Every man in the place was jealous of Creed, wishing to be him, if only for this one moment. They waited breathlessly for his reply.

"I think not," said Creed. He turned his back to her and placed his bet, a ten-cent chip, on twenty-three red.

No man had ever turned his back on Charlotte. She was annoyed by his attitude, but she refused to show her feelings as she said, "Is that your lucky number, stranger? Or on a scale of a hundred, is that how smart you are?"

"My age," said Creed without looking at her.

Charlotte's anger turned to amusement. She took a double eagle from the black velvet drawstring purse dangling on her left wrist and put it on top of Creed's wager. "Spin the wheel, croupier," she said.

"Oui, mademoiselle," said the croupier. He spun the wheel in one direction and the ball in the other.

Everyone continued watching them, all shocked by Creed's behavior and by the fact that Charlotte was betting on roulette. They were equally surprised when the ball dropped into the slot for twenty-three red.

"Vingt-et-trois rouge," announced the croupier. He paid off the bets.

"Let it ride," said Creed.

The croupier looked at Charlotte, who said, "Mine, too."

This brought gasps from several other patrons.

The croupier looked at the other men around the table, but no one else placed a bet, no one wishing to interfere with the little drama unfolding between Creed and Charlotte. The croupier set the ball into motion. Around and around it went until it dropped into a slot on the wheel. *"Vingt-et-trois rouge!"* he announced with some surprise. Amid gasps and mumbled conversations around the casino, he paid off the bets again.

Creed dragged his winnings from the table.

"You aren't going to press your bet again?" queried Charlotte.

Creed turned to her, looked her straight in the eyes, and said, "I already have."

Charlotte smiled at Creed, then said aside, "Croupier, cash me in and put it in my account." Then, to Creed, she said, "Ever play lotto?"

"No."

She took his arm and said, "Well, come with me and I'll show you how it's played."

"No, thanks," said Creed, not moving an inch. "My appetite needs satisfying right now, if you don't mind."

"Are you talking about food or something else?" she asked.

"Food . . . for now," said Creed evenly. "Could you recommend a good restaurant?"

"John's on Bourbon Street," said Charlotte. "I dine there frequently. The French cuisine is excellent."

"How's the American cuisine?" asked Creed, not really knowing what she meant by cuisine.

"Not as good as the French."

"You'd better recommend another place then," said Creed.

"Nonsense!" she said laughing. "John's is the best. Come along and I'll show you."

This time Creed allowed her to lead him away, and every man in the casino envied him again.

They dined, then Charlotte took Creed back to her house for a drink. He had the drink and wound up staying for the night. He went gambling with her the next evening, had a bit more luck at roulette, took her to dinner, and went home with her again. On their third evening together, he was suddenly struck with the thought that he wasn't so much her paramour as he was her trophy. He didn't like the feeling and told her so.

"That's not how I think of you," said Charlotte in a pout. "I'm in love with you, Sugar."

"That's another thing, Charlotte," he said. "You never call me by my name unless you want something from me. All the rest of the time, you call me Sugar."

"That isn't true," she said.

"No, Charlotte? Think about it for a second."

She did, then said, "I didn't realize it, Sugar."

He smiled and said, "See? You're still doing it."

"I'm sorry, Sugar, I mean—"

He held up his hand to stop her and said, "I know what you mean, Charlotte. It's all right. I've truly enjoyed every minute with you. You are something special." He kissed her softly, then looked into those striking eyes of hers. "You're really something special, Charlotte. You just remember that, but don't let it spoil you any more than it already has." He kissed her again. "I'm going home to Texas now, Charlotte. I'll see you again someday."

And with that, he walked out of her life.

Now he was walking back in, hat in hand, so to speak. He knocked at the back door and was greeted by Charlotte's housekeeper, a middle-aged Irish woman named Meg.

"Well, if it ain't Mr. Slater from Texas," said Meg with a broad smile. Her brogue was like a breath of fresh cool air off the ocean at the end of a steamy day riding the range. "What brings you around to the back door, Mr. Slater?"

Creed smiled and said, "For starters, Meg, I'm not Mr. Slater anymore."

"That answers me question. So what is it I should be calling you now?"

"Creed. Slate Creed."

Meg tilted her head and squinted at him, trying to size him up. Satisfied that she had, she said, "Sounds fairly close to your real name, don't it now? And knowing how you walked out on Miss Charlotte last spring, I'd say there's a woman in it. The trouble you got yourself in, I'm meaning. That's it, ain't it? You're in trouble with the laws because of some woman, right?"

Creed laughed and said, "Something like that, Meg."

"And you're innocent, ain't you?"

He wrinkled one brow, aimed his right index finger at her as if he were shooting a gun, and said, "You got it, Meg."

"It's them Yankees, I'll bet," said Meg.

Creed laughed again and said, "Meg, how do you know all this stuff?"

"Woman's intuition, Mr. Slater, er, I mean, Mr. Creed. That'll take some getting used to. Calling you Mr. Creed, I mean. I take it that name has something to do with your principles. Would I be right about that one, too?"

"On the head, Meg."

"As I thought. Well, come on. Miss Charlotte is just finishing her bath. Now won't she be surprised to see you waiting in her parlor?"

11

Meg was right. Charlotte was surprised to see Creed—and very, very happy, too.

"Sugar, you came back," she cooed upon entering the parlor. She glided across the room to him, threw her arms around his neck, and kissed him ardently.

Although Creed didn't reciprocate her ardor, he did return the kiss. "And I'll leave again, too," he said when they broke off the kiss, "if you don't stop calling me Sugar."

"Why, of course, Clete," she said demurely, remembering that was the reason why he had left her before.

"It isn't Clete anymore either," said Creed. "It's Creed now. Slate Creed."

Charlotte tilted her pretty head, peered up at him, and said, "Don't tell me you're in trouble with the law."

Creed's eyebrows rolled up his forehead as he said, "You might say that." He shrugged and added, "It's a long story."

She smiled like a schoolgirl eager to hear the latest gossip and said, "I'd love to hear it, Sug— uh, Slate, was it?"

Creed smiled and said, "That's right. Slate Creed."

She took him by the hand and led him to the sofa. "I don't know that I'll be able to get used to that name, but I'll try. Come sit with me and tell me all about it."

They sat, and Creed told her everything: from the day he left her the previous spring until the moment he put Nimbus in the carriage barn in back of her house.

"And you came to me for protection," said Charlotte when he was finished with his tale. "Why, sir, I do believe that I'm quite flattered."

"Well, the only people in this city that I really know are you, M. Cavaroc at the slaughterhouse, and a bunch of Yankee officers," said Creed. "I know those Yankees would be glad to see me, but

I'm not exactly anxious to see them. Since your house was closer to the docks than M. Cavaroc's stockyards, I came here."

"You mean you would have preferred to hide at the stockyards?" queried Charlotte.

Creed laughed and said, "No, of course not. Cows don't smell nearly as sweet as you do."

Charlotte threw her head back and laughed. "That's what I adore about you, Sugar, uh, I mean, Slate. You never say the things other men say to me." She kissed him again.

Creed let her finish the kiss, then said with severity, "Charlotte, I've told you about Texada. You and I can't pick up where we left off last spring, if that's what you're thinking."

"As a matter of fact, I was thinking that, but if you're going to keep reminding me of this girl back in Texas, then I'll have to think of other things, won't I?"

"Yes, you will," said Creed, touching the end of her nose gently with the tip of his finger as a mild chastisement.

She sighed and said sincerely, "So what can I do to help you out of this difficulty you're in?"

"Allow me to stay here for the time being," said Creed. "And you could make a few discreet inquiries about me around town, especially asking some of your Yankee friends about me."

"I could do that," said Charlotte coyly, "but what's in it for me?"

"You'll have my undying gratitude."

Charlotte leaned against him, pressing her breasts hard against his shoulder, and she reached down to his thigh and ran a finger lightly up the inside of it from the knee toward his crotch. "I don't want your gratitude, Slate," she said.

Creed tensed as he felt his member hardening. He took Charlotte's hand, put the palm to his lips, kissed it, and said, "That's the best I can do, Sugar."

Charlotte sighed and said, "Well, if that's the best you can do, I guess your gratitude will have to do for now." She sighed again. "So what do you want me to find out from my Yankee friends, as you call them?"

"Find out if they're looking for me as Creed or as Slater."

"Does that make a difference?" she asked.

"I don't know," said Creed. "They were waiting for me on the dock when the *Crescent City* tied up. It's my guess that Kindred telegraphed the Army here and told them I was on the ship. I'm wondering if he told them that I am now using the name Slate Creed. So far as I know, I am not wanted by the Army under that name, but I am wanted as Clete Slater. If they realize that Creed and Slater are one and the same man, then I might have to find another name to go by."

"I see," she said. "Then what?"

"Then find out how badly they want me. Find out if they're searching real hard for me, or if they're just putting out the word on me."

"All right, I can do that. What else?"

"See what you can do about getting me and my horse out of New Orleans and on our way to Nashville."

"You and your horse?"

Creed nodded and said, "Yes, me and my horse. I don't want to be dependent on boats, stagecoaches, and trains to get me where I want to go. Nimbus has been with me since I left Glengarry to enlist back in '61. He's never let me down, and I don't plan to let him down by leaving him behind now."

"All right, I'll see what I can do," she said, "but enough of this talk now. You have a very distinct odor about you, Slate, and I do believe a bath is more in order now." She picked up a little porcelain call bell from the end table and rang it.

Meg appeared almost instantly. "Yes, Miss Charlotte?"

"Meg, I'd like you to draw a bath for Mr. Creed, and see if we have some clothes that would fit him. A nice tan suit perhaps. And have Arthur tend to Mr. Creed's horse in the barn. And tell Arthur to be discreet. You know."

"Yes, mum," said Meg. "I'll be sure to tell him to keep his yap shut." She curtsied and departed.

"Now, sir, you must make yourself scarce," said Charlotte. "I have guests coming, and I don't think it would do to have them see you here."

"No, I think not," said Creed.

"My guests are not permitted on the third floor," she said, "so please stay up there until I come up and tell you it's all right for you to come down. Have you eaten recently?"

"No, and I'm famished."

"I'll have Meg bring something up to you, but remember, Slate dearest, stay on the third floor until I tell you it's all right to come downstairs."

"How long will that be?" asked Creed.

Charlotte's brow furrowed as she said, "My guests could be here for two or three days."

Creed shrugged and said, "Well, I suppose it wouldn't do to change your plans now, but to be safe," he opened his coat, showing his two Colt's pistols to her, "I'll keep these close to me at all times."

"You don't expect any trouble, do you?" she asked.

"Charlotte Sugar," he said with a sigh, "trouble has a very nasty way of finding me lately."

12

A bath, a little food, and some sleep were exactly what Creed needed. When he woke that evening, he was ready to face whatever might come his way.

Charlotte had told Creed to confine himself to the rooms of the third floor until she told him that it was all right to come downstairs, but she didn't tell him that he had to keep away from the windows, the balconies, or the roof. He stepped out on the rear terrace for a breath of fresh air and was enjoying the starry night when the sound of Charlotte's voice on the balcony below drifted up to him.

"Percy, I've told you not to come here when I have guests," she was saying.

"I know you have, Charlotte," said McGrath, "but business has been bad at my place lately and I'm leaving town soon."

"Oh, really? Where are you going?"

"Memphis."

"Memphis? Why Memphis? I thought you always went to St. Louis or Pittsburgh when you took to the boats."

"Actually, I'm going to Kentucky," said McGrath. "Bowling Green, to be precise. For the horse races."

"Horse races in Kentucky at this time of year?" asked Charlotte. "Since when?"

"Since I saw this young colt down on the docks this afternoon," said McGrath.

Charlotte peered curiously at McGrath and said, "Are we talking horses," she paused, "or boys?"

"Both," said McGrath with a wicked grin. "A young lad from Kentucky has a Thoroughbred colt that looks like he could outrun a hurricane. They arrived this noon on a steamer from Texas and are headed home to his fair state up north. I'm surprised you haven't heard about them already. The colt is the talk of the town."

Scott Houchin and Pride? wondered Creed, his interest totally piqued. He leaned closer to the wrought-iron railing surrounding the terrace but was careful not to be noticed by Charlotte and McGrath.

"No, I haven't heard anything about a Thoroughbred colt," said Charlotte. "But I did hear about some escaped prisoner from one of the steamships."

"That was nothing," said McGrath. "Just some murderer. The waterfront is full of them. The soldiers searched the docks for a bit, then gave up."

"So what about this boy and his horse?" asked Charlotte. "Does he know about your affinity for boys?"

"It makes no difference," said McGrath, annoyed by her question. "My primary interest is in the horse. He could make me rich. The boy is merely a trifle. A pleasure, to be sure, but quite expendable. The world is filled with boys like him, but there are very few horses like this Pride of his."

Good Lord! thought Creed. The son of a bitch is talking about Scott Houchin and Pride.

"What do you intend to do with this horse?" asked Charlotte. "Steal him?"

"Only as a last resort. The horse was stolen once. During the war. The boy and his brother tracked him down and found him on a ranch in Texas. The brother left them in Texas, and now the boy is taking the colt back to Kentucky by himself. I thought I would go along and see if I couldn't make a business arrangement with the boy's father."

"A business arrangement?" queried Charlotte.

"Yes, something along the lines of a manager or agent. I'd prefer to be owner, but from what the boy tells me, that's out of the question. The father intends to use the colt as a stud. I didn't press the matter, but I know that the horse will be able to demand higher fees if he's won a few races."

"And you intend to arrange these races for them?" queried Charlotte. "Is that it, Percy?"

"Precisely."

"So why are you telling me all this?" asked Charlotte, as if she didn't already know the answer.

"I'm in need of a partner or two in this venture," said McGrath confidently, "and you were my first choice, Charlotte, seeing that we once had a convenient arrangement between us."

"That's in the past, Percy, and you know it."

"Of course, it is, Charlotte, but that's no reason why we can't get together on this deal."

"What deal, Percy? All you have is a boy with a horse that's never run a race. That's hardly anything to base a deal on."

"I'll admit it's a bit thin right now, Charlotte," said McGrath, "but it shows great promise."

"You know I don't gamble, Percy, and this deal, as you call it, is riskier than DuMorney's roulette table."

"Yes, Charlotte, I know, but the possible return on your investment makes the risk worth taking."

"What sort of return are we talking about here, Percy?" asked Charlotte the businesswoman.

"It could mount into the thousands in no time at all," said McGrath eagerly, feeling that he had her on the hook.

Charlotte gave his proposition another few seconds of thought, then said, "Sorry, Percy, I'm not interested."

Good for you, Charlotte, thought Creed.

"Not interested at all?" queried a disappointed McGrath.

"I'm not interested in being your partner," said Charlotte, "but I am willing to let you work for me."

"Work for you? Preposterous!"

Charlotte said nothing. She bided her time, a moment at best, while McGrath considered listening to her proposal.

"I won't do it," said McGrath. "I won't work for a woman."

"Then you must not want this horse very much," said Charlotte. "Fine. You're wasting my time, Percy. Good night."

"Now wait, Charlotte. There must be some arrangement we can work out here."

"Not on your terms, Percy."

"Surely, we can compromise here, Charlotte."

"Not on your terms, Percy," she said persistently. "I either call the shots or there will be no arrangement between us at all."

"All right, Charlotte, what have you got in mind?"

She turned away and said, "Tomorrow, Percy. Come back tomorrow, and I'll tell you what I've got in mind."

"Tomorrow? Tomorrow could be too late!"

"I don't think so, Percy. If this boy and his horse were leaving right away, you would have accepted my proposal right off out of desperation. So tomorrow will be soon enough. First thing after breakfast. Don't be late or I might change my mind. Now get out of here. I'm already delinquent in attending my guests. Now go."

They went back into the house, and Creed heard no more conversation between them. He returned to his room and started to ponder what had just transpired. He was still thinking about it when Charlotte gently knocked on his door, then entered before he could answer.

"So what do you think?" she asked.

"About what?" answered Creed.

"About McGrath."

"McGrath?" he queried.

She giggled and said, "I know you were on the terrace listening to us. I saw your shadow on the building next door, Slate."

Creed's face started to redden, but he quickly regained control of his emotions. "All right, I was listening. I can't believe what I heard, but I heard it."

"Good," said Charlotte firmly. "Now I won't have to repeat everything. I'll just get right to the point. As you heard Percy say, the Army stopped looking for you fairly soon after you got away from them. My guests said nothing about you by name, and no one mentioned the escaped murderer on the docks, so you must not be so important. That's good because I have plans for you, Slate dearest."

"Sorry," said Creed. "I've got plans of my own."

"And they include going to Tennessee, the same as Percy and that boy with the racehorse. It's my hunch that he's the same boy you told me about, the one who helped you escape from the steamer. If he is, I know you'll want to repay him by protecting him from someone like Percy McGrath. Isn't that so?"

It was as if she could read his mind. She knew that she was right, but he didn't want to let on that he knew that she knew. "Go on," he said.

"Percy McGrath is a dirty bugger," said Charlotte. "He likes teenage boys. I think that's disgusting, and I think he's disgusting."

"Then why do you associate with him?" queried Creed.

"I don't. Not anymore. Not since I found out the truth about him. That's when I went on my own. When I learned the truth about him, I mean."

"So why are you considering helping him now?"

"I don't plan on helping him," said Charlotte. "I plan on helping me. And you. And the boy."

"How's that?" asked Creed.

"I'll tell you later." She smiled and kissed him gently. "After I make my excuses with my guests. I'll be up, and we'll talk about it then." She kissed him again. "I hope you're well rested, Sugar." She turned and left the room.

She called me Sugar, thought Creed. Damn!

13

Creed wasn't totally unhappy with the price that Charlotte Beaujeu extracted from him for her help in aiding Scott Houchin. She could have wanted more, and he would have paid it, too, because he knew that she was right when she said, "If I don't work this deal with Percy, someone else will, and that will mean real trouble for your young friend, Sugar."

Percy McGrath arrived at Charlotte's house at the appointed hour the next morning. He was a dapper gent, nattily dressed in a blue-pin-striped charcoal suit, white spats, and a black plug hat. His hair and beard were black and very clean. He had brown eyes that appeared to be afraid all the time, and his skin was quite pale because he seldom went outdoors during daylight hours. Everything else about his person was rather common and indistinguishable. Meg showed him inside to the parlor where Charlotte and Creed were waiting for him.

The trio stood in the middle of the room. Charlotte introduced the two men, and McGrath offered to shake Creed's hand. Creed refused to grip the gambler's hand, but looking him directly in the eyes, he said evenly, "I know what you are, McGrath, and I wouldn't have anything to do with you if not for Charlotte. I want you to know straight out that if you do anything to cross me or Charlotte, I *will* kill you."

McGrath was taken aback. He flinched, looked to his hostess for assistance, and said in a quavering voice, "What's all this about, Charlotte? Who is this fellow?"

"Now, Slate," said Charlotte a bit uneasily, "there's no need to make any threats like that. I'm sure you and Percy will get along just fine."

Seeing how Charlotte spoke to Creed, McGrath resorted to anger and said, "Who the hell is this son of a bitch, Charlotte?"

Creed started to reach for McGrath's lapels, but Charlotte stepped between them and said, "Why don't we sit down, gentlemen?"

Charlotte and McGrath sat, but not Creed. Leaning over and glaring at the foppish dude, he said, "I'm the man who's going to keep you walking the straight and narrow line of decency and honesty, McGrath."

McGrath turned to Charlotte. His eyes bulged with fright; they questioned her, but his lips were unable to move.

"Percy, you aren't to be trusted," she said bluntly. "Mr. Creed is my insurance that you will behave yourself on this trip."

"Charlotte, you cut me to the quick," said McGrath, intentionally overacting the part of the injured party. "Would I ever cross you?"

"First chance you got, Percy," said Charlotte. She picked up the porcelain bell on the coffee table in front of them and rang it twice.

Magically, Meg appeared. "Yes, Miss Charlotte?"

"The box, Meg," said Charlotte.

"Yes, ma'am," said Meg. She curtsied, left, then reappeared a moment later, carrying a small jeweled silver box, which she placed on the table in front of Charlotte.

"That will be all, Meg," said Charlotte. She waited for the servant to leave, then she lifted the hinged lid, revealing the box's contents: four three-inch stacks of gold coins, all double eagles. Her eyes shifted from McGrath to Creed and back to McGrath. They saw what she expected to see. Creed was glaring at McGrath, and McGrath was staring avariciously at the gold. "There's two thousand dollars there," she said. "That should be more than enough to buy the horse and to back him in a few races. That is all you are to do with the money, Percy. If you do any gambling on the boat, then do it with your own money. Is that understood?"

"It goes without saying, Charlotte," said McGrath.

"No, it doesn't, Percy," said Charlotte. "There will be no gambling by you with my money. Understood?"

"Yes, of course, Charlotte."

"Now if the horse isn't for sale," said Charlotte, "then talk the owner into racing him. You are to back him in three races, and three races only, unless he wins at least one of the three. Then you can back him in one more, but if he loses that one, then the game is over. Is that understood?"

"Yes, Charlotte," said McGrath.

"Slate is going along with you, Percy, to make sure you don't slip up."

"That really isn't necessary, Charlotte," said McGrath, protesting mildly.

Charlotte sighed and said, "Yes, it is, Percy. I've already told you that I don't trust you. I trust Slate. I know that he'll see to it that you take care of my business and nothing else. Have I made myself clear on that, Percy?"

McGrath looked at Creed, then said, "Yes, Charlotte," like a whipped puppy.

She took five coins from the box and handed them to McGrath. "Here's a hundred dollars," she said. "Find that boy and see if he's been able to book passage yet. If he has, get on the same boat with him, no matter what it takes. Book passage for yourself and Slate and Slate's horse. If the boy hasn't found a boat yet, then find one for all three of you and both horses. Understood?"

"Yes, Charlotte," said McGrath, again staring at the money in the box.

"And when you've done that, come back here," said Charlotte.

"What about the rest of the money?" asked McGrath.

"Slate will carry it," said Charlotte. "If you should need any more, you can get it from him. Now go on and do as you were told. I have other things to tend to." She looked lasciviously at Creed.

"So I see," said McGrath a bit jealously.

"He's not your kind, Percy," said Charlotte.

"Too bad," said McGrath with an evil smile.

Creed's anger pierced his silence. "Remember what I said about crossing Charlotte or me, McGrath. I *will* kill you, and I won't think twice about doing it."

"I believe you," said McGrath nervously. "I'll see you later, Charlotte." He left.

After McGrath was gone, Creed said, "I don't understand why you need him, Charlotte. I could offer to buy Pride from Scott's father just as well as McGrath could."

"I told you, Sugar," said Charlotte. "If I don't include Percy in this plan, he'll get someone else to help him, and that would put him against you instead of with you."

"I think I'd prefer that."

She frowned and said, "I do wish you hadn't threatened him like that. He's not one to take a threat too lightly. He can be dangerous, Slate. He's a real snake in the grass who will bite you when you least expect it. Remember that, Slate. Percy McGrath is a thoroughly dangerous man."

"I'll try to remember that," said Creed—but only half-seriously.

"I mean it, Slate."

"Yes, I know you mean it," said Creed. "I'll keep a close watch on McGrath. Now don't worry about it anymore."

"All right, if you say so."

"I say so," said Creed, although he still wasn't taking her warning about McGrath completely seriously.

14

McGrath returned that afternoon and told Charlotte that he had booked passage for himself and Creed on the *Princess*, a packet boat bound for St. Louis at dawn the next morning. Yes, Scott Houchin was also booked on the riverboat, although he would be traveling below decks, while Creed and McGrath would be berthed in the first-class cabins on the third deck.

The departure time suited Creed just fine. He could ride Nimbus down to the riverboat docks between Felicity and Thalia streets under cover of darkness and put the stallion aboard the *Princess* without too many eyes seeing them. He would stay with the horse until the boat cleared the port and was well under way for its first stop, at Baton Rouge.

Charlotte wanted one more substantial payment from Creed for the service that she was rendering him, but her customers demanded too much of her attention for her to make a proper collection. She settled for a *liaison rapide* on the chaise longue in her boudoir. Creed was all too happy to be free of this New Orleans minx when he left that morning for the *Princess*.

Scott Houchin was delighted to see Creed when he brought Nimbus aboard the ship. He helped put the Appaloosa in a stall next to Pride's, and even the horses acted as if they were glad to see each other.

"That boy, Charlie, and his family are also on board," said Scott. "He'll sure be happy to see you again. His stepdaddy lost all their traveling money gambling on the *Crescent City*, and his ma had to use her sock money to buy them passage on the *Princess*. Charlie's real upset about it. He said he wished he had a gun so he could shoot his stepdaddy."

"That's not good," said Creed. "Well, as soon as we get out of New Orleans, you tell Charlie I'm here."

The fore and aft lines were cast off, and the *Princess* slid away from the pier. The twin stacks belched heavy black smoke, and the dual side wheels churned up the water. In minutes, the riverboat was in midstream and paddling north.

As soon as the *Princess* was clear of the city, Scott returned to the hold with little Charlie. He hadn't told the boy why he wanted him to accompany him below, so seeing Creed was a big surprise for Charlie.

"Mr. Creed!" exclaimed Charlie. "How'd you get back here? Where have you been? Were you shot by the Yankees? How'd you get away? Boy, am I glad to see you! Are you all right?"

Creed laughed and said, "Whoa, boy! Slow down a bit, will you? Let me answer one question, will you, before you go asking all those others?"

"Oh, sure, Mr. Creed," said Charlie, blushing slightly. "Gosh, it's great to see you again. How'd you get here?"

"There you go again, Charlie," said Creed.

"Oh, yeah. Sorry."

"Sit down here," said Creed, pointing to a bale of hay. They sat, and Creed asked, "What happened aboard the *Crescent City* after I escaped?"

"I got a whupping from my new stepdaddy for helping you," said Charlie. "It didn't hurt, though," he quickly added with a smile. "It was worth it, too, because I got to help you get away. That was really keen how you jumped Nimbus off the boat onto the dock like you did. Gosh, I don't think I'll ever forget that. No, sir. I'll never forget that."

"Anything else happen that you know of, Scott?" asked Creed.

"The captain gave me a good lecture about helping criminals," said Scott, "and the Yankee officer who spoke to me was real mad about you getting away. He said you're name was Cletus Slater and that you was wanted in Texas for some raid on an Army supply train up in Mississippi last summer. That don't quite make sense, Mr. Creed. How come you're wanted in Texas for something that you was supposed to have done in Mississippi?"

"They tried me in Texas," said Creed, "I guess because that's where I was when they arrested me. They'd determined that I was guilty before the trial, so why should they go to all the trouble to send me to Mississippi or even to

New Orleans for a trial that they could hold right there in Texas?"

"I see," said Scott.

"So did you hear anything else?" asked Creed.

"Nothing in particular," said Scott. "They said something about a search, but they figured that would be hopeless in a city this big." He nodded toward the horses and said, "I guess they didn't think about Nimbus there. How many men in New Orleans would be riding around on a horse like that? If I was the one hunting for you, that's what I'd look for. A man on a gray horse."

"Well, I'm glad you're not the one hunting me, Scott," said Creed. "Of course, these are only Yankees looking for me. That's like trying to outsmart a bunch of dumb mules. It doesn't take much wit to do that."

"No, sir," said Charlie with a knowledgeable grin. "Them Yankees ain't too bright, that's for sure. I told them you made us help you get away, and they believed me."

"Good for you, Charlie," said Creed. "Scott tells me your stepdaddy gambled away all your traveling money on the *Crescent City*. That's too bad. Maybe he's learned his lesson now."

"I hope so," said Charlie, "because Ma ain't got much money left for us to eat on."

Creed gave that a thought, then said, "Sit right here, boys. I'll be right back." He got up and went to his saddle and gear in Nimbus's stall. He took the string purse of gold coins from his saddlebags, then picked two double eagles out of the bag. He replaced the purse in his saddlebags, then returned to Charlie and Scott. "Here, Charlie," he said, giving the boy one of the coins. "You give this to your mother. Tell her it's the money I gave you on the *Crescent City* for helping me escape, and when she asks you why you didn't give it to her earlier, tell her you were afraid the Yankees would take it away from you." He gave Scott the other coin and said, "You earned this, Scott. Thanks for your help."

"You don't have to do this," said Scott, trying to give the money back to Creed. "I just wanted to help."

"You risked your neck for me," said Creed. "Both of you did, and I still owe you both. This money can't begin to tell you how much I appreciate your help. So you boys keep it and use it wisely."

"Thanks, Mr. Creed," said Charlie.

"Yeah, thanks, Mr. Creed," said Scott.

"Now there's something I need to tell you boys about. I'm going all the way to Kentucky with you, Scott."

"You are?" queried Scott. This was good news to him.

"Yes, I am. I'm traveling with another man. I believe you already know him, Scott. His name is McGrath."

"Yes, sir, I know him," said Scott evenly.

"He's a gambler, Scott, and he's not to be trusted. Do you understand that?"

"But if he's a friend of yours—"

"I didn't say he was a friend of mine," said Creed. "I'm working for a lady back in New Orleans who wants to buy Pride from your daddy."

"Pa won't sell Pride," said Scott, shaking his head to emphasize his statement.

"That's what I figure," said Creed, "but this lady in New Orleans wants McGrath to ask him anyway. If he won't sell, then McGrath is supposed to back him in three races and split the winnings with your daddy."

"Pa might go for that one," said Scott.

"Well, that's what's supposed to happen," said Creed. "I don't trust McGrath, and I don't want you to trust him either. Stay clear of him as much as you can, and don't let him get you alone." His eyes regarded Charlie with concern, and he said, "Either one of you."

"Why not?" asked Charlie.

"Just don't let him get you alone, that's all," said Creed sternly. "He's a . . . he's not a nice man, that's all."

"All right, if you say so," said Charlie with a shrug.

"I say so," said Creed. He thought for a second, then said, "Charlie, your parents know what I look like and they know about the incident on the *Crescent City*. If they see me on board, they're liable to tell the captain, and I'll be right back where I was on the *Crescent City*. I'll have to stay in my cabin most of the time, so I won't be able to keep an eye on McGrath as much as I'd like to. I'll need you two to watch him for me, but he can't know that you're watching him. Do you know what I mean?"

"Sure, we do," said Charlie. "Don't we, Scott?"

"Yeah, that's right," said Scott eagerly. "We'll watch him for you, Mr. Creed. You can count on us."

"I thought I could," said Creed. "Scott, you point out McGrath for Charlie. I suspect he'll be playing a lot of cards on this trip, so he'll be in the main salon a lot. But when he leaves the main salon, follow him, then come tell me what he's up to. I'll decide what to do then. Understood?"

Both boys nodded that they did.

"Good," said Creed. "Now go make sure your parents aren't out on deck, Charlie. I'd like to get to my cabin without being seen by them."

"Yes, sir," said Charlie, and he left.

"Scott, will you take care of Nimbus for me on this trip?"

"Sure thing, Mr. Creed."

"I don't usually trust him to anyone else, but seeing how much you love horses, I know I can trust you with him." Creed laughed, then said, "I don't think I'd know what to do with myself if I didn't have Nimbus with me." He nudged Scott and said, "Come on and help me carry my gear to my cabin."

15

Creed stayed in his cabin the rest of the day. When the *Princess* tied up for the night at Baton Rouge, he ventured out, figuring Charlie's parents weren't likely to come up to the upper deck after dark. He wandered down to the main salon because Scott had told him that he was right about McGrath, that the gambler would spend his time there gambling at cards.

McGrath was in the middle of a poker game when Creed entered the spacious compartment. Several tables had poker games. A few had faro, and one had three-card monte. Creed wandered about the room for a few minutes before settling down at a vacant table in one corner. A waiter came up to him and asked if he could get him anything. Feeling a thirst but wary of having any alcoholic beverage, he ordered tomato juice with a wedge of lemon and a dill pickle. The former slave brought him the drink, then Creed leaned back and watched the action.

Creed wasn't sure, but the three-card-monte thrower looked familiar to him. He knew the goateed face, but he couldn't recall the name and the place that went with it. Such a curiosity! It disturbed him. He started to get up and walk over to the gent to inquire about his identity, but he held his place when he saw another familiar face just then. It belonged to Canada Bill Jones, a man of very distinct features.

Jones was medium-sized, chicken-headed, and tow-haired with mild blue eyes and a mouth that spread nearly from ear to ear. Wearing a checkered suit that was at least three sizes too large for him and a derby that appeared to be too small even for his head, Jones shuffled up to the gaming table, grinned like an idiot, and placed a wager.

Creed shook his head as the name of the thrower came to him. It was Devol, George Devol, a gambler that he had met at DuMorney's the previous spring. They had spoken briefly about the virtues of various games, Devol proclaiming faro to be the most exciting game for him, while Creed felt roulette was the easier to win at. Creed had watched Devol drop a few hundred at faro, then he left to play roulette and eventually met up with Charlotte Beaujeu. Later, while in Charlotte's company, he had again come across Devol, who then had Jones with him. Upon meeting Jones, Creed couldn't believe that a man who had the appearance of the classical court jester could be so intelligent and articulate. Charlotte explained later that Jones used his fool's aspect to his advantage in the sporting world, that he and Devol were as fine a pair of sharpers as the river had ever known. Creed believed her, but he didn't get the opportunity to see them work.

Now was his chance.

Picking up his drink, Creed sauntered over to Devol's game to observe. He stood behind a short man, a Yankee business-man from the looks of him, who was intent on watching the game.

"Who will go me five?" asked Devol, a large man with thick hands and fingers that seemed inappropriate for shuffling and dealing playing cards.

"Aw, shucks," said Jones, "I'll give it a go." He put a silver dollar on the table and pointed to one of the three cards placed facedown near it.

"No, sir," said Devol. "I said five."

"Yeah, I know, but I ain't got no change."

Devol smiled benevolently and said, "Sir, I'm talking dollars here, not cents."

"Dollars?" queried Jones on cue.

"Yes, sir, dollars."

Jones scratched at his hair as if it were thatch giving him a serious itch, tilting his derby forward. "Well," he said, drawing out the word, "all right, a dollar then."

"Sir, I asked for a wager of five," said Devol. "If you want to play, you'll have to put up five dollars."

Jones screwed up his face and said, "Five, you say?"

"Five, yes."

"Well, all right." Jones dug deep down into his trou-sers pocket and drew out four more cartwheels. He stacked them on the other one, then pointed again. "That one," he said.

Devol shook his head, smiled, and said, "No, sir, you don't

understand. Now I get to mix them up, then you get to choose which is the ace of hearts."

Jones appeared not to understand at first, thought for a second, then smiled and said, "Oh, sure, I gotcha. Go ahead. Mix them up. I'll still get the right one."

"Thank you," said Devol, patronizing the imbecile. He moved the cards over the felt, slowly at first, then a little faster. In a few seconds, he stopped and said, "Now, sir, which one is the ace of hearts?"

Jones grinned ear-to-ear, pointed, and said, "That one," indicating the one on Devol's right.

"This one?" queried Devol. "Are you sure you want that one?" He seemed a bit nervous.

"Yep, that one," said Jones.

Devol turned over the ace of hearts and said, "You win, sir." He slid a five-dollar gold piece across the felt to Jones and asked, "Would you care to go again, sir?"

"Sure thing, mister," said Jones. "Why not? That was easy pickings." He chuckled insultingly.

They replayed the same scene, and Devol paid off again. Jones and Devol repeated the play once more for twenty dollars, and after being paid, Jones said he'd won enough and quit the game, leaving the table behind him.

"Who else will give it a go?" asked Devol.

"Can you take fifty?" asked the Yankee businessman.

Devol appeared to be taken aback at the mention of that amount. "Fifty, sir?" he said.

"Yes, fifty dollars," said the Yankee. "Hard cash money." He produced five ten-dollar gold pieces and put them down on the table.

Devol stroked his beard in thought, then said, "Should I lose, I will be strapped, sir. I think . . . maybe—"

"Aw, go on," said Creed. "Take his bet."

The Yankee glanced over his shoulder and saw Creed grinning at Devol, then he turned back to Devol, who was looking past the businessman. He didn't see Devol's eyes widen for an instant when the gambler recognized Creed.

Devol's orbs regained their feigned seriousness for another second before brightening into mirthfulness. "Yes, I'll take your wager, sir," he said. "I guess that's why they call it gambling."

"That's right," said the Yankee with a hint of avarice in his voice. "Shuffle, mister."

Devol did just that, but this time he was a little faster than when Jones was playing. His hands were a bit more adept, making moves that they hadn't made previously. Finally, they stopped, and Devol said, "Pick your card, sir."

"That one," said the Yankee, pointing to the one on Devol's right.

"This one, sir?" queried Devol, indicating the same card and giving the appearance of worry.

"Yes, that one," said the Yankee impatiently.

Devol turned over the deuce of spades and said, "Well, what do you know? I win." He quickly scooped up the Yankee's fifty dollars and asked, "Care to play again, sir?"

"No. No, I think not," he said with cold sweat breaking out on his face. He looked around him, embarrassed by his loss, then left Creed and Devol alone.

"How about you, sir?" asked Devol, looking at Creed. "You appear to be a man with a quick eye."

Creed smiled back and said, "Maybe so, but I don't think it's as quick as your hands."

"Come now, sir," said Devol. "The hand can never be quicker than the eye."

"Pity we won't find that out with my money," said Creed with a friendly smile.

Devol smiled back and said, "Yes, a pity."

"George Devol, isn't it?" asked Creed.

"Yes, and yours would be . . ." He chuckled and said, "Excuse me for not remembering it, sir, but although I can remember the place and the lady on your arm, I can't for the life of me think of your name."

"That's good," said Creed.

"It will come to me," said Devol.

"Until it does, you can call me Slate Creed."

"No, that's not it," said Devol, still thoughtful.

"It will have to do for now," said Creed with a gentle admonition.

Devol studied Creed's face for a second and realized that it would do no good to pursue his quest for Creed's real name at this time. He nodded and said, "Yes, of course. Then Slate

Creed it will be." He offered his hand in friendship and said, "How good to see you again, Mr. Creed!"

"The pleasure is all mine, Mr. Devol," said Creed, shaking Devol's big hand. He noted how soft it felt, softer than a woman's. He surmised that that was how Devol maintained such a delicate touch with the cards.

"You were with Charlotte Beaujeu the last time I saw you, if I recall correctly," said Devol.

"Your memory is improving," said Creed.

"Ah, yes, Charlotte Beaujeu! Quite a lady. Very attractive, too. And particular as well. How did you manage to . . . to land in her good graces, so to speak?"

"Lucky, I guess," said Creed.

"Well, whatever it was, you were the envy of every red-blooded man in New Orleans last spring. I can tell you that, Mr. Creed. Yes, sir, every man who's ever seen Charlotte envied you. Some even talked of challenging you to a duel, but none dared to do it, because we all knew that Charlotte would never approve. Isn't that an irony?"

"It certainly is," said Creed.

"Tell me, Mr. Creed, is she everything they say she is?"

"More," said Creed with a self-satisfied smile. "Much, much more." He didn't know how true that statement was. Not yet anyway.

Devol shook his head and said, "I believe it. Yes, I do. Charlotte is a rare gem. A very rare gem indeed. Have you seen her lately?"

"Just these last two days," said Creed.

"Really? In New Orleans? I thought she had a game at her place the last two days."

"She did," said Creed. "I was an unexpected houseguest."

"I won't ask anything more about that except to inquire about why you are on the *Princess* this very night."

"Business trip," said Creed, telling him half the truth intentionally. He saw no sense in relating his other reason for heading north at this time.

"Business?" queried Devol.

"Yes, I'm on my way to Kentucky to see a man about a horse," said Creed.

"A racehorse?" asked Devol.

"As a matter of fact, yes."

"And would this horse be aboard the *Princess* at this very minute?" asked Devol.

Devol knew more than Creed had thought. Evidently, McGrath had been talking. "As a matter of fact, yes," he said. He stared at Devol and asked, "How did you know?"

Devol leaned a little closer to Creed and said, "You aren't mixed up with McGrath, are you?"

Creed tilted away, noted the concern in Devol's face, then said, "Mr. Devol, I think we need to go somewhere and have a little talk."

"Yes, we should," said Devol, "and maybe I should have my associate meet us. Do you remember Mr. Jones?"

"Seeing him is how I remembered your name," confessed Creed.

"Do tell," said Devol, suddenly brighter and less conspiratorial. "I'll have to tell him. He'll be impressed. But for now, let us repair to my cabin."

As he and Creed crossed the salon, Devol caught Jones's eye, tugged at his right ear, then put his hand over his heart. This was Devol's signal to Jones to follow them. He and Creed walked leisurely out on deck and up the ladder to Devol's cabin on the second deck. Jones joined them within the minute.

"Do you remember this gentleman, Bill?" Devol asked his companion.

Jones twisted up his face and said, "No, I don't recall him." Then he took a second look and said, "Wait a minute. Aren't you the lucky bloke what was with Charlotte Beaujeu last spring? Let me see. Slater, isn't it?"

"Right you are, Bill," said Devol with a jovial laugh. "Only now his name is Creed. Slate Creed." He perused Creed's face and said, "Hm-m. Cletus Slater is now Slate Creed. Very curious, sir. Running from the law, are you?"

"To make a long story short, yes," said Creed.

"No need for further explanation," said Jones. "We've been there ourselves. Anything we can do to help, you just name it. Any man who can gain Charlotte Beaujeu's favor is aces in my book."

"Mine, too," said Devol, "which is precisely why I brought you here. To warn you about McGrath."

"McGrath?" queried Jones. "You aren't mixed up with Percy McGrath, are you?"

"Unfortunately, yes," said Creed. "It's not my doing, though. Charlotte asked me to do a favor for her, and who am I to refuse a lady a favor?"

"What sort of favor?" asked Devol.

"McGrath came to her and told her about the racehorse," said Creed. "He wanted Charlotte to back him, but she wouldn't have anything to do with that."

"Good for her!" said Jones.

"But the horse belongs to a young man I met on the boat from Texas to New Orleans. I was afraid that McGrath might do the lad harm in some way or another, and Charlotte realized this, too. So she came up with this plan where McGrath is working for her as her agent to buy the horse legally or at least to back him in a few races if the boy's father will permit it. If he doesn't go for the bargain, then McGrath is supposed to back off and leave the boy and his horse alone."

"Sounds simple enough," said Devol. "What do you think, Bill?"

"It's too easy," said Jones, his face wrinkling seriously. "Did McGrath go along with this plan willingly?"

"He seemed willing enough to me," said Creed.

"I was afraid of that," said Jones. He pinched his lower lip between thumb and index finger as he gave the matter some thought. He removed his hand from his mouth and said, "My friend, you'd better keep an eye on McGrath. I think he's up to something. He's been talking about the horse ever since he came aboard this morning. He's talking about this stallion as if he were the next Lexington."

"Lexington?" queried Creed. "A great racehorse, I take it."

"The greatest this country has seen so far," said Jones.

"Well, Scott's horse hasn't even run a single race yet," said Creed. "How can he compare a raw colt to a great racehorse?"

"That's my point, Creed," said Jones. "McGrath is up to something. Something bad, too. You can bet on that. As I said before, you'd better keep a close eye on him at all times. I saw him in the main salon playing poker." Jones snickered and said, "He's cheating, too."

"Cheating?" queried Creed. "How?"

"He's dealing off the bottom of the deck," said Jones, "and he's dealing seconds."

"How do you know?" asked Creed.

Devol laughed and said, "You must be joking, Creed. We're gamblers. We know all the tricks of the games."

"But I don't," said Creed. "How would I recognize his cheating . . . if I was to sit in on his game?"

Jones and Devol exchanged questioning looks before Devol asked, "Is that what you're considering doing?"

"Yes, I suppose," said Creed, a bit unsure of himself.

"Why?" asked Jones.

"To keep a closer eye on him, I suppose," said Creed. "What better way to do that than to play in his game?"

"Good point," said Jones. "But remember this, my young friend, if we tell you how to catch him cheating, you must promise never to reveal who told you."

"I promise you that," said Creed.

"Good enough," said Devol. He nodded at Jones. "Go ahead and tell him, Bill."

"Watch his thumb," said Jones to Creed. "His left thumb. When he deals from the bottom, he'll slide it forward on the deck as if he's pushing the top card forward to be dealt, but really he's pulling the bottom card from the deck to deal. And when he's dealing seconds, he'll slide his thumb backward, taking the top card with it so he can deal the second. He'll do it fast, so don't blink or you'll miss it."

"Thanks for the tip," said Creed.

"Are you planning to get into his game right away?" asked Devol.

"I might be," said Creed.

"Then you'd better arm yourself," said Devol. "If you call McGrath for cheating, he'll draw down on you. He carries a little Smith and Wesson .32 all the time. He'll use it in an instant if his hand is called. And I do mean an instant, Creed. Percy McGrath is very fast with his hands, and damn dangerous, too. He's killed some good men on this river. Three that I know of. Maybe more. McGrath is a poor loser, too. I know of at least one fellow who took him for a bundle and never lived to spend it. He's a snake, that McGrath."

Odd, thought Creed, Charlotte had used that same word to describe McGrath. That was too much coincidence not to be taken seriously.

16

It didn't take much for Creed to get into McGrath's poker game in the main salon. All he had to do was produce some hard cash, and he was in.

McGrath eyed Creed as if he were an unwelcome stranger and asked, "Are you sure you want in this game, sir? The stakes have no limit. We play for cash only. No credit here. Pots go as high as two, three thousand at times. Can you go that much?"

Creed frowned at McGrath and said, "I can go that much. What's the game?"

"Stud," said McGrath. "Seven-card. A dollar ante to see three cards."

Creed tossed a silver cartwheel into the middle of the table and said, "I'm in. Deal." He sat down at one of the three vacant spots at the table and put his bank, a thousand dollars of Charlotte's money and two hundred of his own, in front of him. He squirmed a bit until the Colt's under his coat stopped gouging at his gut.

McGrath dealt the cards, and the game began. Besides Creed and McGrath, three other men sat at the table.

One was a cotton buyer from New England who had chosen to travel on a riverboat instead of taking a sea voyage or riding the rails home, because it had always been his desire to make at least one trip up the Mississippi before his end came. McGrath introduced him as Mr. Pickering. He was short, thin, bespectacled, and austere in dress and aspect.

The second man was Herr Johan Heinrich Nahams, a St. Louis *meisterbrauer* who had been on holiday in New Orleans. He was a large man with rosy cheeks, dishwater blond hair, a silvery mustache that was properly waxed to hold its curls, and jolly blue eyes. His Falstaffian girth stated plainly that he sampled his brew frequently.

Potter Palmer introduced himself. He was a Chicago real estate speculator and mercantile magnate who had gone down to New Orleans for a vacation from the cold north winds coming off Lake Michigan and to escape the even colder stares of his business associates, who disapproved of his choices of entertainment—that is, fast horses, fast games, and fast women. "In New Orleans," he said, "no one knows me, and besides, even if they did, they wouldn't stick their Creole noses in my affairs like those transplanted New England prudes in Chicago so often do."

The game proceeded without incident or excitement through the night. No one player could gain much of an advantage over the others, as their skill of play and their luck ran fairly equally. When dawn came and the *Princess* prepared to pull away from the dock in Baton Rouge, McGrath suggested that they take a break for some hot food and coffee in the riverboat's dining salon, and everyone agreed to the idea.

Creed used the opportunity to confer again with Devol and Jones in Devol's cabin.

"I can't seem to catch him cheating," said Creed.

"When I've been watching," said Jones, "he's not doing anything that I can see except playing straight cards. What about you, George? Have you seen him doing anything suspicious when you've been watching?"

"Not a thing," said Devol, "and that makes me all the more suspicious of him. He's setting up something."

"What do you think it is?" asked Creed.

"Could be any number of things," said Devol. "Bill, did you see anyone come aboard at Baton Rouge?"

"No one," said Jones.

"But I thought several new passengers came aboard at Baton Rouge," said Creed, perplexed by their dialogue.

Devol smiled and explained, "We meant other members of our profession. Just as Bill and I team up, so do many others. McGrath has several cronies on the river. I was asking Bill if he'd seen any of them come aboard in Baton Rouge."

"I see," said Creed.

"He could have some new talent that we haven't seen before," said Jones.

"That's possible," said Devol. "Let's see who gets in the game when it resumes. If it's one of the new passengers, then it's a good bet that he's tied in with McGrath. If it's someone who's been on the boat since New Orleans, then we're back where we started guessing what he's up to."

"Well, I suppose the only thing for me to do is get back to the game," said Creed. He left the cabin and headed to the main salon. Along the way, he thought he'd check on Nimbus in the hold and possibly see Scott Houchin as well. As he expected, Scott was doing the same with Pride.

"Morning, Mr. Creed," said Scott.

"Morning, Scott," said Creed. "How's Pride faring this trip up the river so far?"

"Lots better than he did that voyage on the *Crescent City*. He's eating better anyways."

"That's good. Have you seen little Charlie this morning?"

"Can't say that I have. You need him for something?"

Creed shook his head and said, "No, I was just wondering how he was doing. That's all."

Scott nodded and said, "How are you doing, Mr. Creed? In the poker game, I mean."

"I'm holding my own. In fact, I'm ahead a few hundred."

"No fooling? Gee, that's great!"

Creed smiled sheepishly and said, "Well, it ain't bad, and that's what worries me. McGrath is a gambler, and gamblers are renowned cheaters. Trouble is I haven't seen him cheating yet. I know he's going to cheat, but when and how is the wonderment."

"Maybe he's afraid to cheat because you're in the game," said Scott. "Or maybe he's playing it honest because he's supposed to buy Pride and he don't want anything bad to be said about him or something like that."

"That could be, Scott. Well, we'll just have to see. It's still a long way to Memphis. Anything could happen yet."

Creed patted Nimbus on the neck and stroked the stallion's jaw. The Appaloosa nuzzled him in return.

"From the scars on him," said Scott, "you two must have been in a lot of battles during the war."

"A few," said Creed. "Too many to recall, I guess." He was thoughtful for a second, the sounds of muskets, rifles, shotguns, pistols, cannons, clashing swords, and the screams of wounded and dying men reverberating in his mind; then he said, "Well, I'd better get back to the game." He held up a finger of caution and said, "Scott, you watch out for yourself now. Be prepared for anything and everything, you hear?"

"Yes, sir. You mean, I should be on my guard all the time, right?"

"That's right." As if he were a sage in his long-tooth years instead of the young man that he really was, Creed patted the youth on the shoulder and said, "That's right, Scott. Always be on your guard."

Creed returned to the main salon and discovered that he was the last to rejoin the game and that two new players were seated at the table.

Much to Creed's surprise and chagrin, one was Charlie's step-father, Mr. Carrier, the discharged Yankee soldier who claimed to own a farm in Michigan. He was a stout man with a ruddy complexion, bloodshot eyes, no neck, and prematurely graying hair. From the look of him, Creed surmised that Carrier drank much more than he should. He looked at Creed and nodded as if they had met before, but Creed couldn't recall having seen the man aboard the *Crescent City*. Even so, they knew each other by name, and this worried Creed a bit, although it seemed not to make any difference to Carrier.

The other newcomer was the ship's master, Captain Otis Ritter, a pudgy fellow with watery blue eyes that seemed bent always on tears, whether of joy or anger, it didn't matter. His clean-shaven face was rough, raw, and pockmarked. He had a mouth that didn't smile naturally but that had to be forced into a grin, which appeared counterfeit.

"Whose deal is it?" asked Ritter.

"Mine, sir," said McGrath. "We play seven-card stud here, Captain, if that suits you."

"Suits me fine," said Ritter with a jovial smile.

"Me, too," said Carrier quite seriously.

"A dollar ante, sir," said McGrath to Carrier, patronizing him with syrupy sweetness.

All tossed in their antes, and the game was begun.

Just as things had gone the night before, no player was able to gain much of an advantage over the others. Three hours of play transpired, and the only player with any appreciable increase in his bank was Creed.

The captain excused himself, saying he had to make a round of the boat to make sure every man was doing his job. He would return to play again.

"Well, since our good captain has taken a break," said McGrath, "I suggest the rest of us do the same."

"We don't need any goddamned break," groused Carrier. He had been drinking since the first hand but wasn't seriously drunk, having put away no more than a tumbler of whiskey in that time. "Deal the cards, McGrath."

McGrath scanned the faces of the other players, then said, "Mr. Carrier, I think the majority would appreciate a few minutes from the table. Am I correct, gentlemen?"

"I would like to relieve myself," said Herr Nahams, his accent distinctively German but not all that heavy. "*Ja!* I go to do that now." He slid away from the table, rose, and left.

"A trip to the hurricane deck for a breath of fresh air sounds like a good idea to me," said Palmer. "Care to join me, Mr. Pickering?"

"Yes, sir, I would," said Pickering.

Both men got up and headed for the upper level of the boat.

"What about you, Creed?" asked Carrier. "You running out, too, like you did on the *Crescent City*? Don't deny it, Creed. I saw you." He snickered. "Actually, I rather admired your sand. Imagine, leaping a horse from a ship onto a dock and racing away with a squadron of good Union soldiers firing a volley at your back. An admirable bit of bravado, Creed. Even if you are a Reb."

"Was," said Creed, forcing himself to take Carrier lightly when he really wanted to throttle the man for his snide remarks and the way he was treating little Charlie and his mother. "The war has been over for several months now, Mr. Carrier. As far as I'm concerned, we're all Americans again and not Federals and Confederates."

"To hell with all that political bullshit," said Carrier. "Let's play some poker."

Creed glared at Carrier. The man was abrasive, obtuse, and obnoxious. He needed to be taught a lesson and quick.

"All right, I'll play with you," said Creed, "if you're that anxious to lose your money."

Carrier grunted and said, "I don't aim to lose, Creed. You've got a nice little pile of gold there that would look better sitting in front of me. Deal, McGrath."

"If you insist," said McGrath.

It took Creed and McGrath less than fifteen minutes to break Carrier and send him away from the table bitching about their uncanny luck.

"Now, McGrath, I think I'll take that break," said Creed.

"As will I," said McGrath.

Creed sought out Scott Houchin and told him to find little Charlie as quickly as he could and to send the boy to Creed's cabin. It took less than five minutes for Scott to find Charlie and for Charlie to report to Creed.

"Charlie, your stepfather was in the poker game," said Creed. "I thought Scott said he lost all your money on the *Crescent City*."

"He did," said Charlie. "Ma had some sock money left that she used to buy us tickets to St. Louis, and old Carrier sweet-talked her into giving him what was left so he could win back what he lost on the *Crescent City*."

"I see," said Creed. "How much was that, Charlie?"

"I don't know," said the boy. "Fifty dollars, I guess. Maybe more."

Creed pulled a poke from inside his coat and dug out some double eagles. "Here, Charlie," he said, handing the money to the youngster. "You give this to your mother. It's the money I won off your stepfather. Tell her not to let him have it again, because the next man who wins it from him might not be so generous, and that includes me. You understand, Charlie?"

"Yes, sir, I do," said Charlie, his face twisted up with adult seriousness. "I'll give this to Ma, and I won't tell old Carrier nothing about it. You can bet on that, Mr. Creed."

"You best learn a lesson from all this, Charlie. Gambling is serious business. There are men on this river who would cut you up into little pieces to win a hand of cards from you. Do you understand that, Charlie?"

"Yes, sir, I do. Gambling ain't for me. No, sir. Not for me at all."

"Good lad," said Creed. "Now take that money to your mother."

"Yes, sir," said Charlie, and he left.

Creed splashed some water on his face, wiped himself dry, then put on a clean shirt. He replaced the thousand dollars of Charlotte Beaujeu's money in its hiding place, then returned to the game.

All the other players with the exception of Carrier were present and waiting for Creed. He sat down, and play resumed. Unlike the previous sessions, when no player could gain the upper hand and no player lost too badly, with the exception of Carrier, Mr. Pickering bet more heavily than before, took some lumps, and was quickly forced to withdraw midway through the afternoon. Herr Nahams was the next player to see his bank dwindle rapidly, and he, too, took his leave. This left Creed, McGrath, Palmer, and Captain Ritter.

"Gentlemen, I will have to retire within the hour," said Ritter. "We are nearing Natchez, and I must report to the pilothouse soon."

"At that time," said McGrath, "I believe we should suspend play until after the boat is tied up in Natchez. Agreed, gentlemen?"

"Sounds good enough to me," said Palmer.

"I'll go along with that," said Creed.

"Excellent," said McGrath. He dealt the next hand.

Creed wasn't sure, but he thought he saw McGrath pass over the top card on the deck and deal the second to Palmer. On the next round, he was sure he saw McGrath slip the bottom card to Palmer. On the third round, he dealt another second to Palmer. It was an ace. Creed had a king showing, Ritter a seven, McGrath a six. Palmer bet twenty dollars on his ace without looking at his hole cards. The other three players called his wager, and McGrath passed out the fourth round of pasteboards. Creed paired up; Ritter got an eight; Palmer caught a deuce of the same suit as his ace; and McGrath drew a ten. Creed threw two double eagles into the pot and said, "Twenty on each of my lords." Ritter called; Palmer studied his cards a second and did likewise; but McGrath raised twenty dollars.

Creed studied each man's hand. Palmer could have anything from three aces or a straight flush going down to an ace and nothing. Ritter had two cards to a straight showing and could have two more cards to that straight in the hole. McGrath also had two cards to a straight, but they were at the ends of the line, meaning he would be betting on drawing to an inside straight, which wasn't likely, because, as any good gambler knew, the odds against hitting an inside straight were quite poor at best.

To see if McGrath was holding more than he showed, Creed raised him back twenty dollars.

"Forty to me?" queried Ritter. He knew the answer without being told, and he threw in the wager.

Palmer did likewise, and McGrath called Creed and dealt the next round. Creed's card was a queen; Ritter's was a nine; Palmer's another ace; and McGrath's a five. Palmer had control, and he bet fifty dollars. McGrath immediately raised him fifty. Creed peeked at the king he had in the hole and raised another fifty, while still wondering what McGrath was betting on. Ritter called. Palmer made the last raise, another fifty. McGrath stayed in, as did Creed and Ritter.

As McGrath dealt again, Creed summed up the other players' hands. Ritter had three cards to a straight. Palmer had a pair of aces. McGrath had nothing in sight.

Creed caught a ten, Ritter a ten, Palmer another ace, and McGrath an eight.

"Three aces, gentlemen," said Palmer calmly. "One hundred on each one." He tossed the gold into the pot.

"I'll call," said McGrath without hesitating, putting three hundred dollars in the middle of the table.

Creed was beat on the board, but there was still a good chance that he could win. He might catch another queen or a ten to give him a full house, or he could catch a jack that would give him an ace-high straight. He might even catch the fourth king. One thing he knew for sure. Palmer wasn't going to beat him with four aces.

Creed called, and so did Ritter.

"Pot's right, gents," said McGrath. He dealt the last round of cards facedown, then said, "I believe it's still your bet, Mr. Palmer."

Palmer peeked at his three hole cards, was pensive for a few seconds, then said, "It will cost each of you a thousand to see my hand, gentlemen." He slid a stack of one hundred dollar gold pieces into the pot.

McGrath raised five hundred without hesitation, which didn't surprise Creed, because he had seen McGrath deal the last card to himself from the bottom of the deck.

Creed's final card was a queen, giving him a full house. Palmer could have him beaten, but he couldn't fold on a full boat. Or could he? McGrath was cheating, and Creed knew it. If he bet, he would certainly lose, and that would break him. He placed his cards facedown and said, "I fold."

"I'll call," said Ritter.

Palmer eyed McGrath, apparently wondering what the gambler had for a hand. Obviously, the man had a straight, but there was no way he could have a flush because his four up cards were all different suits. So what was he raising on? A full house? That was distinctly possible. McGrath was a professional gambler, and the pros usually folded on the first up card unless they had a pair, three cards to a straight, or three cards to a flush. No matter what McGrath had, Palmer had a straight flush, and that beat a full house.

"I'll raise another five hundred," said Palmer. He put the bet in the pot.

Calmly, McGrath said, "I'll call your five hundred and raise you another thousand." He counted out the money and put it in the middle of the table with the other bets.

Captain Ritter considered his cards for a moment, then said, "Gentlemen, I haven't got enough cash to call you with. Would you accept title to the *Princess* as collateral until we reach Natchez?"

Palmer smiled and said, "Sounds reasonable to me, Captain. I've always wanted to own a steamboat like this one."

"I'll accept that, too," said McGrath.

"Don't go getting your master's papers yet, Mr. Palmer," said Ritter jovially. "I call."

McGrath turned up his hole cards. Three sixes to go with the one he had up.

"That beats me," said Palmer, shrugging and throwing his cards in the pot nonchalantly.

Creed couldn't stand it any longer. He slid his chair away from the table, put his hand on the butt of his Colt's, and said, "You cheated, McGrath."

"What did you say?" demanded McGrath, also sliding away from the table.

"You cheated," said Creed. "I saw you deal that last card from the bottom of the deck, and you dealt seconds to Mr. Palmer earlier. I saw you."

McGrath acted as if he was going to pull his gun.

Creed did pull his and would have killed McGrath if not for Ritter slapping him with a backhand, spoiling his aim. The ball nicked McGrath's left earlobe, and the flame from the revolver's blast singed his beard.

McGrath screamed and grabbed his face.

Ritter struck Creed again, shouting, "Hold on there!"

Palmer sat quietly, seemingly rather amused by the scene before him.

Creed was astonished by Ritter's attack. He leaned away from Ritter's blows and forgot about shooting McGrath again.

"Hold on there!" shouted Ritter again. He grabbed at Creed's gun hand, seized it, and forced Creed to aim at the deck. "I have the winning hand, Mr. Creed."

Creed's mind went into an instant blur. Was he hearing right? Did Ritter say he had the winning hand? He heard himself ask, "What?"

"I have the winning hand," said Ritter. "See for yourself."

Creed ceased to struggle with the captain.

"I'm injured!" cried McGrath. "I'm injured!"

Palmer turned over Ritter's cards for everyone to see.

Four sevens stared hard at Creed.

17

"I'll kill that son of a bitch!" whined McGrath.

"You'll do no such thing on my boat," said Ritter.

At the captain's command, two waiters had come over to the table, disarmed Creed, then restrained him by the arms. Not that he was threatening anyone or was struggling to get away; it was just a precaution.

"You're not hurt that bad," said Palmer, still amused by the incident.

"I tell you he was cheating," said Creed a bit angrily. "I saw him dealing seconds, and he dealt the last card to himself from the bottom of the deck."

"If he was cheating," said Palmer, "then he cheated himself, don't you think, Mr. Creed? After all, he lost, and the captain won. Cheaters usually play it so they can win. And that's not to mention that you lost the least on this hand." He turned over Creed's cards. "Now this is interesting. You were holding kings over queens in a full house, and you folded. Why did you do that, sir?"

"Because I knew McGrath was cheating," said Creed. "Don't you see it, Mr. Palmer?"

"Frankly, I don't," said Palmer.

"And neither do I," said Ritter, "and my word is the only one that counts on this boat. I am the law here, Mr. Creed, and you discharged a weapon on my boat. I won't allow that, sir. You leave me no alternative but to put you ashore immediately. Gather your things, Mr. Creed."

"Throw him in the river!" shouted McGrath, still holding his injured ear.

"Don't be ridiculous, McGrath!" snapped Ritter. "We'll pull in close to shore and put out the gangplank."

Creed glared at McGrath. He wanted to say something to remind McGrath that they were supposed to be making this trip on behalf of Charlotte Beaujeu, that her business had nothing to do with this affair. But it would do him no good to announce his association with McGrath after accusing the bastard of cheating at poker. It would—

No, wait! Maybe that was exactly what McGrath was counting on. McGrath had cheated at cards; nothing would convince Creed otherwise. Maybe McGrath wanted to be accused of cheating just so he could discredit Creed, and when Creed made the claim that he and McGrath were traveling together in order to buy a horse in Kentucky, McGrath could deny that, too, and further discredit Creed, not just in the eyes of the captain and the other gamblers but more importantly in the eyes of Scott Houchin, whose word would carry a certain amount of weight when it came time to deal with his father over Pride.

Yes, that was McGrath's plan. But was that all of it? The captain won the hand, and he did act rather quickly to stop Creed from shooting McGrath. Yes, of course! The captain and McGrath! They were in it together. Now he saw it. McGrath needed Creed out of the way so he could deal with Scott Houchin without Creed's interference, and what better way of getting Creed out of the way than to have him put off the boat long before it reached Memphis? Yet, would he be too far from New Orleans to return there to catch a train to Kentucky before the *Princess* arrived in Memphis? Of course, he could catch a train from Baton Rouge, but there was no direct route from the Louisiana capital to the north; he would have to change trains so many times that the delays would prevent him from reaching Kentucky on time to stop McGrath.

Damn! thought Creed. The dirty little bugger had suckered him! And he was powerless—for the moment—to do anything about it.

The first mate and a few husky stevedores were summoned to assist Creed in gathering his belongings. He scooped up his gambling bank from the table and eyed McGrath one more time. "I will deal with you yet, McGrath," he said.

"If I ever see you again," said McGrath defiantly, "I will shoot you on sight."

"Then you better pray that you see me first," said Creed. He started for his cabin with the escort at his heels.

Word of the shooting in the main salon spread around the ship like a coal oil fire. Little Charlie heard about it and told

Scott Houchin. They raced to the main salon but were too late
to see Creed there. Having been told that Creed was to be put
off the boat, they ran for his cabin.

"Stay away," said the burly first mate.

"We want to talk to Mr. Creed," said Scott.

"He ain't allowed," said the mate. "Now get away."

"Scott, would you take care of Nimbus for me?" asked
Creed.

"Take care of Nimbus?" queried Scott.

"You ain't allowed to talk to them neither," groused the mate
at Creed. "Now keep your mouth shut, or I'll have to shut it
for you."

Creed glared at the mate but said nothing.

"Come on, Scott," said Charlie.

The two boys left and went to the hold.

"What do you think he meant about taking care of Nimbus?"
asked Scott. "You don't think the captain is going to put him
off without his horse, do you?"

"Maybe," said Charlie. "Just in case, maybe you should saddle
up Nimbus so Mr. Creed can ride out of here like he did back in
New Orleans."

"Good idea," said Scott, and he began the chore.

The *Princess* was just then approaching the Minor Plantation
on the west bank of the river. Captain Ritter maneuvered the
packet toward the broken-down Minor levee, and the deckhands
started to swing the gangplank into position.

After hurriedly packing his belongings, including his extra
Colt's and the poke that Charlotte had given him and which
he had hidden inside a pair of rolled-up trousers, Creed slung
his saddlebags over his left shoulder and left the cabin for good.
He turned toward the bow of the boat and walked along the
promenade to the ladder that went down to the main deck. He
descended the steps and saw Scott Houchin bringing Nimbus
up from the hold. The gangplank was in place and waiting for
Creed. Scott handed him the reins to Nimbus.

"Will you still be going to Kentucky to see my pa, Mr. Creed?"
asked Scott.

"I told you, boy," said the mate. "No talking to him."

Palmer stepped forward, carrying Creed's other Colt's. He
offered it to him butt first. "You might be needing this in the
future," he said.

"Hey, you can't give him that," said the mate.

"I can and I will," said Palmer sternly. "I'm sure Mr. Creed won't use it on you."

"Thank you," said Creed, taking the gun from Palmer. He shoved it inside his waistband, then looked at Scott Houchin. "Yes, Scott, I'm still going to Kentucky. I'll see you there." He noticed little Charlie and said, "Remember what I told you, Charlie. Always be on your guard."

"Yes, sir," said Charlie. "I hope to see you again someday, Mr. Creed."

Creed smiled and said, "You said that once before, Charlie, back on the *Crescent City*."

"Yeah, that's right," said Charlie, blushing.

"Well, like I said then," said Creed, "I hope to see you again, Charlie." And with that, he turned and led Nimbus off the boat.

Creed watched the *Princess* move away from the bank and continue its northward journey. Scott and Charlie stood at the rear of the hurricane deck, waving good-bye to him. He waved back, hoping that both would fare well in the future. As for him, he had other fish to fry.

18

Unsure of his exact whereabouts, Creed waited until the next morning before riding north to Vidalia to take the ferry across the Mississippi to Natchez Under the Hill. While he waited to be taken across the river, he wrote a letter to Texada with the thought of posting it as soon as he reached Natchez on the Bluff.

New Orleans frequently proclaimed that its waterfront was the wickedest on the river, and Vicksburg often asserted that its underworld could outshade and outstrip anything the Creole city offered. Both claims were based on fact, but neither city could really match Natchez Under the Hill in the depths of crime and debauchery.

For nearly fifty years Natchez Under the Hill had worn the crown for flaming, freewheeling gaiety. Anyone who had ever been there would boast that lower Natchez had whatever one liked, whatever way one liked it, at any time of the day or night, as long as one could pay the price. Natchez Under the Hill was Hell on earth—with bells attached.

At the foot of the hill where Natchez on the Bluff stood, the Mississippi had deposited an irregular shelf of silt a half to three-quarters of a mile long. Over it, jerry-built, weather-beaten shacks lined crisscrossed narrow streets and filled nearly every square foot of ground, extending to the water's edge, where they perched on stilts. No flowers, no grass to beautify and color the place, only a green scum covering the wetter places.

In its heyday, hundreds of vessels, all bobbing in a shifting line, would be moored at the landing under the hill: flatboats like heavy rafts with huts on top, laden with wheat and corn, turkeys and pigs; keelboats with crews of twenty-five to thirty hard-drinking, iron-fisted men; barges and skiffs and an occasional seagoing vessel; and, later, the steamboats. Yellow-skinned hawkers, mulattoes whose accents were still tainted with French, lured their listeners, like the Sirens of Homer's *Odyssey*, to the joys of Silver Street, the main thoroughfare under the hill. Few, if any, establishments ever closed their doors or were silent for very long. Noise—the pounding of tinny pianos, the high-pitched laughter of lewd women and lecherous men, the squawking of parrots, the clatter of gambling games—was never deafening but was always constant. Half-naked girls leaned out of windows touting their charms, the more endowed hefting them lasciviously and inviting the passerby to have a taste or a feel. Drunken men, whether white, black, yellow, or red, lurched past. Soldiers, sailors, merchants, lawyers, farmers, and even an occasional planter who had slipped away from the fastidious life on the hill, drank and ogled and exchanged amused comments and sometimes sampled the women or tried their luck at the tables. And if two gentlemen of acquaintance on the hill should meet under the hill, neither took notice of the other, as that was the unspoken law of Natchez Under the Hill: everyone minded his own business.

Every few years or so the mighty Mississippi took umbrage at the debauchery along its banks and flooded the lower town. Sometimes rising gently and gradually, the Old Man, as many called the river, gave warning of his anger and allowed the denizens under the hill to retreat to higher ground. But there were those other times when he failed to offer them the chance to retreat before his ominous onslaught. At these times, Natchez Under the Hill was washed clean but only for a short time, because as soon as the river resumed its normal course so did life below the bluff.

With the onset of the War Between the States, river traffic came to a near standstill, and with it, life under the hill slowed to a snail's pace. Some people continued to live there, but most moved away, especially after the Federal gunboat *Essex* bombarded the town in September of '62.

Not as strategically important as Vicksburg, Natchez was bypassed by the Federals until July of '63. When they occupied the town, they set up their headquarters and housed their officers in many of the mansions on the hill, and they built a fort and a hospital on the northern bluffs. Almost immediately mobs of hungry ex-slaves, freed by the Emancipation Proclamation, assailed the Yankees, seeking food and protection. Not sure of what to do about the problem, the Federals built a stockade of sorts under the hill and ordered the Negroes to confine themselves there until Washington sent orders telling the soldiers what to do with them. The place became known as the Corral. It had no sanitary facilities and little protection from the elements. The Army fed the people, but no medical care was given them. Hundreds died miserably from scarlet fever, measles, bloody dysentery, cholera, and yellow fever, and they were buried in trenches near the stockade, their bodies stacked up like cordwood and covered over with a few inches of dirt.

When Creed landed in Natchez Under the Hill three days after Christmas of '65, most of the Corral had disappeared from sight but not from memory. The freedmen of the area would long remember it; of that, there was no doubt.

Creed rode up the bluff along Silver Street to Market Street. He saw one sign advertising a restaurant and another indicating the post office. He was hungry and wanted to stop for a bite to eat but knew time was working against him. Maybe a cup of coffee and a piece of pie and then on to the railroad station. But first he had to post his letter to Texada. With that chore done, he rode to the restaurant, where he tied Nimbus to a hitching post out front and entered the establishment.

The restaurant was full of Yankee soldiers. Just what Creed wanted to see. Three yellow-skinned, black-haired, almond-eyed waitresses rushed here and there taking orders and delivering food to tables. Creed spotted a short counter and took a seat at it. A fourth woman, pale and haggard, tended the bar trade. "Coffee, mister?" she asked gruffly.

"Yes, thank you, ma'am," said Creed.

His Texas accent and his Southern manners obviously pleased the waitress, because she smiled a toothy grin back at him and wiped the dust from a cup with her apron before she poured his coffee into it. She brushed a few strands of red hair back from her forehead with her arm, then said, "Anything else I can get you?" Her tone was softer, warmer, friendlier.

"You wouldn't have any fresh pie around, would you, ma'am?" asked Creed, returning her smile and friendliness.

"How does pecan pie sound to you?" she asked.

Creed's mouth started to water at the mention of his favorite pastry. "Ma'am, it sounds like home to me," he said.

A Yankee sergeant two seats down from Creed overheard their conversation and didn't like it. "Hey, Maggie, I thought you said you didn't have any pie left," he groused.

"I said I didn't have any left for the likes of you, McCall," said Maggie, now using her brusque, hardcase tone.

"But you've got some for this man, is that it?" asked the sergeant. "What makes him so special?"

"He asked me nice," said Maggie as she produced the pie from beneath the counter. She cut a wedge, put it on a salad plate, and set it in front of Creed.

"Oh, I get it," said McCall. He turned to Creed and said, "You're one of them Southern gentlemen, ain't you?"

"You wouldn't know a gentleman if one walked up and introduced himself to you, McCall," said Maggie.

"Sergeant, I'd be more than happy to share this pie with you," said Creed as friendly as he could be. "In fact, you can have the whole piece, if it will make you happy." He slid the plate over to the sergeant.

"I don't want your goddamned pie, Reb," said McCall. He was getting louder with every word. "Here! You eat it!" He picked up the pie and crammed it into Creed's face. "Taste good, Reb?" He laughed obnoxiously.

By now, every ear in the restaurant was listening, and every eye was watching Creed and McCall.

Creed used his index fingers to remove the pie from his eyes, then he licked the digits clean, smacked his lips, and said, "As a matter of fact, Sergeant, it's delicious, but I'd rather eat it off a plate than off my unshaven face. Ma'am, could I trouble you for a cloth to wipe my face with?"

Without hesitation, Maggie handed him a towel, and Creed wiped away the pie filling.

"What's the matter, Reb?" asked McCall. "Are you so yellow that you're gonna just sit there and let me get away with that?"

Creed ignored McCall and turned to the other diners. "Is there a ranking officer present?" he asked.

"I'm a captain," said a man sitting at a corner table with two lieutenants. He stood and asked, "Will I do?"

"Captain, I'd like to take Sergeant McCall out behind this establishment," said Creed, "and teach him something about courtesy and Southern hospitality, but I'd like to be assured that I won't have to teach anyone else the same lesson after I'm finished with him."

The captain laughed and said, "Well put, sir. You have my word as a Union officer that no one will interfere with your class in etiquette, although I would like to observe your method of teaching, if you don't mind." He looked around. "In fact, I'm sure every man in here would like to see how you, a Southern gentleman, would instruct a Northerner like McCall in good manners. Would you mind, sir?"

Creed smiled, bowed, straightened, and said, "The honor would be mine, sir, but as I stipulated, only as long as I have to teach just this one student."

"You have my word, sir," said the captain.

"Beg pardon, Captain Callaway," said McCall, "but what the hell was that all about?"

"Why, Sergeant McCall, I believe this gentleman intends to thrash you," said Callaway.

McCall winced, then frowned and said, "Is that so?"

"After you, Sergeant," said Creed, motioning toward the rear door of the restaurant.

"No, after you, Reb," said McCall.

Creed started to step past the sergeant, and as he came even with McCall, the Yank came out of his seat and aimed a haymaker for Creed's jaw. Creed had expected as much from a blowhard like McCall. He was prepared for it. He ducked, spun clockwise, and slammed his elbow into McCall's right kidney, sprawling the man on the floor.

Two enlisted men made moves toward Creed. "Hold on there!" ordered Callaway. "Leave them be!" The soldiers looked askance at Callaway. "That's an order, men!"

"That's your first lesson, Sergeant," said Creed as he stood over the gasping soldier. "Never try to hit a man who isn't facing you, because he just might have eyes in the back of his head." He offered McCall a hand up and said, "Now, shall we continue this outside?"

McCall accepted the aid with his left hand, came to his feet, and tried to slug Creed with his right. Creed blocked the punch with his free hand, then spun around, twisting McCall's left arm as he did. Bending the limb behind McCall, Creed pushed him against the counter, bent him over it, and said softly in his ear, "Sergeant, I can break your arm right now if I want, but I'd rather take you out back and break your face. Now we can end this right here and now, or you can be a man and stop this underhanded bullshit and come outside with me where we can have a fair, clean fight. What's it going to be, Sergeant?"

"All right, all right! No more funny stuff. We'll settle it outside."

Creed eased up on the hold and said, "After you then."

McCall moved hesitantly toward the rear door, and Creed followed. There was a clatter of chairs being pushed away from tables and boots pounding on the wooden floor as the other soldiers rushed to follow the combatants outdoors.

"Remember, men!" shouted Callaway over the din. "There will be no interference between McCall and the Reb."

Creed heard the last and thought, Maybe they *are* all alike.

McCall stepped outside into a small fenced yard. Creed joined him. The other soldiers surrounded them. Maggie and the other waitresses stood at the doorway to watch.

"Now, Sergeant," said Creed, "in the South we don't speak to women the way you just did to that lady inside."

"She ain't no lady, Reb," sneered McCall. He lunged at Creed, missed when Creed sidestepped his attack, and fell to the ground. He rolled over, expecting Creed to come at him with a boot, but was surprised when no such assault was forthcoming.

"Down here, Sergeant," said Creed, "we give every female the benefit of the doubt until she states the contrary."

"She's one of your Southern whores," growled McCall, again on his feet. He moved toward Creed with doubled fists.

Creed stood motionless, waiting.

McCall swung. Missed.

Creed slammed his forearm into McCall's solar plexus, blasting the wind from his lungs and doubling him up. The soldier's eyes bulged as he gasped for air. Creed used the opening to slug McCall in the jaw, staggering him but not felling him. He came around again, and Creed landed a solid right to the man's chin. Again, McCall stumbled about but refused to go down. Creed hit him in the stomach twice more. This time McCall dropped to his knees. Creed smashed his fist into the sergeant's nose. The crunch of bone was audible to everyone present. Blood spewed from McCall's nose as he rocked backward on his knees, arms falling loosely to his sides. His head lolled; his eyes rolled up; his mouth fell wide open. He was done for.

Assured that McCall would offer him no more resistance, Creed looked warily around him. Not one soldier moved, but most of them wanted to come after him. Only Callaway's presence held them at bay.

"Well, sir," said the captain, "that was a fine display of fisticuffs. I salute you, sir." And he did. "Some of you men take McCall to the company surgeon at once. I believe he needs a physician's care immediately."

A half dozen soldiers moved to aid McCall.

"Sir, could I buy you a drink?" asked Callaway of Creed.

"Thank you all the same, Captain," said Creed, "but I'd just like to finish my coffee and pie and be on my way."

"Why the hurry?" asked Callaway.

"It's a long story, Captain," said Creed as he returned to the restaurant. "Let's just say that I have to catch a train and get to Kentucky as soon as I can."

"Catch a train? Where? Here in Natchez?"

"Well, I was hoping to get one out of here," said Creed.

Callaway burst into raucous, uncontrollable laughter.

Creed peered sourly at the captain and wondered what the hell the joke was. He didn't have an inkling that the joke was on him.

19

What else could go wrong? Creed wondered. He was put off the *Princess*, and now no trains were running out of Natchez. In fact, the only railroad tracks that ran from Natchez to anywhere had been put down almost thirty years earlier, and those rusty rails only went to nearby St. Catherine.

That left the Trace. Not much of a choice, but it was the only option open to him if he wanted to get to Kentucky in time to keep McGrath from whatever evil he was up to.

Creed didn't wait around Natchez. He finished his coffee in the restaurant, cinched up his saddle for the long ride ahead, then struck out on the Trace for Jackson. But before he left, Captain Callaway warned him that the Trace was once again a haven for outlaws and highwaymen.

"They come in all colors now," said Callaway. "President Lincoln freed the Negroes, and now Congress is trying to give them rights equal to whites. But they've already seen fit to make themselves equal to whites when it comes to lawbreaking. Between them and the various groups of Southern whites, we've had a devil of a time trying to maintain law and order in these parts. Oh, I'm not saying every Negro is a lawbreaker. Heavens, no! Nor are all you Rebels. Oh, excuse me. I should say, you former Confederates. But there are enough troublemakers of both colors to keep us on our toes. I warn you, sir. Keep your guard up on the Trace. It is still a dangerous road."

Callaway was right. The Trace had once been a highway of hell and horror.

The first infamous villains of the Trace were the gruesome Harpe brothers, Little Wiley and Big Micajah, those shark-eyed butchers of countless numbers of innocent men, women, and children—including Big Harpe's own child, whose head he bashed into a dozen pieces against a tree when the child's

99

crying annoyed him. After Big Harpe was beheaded with a butcher knife by the husband of one of his victims, Little Harpe joined up with the notorious highwayman and murderer Sam Mason. Little Harpe proved the axiom that there is no honor among thieves when he later killed and beheaded Mason in an effort to collect the bounty on the highwayman's head. The plan failed, however, when Harpe was recognized by a man whose family he had helped his big brother murder. He was promptly tried and hanged for his crimes.

The last of the well-known and highly feared bandits on the Trace was John Murrell, who used cunning as much as he did violence to commit his crimes. Unlike his predecessors, who usually acted on the spur of the moment to rob and murder whoever came their way, Murrell planned his crimes down to the last detail before committing them.

Murrell discovered that the most lucrative product in the South wasn't cotton or tobacco. It was the slave. Good, strong field hands were hard to come by, and planters would pay a premium price for healthy young bucks. By promising him freedom in the North, Murrell would coax an innocent Negro youth into running away from his master. Once they were away from the Negro's home plantation, Murrell would tell him that they needed money to travel and that to get those funds Murrell would have to *sell* the youth. Not to worry, said Murrell; the young Negro would only run away again and meet up with Murrell at a predesignated place. They would move farther north and repeat the selling and running away gambit again and again until too many people were looking for the Negro. At that point, Murrell would murder the innocent youth, then return south to find another accomplice/victim and begin the process all over. The outlaw pulled this dastardly evil again and again and was never caught.

But he was caught stealing horses once. His thumbs were branded with the initials HT for horse thief, and he was sentenced to a year in the penitentiary. He walked into jail defiantly and came out more devious than ever before.

Upon his release from prison, Murrell formed the Council of the Clan of the Mystic Confederacy, a network of outlaws that spread all across the South. With thousands of criminal cronies, he planned a slave uprising that would occur simultaneously on Christmas Day of 1835 throughout the slave states. His motive, however, was not to free the Negroes, but to create an empire of bandits that would pillage and plunder the South and blame the Negroes for their crimes. Fortunately, Murrell was betrayed and his plot exposed. He was convicted of slave-stealing and was sentenced to ten years in prison. When he was released after serving nearly the whole term, he returned to the country around Natchez as a broken man and eventually disappeared from the area in a foggy mist of contradictory legends.

Creed had heard tales about the Harpes, Mason, and Murrell during the war. Soldiers from Mississippi, Tennessee, Alabama, and Kentucky would sit around the campfires and tell the frightening tales of murder on the Trace, each man trying to outdo the one before him. Creed listened with the fascination of a child, but he knew that these bogeymen were far in the past and could never reach out to really touch him.

All that was long before Creed found himself on the Trace, alone, with darkness closing in around him, although the sun was still above the horizon. The farther he rode away from Natchez, the thicker the forest became. The oaks were without their summer plumage, but the evergreens and underbrush crowded in among them to give the woodland a primeval density.

Creed hadn't seen a soul on the Trace since passing the house that was once known as King's Tavern, the unofficial southern terminus of the old pioneer trail from Nashville to Natchez. He had pushed Nimbus at a steady trot all afternoon, which was unusually warm for late December, even in southwestern Mississippi. The stallion had worked up a good lather, and although Creed wanted to reach Port Gibson before dark, he knew that it would be cruel not to give the Appaloosa the breather he deserved. When they came to what appeared to be a fairly straight and level piece of road, Creed reined in Nimbus, patted the horse's gray neck, and said, "I think we should walk a ways, boy." He dismounted, twisted his frame to get some of the kinks out, then started walking.

At the end of the flat stretch, the Trace dipped into a ravine that had a small creek running through it. A cool drink of water sounded good to Creed, and he knew Nimbus would like nothing better right now. They picked up the pace and hurried down to the stream. Nimbus bent his long neck to suck up the water, while Creed got down on all fours to do the same. Getting his fill first, Creed pushed himself up and rested on his knees, taking off his hat and wiping his forehead with his coat sleeve. He looked skyward, saw heavy storm clouds heading north, and hoped they would move far up the valley before they encountered cooler air and dropped their precipitation as either rain or snow. The last thing he needed now was wet weather. Or so he thought.

Nimbus jerked his head from the stream, snorted, and backed away a few feet. Creed was startled by the horse's sudden movement. His lips parted to ask the stallion what was wrong, but the rustle of leaves drew his attention downstream. Nimbus whinnied and backed farther away. Creed grabbed the reins with his left hand and drew his Colt's with the other. He still didn't see what had riled up Nimbus, but he heard it.

Ornk-Ornk! Ornk-Ornk!

Oh, damn! thought Creed. Not many things genuinely frightened him, but the snort of a razorback boar ranked high up on his list of least favorite sounds. He drew back the hammer of the revolver, aimed it toward the noise, then spotted the wild pig bearing down on him. He fired—missed.

The pig came on at full speed.

Creed raised the pistol over his head to drop the spent cap as he cocked the hammer again.

The beast was less than a dozen yards away.

Creed had no time to aim, only point the gun. He fired again and—missed again?

The razorback leaped at Creed, its long teeth bared and eager to rip at the man's throat.

Creed tried to duck out of the way. He succeeded—but not completely. He got his head out of the boar's flight path, but his shoulder didn't make it. The pig struck him full force and knocked him sideways to the ground. The air blasted from Creed's lungs when he hit the dirt. He bounced up for a second, then fell back, striking his head on a large stone at the creek's edge. He heard Nimbus whinny again, blinked his eyes once as he struggled to remain conscious, failed, and was swallowed by darkness.

20

A hen cackling woke Creed up from his forced slumber. At least he thought it was a chicken. Or maybe he dreamed it. He couldn't be sure.

Once he was aware that he was still alive, Creed tried to move but couldn't. He was tied up. He felt rope around his ankles, around his wrists, and a gag in his mouth. He smelled meat cooking, beans and coffee, too. He was lying on his side on the ground, facing away from the fire, the heat of which warmed his backside nicely. He rolled over.

"Look here, Lije," said a crone of a white man dressed like a preacher. He pointed a bony finger at Creed. "He's awake."

"Yessuh, he sure is awake," said Lije, a large, white-haired Negro. He sat beside the fire, turning a pig on a spit. He smiled broadly, showing a full mouth of yellowed teeth. "Sure was good of you, mistuh, to go and shoot this here razorback for us. Him sure gonna taste good."

"Of course, you won't find that out for yourself," said the crone. He cackled like an old woman.

So you're the hen I heard, thought Creed. And that's the boar that attacked me and knocked me down. And I hit my head on a rock. Oh, yeah! Damn! My head hurts! Nimbus! Where's Nimbus, you old son of a bitch?

"AIR EYE ORE?" asked Creed through the gag, a dirty red neckerchief tied tightly between his jaws.

The crone cackled again. "Listen to that, Lije," he said. "The damn fool's trying to talk."

"He sure is, Mr. John," said Lije. "Maybe I should loosen the gag so we can hear him talk some."

"Yes, you do that, Lije," said Mr. John.

Lije left the spit and bent over Creed. He loosened the knot behind Creed's neck and pulled the neckerchief away from his mouth.

Creed swallowed hard. His lips and mouth were dry. He had a powerful thirst. "Water," he rasped.

"Water?" queried Lije.

Creed nodded.

Lije looked at Mr. John, who said, "Sure, Lije, give him a drink. We got plenty of water around here."

The old Negro went to the stream—was it the same creek where he'd been attacked by the razorback? wondered Creed— and fetched a cup of cool water for Creed. He came back, propped Creed into a sitting position, and poured the water slowly into his mouth, spilling only a few drops.

"Thank you," said Creed softly. He cleared his throat.

"Polite rascal, ain't he, Lije?" cackled the crone.

Fat crackling in the fire reminded Lije that he had better return to the spit or their supper would burn.

Creed could see both men better now that he was sitting up. He gave each man's face a quick perusal and realized he was in real danger.

The white man appeared to be crazed or senile or both, and the Negro was the crazy man's willing servant. Both of them had wild eyes. Mr. John had two pistols—flintlocks—stuck in his waistband. He toyed with a large hunting knife. His clothing was old, tattered, and dusty. He wore a long coat and a stovepipe hat that had been crushed more than once.

Creed felt a definite need to go slow here.

"My name is Slate Creed," he said.

"Don't care what your goddamned name is, boy!" snapped the crone. "We ain't putting up a marker for you after we slit your gut open and leave you for dead." He made a slashing motion with the knife. "Coons and possums won't care what your shittin' name is when they're eating what's left of you, so why should we?"

The man did have a point, thought Creed. Better go slower.

"Mr. John is only funning you," said Lije apologetically as he continued turning the spit.

"No, I ain't, you lazy nigger!" snapped Mr. John. "I aim to cut him open and watch him die the way the Harpes used to do to folks way back when."

Mr. John, thought Creed. Mr. John? He looked at the old crone's hands. He wore gloves that had the fingers cut off them but not the thumbs. Strange! Why would he leave the thumbs on the gloves? To hide something? Yes, of course! Branding marks! And his clothes. An itinerant preacher's costume. And Lije calling him Mr. John? Mr. John Murrell? It was worth a try.

"He keeps calling you Mr. John," said Creed, going into his down-home simpleton act. "Is that your name, sir?"

"None of your goddamned business!" growled Mr. John.

"Of course, it's his name," said Lije a bit belligerently. "Why else would I be calling him that if it weren't?"

"What I meant was," said Creed, "is your name John Murrell?"

Lije quit turning the pig on the spit as the two old men exchanged glances.

Creed had hit a nerve.

"Murrell is dead," said Mr. John.

"Yessuh, that's right," said Lije.

"No, he's not," said Creed. "You're John Murrell." He smiled to show that he was pleased he had guessed the old man's identity. "I know you're John Murrell."

"No, I ain't," said Mr. John angrily. "Murrell is dead, I tell you. Do you hear me? Murrell is dead!"

"Well, you can keep telling me that all night," said Creed, "but I still won't believe you. You're John Murrell, and I'm real proud to meet you, sir."

"Say what?" asked Mr. John.

"He say he's real proud to meet you," said Lije.

"Shut your mouth, boy!" snapped Mr. John.

"You don't have to worry about me, Mr. Murrell," said Creed. "I won't tell anyone you're still alive."

"You sure got that right," said Mr. John. "You'll be dead soon, and dead men don't talk."

"Well, that's all right," said Creed. "You can go ahead and kill me. I won't mind because I'll know that it was the great John Murrell that did me in."

"What the hell are you talking about, boy?" asked Mr. John. "Are you crazed in the head or something?"

"No, sir, I'm not," said Creed. "You see, sir, I've heard stories about you all my life, and I've always admired your bravado and daring, sir."

"Bravado and daring?" queried Mr. John, suddenly taking a lighter tone.

"Yes, sir," said Creed. "Why, I guess you're the greatest highwayman that ever lived. I always wanted meet you, Mr. Murrell, and maybe join up with you. Of course, that's just the dream of a young boy, I guess."

"Greatest highwayman that ever lived, you say?" queried the old man.

"Yes, sir, the greatest," said Creed.

"Well, I knew I was famous," said Mr. John, "but I didn't know that folks considered me to be the greatest highwayman that ever lived. You do me honor, young sir."

"Oh, no, sir," said Creed, moving his charade into another stage, "the honor is all mine."

"You hear that, Lije?"

"Yessuh, I hear it," said Lije, looking at Creed with suspicion.

"You know, Mr. Murrell," said Creed, "this must be an act of Providence. Our meeting, I mean."

"Act of Providence?" queried Mr. John. "How do you figure that?"

"Well, sir, I don't know for sure," said Creed, "because I don't know what happened after the razorback knocked me to the ground and I hit my head on a rock."

"Well, we heard you shooting," said Lije, "and we come running from our camp here. We found you laying next to the creek, and the razorback was laying next to you."

"What about my horse?" asked Creed.

"We brung him back here with you," said Lije. "I got him staked out in the meadow. He's all right."

"Never mind the horse," said Mr. John. "Go on about why you think our meeting is an act of Providence."

"Well, sir," said Creed, "during the war, I heard lots of stories about you, Mr. Murrell, and I made up my mind that if I survived the war, I'd come looking for you and see if you'd let me join up with you. Well, I survived the war, as you can see, and I came looking for you. Now, I was in lots of battles during the war, and the good Lord kept me safe through all of them. And since the war, I've been riding up and down the Trace looking for you, Mr. Murrell, and I couldn't find you. Now, I've stopped at lots of streams to get me a drink of water and to let my horse get a drink, but I've never had any trouble with any razorbacks before today. Now, I know this camp isn't right on the Trace, and I probably would have mounted up and rode off again if it hadn't been for that razorback attacking me like it did. The way I figure it, Mr. Murrell, the good Lord sent that hog after me so I'd have to shoot it and you'd hear my shooting and you'd come to see what it was all about and we'd finally meet. That's why I think it was the hand of Providence that brought us together, Mr. Murrell."

Mr. John stared at Creed for a second, looking quite serious as he studied the Texan's face. He shifted his eyes at Lije, then started to cackle louder than ever.

"What's so funny, Mr. John?" asked Lije.

"Untie him, Lije," said Mr. John. "We can't cut up a boy who can tell a yarn like that."

"A yarn?" queried Lije, not catching on.

"Just untie him, boy," said Mr. John, suddenly quite lucid. "What did you say your name is, son?"

"Slate Creed, sir."

Lije began to untie Creed's feet.

"Well, Mr. Creed, tell me this, will you?" said Mr. John. "How'd you know I'm John Murrell?"

"Well, sir, I have heard a lot about you and your illustrious career," said Creed, dropping his simpleton act, "and I remember that you'd been caught and convicted for stealing a horse and that you'd had your thumbs branded for it. When I saw your gloves, I figured you had something to hide. That and the fact that Lije was calling you Mr. John, and your attire, sir. I'd heard how you used to disguise yourself as a preacher to fool folks on the Trace. I added all that up and figured you were John Murrell, the most famous highwayman to ever walk the Trace."

Lije finished untying Creed's feet and started on his hands.

"A very good piece of deduction, Mr. Creed," said Murrell. "I am very much impressed."

"Oh, yes," said Creed, "and those flintlocks you're carrying in your belt. I'd heard about those, too."

Murrell cackled again, then said, "I haven't used these in years. I don't even know if they work anymore."

Creed's hands were free again. He rubbed his wrists and ankles to help restore some of the lost circulation in his hands and feet.

"You want some of this pig and beans?" asked Lije.

"Sounds real good, Lije," said Creed. He glanced around the little camp. "You two been here long, Mr. Murrell?" he asked.

"How long's it been, Lije?" asked Murrell. "Ten, twenty years now?"

"Closer to twenty," said Lije. "Ever since you stole me off Massuh Jeff's island plantation. What year was that?"

"I don't recall, Lije, but I remember it was when he was off fighting down to Mexico."

"Wait a minute," said Creed. "Are you saying you were a slave on Jefferson Davis's plantation?"

"Yessuh, that's right," said Lije. "Do you know Massuh Jeff, Mr. Creed?"

"Well, not personally."

"But you've heard of him, I suppose," said Murrell.

"He was president of the Confederacy, Mr. Murrell."

Murrell bolted upright and said, "You mean the Mystic Confederacy is still alive after all these years? I can't believe it. And you say Jefferson Davis was its president? This is incredible, Lije. The Council of the Clan of the Mystic Confederacy still lives. Isn't that something, Lije?"

"Yessuh, it sure is," said Lije as he handed Creed a plate of meat and beans.

"You know, Mr. Creed," said Murrell, puffing himself up like a peacock, "I started the Council of the Clan of the Mystic Confederacy back in . . ." He looked skyward as he tried to recollect the date. "Now, when was that? Was it '34 or was it '35? One of those years. It makes no difference now, I suppose. We were going to free the slaves and set up a new regime in the South, but they called it treason and put me in prison for it." He was sullen for a moment, but only for a moment. "But now you tell me the Mystic Confederacy survived and Jefferson Davis was its president. Is he still the president?"

"No, sir," said Creed, not knowing if he should tell Murrell that the Confederacy he was speaking of and the one Murrell was reminiscing about were two different animals. When he saw the light in Murrell's eyes, he realized it would serve no purpose to explain the difference to him.

"Who's president now?" asked Murrell.

"I'm not sure," said Creed. "The Confederacy has sort of passed on, I guess."

"Passed on? What do you mean?" demanded Murrell.

Thinking fast, Creed said, "Well, it's now called the Order of American Knights. I think that's it, anyway."

"The Order of American Knights?" queried Murrell. He gave the name a second of thought, then sucked in his breath and said, "Oh, I like that. I wish I'd thought up that name. Yes, indeed. That's a dandy name."

"It's a very secret organization," said Creed. "I don't know much about it myself. I'm not a member or anything."

"You're not? Then what are you?"

"I'm a Texan," said Creed as if that should say it all.

"A Texan? From Texas?"

"Yes, sir."

"I'd have never taken you for a foreigner," said Murrell, cackling again.

Creed laughed and said, "Texas is a state now."

"A state? Since when?"

"Since '45," said Creed.

"Since '45," repeated Murrell, shaking his head in amazement. "I can't believe how much has happened these last few years. Texas a state. Incredible!"

Creed realized that Murrell and Lije had been out of touch with the real world for some time. That, or they were crazy. Or maybe both. If they were crazy, they could turn on him at any minute. He looked around the camp again, and this time he saw what he wanted to see: his saddlebags and its Colt's.

Murrell saw what Creed was looking at and said, "Yes, it's all there, Mr. Creed. Your guns and your gold. We didn't take any of it. Go ahead and see for yourself."

"No. That won't be necessary," said Creed.

"You trust us?" asked Murrell. "Are you crazy, Mr. Creed? I'm John Murrell, the greatest highwayman of all time. You shouldn't trust me. I could kill you at any minute I choose."

"With what?" asked Creed. "That hunting knife?"

"Yes, with this," said Murrell, brandishing the blade.

"Not unless you can throw it faster than I can move aside," said Creed. "I know you wouldn't try to come at me with it. I'm much too strong for you."

Murrell cackled and said, "You are so right again, Mr. Creed. Yes, sir. Quite correct. A man like you deserves to live a long and happy life. So tell me, what are you doing on the Trace? At this time of year? And this time of day? And all alone?"

21

When Creed rolled out from beneath his blanket the next morning, John Murrell and Lije were gone, vanished as if they had never been there, as if they'd been specters in the night. The fire was dead, and the air was cold with a threat of rain. Nimbus was tied to a nearby tree, saddled and ready to ride. Creed shook the sleep from his head and wondered if the night before had been a dream.

No time to think about that now, he told himself. McGrath was getting farther away, and he wasn't getting any closer to Kentucky standing there in the forest. He stretched, mounted up, and headed into Port Gibson, where he had breakfast before setting out for Jackson. He could have gone to Vicksburg to catch a train, but he figured he'd have a better chance of making a connection in Jackson, because the Mississippi Central and Southern Mississippi lines junctioned in the capital city. He was right.

Night was falling when Creed reached the Mississippi Central depot. The agent was closing up for the day just as Creed came riding up.

"Pardon me, sir," said Creed, still in the saddle, when he saw the agent locking the station door behind him.

The skinny, diminutive man wore spectacles, a well-worn felt hat, and a black frock coat. He squinted up at Creed and said, "Something I can do for you, sonny?"

"Yes, sir," said Creed, smiling because the man had used an appellation normally reserved for much younger males. "Could you tell me when I can catch the next train for Nashville?"

"Nope!"

Creed wasn't prepared for that answer. "Aren't you the station-master here?"

"Yep!"

"Then why can't you tell me when the next train is leaving for Nashville?"

"You didn't ask me that," said the codger.

"I didn't?" This was news to Creed.

"Nope, you didn't," said the agent. "You asked me when *you* could catch the next train for Nashville. You can catch whichever one you want, but I sure as hell can't tell you which one you'll catch."

Creed smiled politely and said, "I see what you mean, sir. Then could you tell me when the next train for Nashville will be leaving this station?"

"I could."

"Then would you please do it?" asked Creed, getting a little edgy with this fellow.

"Be glad to. All you had to do was ask. The answer is it ain't."

"What do you mean by that?"

"I mean, there ain't no train leaving here for Nashville, that's what I mean. What's the matter, boy? Don't you understand American?"

Creed took off his hat, wiped his brow on the sleeve of his coat, heaved a sigh, then said, "What you're saying is there isn't a train that runs from here to Nashville. Is that it?"

"That's right, sonny."

"Then where do trains go when they leave here?"

"Some go north, and some go south."

"But none of them go to Nashville?"

"Not a one," said the agent.

Creed replaced his hat and said, "Let me ask you this then. If you were me and you were trying to get to Nashville and from there to Bowling Green, Kentucky, and you wanted to get there in a hurry by train, how would you go about doing it?"

"First off, I'd go over to the Southern Miss depot, and tomorrow I'd take the day coach to Meridian, where I could catch the Mobile and Ohio to Humboldt, Tennessee, where I could catch the Memphis and Ohio to Bowling Green. That's what I'd do, if I was you, sonny, and I was in a hurry to get to Bowling Green."

"But why should I go over to Meridian and catch a train going north? Doesn't this line go to Tennessee, too?"

"Sure it does," said the agent, "but it ain't going there until the day after New Year's Day."

"The day after New Year's Day?" queried Creed. "How come so long before the next train?"

"Sonny, we had us a war down here not too long ago. Maybe you heard about it. The South against the North?"

"I heard about it," said Creed.

"Well, the Yankees came down here and destroyed most of our rolling stock and what they didn't destroy is in piss-poor shape. We're lucky we got two engines running at any one time."

"I see," said Creed.

"Of course, the other lines ain't much better off. The war was hard on all of us."

"I know what you mean," said Creed.

"You fight for the Gray?" asked the agent.

"Yes, sir, I did."

"Around here?"

"Some."

"Uh-huh. Well, you best be getting over to the Southern Miss station and check on that train for tomorrow. I could be wrong about that, you know."

"That thought hadn't occurred to me, sir." Creed nodded, replaced his hat, and said, "Thank you, sir." And he rode off.

The stationmaster for the Southern Mississippi depot was already gone when Creed arrived there. He groused at himself for being late, then decided that would achieve no good. Before he could think of what to do next, extreme fatigue overwhelmed him. He hadn't eaten since morning, and he knew Nimbus was worn out as well. Both of them needed a good meal and a solid night's rest. He took a room at a hotel, put Nimbus in the nearby livery, ate a hot supper of catfish, fried hominy, and rice and red beans, then went to bed, leaving a message at the desk that he wanted to be awakened in time to eat breakfast before catching the morning train for Meridian.

Creed was up in plenty of time to do what he wanted the next morning. At the Southern Miss depot, the agent proved to be very similar to the one at the Mississippi Central station the previous eve. He was short, old, thicker set, and just as cantankerous.

"You can't take the horse with you," said the agent.

"I'll pay for it," said Creed.

"You don't understand, sonny." There it was again. Why did old men insist on calling young men sonny? Was it to put them in their place or something? "There's no livestock car on this train."

"Then he can ride in the express car or something," said Creed rather adamantly.

"That's against regulations," said the agent. "Can't do it, sonny."

Creed heaved an exasperated sigh, then said, "How much?"

The agent cocked his head and said, "How much what?"

"How much do I have to give you to put my horse on that train?" asked Creed.

"Are you offering me a bribe, sonny?"

Creed produced a double eagle from his pants pocket, held it up for the agent to see plainly, and said, "Yes."

An avaricious gleam shone in the old man's eyes as he stared at the coin. "I could lose my job," he said.

"Mister, I'm only offering you half of this," said Creed.

"All of it, or the horse walks to Meridian on his own," said the agent.

"Done," said Creed, "as soon as he's on the train."

"Agreed."

The train from Vicksburg pulled into the station at ten o'clock, only a half hour late. Creed led Nimbus to the express car, but the clerk refused to let the stallion on board.

"I ain't going to have no horse in here, shittin' all over the place and stinking up my express car," said the clerk, another little man, although not as old as the two agents that Creed had encountered in Jackson. This man had a brown beard, thinning hair, freckles, spectacles, and a chip on his shoulder that many short men seemed to carry around with them, because God had seen fit to endow them physically with less than most men and a lot of women as well.

Creed smiled at the man and said, "Sir, I've come a long way with that horse, and I have a long way to go yet. I'd appreciate it if you'd let him on the train."

"No, sir."

"Let him on the train, Junkin," said the stationmaster.

"I ain't doing it, George," said Junkin defiantly.

Creed had had his fill of these little runts. He reached up into the express car, grabbed the clerk by his shirt, and jerked him outside, holding him off the ground and drawing him close until they were almost nose to nose. "Listen to me, you little piss ant," growled Creed. "That horse went all through the war with me. He's got more battle scars than a whole regiment of little turds like you. As far as him shittin' in your express car, you should be honored to ride in the same car with him. That horse is a hero."

"I don't care," said the clerk after swallowing hard and summoning up the courage to defend his position. "He's not getting in that car with me."

"All right," said Creed, "have it your way." He turned to the frightened stationmaster and said, "You got an outhouse around here?"

"Right over there," said the agent, pointing to a privy several feet beyond an equipment shed.

"That'll do," said Creed. He threw the clerk over his left shoulder like a sack of potatoes and headed off toward the outhouse.

"Put me down!" screamed the clerk. "Put me down!"

Creed drew his Colt's, held it over his right shoulder, and said, "You see this gun in my hand, Mr. Junkin?"

"Gun?"

"That's right," said Creed, cocking it. He jammed the muzzle against Junkin's butt and said, "If you don't stop fussing, Mr. Junkin, I'm going to blow a new hole in your ass."

"Yes, sir," stammered Junkin.

The stationmaster, the train's crew, and anyone who happened to be around the depot followed Creed and Junkin to the privy. When they reached the little-house-in-back, Creed uncocked his Colt's, replaced it in his belt, pulled open the outhouse door, and threw Junkin inside, slamming him against the wooden seat and back wall and knocking the spectacles from his face and the wind from his lungs. Not satisfied yet, Creed grabbed Junkin again, stood him up, turned him around, then forced him to bend over, shoving his head through the hole.

"You smell that, Mr. Junkin?" asked Creed. "That's real people shit down there, and I'll bet some of it is yours, too. It doesn't exactly smell like roses, does it, Mr. Junkin?"

Junkin couldn't answer him. He was too busy wretching. Creed pulled him up for a rush of better air. The man's color had a deathly pallor to it, and his bloodshot eyes dripped like a pair of old faucets.

"Now, Mr. Junkin," said Creed softly, "do you think my horse's dung will smell as bad as that?"

Junkin shook his head weakly.

"Good," said Creed. "Then he can ride in your express car with you, can't he?"

Again, Junkin shook his head weakly.

"Damn!" swore Creed. "You are a stubborn little bastard, aren't you? Well, back in the hole." And Creed shoved the clerk's head through the hole a second time.

Junkin heaved again and again until his stomach was empty of every drop of fluid. At that particular moment, he could have sworn that someone was jabbing his testicles with a carving fork. His eyes felt like they were about to explode from their sockets and fall into the feces below.

Creed pulled Junkin up again and said, "Well, Mr. Junkin, does he ride in your car or do you go down in that hole for the third time?"

Junkin nodded feebly, then passed out.

22

Mr. Turner, the express car clerk on the Mobile & Ohio train, was almost as nasty about having Nimbus riding with him as Junkin had been. Then he heard from the stationmaster, who had gotten the story over the telegraph wires, what Creed had done to his counterpart on the Southern Miss.

"Sure thing, Mr. Creed," said the Mobile & Ohio expressman nervously. "I'd be glad to have your horse on my train. I'll even feed him for you."

"That's mighty nice of you, sir," said Creed. He gave the clerk a double eagle and said, "See that he gets the best oats. He's quite a horse, and he deserves the best."

"Yes, sir," said Turner, grateful for the reward.

Creed relaxed as best as he could in the coach. The car wasn't crowded, which allowed him to have one full bench seat all to himself. That was nice, but the seats were too small for him to stretch out across just one. He needed two, but that meant lying over the aisle. That was no good. He tried to lean back and stretch out, but the seats were also too close together for him to fully extend his legs. He made do, though, alternately curling up on the bench until his limbs became stiff, then sitting up and staring out into the night or, when it was daylight, at the passing countryside.

The Mobile & Ohio train had left Mobile at seven that morning, the next to last day of 1865. It had arrived in Meridian an hour after the Southern Mississippi train, although the M & O train had fifty miles less distance to travel than the Southern Miss locomotive. The extra time was due to the condition of the line. The tracks, the bridges, the rolling stock, and the engines of the M & O had all been neglected during the war. This was due to the fact that the railroad started in Kentucky, ran across Tennessee, descended nearly the whole length of

116

Mississippi, then veered into Alabama about sixty miles north of Mobile.

When the war started in '61, Kentucky had declared itself neutral, which had no effect on the Mobile & Ohio; the railroad's business went on as usual and actually increased. In late summer of that first year of the conflict, the Confederate Army under General Leonidas Polk moved into Kentucky and occupied Columbus, the railroad's northern terminus on the Mississippi River. Five months later Polk was ordered to retreat to Tennessee, leaving Kentucky in Union hands, and the Mobile & Ohio felt its first twinge of combat fatigue. When the Federal Army penetrated as far south as Corinth, Mississippi, the railroad was suddenly split into two parts, being limited to a Yankee operation in Kentucky and Tennessee and running back and forth in Mississippi under the supervision of the Confederate Army, which meant very little money was coming into the company treasury. Fortunately, the war ended before total bankruptcy befell the firm.

Creed didn't care about the Mobile & Ohio's financial troubles, past or present. He wanted speed from the train, but he wasn't getting any. Normally, before the war, the trip from Meridian to Corinth took ten hours, give or take an hour, depending on weather conditions. But now, with the track in such disrepair, the engineer dared not go any faster than half-speed, and with rain coming down in torrents, the journey was drawn out an extra day, so that the train didn't pass through Corinth until after dark on New Year's Eve.

The storm had raged the whole time since Creed had boarded the train in Meridian. The roof of the coach in which he rode leaked badly as water dripped from every seam in the ceiling. It was cold, too. He was quite uncomfortable, and he longed to be in Texas with Texada snuggling in his arms. His mind wandered. He tried not to let his impatience to get to Kentucky and catch up with McGrath dominate his thoughts, but it was hard to stop thinking about the little weasel. At least it was until a flash of lightning near the track lit up the countryside and reminded him of the war. Images of the battles, raids, and skirmishes in which he had participated kaleidoscoped in his brain. Before he was able to focus on any single incident, another lightning bolt struck near the train, this one closer and louder than the previous one.

Rousted from his morbid reverie by the crack of thunder, Creed jerked upright in his seat, and no sooner had he done this than the train was jolted, throwing him forward against the back of the seat in front of him.

The other passengers, two peddlers and two ladies, were similarly ruffled, the women screaming in fear that a great disaster was about to befall them.

The train came to a grinding, squealing halt.

Creed peered through the black window, hoping to see something, anything that might explain why the train had stopped. He saw the glow of the engine's headlamp ahead, indicating that the train had paused on a curve. Another flash of lightning lit up a hillside beside the track. He leaned closer to the glass, only to have his breath fog up the window. He wiped it clear again and saw a man with a lantern—Mr. Quinn, the conductor, he assumed—emerge from the train and move along the track toward the locomotive. A second man with a lantern—presumably the engineer—stepped down from the cab and met the conductor. They walked to the front of the engine, stopped, conferred for a minute, then returned to the train, the engineer to his post at the controls and the conductor to the express car.

"So why did we stop?" asked one of the peddlers.

"Beats me," said the other.

"Well, why don't you go find out?" said the first.

"Why don't you?" suggested the second.

They argued, but without conviction.

Annoyed by the two carpetbaggers, Creed heaved a sigh, stood, and exited the coach for the express car to make certain that Nimbus was all right. He was just opening the door when out of the darkness came a terrifying crash that rocked him back into the car, staggering him against the first bench, which caused him to fall awkwardly onto it.

The women screamed in terror, and the salesmen cursed the night, the storm, and each other.

Creed righted himself, stood, then grabbed the door latch, lifting it and jerking the door open. Rain and an icy wind immediately stung his face, forcing him to step back for an instant before moving out into the darkness. He pulled his collar up and his hat down around his ears, then jumped from the coach's platform to the express car's, tried the next door, but couldn't get it open. The rain and wind continued to beat at him as he tried the door again. He stopped when he thought he heard Nimbus whinnying within the car.

Something's wrong with Nimbus! he thought. He threw himself against the door. It refused to give. He crashed against it again, but it still wouldn't budge. He stood back for a second, then went to the steps and peered around the corner of the car.

Son of a bitch! he swore silently.

A tree, a big tree, a huge oak tree had fallen on the express car, crushing it in the middle. Light glowed around the tree's branches, giving them an eerie essence.

Nimbus!

Creed leaped into the mud beside the tracks and fell forward, but caught himself before his face kissed the ground. He pushed himself erect and ran up to the fallen tree. He climbed onto the trunk and fought through the broken branches until he was inside the car.

The conductor and the clerk were lying facedown on the floor, pinned there by the tree. Nimbus was on his feet at the far end of the car. He appeared to be unharmed. Rain poured in on the three men, but not on the Appaloosa. Lanterns hanging at each end of the car swung back and forth, spilling their light over the scene.

"Help me!" the conductor called out. His face was scratched and bleeding. "Help me!"

"How bad are you hurt, Mr. Quinn?" asked Creed, trying to get closer to the man.

"I don't know. I'm not sure."

"Don't move," said Creed. "I'll get more help." He looked over at the express clerk, whose face was turned away from Creed. "Are you all right, Mr. Turner?" No reply. "I'd better get some help," he said to the conductor.

Aid was already on the way. The fireman, the brakeman, and the engineer had heard and felt the crash of the tree. They came running up to the car before Creed could jump down and come looking for them.

"Anyone hurt?" asked the engineer over the storm.

"Don't know yet," said Creed. "Conductor and Mr. Turner are trapped under the tree. Come on up."

The three railroadmen climbed into the car and surveyed the damage. The tree had crashed through the car almost directly in the middle of it, caving in the center roof and both side doors.

"Help me," said the conductor. "I'm bleeding."

The engineer stepped carefully over the branches to get to Quinn. He knelt down beside him and said, "You hurt bad, Fred?"

"I can't tell," said the conductor. "I can't feel all my parts. Some hurt, and some are numb. Mostly numb. But I can't move."

"Have you tried, Mr. Quinn?" asked Creed.

"No," said Quinn. "I'm afraid to."

"Try wiggling your toes," said Creed.

The conductor did as instructed and said, "I can move them. Now what?"

"Well, at least your back isn't broken," said Creed. "Try your fingers."

"They work," said Quinn. "Now what?"

"Now let's get you out of there," said Creed. He lifted up on a large branch, and the other men helped. "See if you can crawl out of there, Mr. Quinn."

"But I'm bleeding," argued the conductor.

"Just your face," said Creed firmly. "Now give it a try before we drop this tree on you again."

Quinn bent his knees up, gave a little push, didn't seem to feel any pain, and crawled out from under the tree.

"Good," said Creed. "Now let's see about Mr. Turner."

Turner was unconscious. He'd fainted with fright when the giant oak came crashing into his working place. When Creed shook him, he came around rather quickly. "Good Lord! Am I dead?" he asked with incredible confusion.

"No, you're still alive," said Creed with a grin of relief. "Are you hurt?"

Turner thought about it for a second, then said, "I don't think so. Should I be?"

"Yes, you should," said Creed, "but I guess you're all right. Can you get out of there without our help?"

"I'll try," said Turner. And without further ado, he slid out from under the oak branches. "Where's Fred?" he asked.

"He's over there," said Creed. "He's scratched up a bit, but he's all right."

"That's good," said Turner. He stared at the oak. "My God, that's a big tree. You could build a house out of that tree."

"Why did we stop?" asked Creed of the engineer.

"Landslide," he replied. "Part of this hill caved in over the tracks ahead."

"How long before you can clear it off and we can get under way again?" asked Creed.

The engineer laughed and said, "We're not going to clear away anything, mister. That takes a line crew, and we ain't got one. And now with this tree here, we ain't going no place for a while." He peered at Creed, then asked, "If you were in a hurry, mister, you should have taken a steamboat up the Mississippi."

Creed could have done without that last bit.

23

Creed found something that resembled a road, guessed that it ran north and south, and, with the icy rain beating in his face, set out toward what he hoped was Tennessee. He wanted to sleep but couldn't, of course; the weather wouldn't let him. He plodded on with Nimbus, sloshing through the mud and mire until dawn, when the rain finally quit.

Exhaustion dictated Creed's decision to dismount at a stand of pines. He tied Nimbus to a small oak that put the stallion out of the wind, unsaddled the horse, then made camp beneath the branches of the largest evergreen. In no time, he was stretched out and asleep.

When he woke up at midday, Creed was famished. Part of him wished that he'd stayed with the train and gone back to Corinth, while the other part told him to saddle up and get moving, daylight was wasting. He chose to listen to the latter voice.

An hour down the road, Creed suddenly felt something strange awaken within him. A familiarity. Then he saw it. He had been here before. This was Shiloh.

The fighting had started at dawn the day before, April 6, 1862, when General Albert Sidney Johnston ordered his Confederate Army of the Mississippi to attack General U. S. Grant's Union Army of the Tennessee, which had landed north of Corinth at Pittsburgh Landing on the Tennessee River.

Some of the green troops on both sides ran to the rear at the first sounds of battle. The Yankees who ran hid under the bluff at the landing, while their Confederate counterparts retreated to the woods, where their reserves waited to get into the battle.

Among those units being held out of the fight on the Southern side was Colonel John A. Wharton's regiment of Texas Rangers, which was made up of companies from several different Texas cavalry regiments, including Company F of the 8th Texas Cavalry, Creed's unit. Only then he was Clete Slater, and he was barely twenty years old.

As the battle raged and the Yankees were driven from their camps, the Confederate reserves moved up to be near the forward units in case they were needed. The Texans wanted to get into the fight and resented being kept behind the lines. Their officers had their hands full trying to keep the men out of the fray until they were ordered into the fight.

When the afternoon sun began to fade in the west and the battle seemed to be won, the Texans couldn't restrain themselves any longer. They burst from their ranks and rode through the deserted Union camps, taking everything they found that would be of use to their side. Very few of them came close to the real fighting.

When dusk settled over the battlefield, Grant's Army found itself pushed far back from its original camps, and the prospects for the morrow seemed miniscule.

On the Confederate side, jubilation reigned. General P.G.T. Beauregard was confident that all he had to do the next day was attack again and the Yankees would run all the way back to Kentucky.

A downpour struck that night. Ten thousand wounded men lay on the battlefield with little or no shelter. Many of them died because of exposure and a general lack of medical attention. Hell soon had a new name: Shiloh.

Grant launched a surprise attack at dawn April 7. The Rebels were caught unawares. Just as the Federals had done the day before, the Southerners ran off at first, then were rallied by their officers to make a stand against the Union onslaught.

The Texans finally saw action when Colonel Wharton was ordered to ride around the Federal right flank and attack the Yankees in the rear. He was doing this when a Union infantry brigade suddenly appeared ahead of him and opened up on his cavalry with a half-dozen volleys of rifle fire that toppled many of Wharton's men from the saddle. Realizing he was in an untenable position, Wharton fell back, dismounted his regiment, and began skirmishing on foot. After receiving word that the Union reserves were attacking Wharton in force, Beauregard ordered the Texans to retreat to Shiloh church.

Wharton commanded Captain Louis Strobel and Captain Frank Clemons to cover the regiment's retreat with their companies, F and D, respectively.

Captain Clemons climbed onto a log that the Rangers were using as a rampart and shouted, "Hold your ground, boys! Rally for the South, boys!"

"It ain't my ground," said Jess Tate. He looked over his shoulder and saw the other companies riding away to safety. "I'm skedaddling out of here. You coming, Clete?"

Clete Slater didn't hear the question; he was too busy drawing a bead on a Yankee. He fired his shotgun, and the bluecoated soldier fell dead. Reloading, Slater looked around him and noticed that the other men in his squad had mounted up and were riding off after the main body of the regiment. He heard Clemons shout again. Looking up, he saw three Yankees stick the captain with their bayonets, but before Clemons died, he ran his sword through two of his killers, taking them with him to the Hereafter.

Yankees were swarming around what was left of Slater's company now.

"Son of a bitch!" swore Slater. He turned to run.

"You hold your ground!" shouted Sergeant Dickerson, pointing his pistol in Slater's face. "Or I'll shoot you myself!"

Slater started to argue, but before he could utter a word, a Yankee minié ball creased his skull.

When he awoke, Slater was lying where he fell, rain pouring down on him and a big ugly Bluebelly staring down at him.

"You'll live, Reb," said the Yankee. He reached down, picked up Slater by his coat collar, and shoved him toward a line of other Confederate prisoners.

After spending a night in the open, Slater, and the other prisoners who survived the foul weather and their wounds, were put on board river transports and sent north on the Tennessee River. Two days later they were in Kentucky, and all but Slater figured the war was over for them.

Slater had one thought on his mind: Nimbus, his horse. While he was being marched aboard the steamer with the other prisoners, he had seen the Appaloosa stallion tied up in front of some officer's tent. That would never do. Nimbus was his horse, and no Yankee was going to own him, and that was that.

His desire to get his horse back drove Slater to escape. Having not been fed much by his Yankee captors, he'd gotten skinnier over the past few days, which allowed him to slip the chains from his ankles. He waited for the right moment, when the guards weren't looking, then jumped over the side into the turbulent river. The Yankees didn't bother firing at him, figuring he would drown in the swift current; but when he reached the bank safely, they gave him a volley that came nowhere near him. His fellow Southerners aboard the steamer gave him a cheer for the feat.

Slater didn't know that he was in Kentucky, but he did know that he was a few hundred miles from where he'd last seen his horse. Of course, he also knew that there was no guarantee that Nimbus would still be at Shiloh. Hell, the Yankees were on the move. They could be anywhere by now. Corinth, even. He had to get back to Shiloh as fast as he could, and the fastest way was on horseback.

Kentucky was real horse country. It seemed to him that every man had a decent horse for pulling a light buggy and a second for riding. All Slater had to do when he came across a farm with two horses was to figure out which was for the saddle and which was for hitching to a rig, and then steal the first one. Near a place called Aurora he came across a fair-sized plantation that had several horses grazing in a small pasture near a big stock barn. He found a rope, lassoed a likely gelding, climbed on him bareback, and headed south at a gallop.

Three days later Slater saw the first Union pickets several miles north of Shiloh. He jumped one who was half asleep. After a brief scuffle, he had the sentry's Springfield in his possession. Pointing it at the surprised Northerner, he said, "All right now, Yank, get that uniform off."

"Take off my clothes?" queried the Yankee.

"Just the coat and pants," said Slater. "And the hat, too."

"What do you want them for?" asked the Yank.

"You never mind that. Just get that uniform off and do it pronto like."

"Pronto like? What the hell does that mean?"

"Damn! You Yanks are ignorant," said Slater. "That's Texan for you'd better get your ass moving, boy, or I'll shoot it off."

"You're a Texan?" queried the Yank as he began unbuttoning his tunic.

Slater recognized the fear in the Northerner's voice and said haughtily, "That's right. I'm a Texan. What of it?"

"Nothing, sir," said the Yankee, suddenly filled with respect for his captor.

"All right then. So hurry your ass up, boy!"

The Yankee undressed as quickly as he could and placed the clothes in front of Slater. "Now what are you going to do to me?" he asked in a quavering voice.

"Turn around," said Slater.

The Yank turned around as ordered and said, "You ain't going to stick me with my own bayonet, are you?"

"Put your hands behind you," said Slater, "and quit asking all those fool questions."

The Yank obeyed again, and Slater took the rope he'd used to lasso his stolen horse in Kentucky and tied the Union soldier's hands behind his back. Then he tied him to the nearest tree and gagged him with his own neckerchief.

"I don't like leaving you like this, Yank," said Slater, "but I can't kill you in cold blood. It ain't my way. Not even in this war. Now you remember that next time you got one of ours in your sights and you got the choice of killing him or taking him prisoner. You hear me, Yank?"

The Yankee nodded that he did.

Slater donned the blue uniform of an infantryman from the 24th Indiana Regiment. Noting the numeral insignia, the thought occurred to him that it might be helpful if he knew something about this Yank. He removed his prisoner's gag and asked a very pointed question. "What outfit you with, Yank?"

"Company B, 24th Indiana," the soldier replied.

"Who's your company captain and who's your regimental commander?"

"Captain Bendix heads up the company, and Colonel Hovey is the regiment's commanding officer."

"Who's your general?" asked Slater.

"General Lew Wallace."

"And what's your name, boy?"

"Sam Holloway."

Slater nodded, replaced the neckerchief in the Yank's mouth, and said, "I hope you make it through the war, Sam Holloway." Then he continued his journey back to Shiloh.

Wearing a Yankee uniform was a good idea on the one hand because it let Slater move through the Union lines without much trouble, but on the other hand, if he were caught, he could be shot as a spy. That was the risk of war, but Slater didn't know how big a risk it was as he slipped into the main camp of General William Tecumseh Sherman's Fifth Division.

Sherman had been wounded during the Battle of Pittsburgh Landing, as the Yanks were calling Shiloh, and three horses had been shot out from under him on the first day alone. When he heard that Sherman, a fellow Ohioan, was without a good horse, Colonel Sam Steadman of the 68th Ohio had presented him with the gray Appaloosa stallion that his men had captured on the second day, when they ran headlong into a Rebel cavalry regiment and drove it from the field.

Slater saw Nimbus tied to a picket line near Sherman's tent. Daylight was dying in the west. He would wait until dark before taking his horse and getting the hell out of there.

Now standing below the bluff at Pittsburgh Landing waiting to be ferried across the Tennessee River, Creed recalled how impervious he had been to the Yankee sentries that night more than three years ago, only because they had been asleep for the most part. Those that weren't had offered him no interference.

He patted Nimbus on the neck and said, "I almost lost you then, boy." He stroked the horse, feeling all the love a man could have for an animal, and he thought of Scott Houchin and Pride.

Scott and his family had gone through a lengthy ordeal to recover his horse. Scott's adventure hadn't been as dangerous as the one that Creed had endured, to be sure, but Pride was certainly just as important to Scott's life as Nimbus was to Creed's.

"Folks who will go to that much trouble for a horse are our kind of people, Nimbus," said Creed. "We've got to get to Kentucky as fast as we can and help those people."

24

Middle Tennessee was country that Creed knew well; he'd ridden through it often enough with Colonel John Hunt Morgan during the War Between the States. Those were daring times, he recalled as he rode from Savannah to Columbia during the next two days. Even Nimbus seemed to sense a homecoming of sorts as they passed through the countryside. But Creed knew that he had no time to wax nostalgic. There was another job to be done now.

At Columbia, Creed booked a ticket for himself and space in the express car for Nimbus on the Decatur & Nashville train to Nashville, where he could make connections for Bowling Green. The D. & N.R.R. seemed to Creed to be in better shape than the Mobile & Ohio had been. The coach wasn't as drafty as the one in which he'd ridden in Mississippi, and the trainmen were a nicer lot. Creed slept well during the short trip to Nashville.

Creed's cavalry company had been one of the last to arrive and one of the first to leave Nashville when the Union Army under General Don Carlos Buell approached the city in the winter of '62. The Texas regiment had left to aid in the evacuation of troops from Fort Donelson below Nashville on the Cumberland River. The next time he saw the city he was riding under Morgan's command when that valiant leader raided the city with General Forrest in the summer of '62.

As on those two previous occasions, Creed was just passing through Nashville, although he wanted to stay there for a while and look for Blackburn and the others who had dropped the blame for their crime on his shoulders. He would return, he told himself, and find all of them and make them tell the truth—one way or another. For now, he would visit the post office and ask if there was a letter for him. There was. He read it while he waited to change trains and railroads to continue his trip north.

True to her word, Texada had thought of Creed and prayed for him every day since he had left Hallettsville. She had written down some of her thoughts of him with the news from back home.

My dearest darling Clete,

Jake brought me your letter from Victoria. I am glad you decided to go looking for Blackburn and the others right away instead of coming home as you really wanted to do. I wanted you to come home, too, my darling, but as I wrote to you before, it is not safe here for you yet.

Kindred was made a deputy marshal by an appointment from Austin, and he made the Detchens his deputies. They rode out of town with Markham to capture you in Victoria. Jake said he saw them on the road after he saw you safely out of Victoria. I suppose they will follow you from there if they have the grit to do so, which I do not think they do.

Christmas is nearly here, and Granny seems to be holding her own these last few days. I think she will live through the holidays, but I do not think she will survive the winter. She is suffering so, but she never complains about it. I wish I could ease her pain for her, but there just is not anything I can do for it. In a way (and I know this is an awful thing to say) I wish the Lord would hurry up and take her and get it over with. Not for my sake but for hers because of the pain she is in.

Malinda came by yesterday, and I told her the latest news that I had about you. She sends her love. I did not tell her that you had gone to Tennessee to look for Blackburn and the others, because she said not to tell her where you are for fear that she might accidentally say something to Markham about you.

Although I detest Markham for what he did to you last summer, I can understand why Malinda loves him. He does treat her well. I envy her that. She has her man, and I only have my dreams of you.

I do love you so, my darling Clete. I wish the day when we can be together again would hurry and get here. I get so impatient for that day. If only I knew when it was, I think I could be more patient. It is this not knowing that makes me a little crazy when I am alone. Oh, my darling, I miss you so. Please hurry and find Blackburn and the others and make them tell those damn Yankees the truth so you can come home again and be a free man again.

Well, Jake has just come in. I suppose I should finish this letter so he can take it and post it up to Oakland for me.

I love you, my darling. May the Lord keep you safe until the day when we can be together again.

> Your ever loving,
> Texada

Creed bought a ticket for himself and booked space in the express car for Nimbus on the Louisville & Nashville train for Bowling Green. While he waited, he read Texada's letter several more times, and each time he felt the tugs at his heartstrings. As much as he wanted to go home, he knew he couldn't. Not yet. He had a train to catch, and within an hour he was once again on his way north.

The Louisville & Nashville train pulled into the Bowling Green station shortly after dark on January 4, 1866. Creed disembarked, off-loaded Nimbus, then walked to the nearest livery, where he boarded the Appaloosa for the night. Satisfied that his horse was secure, he found a hotel, where he checked in for a hot meal and a good night's rest. The next morning he checked out, asked directions to Edmondson County, retrieved Nimbus, then rode off to find Scott Houchin's home.

Nine days had passed since Creed had been put off the *Princess* below Natchez. He was sure that it hadn't taken Percy McGrath and Scott Houchin that long to get to Bowling Green. His estimate had them arriving in Edmondson County no later than January 2, maybe even as early as New Year's Eve, depending on how easily they had made railroad connections at Memphis.

Creed reached Brownsville, the county town for Edmondson County, by mid-afternoon. His first impression of the town was favorable; it seemed to be prosperous.

The first place Creed visited was the post office, which was located in the general store. He figured the postmaster would know where he could find the Houchin farm. Barring that, he would ask the sheriff.

"Who wants to know?" responded the postmaster, a skinny fellow who made up for his bald head with an abundance of beard.

"My name is Slate Creed. I'm from Lavaca County, Texas. I met young Scott Houchin on a boat from Indianola, Texas, to New Orleans. His father owns a horse that interests me. I've come here to speak to him about it."

"That would be Davis Houchin," said the postmaster. "Scott is his son. Just got home the other day, he did. Had some fellow with him, too."

"Is his name McGrath?" asked Creed.

"Who?"

"The fellow with Scott," said Creed. "Is his name McGrath?"

"Don't know for sure. You can ask him yourself. He's staying over to the hotel. You can't miss him. He's got a little bandage on his right ear. Or is it his left? Can't rightly recollect, but I know it's on one of his ears. 'Tain't on his nose. I know that for sure. One ear or the other."

"Much obliged," said Creed, nodding. He left the store and headed over to the north side of the town square, where the Bob Hazelip Hotel was located.

Bob Hazelip was the desk clerk; he was also the barkeeper and the owner of the establishment. He greeted Creed with a pinpointed stare, saying, "Afternoon, sir. Something I can do for you?"

"I hope so," said Creed. "I'm wondering if one of your guests is named Percy McGrath."

"Who wants to know?" asked the clerk.

Tight-lipped bunch around here, thought Creed. "My name is Slate Creed," he said. "I'm a friend of Scott Houchin."

Hazelip's eyebrows pinched together over his nose as he scanned Creed and asked, "Where do you know Scott from?"

"We met on the boat from Texas to New Orleans just before Christmas," said Creed, becoming a little exasperated with the clerk. "So what about McGrath?"

"What about him?"

"Is he staying here?"

"Sure, he is," said the clerk.

"Thank you," said Creed. "Is he around?"

"Around where?"

"Never mind," said Creed, having finally had his fill of the man. "How about a room?"

"Why didn't you say you wanted a room in the first place?" Hazelip turned the registry around for Creed to sign. "That'll be fifty cents for the room, and a dime for each meal you want to eat here in the dining room. Will you being staying long?"

"Maybe," said Creed. "I don't know yet." He signed the registry with the pencil that was in the crease of the book.

"Are you interested in buying the Houchin horse, too?" asked Hazelip.

"You mean there are others?" queried Creed.

"Just one so far," said Hazelip.

"McGrath?"

"Yep," said Hazelip, nodding.

"I thought so," said Creed. "Well, as a matter of fact, I am interested in buying the horse."

"Well, I wouldn't count on buying it, if I was you. Davis Houchin ain't planning to sell."

"How do you know this?" asked Creed.

"There's been Houchins around here since the days of Daniel Boone," said Hazelip. "Ain't none of them ever owned a horse like this one Davis has got now. I've known Davis Houchin all my life. I can't see him selling that colt at all."

"I see," said Creed. "Could you tell me how to get out to the Houchin farm?"

"Which Houchin farm?"

"The Davis Houchin farm," said Creed with a sigh.

"There's a sign on the square that points out the road that leads out to Houchin's Ferry. Don't go there, because that's the wrong Houchin. That's the ferry Johnny Dick Houchin started up back about the time of the last war with England. You don't want that one. Davis Houchin has a ferry at his place. That's the one you want. His ferry crosses the Green at Turnhole Bend. That's a half dozen miles east of town. You go that way. East, toward Elko. Just follow the signs to Elko, and you'll come to one directing you toward Davis Houchin's ferry at the Turnhole. You can't miss it."

25

The day was too far gone for Creed to be riding out of Brownsville that afternoon to look for the Houchin farm, so he opted to have a look around the town instead and possibly find Percy McGrath.

Brownsville was situated in a dingle between two ridges that sloped down to the Green River, which coursed by the town to the northwest. The village wasn't much bigger now than when its founders platted the site in 1825. Its population hadn't grown much since founding either, being barely over a hundred souls and the core of the town hadn't changed: the courthouse square surrounded by Main, Washington, Main Cross, and Green streets. All of the businesses, including the Bob Hazelip Hotel, faced the square. The village smithy and livery stable were the only businesses on the road going east from town. The road west led down to the river, the town ferry, and the boat landing.

Satisfied that he'd seen enough of the municipality, Creed returned to the hotel for supper.

Bob Hazelip's hotel was a two-story affair built into the side of the hill that protected Brownsville from cold north winds in winter. The hill was so steep that the horse hitching posts and rails on the street were a full story below the hotel's porch. The dining room of the establishment was nothing elaborate, not being a whole lot bigger than one in a fair-sized boardinghouse. It had four square tables that were unadorned by covering cloths, and each table had four chairs, not all of which matched. The ceiling and walls were vertical tongue-and-groove boards heavily coated with creamy milk paint. One door led to the so-called lobby, while the other opened into the kitchen. Two windows in the front wall allowed diners a perfect view of the town square and courthouse, and the one on the side let them see who might be approaching from the west along Washington Street.

When Creed arrived that night, one of the tables was occupied by four muscular men who, from the looks of their clothing, appeared to be laborers. They gave Creed a casual glance as he pulled up a chair at one of the three vacant tables and waited to be served.

Bob Hazelip entered the room and said, "We don't serve nothing too fancy around here, Mr. Creed. For supper tonight, we got corn bread, bacon, and sweet potatoes. Is that good enough for you?"

Creed ignored Hazelip's impertinence and asked, "Have you got coffee, too?"

"Of course, we got coffee," groused Hazelip. "What do you take us for? A bunch of Illinois suckers?"

"Then corn bread, bacon, and sweet potatoes will do me fine, Mr. Hazelip," said Creed with a condescending smile.

"Strangers," harrumphed Hazelip. He left Creed and went to get the food.

As Hazelip departed through one door, Percy McGrath appeared in the other. He looked around the dining room and saw the four customers at the other occupied table; then he saw Creed. Fear swept over him.

Creed saw McGrath at the same instant. Anger flared inside the Texan.

McGrath started to reach inside his coat for his Smith & Wesson .32 but thought better of it when he saw Creed slide his hand inside his coat and grasp the grip of his Colt's. McGrath stayed his hand. He and Creed were both strangers in this town, but in McGrath's estimation, Creed was a country bumpkin like the locals. McGrath felt that this very fact put him at a distinct disadvantage if he should start something with Creed here and now in front of witnesses and then have to explain it to the sheriff later. He decided that another tack was called for here.

"Creed, my friend!" said McGrath, overflowing with feigned effervescence. He rushed toward the Texan with an extended hand. "You made it! Thank God!"

Creed didn't know what McGrath was up to, but when he noticed that the four men at the other table were watching them, he decided to play along with the gambler. "Percy," he said calmly, "how are you?" He accepted McGrath's handshake.

"Percy?" queried one of the four men to his companions. "What the hell kind of name is that?"

The others guffawed, then went about eating again.

McGrath gave the laughers a sideways glance, then seated himself across from Creed. "How are you, Creed?" he asked. He let his hands fall into his lap.

McGrath's movement didn't escape Creed's notice. "Keep your hands where I can see them, McGrath," he said in a low growl. To emphasize the command, he cocked his Colt's.

The click of the six-gun's hammer moving into firing position was quite audible to McGrath. He got the message and put his elbows on the table, hands empty in front of him. "You'd better ease back there, Creed," said McGrath with a twinkle in his eye. "You wouldn't want that thing to fire accidentally now or you just might leave here half-cocked." He snickered at his own joke.

Creed ignored McGrath's attempt at levity and put the hammer back in the safety position. "You'd better worry more about your own hide staying in one piece, McGrath," he said.

McGrath quit laughing and said softly, "I really didn't expect to see you again, Creed. I thought you would have taken Charlotte's money and gone back to Texas by now."

"You figured wrong, McGrath," said Creed in an even voice. "I made a deal with Charlotte, and I intend to keep my end of it."

"Yes, I can see that now," said the gambler.

"I warned you in New Orleans, McGrath, that if you crossed me that I'd kill you."

"Hey, wait a minute, Creed," interjected McGrath anxiously. "I wasn't the one who called you a cheater. You called me one."

"That's because you were cheating," said Creed. "You and that captain were in it together. You're lucky he spoiled my aim, McGrath."

The gambler blanched and touched the bandage on his ear. "All right, so what? You weren't the mark. Palmer was. I just cut the captain in on the deal is all. What's the matter? Are you angry because I didn't cut you in, too?"

"I don't feel a need to cheat in order to win," said Creed.

"That's not what Charlotte says. She told me how she helped you win at roulette when you first met her at DuMorney's."

"Helped me win? What the hell are you talking about?"

McGrath snorted a laugh and said, "You are the innocent, aren't you, Creed?" He snickered again. "DuMorney's croupier let her win. The table is rigged. You weren't hurting anything, so she gave them the nod to let you win a little. If you hadn't broken off the game when you did, Charlotte would have given him another nod and you would have lost it all back to the house that quick." He snapped his fingers for emphasis, which drew the attention of the other diners. Seeing this, McGrath spoke quietly again. "You got luckier than you think, my friend."

"What difference is that to you, McGrath?"

"None," said the gambler nonchalantly. He looked Creed straight in the eye and said, "I think you know what my style is, Creed. Charlotte is the one that I envy." He smiled evilly.

"McGrath, the only thing that's keeping you alive right now is the presence of those four men over there."

"I might say the same thing to you, my friend. You were lucky on the *Princess*, Creed. If I'd suspected that you might start something, I would have killed you the second that you called me a cheater. I'm glad that I didn't, though."

"Is that so?" said Creed.

"Yes, it is. If I had, you wouldn't be here now, and my chances to obtain Pride from the Houchins would be nil."

"The deal is we buy the colt for Charlotte," said Creed, "if Scott's father is willing to sell."

"That's what I meant," said McGrath. "Our chances to buy Pride from the old man would be nil without you and Charlotte's money, of course."

Creed began to relax. As much as McGrath disgusted him, he still had to work with the gambler. He might as well make the best of it.

"All right, McGrath, tell me what's happened since we parted company on the river."

"Nothing much," said McGrath. "We arrived in Memphis, then took the train to Bowling Green. I bought a horse there, and young Scott and I rode up here." He glanced around the room. "Rather quaint, don't you think?"

Before Creed could answer him, Hazelip came into the room and set a plate of corn bread, bacon, and sweet potatoes in front of Creed. He left again but returned a few seconds later with a cup and a pot of coffee. He put the cup down beside the plate, then filled it three-quarters full.

Creed nodded and said, "Thank you, Mr. Hazelip."

Hazelip eyed McGrath and asked, "You eating, too, Mr. McGrath?"

"Yes, I believe I will," said the gambler.

Hazelip left them alone again.

"So what have you done since you got here?" asked Creed.

"Nothing really," said McGrath. "The boy took me out to his family's farm, and I met the old man and his family."

"That's all? You haven't tried anything funny with Scott?"

"I'm not a fool, Creed. The horse is worth too much for me to foul up the deal that way. Like I said, I met the old man and the family."

"And what did you talk about?"

"I talked to the old man about the horse a little bit. He told me the horse wasn't for sale, but I told him I couldn't make him an offer until you got here. He asked me when that would be, and I told him that I expected it would take you a couple of weeks to get here, at least. You fooled me, Creed. I didn't expect you to get here at all, and then you got here in half that time. I'm impressed, my friend."

"Save your flattery, McGrath," said Creed. "It won't hold any water with me."

"Suit yourself," said McGrath with a shrug. "I was just trying to be friendly."

"This is business, McGrath, and that's all. Except when it comes to the horse, I don't want anything to do with you. Do you understand that?"

"Sure, Creed, sure. We'll be all business from here on. All right?"

Hazelip brought McGrath his meal, and the two men ate in silence.

"What now?" asked McGrath when they had finished eating.

"I plan to get a good night's sleep," said Creed, "and tomorrow I'm going to ride out to the Houchin farm and talk with Scott and his father."

"What about me?" asked McGrath.

"You just stay out of my way, McGrath. You can't be trusted to handle this business for Charlotte, so I guess I'll have to do it for her. You just stay out of my way until I need you. Is that understood?"

McGrath didn't like it, but he agreed, while under his breath he determined that he wouldn't put up with very much of this sort of treatment for very long.

26

Back before the turn of the century, five Houchin brothers—John, Charles, William, Kanus, and Francis—left their homes in Virginia and trekked over the Appalachians to "Kentucke," where they settled along the Green River within a mile or so of each other, on lands that were granted to John and Charles for their service in the Revolutionary War. John, Charles, William, and Kanus took up the plow on low-lying land, while Francis staked his claim to a hill south of a bend in the river known as the Turnhole. Although he worked just as hard as his brothers, Francis was unable to coax a living as good as theirs from his hilltop farm.

The Houchins were a prolific bunch, starting with John, the oldest brother, who had five sons and four daughters who reached their majority. Francis had his share of sons, too, including Scott Houchin's father, William Davis Houchin, who was named for Francis Houchin's two neighbors and good friends, William Thompson and Robert Davis.

Wanting no part of his father's rocky knoll farm as a young man, William Davis Houchin took up surveying and went to work for the county laying out roads. He ran his cousin's ferry near Brownsville for a while, married, and had his first family. Tiring of working for others and having sons who were old enough to work beside him in the fields, he bought a piece of his father's land that bordered on the Green River at Turnhole Bend, took up farming, and established his own ferry. He built his cabin right on the bluff overlooking the river so he could hear anyone hailing him from the other side, day or night, when they wanted to be ferried across the Green.

When Creed rode out of town in search of this particular Houchin farm, he followed all the directions he was given by Hazelip and arrived at the Houchin farm by mid-morning.

138

"Stranger coming around the bend, Pa," said John Wesley, the third of Davis Houchin's children by his second wife, Edith Elizabeth. The boy ran up to the porch, to his father, who was sitting in his rocker.

Davis Houchin was in his sixty-second year, and he looked it. His hair was white, and so was his beard. His shoulders were beginning to turn in, putting a stoop in his back. Even so, his eyes, though not as sharp as they had been once, were as bright as ever, and so was his mind. He squinted to see Creed approach.

Edie Houchin stepped outside, wiping her hands on her apron. She was a smallish woman in size but not in stature. Fate had dropped lemons on her life since childhood, but she had squeezed those lemons until she had enough juice to make gallons of lemonade and several big meringue pies, too. Orphaned at an early age, Edie and her sister Mary were taken in by Davis and his first wife, Elizabeth, as their wards. When Liza Houchin took sick and suffered a stroke, Edie assumed the role of woman of the house, including the connubial duties of a wife. Liza's children openly resented Edie for supplanting their mother. Edie was hurt by their attitude, but she never let it show. She nursed Liza as best as she could, doing everything possible to make the sick woman comfortable as she slowly wasted away. Although helpless to do anything at all, Liza lingered for several years before dying. With Liza in her grave, Davis finally married Edie just a few weeks before she gave birth to their fourth child. The neighbors whispered that it was about time that he gave his name to Edie and their first three children. Of course, this talk about Edie and Davis started long before Liza died, but no one made anything out of it with the law, because everybody knew that a man needed a woman's comfort, and if he got it from the housekeeper instead of his sickly wife, well, that was all right, they guessed.

"You know who it is, Pa?" asked Edie as she stared down the road at the approaching stranger.

"Can't tell," said Davis, "but he's riding a helluva good-looking horse."

Clarenda and the other children appeared on the porch beside their parents. Clarenda was only fourteen, but she looked older, being amply endowed in the bust and hips. Early physical development was the curse of Houchin women, because mental and emotional wisdom usually didn't keep pace with their bodies, often leaving them with broken hearts and unexpected bundles in swaddling. "What is it, Mama?" asked Clarenda.

"Stranger coming," said Edie.

Scott and Eddie Butler, a Houchin cousin by marriage, who was the same age as Scott, came out of the barn where they had been cleaning out the stalls. Eddie looked at the house and saw the rest of the family gathered there, noticed that they were looking down the road to Brownsville, and naturally turned to see what held their attention so. When he saw Creed coming, he nudged Scott and said, "Rider coming."

Scott was too tired to care until he realized it was Creed atop Nimbus. "It's him," he said softly.

"Who?" asked Eddie.

"Mr. Creed, that's who," replied Scott excitedly. "Come on." He raced off toward the road.

Eddie thought about what Scott said for a second, then realized that his cousin was talking about the man he'd met on the boat down to Texas. Wanting to meet him, he followed Scott as fast as he could.

"Mr. Creed!" shouted Scott.

Creed saw the two Houchin cousins running toward him, recognized Scott, and reined in Nimbus. He jumped down and waited for them, holding the stallion's reins tightly.

"Mr. Creed!" said Scott. He held out his hand in greeting.

"Scott, it's good to see you again," said Creed, accepting the handshake. He looked at Eddie and said, "Is this your brother?"

"My cousin," said Scott. "This is Eddie."

"How do you do, Eddie?" said Creed, offering to shake hands with young Butler.

"How do you do, Mr. Creed?" said Eddie, surprised to be treated like an adult. He shook Creed's hand vigorously.

"I didn't think I'd see you again so soon," said Scott. "You must have ridden day and night to get here."

"There were times when it seemed like that was what I was doing," said Creed. "Actually, I rode a lot of trains as well as Nimbus. Except for a night in Meridian, Mississippi, another in Bowling Green, and last night in Brownsville, I spent the rest of the time on the trail. I see that you and Pride made good time getting home, though."

"Yes, sir, we did," said Scott. "Thanks to Mr. McGrath. The train brought us all the way from Memphis to Bowling Green, and I rode Pride from there. Got home in time to celebrate the New Year with the folks."

Creed nodded, then lowered his eyes as he asked, "You didn't have any trouble with McGrath, did you?"

"No, sir, not a bit," said Scott. "He paid for everything all the way, and he kept his distance, too."

Creed nodded again, then looked past the cousins toward the rest of the family at the house.

Scott turned to see what Creed was looking at, then said, "Come on, Mr. Creed. Pa's real anxious to meet you."

Creed followed the two young men up to the house, where Scott made all the introductions.

"Scott's told us a lot about you, Mr. Creed," said Edie.

"Well, I don't know how much there was to tell," said Creed with a sheepish grin. "We only spent a short time together on the two boats."

"That was plenty," said Davis with all the austerity of a country minister looking for sinners. "The boy said you jumped that horse of yours off the boat in New Orleans. Is that true?"

Creed dropped his head in modesty for a second: then he realized that Davis was doubting his son's word. He looked Davis straight in the eye and said, "Mr. Houchin, although I only spent a short time with Scott, I learned in a hurry to respect him for his honesty and forthrightness. It would be my estimation that he never told a lie in his life, and I'd have to say that was a reflection on the way he was brung up. Wouldn't you agree, sir?"

Davis nodded slowly as he considered Creed's words. Then he pinpointed his view on Creed's eyes and stated firmly, "Scott also said you were our kind of people, Mr. Creed. I can see that he was right about that."

"Thank you, sir," said Creed. "I'll take that as a first-rate compliment."

"Fetch my jug, Ma," said Davis.

"I'll get it for you, Pa," said Clarenda. Without another word, she disappeared into the house.

"Fetch Mr. Creed a chair, John Wesley," said Davis. "Come on and set yourself, Mr. Creed."

"Thank you kindly, Mr. Houchin," said Creed. He stepped onto the porch and seated himself in the chair that John Wesley pulled up for him.

"Well, you menfolk got business to talk about," said Edie, "and I've got dinner cooking already. If you'll excuse me, Mr. Creed, I'd best be getting back to my chores."

Creed rose like a gentleman, tipped his hat, and said, "Certainly, ma'am. It was an honor to meet you, Mrs. Houchin."

Edie blushed, did a quick curtsy, then scurried into the house.

Creed sat down again.

"Where's that girl with my jug?" groused Davis.

Almost magically, Clarenda appeared with the earthenware jug. She handed it to Davis, but her attention was really on Creed. She smiled at him, and being polite, he returned the expression in kind.

Davis pulled the cork, hefted the jug onto his arm, tipped it to his lips, and took a healthy swallow. The white lightning burned his tongue and throat and caused his eyes to water a bit, but he enjoyed the warmth of the fire, expressing his delight with a drawn-out sigh before passing the jug to Creed.

Creed accepted the container, put it to his lips, and took a sip. He was instantly glad that he hadn't tried to swallow more. Tears spewed from his eyes, and the breath was sucked out of him for a moment. A wildfire raced down the back of his throat all the way to his stomach, putting him in a panic for a few seconds. When he regained control, he smiled and said as best as he could, "This wouldn't be some of your own mountain dew, would it, Mr. Houchin?"

"Made it last year," said Davis with a grin of satisfaction. "I like to age her a bit before giving her a good home. Go on and have another drink. It'll take the edge off the first one."

Creed's brow furrowed, but he did as Davis said—quite reluctantly, of course. He tipped up the jug and took another swallow. Damn! he thought. The old man was wrong! The second drink was just as fiery as the first.

"Better, eh?" queried Davis with a grin.

"Yes, sir," rasped Creed. Without further hesitation, he handed the jug back to Davis. "Thank you, sir."

"You don't have to be so formal with me, Slate," said Davis. "You can call me Davis, if you're a mind to."

"Thank you, Davis," said Creed.

"Well, let's get to it," said Davis. "Pride ain't for sale. I ain't parting with him for no price. I want you to know that right up front."

"I understand that, Davis," said Creed. "I wouldn't insult you by even making an offer to buy him. Scott's told me how much store you put in that horse, and I can't blame you. Pride is a real 'Bred."

"Of course he is," said Davis, "and he's going to sire a whole bunch just like him, too. I've already got folks coming around asking me how much for him to stud their mares. One fellow offered me fifty dollars cash money right on the spot. Had his mare with him, too. I told him to come back next month. Pride ain't ready for fooling with no one else's mares just yet, although I have got him in with one of mine."

"He's about three years old, isn't he?" queried Creed.

"Yes, he is," said Davis, and with a wink, he added, "but I figure if I make the fellow wait, he'll pay me sixty dollars next month."

Creed smiled and said, "Maybe more."

"Could be," said Davis.

"Everybody will pay more than that if Pride wins a few races first," said Creed.

Davis twisted up his mouth as he considered Creed's words, then he said, "Maybe. And maybe not. What if he loses? Then what? He won't be worth a whole lot then."

"The lady who's backing my play here, Davis, is willing to put up any money it takes to race Pride."

"That ain't much of a problem around here. Not too many folks in these parts got any real betting money. I could race him against some of the local nags, but there ain't no one so foolish as to put up more than a few dollars against him. Can't see a whole lot of profit in that. And there's the possibility that he might get hurt, too. I can't be risking a valuable horse like Pride for a few dollars."

"Well, that's where I come in, Davis," said Creed. "I'll put up a purse of . . . say a hundred dollars for the winner of a race, and everybody who enters will have to pay . . . say ten dollars to run their horse. That will keep the pikers out."

Davis nodded and said, "That's fine, but where do you plan on racing?"

"At the track, of course."

"At the track? Where do you think you are, Slate? Bowling Green? Nashville, maybe? Or were you thinking this place is Louisville?"

"I take it there's no track around here," said Creed.

"Ain't no one got the land for one," said Davis. "We run quarter miles around here."

27

Quarter-pathers! That's what old Davis said raced around Edmondson County. Pride was no quarter-pather. He was a 'Bred. A real racehorse. One meant for running a mile or more in a race. Not just a sprint of a quarter mile. But how to convince Davis Houchin of that. That was Creed's problem. Creed's and Scott's.

Before Creed could present any argument about Pride's racing potential to Davis, Edie stepped out on the porch to tell Davis that he had a customer waiting on the far landing to be ferried across the river. Scott volunteered himself and Eddie Butler to do the chore, but Davis told him to stay put, that he'd do it just like he had for most of the last twenty-six years. Edie used the opportunity to invite Creed to stay for dinner, and he graciously accepted, saying he'd be honored to sit down at her table. She blushed at the flattery, gave a little girlish giggle that she tried to hide with her hand, then went back to her kitchen.

With Davis occupied by the ferry, Creed found himself surrounded by the Houchin children and cousin Eddie. All but Scott had a million questions to ask him, mostly about Texas and the war. He started to answer them and would have willingly done so for hours, if Scott hadn't put a stop to it at the outset. "Mr. Creed didn't come here to answer a lot of fool questions from you kids," he said. "He's here to talk to Pa about Pride. Now go on and leave him be."

"You heard him," said Clarenda, trying to act older than her fourteen years. "You kids go on now."

"You go on, too, Clarenda," said Scott.

"Me? I ain't going nowhere."

"Yes, you are," insisted Scott.

"No, I ain't, Arlington Scott Houchin," said Clarenda, calling him by his full name because she thought it would make her

145

appear to be more adult in Creed's eyes, "and you can't make me go neither."

"Yes, I can," said Scott as he started toward his sister.

Fully aware of what was going on here, Creed stood up and blocked Scott's path, saying, "Scott, I'd like to have a word with you, if I could, before your father comes back. Could we take a walk somewhere? Just the two of us?"

Scott puffed up his chest, looked at the others, then said, "Sure thing, Mr. Creed. We can walk Nimbus down to the barn. I'm sure he'd like some oats and a drink of water."

"I'll come, too," said Eddie.

"Thanks, Eddie," said Creed, "but I'd rather speak with Scott alone, if you don't mind."

Eddie was disappointed, but not nearly as disappointed as Clarenda was. She watched wistfully as her brother and the handsome newcomer stepped off the porch, took Nimbus by the reins, and led the Appaloosa toward the barn. She heaved a longing sigh, then ran into the house to ask her mother how she felt about this exciting man from Texas.

Creed glanced over his shoulder, saw that they were far enough away from the others now to keep from being overheard, and said, "Scott, your father reminds me a little of my grandfather Dugald. He was a Scotsman, and let me tell you, Scotsmen are as stubborn as they come. I'm getting the impression that your father has a little Scotsman in him, too."

"He's mule-headed, you mean," said Scott.

Creed got that sheepish look of his and said, "I was trying to be polite."

"No need for that here," said Scott. "Pa is as mule-headed as they come. I know that, and so does he. Fact is, he's proud of it. Ask him, if you don't believe me. He'll tell you so himself. He brags that he's part mule and part bull. He calls it fierce determination. Mule-headed is what the rest of us call it. Pure mule-headedness. That's Pa."

"No matter what you call it," said Creed, "we still have a real problem here. Pride is no quarter-pather. He's a 'Bred who should be racing on a track for a sizeable purse, not on a country lane for a jug of whiskey and a plug of tobacco."

"I agree with you completely, Mr. Creed," said Scott as they reached the barn and stopped outside, "but we don't have any tracks in Edmondson County. They got one down to Bowling

Green, and there's one up to Lexington. Louisville and Nashville have got tracks, too, but I know Pa won't let Pride go that far. Not yet anyway. Fact is, I don't think he'd even let me take Pride to Bowling Green after all the trouble we had getting him back here. Leastways, I don't think he'd let me take him now. Maybe later in the year, after Pa gets used to having Pride around again." He opened the barn door and went inside.

"I know what you mean, Scott," said Creed, following young Houchin into the barn.

Nimbus followed the humans willingly. He sniffed the air, then snorted at the smell of other horses.

"Easy, boy," said Creed responsively.

The stallion calmed down for the moment.

"I told Mr. McGrath the same thing the other day," said Scott, "and he said not to worry about it, that Pa would see things his way before too long, and we'd be taking Pride to Bowling Green for the spring meet before you knew it."

"I didn't realize that McGrath was planning on hanging around here that long," said Creed. "I was hoping we could run a few races right away here in Edmondson County, win some bets, and be on our way. I've got other plans that need taking care of now so I can get on with my life."

"Yes, sir, I know," said Scott as he took the Appaloosa's reins from Creed and led Nimbus toward a stall. "So what do you think we should do, Mr. Creed?"

"If there was only a track here in Edmondson County, we wouldn't have a problem, Scott. We could run Pride right here, and that would be it. Win or lose, I could complete my bargain with Charlotte Beaujeu and be on my way."

Scott put Nimbus into the stall and tied the reins to a rail in the rear. Without thinking about it, he began unsaddling the horse. "But I've already said that we don't have a track here in Edmondson County," he said.

"Then we'll have to make one," said Creed.

Scott threw the saddle over the side of the stall and said, "Make one?"

"That's right. We'll have to make our own track."

"How?" queried Scott. "Pa already told you that there ain't enough flat ground around here for a track." He fetched a bucket of oats and fed Nimbus.

"I know he said that," said Creed as he leaned against a loft stanchion, "but there must be at least one piece of flat land somewhere in this county."

"Not that someone would be willing to let you use for a horse track," said Scott. He started toward the barn door. "Good farmland is pretty scarce around here, and no one that I know is going to let you turn his best cornfield into a racetrack."

"Then we'll just have to buy the land we need," said Creed, following Scott outside to the well pump. "How much can forty acres of land cost around here anyway? A hundred dollars? Two hundred? Even if it's five hundred, it would be worth it. We'd get it back in just one race, if we play it right."

Scott primed the pump, then said, "How's that, Mr. Creed?"

"People pay to see horse races, Scott, and the bigger the race the more people will pay to see it."

"Well, that sounds just fine, Mr. Creed," said Scott. He placed a bucket below the pump spout, then took the handle and started pumping it. As soon as the water began to flow, he stopped and said, "I don't know if you noticed it or not, but we don't have a whole lot of folks living in these parts. Where do you think all those paying customers will come from?"

Creed was taken aback momentarily by Scott's question, surprised by the youth's acute sense of business. "We'll get them to come here from Louisville and Nashville and everywhere else if we have to."

Scott picked up the water bucket and said, "How do we do that?" Then he started toward the barn again.

"We put the word out that there's going to be a big race," said Creed as he walked beside Scott.

"But how do we do that?" repeated Scott.

Creed frowned and said, "I'm not sure, but I know there are ways to get people here. We'll worry about that later. Right now, we have to put first things first, and the first thing we need is a racetrack and for that we need forty acres of flat land."

Scott poured the water into the trough in Nimbus's stall, then said, "There's something else that bothers me about this plan of yours, Mr. Creed. How long will it take us to build a track?"

"Good point, Scott," said Creed. "It's so good that I don't have an answer for it."

Scott smiled and said, "Well, maybe Pa does. He may be the most mule-headed man in these parts, but he's nobody's fool when it comes to getting a job done in a hurry."

28

"Flat land, you say?" queried Davis Houchin. He was once again sitting in his rocker on the porch. "The only flat land around here is on my son Willis's place up on the hill, but there ain't enough of it for building a racetrack on."

"Then where would we find enough flat land to build a track on?" asked Creed, sitting in the same chair as before. He leaned forward, resting his elbows on his knees. "In this county, I mean."

"That ain't your problem, Slate," said Davis.

"It isn't?" queried Creed.

"No, sir," said Davis. He craned his neck and spit a gob of tobacco juice onto the ground in front of the porch, then sat back and said, "Slate, your problem is finding a piece of flat land that folks can get to."

"What do you mean, Pa?" asked Scott. He was sitting Indian-style on the porch, with his back against the post in front of Creed.

"What I'm saying is there's lots of parcels with forty acres of flat land on them, but damn few of them are in places where lots of folks can get to them."

"I see what you mean," said Creed. "We need to build the track on land that's got a good road running by it."

"Or that's got a good railroad running by it," said Davis.

"A railroad!" said Creed. "Of course!"

"But, Pa," said Scott, "there ain't no railroad that runs through Edmondson County. The nearest one is over to Glasgow Junction in Barren County."

"That's right, son," said Davis.

"Glasgow Junction? Where's that?" asked Creed.

"Draw him a map in the dirt, Scott," said Davis.

150

Scott stood up and stepped down from the porch. He picked up a little stick and began drawing a map in the dirt just below the porch.

Creed leaned over to watch.

"This is home," said Scott, pointing to his starting point, "and over here to the east is Elko. That's about two miles from here. From Elko, you take the road along Joppa Ridge down to Sloan Crossing, Union City, and Chaumont, then over here to Glasgow Junction."

"How far is that?" asked Creed.

"Maybe fifteen, sixteen miles, wouldn't you say, Pa?"

"About that," said Davis. "Maybe a mile or two more. Makes no difference, though, how far it is from here. It's how far it is to another place that counts."

"Another place?" queried Scott.

"Why sure," said Davis. "Think, Scott. What other place in these parts would folks from other places, say Louisville and Nashville, what other place would they be likely to visit in these parts?"

"The caves?" guessed Scott.

"Which cave in particular?" asked Davis.

"Mammoth!" said Scott, suddenly excited. "Sure, Pa. I understand now. Mammoth Cave and the hotel. Lots of folks would be there at almost any time of the year. You're thinking we should build the track up there, aren't you?"

Creed had no idea what the two Houchins were talking about. He frowned and said, "What is this place? This Mammoth Cave?"

"I suppose you never heard of it, being from Texas and all," said Scott. "Mammoth Cave is this huge cave that's miles and miles long." He puffed himself up with pride and added, "It was discovered by my granddaddy. Ain't that right, Pa?"

"That's the way it was told to me, son," said Davis. "You see, Slate, my daddy was out hunting when he come across a bear. He shot at it but didn't kill the damn thing. He reloaded and took after the varmint. He had chased it for a few miles, trailing the blood, when all of a sudden the blood trail stopped. It seemed to vanish into thin air. Then Daddy spotted this hole in the ground. He bent down for a closer look and saw that it was a big hole, one big enough for a bear to crawl into. He peeked a little closer and saw that it was the entrance to a cave. He poked his head inside and found the blood trail again, but he didn't see the bear. Not wishing to let a wounded bear get away and die somewhere and go to waste, Daddy made up a torch, lit it, and went inside that cave looking for the bear. He went in only as far as he could still see daylight from the entrance, but that was far enough for him to discover that the cave was full of saltpeter for making gunpowder. He could have gone farther, but he wasn't about to get himself lost in there, bear or no bear. He gave up the chase and went home.

"When he got back, he told the whole family about it, and before you knowed it, they was repeating the story all around about this big cave. Only thing was they forgot to tell the whole story, meaning they left out the part that my daddy was the one who chased that bear into that cave. After the cave become famous, every Houchin in these parts started claiming it was his daddy or granddaddy who discovered the Mammoth Cave. Hell, even my cousin, Johnny Dick, claims to have found it. Sure, he found it. A dozen years after my daddy found it first, when Johnny Dick and his brothers first come to these parts, just before the turn of the century. Of course, I know different because it was my daddy who found it. The way I know is that he used to tell me how they'd go over to the cave and dig up the peter dirt for gunpowder whenever they'd run low. They did that, he said, until old Valentine Simon staked his claim to the land above the cave.

"Anyway, over the years, the Mammoth Cave has become famous in these parts. It first become famous when one of the slaves digging at the niter works in the cave found an Indian mummy. That brought in some of them educated book-learning folks from all over the country to see it. That's about all that come at first. Then someone wrote some book about the cave about twenty years back, and all sorts of folks started coming down from Louisville to see the Mammoth Cave then, and they've been coming ever since. They usually stay at the hotel up there for three, four days at a time and go down in the cave every day they're here. Now, I ain't been in the Mammoth Cave myself, but I have been in my own."

"In yours?" asked Creed. "You've got a cave, too?"

"That's right," said Scott proudly. "Over there." He pointed to a spot northwest of the house.

"Of course, it ain't the Mammoth Cave," said Davis, "but it's still a cave, and it's ours. I've been thinking about charging folks to go down in it, but there ain't been no one come asking me about having a look into it yet."

"All right, but what about this Mammoth Cave?" asked Creed. "Who owns it?"

"The last living owner was Dr. Croghan," said Davis. "He died back in '49, I believe. He left the cave and the two hundred acres of land above it to a trust for his nieces and nephews. The way I understand it they receive the profits from the cave and the hotel and the stagecoach line that runs from the station at Glasgow Junction to the hotel. I ain't sure who's running the place now, but I know that whoever it is running it ain't likely to turn down an honest way to increase business over there."

"But, Pa, there's nothing but woods around the hotel. Where were you thinking we could build us a track?"

"When I was a boy," said Davis, "the land for two miles to the southeast of the hotel was open fields. I know old Valentine Simon first settled the land above the cave, but I don't know who all his neighbors on the ridge were. I know they cleared the land much the same as my daddy and uncles did up on our ridge. After old man Simon sold his land and the caves to them Philadelphia businessmen, the fields near the cave were left to go back to forest. Most of the other folks on that ridge realized that their land was better suited for grazing cows and horses, so they let their fields go to pasture. I was still a boy then, so those trees over there ain't but forty to fifty years old, and they ain't so thick together that it would take a whole lot to clear enough land for a horse track. You could get a whole army of men with axes and saws to clear that land for a dollar a day and have the job done in a week or so."

"I'd like to ride over there and take a look at the area," said Creed.

"Sure. You do that, Slate," said Davis. "You can take Scott with you. Right after dinner."

29

Scott and Creed left the Houchin farm right after dinner, taking the trail that Davis had laid out when he bought the land along the Green River from his father more than twenty-five years earlier. The two-track followed the east side of the hollow until it joined the Brownsville-to-Elko road that bordered the Houchin property on the south. They turned east on the county road and started up the slope to Joppa Ridge. At the top of the hill, they came to the junction with the road to Cedar Sink, one of the routes of the highway system that was built by Dr. John Croghan in order to make Mammoth Cave more accessible to visitors. Another mile farther they passed Joppa Church and its cemetery at the crossroads known as Elko. The road split at this point.

"The right fork goes to Sloan Crossing," said Scott, "like I showed you on the map in the dirt back at the house. This is the way to Mammoth Cave." He pointed his father's gelding toward the left fork.

Creed was greatly impressed by the quality of the road. Although he had traveled over several thousands of miles of the South's best turnpikes and highways, as well as deer trails and cow paths during the war, he felt that few of them could match this Kentucky artery. The thoroughfare had been recently graded, and this made the travel easier, especially when they descended into Deer Park Hollow for a short way, then quickly ascended onto Jim Lee Ridge. The downgrade into Bruce Hollow was free of ruts and loose stones, and the two-hundred-foot climb up the other side to Mammoth Cave Ridge was accomplished without stressing or winding the horses.

Creed also marveled at the scenery. It was unlike anything that he had known back in Texas. Whereas his home country was flat for the most part, this part of Kentucky consisted of rugged hills and valleys sculpted from a great plateau by aeons of rain and

154

wind. Of course, he had seen landscapes similar to this one during the war, but those had failed to captivate his imagination, simply because of the times in which he was living—times where death could touch him at any second if he should cease his constant vigilance for survival and allow himself a moment to cast an appreciative eye on the land around him.

Continuing the ascent of Mammoth Cave Ridge, Creed thought of Texada back in Texas, and he longed for her, wishing she were there to share this afternoon with him. How this country would awe her! She would be speechless, he felt, as she gloried in its natural wonders, and he would reach out and touch her and feel that static excitement that only lovers know when they are surrounded by beauty. How wonderful that would be! But alas! A sigh weighed heavily in his chest as he faced the reality that Texada was a thousand miles away and that they might not have even a minute together for many months yet to come.

At the top of the hill, they came to a crossroads.

"The hotel is over yonder," said Scott, pointing to the left. "The cave entrance is around there, I reckon. I don't know for sure because this is all the further I've ever been when I've come over here." He nodded to the right and said, "That's the road to Glasgow Junction. It's about eight or nine miles down the slope. Straight ahead is the way to Munfordsville and Louisville. Munfordsville is the county town for Hart County. You want to go look at the hotel?"

"I guess it wouldn't hurt," said Creed.

The hotel at Mammoth Cave was a large edifice, two hundred feet long by forty-five wide, with piazzas sixteen feet wide extending the whole length of the building on both the upper and lower stories. The original structure was a log building consisting of two rooms on the first floor that were eighteen feet square and that were separated by an open space ten feet wide that allowed a breeze to blow through and cool the rooms. Over the two lower rooms and the breezeway was a second story. The inn was enlarged in 1838 to accommodate thirty to forty guests at a time, and fences and stables were added. When Dr. Croghan bought Mammoth Cave and its accompanying land and buildings in 1839, the hotel was expanded again, reaching the dimensions that it had when Creed first saw it that mild January day of 1866.

As they rode up to the hotel, a bugle sounded behind them, followed by the rumble of horses pulling the stagecoach from

Glasgow Junction. The horn blared again, and the Concord coach came into view, being pulled by four Morgans. Creed and Scott reined their mounts aside and let the stagecoach pass. They watched it come to a halt in front of the hotel, where several freedmen porters rushed out to greet the passengers and take their luggage inside. This was first-class service, treatment that was denied Creed and Scott when they rode up to the carriage stop. They dismounted and tied Nimbus and the gelding to the hitching posts.

"I suppose I should see the proprietor of this place," said Creed, "and speak to him about a track." He looked around them. "Pretty place," he said, noting how the hotel grounds had been laid out with taste, ornamental shrubbery being interspersed among ancient oaks overshadowing a well-kept lawn. "I think I might wish to come here just to get away from a city, if I were a city dweller, I mean. Seems like a leisurely spot."

"I wouldn't know much about that," said Scott as they walked up the wide path to the hotel entrance. "I haven't been to too many real cities, except New Orleans, of course, and maybe Nashville and Louisville with Pa. Oh, yes, and Memphis, too." He thought about what he'd just said and added, "I guess maybe I have been to a few cities. Can't say that I really liked them, though. Too many people."

"Can't say that I blame you there, Scott," said Creed.

They entered between two tall white pillars at the front of the L-shaped wooden frame building that housed the hotel lobby, offices, parlors, and ballroom. A porter held the door for them.

Creed nodded and said, "Thank you." He dug a nickel out of his trouser pocket and handed it to the fellow.

The former slave looked at the coin in his palm first, then, with his face beaming, up at Creed, and said, "Thank you, sir."

The lobby wasn't as fancy as Creed had seen in New Orleans, but it was spacious and decorated pleasantly with a patterned wallpaper above wainscoting, a molded ceiling, and a carpeted floor. Chairs and couches were backed against the side walls and faced the windows, where one could look out over the lawn. A single hall led to the rest of the hotel. The registration desk was straight ahead from the entrance.

Creed and Scott waited for the newly arrived passengers to sign the registry and to receive their room assignments. Then they approached the desk and spoke to the clerk.

"May I help you, sir?" asked the deskman. He didn't appear to be too impressed with Creed's rather plain attire, and he was definitely looking down his sharp nose at Scott's homespun shirt and pants.

"Good afternoon, sir," said Creed, ignoring the man's patronizing tone. "I am Slate Creed. I represent Mlle. Charlotte Beaujeu of New Orleans, and I would like to speak with the proprietor of this . . . ," he allowed himself a disdaining glance around the room before finishing the sentence, " . . . this quaint establishment, and I would like to see him posthaste."

"And what business would you have with Mr. Proctor?" asked the nonplussed clerk.

"That would concern Mr. Proctor and myself," said Creed flatly.

"Mr. Proctor is a busy man," said the clerk.

Creed drew back the left side of his coat to expose the butt of the Colt's sticking out of his waistband and said in a low growl, "So am I."

The clerk's chestnut eyes bulged with fright, and his pale skin turned ashen. He swallowed hard and said, "Yes, sir. I'll get him right away, sir." He disappeared through a doorway behind the desk.

While he waited, Creed noted the bank of cubbyholes behind the desk. Each box had a number, and most of them had keys hanging from them. This told him that the hotel's current occupancy was low. The warmth of confidence spread over him.

An angry, heavy man, with a short black beard, charcoal eyes, thick black eyebrows, and sunken cheeks, emerged through the door behind the desk. The registration clerk followed him.

"I'm L. R. Proctor, sir, the hotel's manager," said the larger man. "How dare you come in here and threaten my employee with a gun!"

"Mr. Creed didn't threaten him at all," said Scott.

"Never mind, Scott," said Creed. "I'll deal with it."

"State your business, sir," said Proctor impatiently, "and make it quick. I am a busy man."

"I doubt that you are all that busy, Mr. Proctor," said Creed evenly. "Not by the looks of all those keys hanging on the wall there."

"The hotel's business is none of your concern, sir," said Proctor, still being quite belligerent.

"Ah, but it is," said Creed, raising a finger and waggling it at Proctor. "You see, Mr. Proctor, I can get all those keys into the hands of paying customers at one time."

Proctor flinched, then said, "What did you say your name was, sir?"

"Creed, sir. Slate Creed. I represent Mlle. Charlotte Beaujeu of New Orleans. And this young lad is Scott Houchin of this county."

"Pardon me, Mr. Creed," said Proctor, his voice becoming less hostile and more congenial, "I am quite acquainted with the Houchin name in this county, but I am unfamiliar with you or the lady whose name I didn't quite catch."

"Mlle. Charlotte Beaujeu," repeated Creed. "She is a lady of business, Mr. Proctor. Her name is well known and highly respected in the best of circles in Crescent City. I'm sure that you would discover this for yourself should you wish to make any inquiries concerning Mlle. Beaujeu in New Orleans."

"I don't believe that will be necessary," said Proctor.

"Very good, Mr. Proctor," said Creed. He looked past the hotel manager at the clerk. "Could we converse alone, Mr. Proctor?"

"Yes, certainly," said Proctor. He turned to the clerk and said, "You may return to your duties, Cox."

"Yes, sir," said Cox.

"Right this way, Mr. Creed," said Proctor as he led the way down the hall to another office. He seated Creed and Scott in straight-back chairs, then sat down behind a large desk. "Now, sir, I believe you mentioned something about increasing the hotel's occupancy."

"Yes, sir, I did," said Creed.

"Just what do you propose, Mr. Creed?"

"Mr. Proctor, it's my guess that you are familiar with all the landowners around here," said Creed.

"Yes, I know many of our neighbors here on Mammoth Cave Ridge," said Proctor. "Were you interested in purchasing land in this neighborhood, Mr. Creed?"

"No, sir. I only wish to rent forty acres for a time, but the forty must be as flat as possible."

"Well, there is plenty of level land on this ridge, Mr. Creed, but you only wish to rent forty acres? For what purpose, may I ask?"

"It's my intention to erect a temporary horse racing track on the land, Mr. Proctor."

"A horse racing track?" queried Proctor rather incredulously. "That's absurd, sir."

"Not at all, Mr. Proctor," said Creed, ignoring Proctor's remark. "The potential gain in such a project is worth the risk, and no matter whether the track is successful or not, you and this hotel stand to gain."

"How do you figure that, Mr. Creed?" asked Proctor.

"Simple, sir. The track will attract patrons of the sport of horse racing from Louisville, Nashville, and many other cities in this part of the country, and those people will have to be accommodated by the inns and hotels in this area. I should think that the hotel that is closest to the track would be certain to receive the most trade from such a patronage."

The plan was beginning to saturate Proctor's business mind, and the possibilities struck him as being quite profitable. "That's quite possible," he said, "but we already have the greatest attraction in these parts, Mr. Creed. Mammoth Cave is known throughout the country and the civilized world. We have visitors come here from all of the nations of Europe."

"Yes, I saw that out front," said Creed facetiously.

"Of course, this is the off-season," said Proctor almost apologetically. "Occupancy is down at this time of the year every year."

Creed eyed the manager suspiciously and said, "I'd be willing to bet, Mr. Proctor, that this hotel's occupancy has been down since the beginning of the war." He watched Proctor closely for a sign that he was right, saw it, and added, "I'd also bet that if you don't get things back to the way they were before the war pretty soon, this hotel will be teetering on the brink of bankruptcy."

Proctor forced a smile and said, "Poppycock, Mr. Creed. The Mammoth Cave Hotel is quite solvent, I assure you."

"The hell it is, Proctor," said Creed, dropping all pretenses now. "You're in trouble here, and you know it."

"There's no need to be crass, Mr. Creed," said Proctor, feigning insult.

"All right, I'll apologize for that, but only if you'll stop beating around the bush here and deal with me evenly."

"Agreed," said Proctor. "So what do you want of me?"

"Introductions," said Creed, "and backing."

"You want me to introduce you to the landowners, and you want me to support your scheme?" Proctor seemed ready to grant Creed's request, but an idea suddenly struck him. "Sounds reasonable enough, but why go to all that bother, Mr. Creed?"

It was Creed's turn to be caught unawares. His brow furrowed as he said, "I don't think it would be that bothersome, Mr. Proctor."

"What I mean, Mr. Creed, is why build a track when one already exists right here at the hotel?"

"You don't have a track here," said Scott.

"Not a racetrack like they have in Louisville or Nashville," said Proctor, "but a track all the same."

"Where is it then?" asked Scott.

"Why, you must have seen it when you came into the hotel," said Proctor. "It's right out in front of the building."

30

Creed and Scott returned to the Houchin farm late that evening. Edie Houchin was the only family member still awake when they arrived. She fed them a cold supper and explained that Davis was having trouble with his "rheumatiz" and had gone to bed early. Without telling her about their meeting that afternoon with Mr. Proctor, Creed and Scott turned in for the night.

The next morning they reviewed the previous day's meeting for Davis. The whole family was gathered in the house to listen to them.

"Mr. Proctor offered to let us use the oval driveway in front of the hotel as a racetrack," said Creed. "I found this to be agreeable and accepted. Then we gave consideration to advertising the hotel, Mammoth Cave, and a racing meet. We agreed that dates for the meet would have to be set, then we could begin to advertise. I suggested we have the meet as soon as possible, and he was agreeable to this and said that sometime within the month would be good."

"And what days did you choose?" asked Davis eagerly.

"We picked the twenty-eighth and twenty-ninth," said Creed. "Saturday and Sunday, three weeks hence."

"Sounds good to me, too," said Davis with a slap on his knee. "That will give Scott time to work with Pride and get him into racing shape." Davis nodded to accentuate his approval, then said, "What about other horses? Pride's going to need some competition. What are you going to do about that, Slate?"

"I'm putting up a guaranteed purse of one thousand dollars to the winner of the meet," said Creed. "Mr. Proctor has agreed to put up a hundred-dollar purse for each of the qualifying races. We'll advertise the purses with everything else. We'll get lots of paying entries from that."

161

"You still thinking about charging ten dollars for an entry fee?" asked Davis, turning more serious now.

"No, we'll make it fifty," said Creed.

"How many entries do you expect to get?" asked Davis.

"That's hard to tell," said Creed. "January isn't exactly racing season, so there might not be any interest at all, or there might be plenty. There's just no telling what sort of response we'll get."

"What about the weather? It could snow, or it could rain. Then what happens?"

"As long as it's not real cold," said Creed, "we'll be all right. The patrons can watch the races from the balcony and the porch of the hotel. They'll be out of any rain or snow. As for the horses and the jockeys, they'll just have to put up with it, unless, of course, there's a high wind with the wet stuff. Then we'll consider canceling the races." In anticipation of Davis's next question, he added, "And if we do have to cancel the races, we'll hold them over to the next Saturday and Sunday, and we'll keep doing that until the races are held."

"So far, it sounds pretty good," said Davis, "but there is one thing that worries me."

"What's that, Pa?" asked Scott.

"The Mammoth Cave is out there all by itself," said Davis. "The nearest town of any size is Munfordsville. How do you plan to feed and care for all the horses and people that might show up for this meet?"

"Mr. Proctor said we could use the old saltpeter works for stables," said Creed, "along with the stables that they have there already. The horses will be out of the weather that way, and he's already ordering hay and feed from the surrounding farms. He's sure he'll get enough to handle a large number of horses.

"As for the people, the hotel has plenty of room and can accommodate four hundred people comfortably. If more than that come out for the meet, then the overflow can stay in Glasgow Junction or Brownsville or any other place where there's lodging available. Just for this meet, the hotel will run extra stagecoaches to any place where there are people wishing transportation to the meet."

Davis considered Creed's words for a moment, then said, "Sounds like you thought of most everything."

"Well, I don't know about it being everything," said Creed, "but it's a start. If you approve, that is."

Davis nodded and said, "Oh, I approve wholeheartedly, son. I can't see that I've got anything to lose in this deal, so I say, let's do it."

Creed and Scott exchanged smiles, both pleased that the senior Houchin approved.

"I suppose you've got to go to Brownsville now on business to start the ball rolling," said Davis, almost as if he were dismissing Creed.

"Yes, I should be going right away," said Creed. "There's really no time to be lollygagging here."

Clarenda nudged her mother, who looked at her daughter for a second without understanding. When Clarenda frowned and motioned her head at Creed, Edie understood completely and said, "Will you be coming back this way soon?"

"As soon as possible, ma'am," said Creed. "I'll be coming back as often as I can to keep you informed on the progress of the arrangements for the meet. And, of course, I'll have to go up to the Mammoth Cave Hotel and talk with Mr. Proctor on several occasions. When I do, I'll be sure to stop by here on the way, if that's what you want, I mean."

"That would be fine," said Edie. "We've enjoyed having you here with us, son."

"I've enjoyed the visit, too," said Creed. "I especially enjoyed your cooking, Miz Houchin. Reminded me of home. Thank you so much."

Edie blushed at the compliment and said, " 'Tweren't nothing really. Just everyday fare around here."

"All the same," said Creed, "it was surely enjoyable."

"Good," said Davis, rising from his chair. "I'm glad you liked the vittles. We'll be looking forward to seeing you again real soon."

Creed took that as his cue to be on his way. He led the way outside, and everybody followed him onto the porch.

"John Wesley, you fetch Mr. Creed's horse for him," said Davis. "And be quick about it."

John Wesley raced down to the barn and fetched Nimbus back to the house for Creed. Scott had gone out earlier and saddled the Appaloosa in anticipation of Creed's departure.

Creed mounted up, said one more farewell to all, then rode off toward Brownsville as the whole Houchin family waved good-bye and watched him go down the track toward the road.

"Do you think he can do us any good, Pa?" asked Edie of her husband once Creed was out of earshot.

"Of course he can, Ma," said Scott.

"Don't be so sure of that, son," said Davis cautiously. "You're forgetting that fellow McGrath. Something tells me he's nothing but trouble."

"You don't have to worry about McGrath, Pa," said Scott. "Mr. Creed can handle him. Mr. Creed can handle just about anything."

"I only hope you're right, son," said Davis. "I only hope you're right."

31

McGrath was eating his lunch when Creed arrived back at the Bob Hazelip Hotel in Brownsville.

"Creed!" said McGrath louder than Creed would have liked. "What happened to you last night? You didn't come back to the hotel. Did that Houchin girl convince you to stay over for a little roll in the hay?" McGrath laughed boisterously as if he'd made a friendly joke instead of a degrading insinuation.

Creed glanced at the other diners—two drummers at one table and a man and woman at another—and noted that they were hanging on every word. Embarrassed and angry, he sat down across the table from McGrath and growled, "You filthy little bastard! If you ever do that again, I'll call you out right then and there, McGrath. Do you understand me, McGrath?"

"There's no need to get huffy, Creed," said McGrath in a lower voice. "I didn't mean anything by it. I just figured you'd got a better offer out at the Houchin place than you would have in this one-horse burg."

"You've got a dirty mind, McGrath, and I don't like it. You can keep comments like that to yourself from now on."

"All right, have it your way, Creed," said McGrath. He took a sip of coffee; then, holding the cup in front of his face, he said over it, "So tell me what happened yesterday. Did you make a deal with the old man or are we still sitting on the dime?"

"I've got things in motion," said Creed.

Excitement glowed in McGrath's eyes as he asked, "You got the old man to sell?"

"No, of course not," said Creed. "But I have started the ball rolling for a racing meet."

McGrath's joy turned to anger. "A racing meet? Here? In this jerkwater town?"

"No, at Mammoth Cave."

"Mammoth Cave?" queried McGrath, totally perplexed. "What the hell is that?"

Creed explained about Mammoth Cave, then he told McGrath all the details of his meeting with Proctor the day before.

"That's all well and good," said McGrath, "but what's my part in all of this?"

"You handle the betting, McGrath," said Creed. "That's what you do best, isn't it? You are a gambler, aren't you?"

McGrath smiled and said, "Yes, I am, and a damn good one, too. Yes, I'll handle the betting. All of the betting. No one gets in on the action without going through me first." His eyes glowed like burning coals. "Yes, I like it, Creed. Good show, my friend." He reached across the table to pat Creed on the arm but withdrew his hand when he saw the disapproval in Creed's eyes. "Well, good show anyway, Creed. Now what?"

"Now I'm going to telegraph Charlotte and tell her what's happening up here," said Creed. "I'll wait here for her answer, then proceed from there."

"Her answer? What answer?"

"It's still Charlotte's money, McGrath. We can't jump into this without her approval first."

"You needn't worry about getting her approval, Creed. She'll go for the deal. You can bet on that."

"You're probably right," said Creed, "but just the same, I think I'll extend her the courtesy of asking for her approval first."

"I suppose it won't hurt anything," said McGrath.

"What about you, McGrath? What are you going to do now?"

"The same as you, Creed. Advertise. I have to put out the word to the boys. I'll go down to Memphis and start spreading the word there. Then I'll take the train to Nashville and do the same thing there. From Nashville, I'll go up to Louisville and make sure word is going up the Ohio. Then I'll come back here."

"Why don't you go to the hotel at Mammoth Cave instead?" said Creed. "It's closer to Louisville and easier to get to than Brownsville. You might as well stay there until the meet."

"Right," said McGrath. "That's what I'll do. So what about you? What will you do after you get Charlotte's approval?"

"I'll move over to the hotel at Mammoth Cave," said Creed, "and help Mr. Proctor with the arrangements for the meet."

McGrath studied Creed for a few seconds, then said, "I'm impressed, Creed. I would never have thought you had it in you to handle this business. Just who the hell are you anyway?"

"You know all you need to know about me, McGrath," said Creed. "Any more could put you in more danger with me than you already are."

McGrath touched his healing ear and said, "You know what? I believe you."

But not really.

32

Charlotte Beaujeu received two telegrams that first Sunday in January 1866. One came from Creed, and the other was from Percy McGrath. She read both with relish, then called her servant into the parlor.

"Meg, pack my things," said Charlotte. "We're going to the races."

"The races, Miss Charlotte?" queried Meg.

"Yes, Meg."

"At Metairie Racecourse?"

"No, at Mammoth Cave."

"Mammoth Cave, Miss Charlotte. Where on God's green earth is that?"

"In Kentucky, Meg," said Charlotte, slightly exasperated. "Now get going. There's a lot to be done, and we've got no time to lose."

Meg walked away talking to herself. "The woman is daft. Races! In Kentucky! In a cave, no less! Saints preserve us!"

Charlotte sent replies to Creed and McGrath, telling each of them the same thing and something different as well. She told both of them that she was coming north for the racing meet at Mammoth Cave, wherever that was, and that she would need hotel accommodations, the best available. She also told them that she approved of Creed's work in setting up the meet in order to showcase Pride. Creed alone she asked to make arrangements for her stay at the Mammoth Cave Hotel, and McGrath was to proceed as she and he had originally agreed in New Orleans.

Creed received his answer from Charlotte on Monday morning at the Bob Hazelip Hotel in Brownsville. McGrath got his at the Planters Hotel in Memphis the same day. Both of them went about their business from there.

The first thing Creed did was pack his belongings and check out of Bob Hazelip's place.

"I suppose you'll be going over to the Mammoth Cave Hotel now," said Hazelip.

"What makes you say that?" asked Creed.

"Oh, everybody knows about the horse racing meet you're planning on staging up there," said Hazelip with a huge grin. "Hell, it's no secret around here that Davis Houchin has that Thoroughbred and he wants to race him. Folks have been talking about that ever since you and that Mr. McGrath came to town. We just didn't have all the particulars until yesterday." He laughed and said, "In case you didn't know it, Mr. Creed, you and Mr. McGrath were the subjects of nearly every sermon preached in this county yesterday. I heard that Brother Locke over to Joppa Church at Elko really raised the Devil over you two. Said you two was the right-hand servants of Old Ned himself. Yes, sir, he did. Said racing horses and gambling was two of the worst sins in this world, and you and Mr. McGrath was leading everybody astray with this horse racing meet you're planning."

"Is that so?" said Creed, rather annoyed by Hazelip's attitude as well as the fact that the local ministers were trying to stir up the populace against the meet.

"That is a fact, Mr. Creed," said Hazelip. "Of course, I wouldn't worry too much about Brother Locke and the other preachers. Most of them are just jealous that they ain't got a horse to enter into the meet themselves."

"What?" asked Creed, quite incredulous over Hazelip's last statement.

"Oh, sure," said Hazelip. "Everybody knows that Brother Locke and the other preachers like to race just as much as the next fellow. Only they don't race on horseback. They race their buggies and buckboards every chance they get. Just depends on who they meet on the road. Hell, you should see them on Sundays. They leave one meeting, jump into their rigs, crack the whip over their horses' ears, and take off like Satan was going to get to the next congregation before they did. Of course, that's on Sundays. On other days, they're just as likely to race anybody they might meet on the road as the next fellow would."

"I see," said Creed.

"I wouldn't go worrying too much about Brother Locke and the others," said Hazelip. "They'll hoot and holler a bit, but if you ignore them, they'll stop after a while and start up on some other sin. Hell, you should have been here when Davis Houchin and Edie were still living in sin. You would have thought the whole county was adulterizing the way Brother Locke and the other preachers carried on. Yes, sir, that was a time."

"I'll bet it was," said Creed. "Well, I'll be going now, Mr. Hazelip. I thank you for your hospitality."

"You're more than welcome, Mr. Creed." He watched Creed start for the door, then another thought came to him. "You might want to stop by the post office and tell Joe Meredith to send your mail over to Mammoth Cave Hotel now."

Creed glanced back over his shoulder and said, "Thanks. I'll do that." Then he left.

At the post office, Joe Meredith gave him pretty much the same speech that Hazelip had but with a slightly different bent to it.

"I'd be careful out there on the road," said Meredith. "If I was you, that is."

"Oh? Why so?" asked Creed.

"It's Monday," said Meredith.

"Monday? What's Monday got to do with anything?"

"This is the day the preachers are out and visiting their church members at their homes," said Meredith. "You're most likely to meet up with one or two of them on the way over to Mammoth Cave. Fact is, I'd bet they'll be looking for you out there today."

"Why me?"

"Well, they'd be looking for the other fellow, too, but everybody knows that he left for Memphis yesterday and that you stayed here. So it only goes to show that you'll be the one they'll be looking for."

"I see," said Creed. He didn't like it, but he realized that there was little he could do about it. If the local ministers wanted to harangue him over a horse racing meet, then so be it. As long as that was all that they did.

33

Creed rode out of Brownsville, toward the Houchin farm, and was almost to the two-track that followed the ridge back to the farmhouse when he saw a bearded man in a black frock coat and black stovepipe hat, driving a buckboard down the road toward him. A sense of pending doom swept over the Texan, especially when he saw the buggy stop at the entrance to the Houchin place, effectively blocking his path.

"Hold there, friend," said the bearded man.

Creed halted because the request was made sternly but with politeness. He smiled, tipped his hat, and said, "Good day to you, Parson Locke," guessing at the man's identity.

The driver's bushy eyebrows wrinkled up into one long fuzzy caterpillar for a second as he asked, "Do you know me, sir?"

"No, Parson, I don't," said Creed honestly, relieved that he was right and now had the minister off his guard. He added, "But I have heard much about you, sir."

"Yes, I'll bet you have," said Locke, making a poor choice of phrase to express himself and instantly realizing it.

"Just this morning," said Creed, not wishing to let Locke get in too many words too soon, "your name was mentioned to me by two different gentlemen in Brownsville. Both of them had great praise for you, sir."

"Great praise, you say? Who were these flattering fools you speak of?"

"Mr. Hazelip at the hotel and Mr. Meredith at the post office, Parson."

"As I thought," said Locke a bit disgustedly. "Two of the biggest tongue-waggers in the county. And you say they had praise for me. In what context, sir?"

"Both gentlemen praised your preaching style, Parson. They

171

said that you could raise the Devil in one instant and send him back to Hell in the next."

"Oh, they said that, did they?" queried Locke, a bit annoyed by this talk.

"Yes, sir, they surely did," said Creed, really getting into his down-home routine now. "They said you could speak hellfire and brimstone with the best of them. Made me wish I'd been in your church yesterday morning and heard you preach."

"My sermon yesterday concerned horse racing, gambling, and two men who are trying to lead the good people of this county from the path of righteousness by holding a horse racing meet. Do you still wish that you'd heard me preach yesterday?"

"Why, certainly, Parson."

Locke eyed Creed suspiciously, then said, "I heard that one of the two men that I preached about was named Creed and that he would be riding an Appaloosa stallion if I was to come across him on the road. That would be you, I take it."

Creed smiled proudly and said, "Yes, sir, Parson. My name is Slate Creed from Lavaca County, Texas."

"I thought so, sinner!" blared Locke.

That was one of the words that Creed refused to allow any man to call him. In an instant, he dropped his good old boy facade and his face took on a cold, blank expression. In a tone as even as he could muster, he said, "Parson Locke, the Good Book states plainly that only a man without sin can judge another. I believe it was Jesus who said, 'Let him who has no sin cast the first stone.' Is that right, Parson?"

Locke was absolutely incensed with outrage. He jumped to his feet, pointed a bony finger at Creed, and screamed, "That's blasphemy! How dare you quote our Lord Jesus! You, a sinner in league with the Devil himself! You blasphemous minion of the Antichrist! You'll burn in Hell, sinner!"

Creed had had enough of this. He opened his coat and slowly drew his Colt's from his waistband, making sure that Locke saw every bit of the movement.

"You can't kill me, sinner!" screamed Locke. He reached down in the seat beside him and picked up his Bible, brought it up to his chest, and said, "I have the Holy Word to protect me."

Creed didn't point his revolver at Locke. Instead, he leaned forward on Nimbus's neck, aiming the gun to one side away from Locke, cocked it, and said, "Hazelip and Meredith were right about your style, Parson. You sure can raise the Devil with the best of them, but I think I'd prefer that you raise him somewhere else." He squeezed off a round into the dirt.

The gunshot startled Locke's horse. The Morgan reared up in fright. Locke grabbed the reins and tried to control him, but Creed's second shot put an end to that notion. The mare lurched forward, throwing Locke back over the seat of the buckboard. Although sprawled on the back of the buggy, Locke held onto the reins and his Bible. Another shot from Creed's gun was the final straw for the Morgan. She bolted.

With no minor degree of satisfaction, Creed watched Locke struggle to regain control of his rig as the Morgan raced down the road toward Brownsville. He continued to watch for a few seconds, then realized that Locke was in real trouble with his horse and buggy. "Aw, hell!" swore Creed. He replaced his Colt's in his waistband, and said, "Come on, Nimbus. We'd better go after him." He kicked the stallion, and the Appaloosa burst into a full run.

Locke was holding onto his Bible, the reins, and the back of the buckboard seat—all for dear life—as he tried to right himself, control the Morgan, and pray at the same time. "Whoa, Pansy! Whoa!" he shouted at the mare, but to no avail.

Although the Morgan had a head start on Nimbus of a good one hundred yards, Creed had little trouble in catching the buggy, because the out-of-control mare had to pull the rig uphill, which was a lot more difficult than carrying a single rider who was in control of his mount up the same hill. Creed and Nimbus were on the right side of the buckboard when they came to the first hairpin turn in the road.

"Hold on, Parson!" shouted Creed.

Locke barely heard him, and he ignored the command anyway. He would have rebuked Creed if he hadn't been so busy holding onto everything, especially his life.

They made the turn and started up the second leg of the incline to Indian Ridge. Creed maneuvered Nimbus alongside the Morgan, then reached over to grab the mare's harness. As soon as he had a firm grip on the headstall, he started to ease back on Nimbus's reins, while simultaneously trying to coax the mare into slowing. "Whoa, girl!" he shouted in a firm voice. And before they reached the second hairpin, he had the Morgan under full control. Placing Nimbus in front of the mare and still holding onto the bridle, Creed looked back at Locke and said, "Are you all right, Parson?"

Locke didn't answer. Instead, he pulled himself over the buckboard seat and reached for the whip.

Seeing what Locke was up to, Creed released his hold on the Morgan, drew his Colt's in a flash, cocked it in the same movement, took aim at Locke's right hand, and said, "I can't let you do that, Parson. Preacher or not, you're still a man, and no man takes a whip to me. I'd rather not shoot you, Parson, but I will if you pick up that whip."

Locke stayed his hand for the moment, his eyes shifting back and forth between the whip and Creed's face. Then he sat back in the seat, put his Bible down beside him, took a firm hold on the reins, and said with all the hate and venom he could draw from his soul, "Out of my way, Mr. Creed."

Creed nudged Nimbus with his knees, and the stallion moved ahead a few paces, clearing the way for Locke and his Morgan to move on up the grade.

Locke snapped the reins and said, "Giddap, Pansy!"

The Morgan moved out on command.

Creed kept his eyes on Locke as the minister passed him.

Locke never looked to the side. He drove up the hill and out of sight.

Creed uncocked his revolver and replaced it inside his waistband. Shaking his head, he said, "Dammit all, Nimbus! How am I going to make this up to the Lord?"

34

Armed with a shotgun and sitting atop the Houchin's gelding, Scott waited for Creed at the bottom of the hill. "What was all the shooting about?" he asked when the Texan rode up.

"Snake," said Creed simply, passing Scott and heading on toward the farmhouse.

"Snake?" queried Scott, his nose wrinkling at Creed's answer. "At this time of the year?" Then realizing Creed wasn't going to stop, he kicked the gelding and followed his friend.

Davis stood on the porch holding his shotgun across his left arm. He looked beyond Creed and Scott to see if anyone was chasing them. When Creed halted at the hitching post and dismounted casually, the senior Houchin relaxed his vigilance and called out, "It's all right, Edie. It's just Slate Creed." He tottered over to the steps and held out his hand to greet the Texan. "What was all the shooting about, Slate?" he asked.

Creed accepted the handshake and said, "Snake."

"Snake?" queried Davis, the same as his son had. "There ain't no snakes around here at this time of the year. Are you sure it was a snake?"

"Oh, he's a snake, all right," said Creed.

Scott rode up, jumped down, and tied the gelding to the hitching post. Running up on the porch, he said, "Snakes aren't out at this time of the year, Mr. Creed."

"This one was," said Creed.

"What do you mean 'he'?" asked Davis.

Creed heaved a sigh and said, "Your parson, Mr. Houchin."

"My parson? Who would that be?"

"I believe his name is Brother Locke," said Creed.

Scott looked disbelievingly at his father, who was standing there with his mouth hanging open.

Edie Houchin stepped outside and said, "You was shooting at Brother Locke, Mr. Creed?" Her face and voice were filled with disbelief and fear.

"No, not at him," said Creed, looking sheepish. "I shot at the ground, trying to scare the man's horse."

"Scare his horse?" queried Edie. "What on earth for?"

"He was being obnoxious," said Creed.

"That's Brother Locke, all right," said Davis with a gentle chuckle.

"Now, you oughtn't to say that, Pa," said Edie. "Brother Locke is a man of the cloth."

"So what if he is?" growled Davis. "He's the one who made all the fuss about you and me living in sin and all. He interfered with our lives, and I can't abide a man who sticks his nose into my business. Hell, he wouldn't even marry us."

"He got Brother Morrison to marry us, didn't he?"

"Brother Morrison? He wouldn't have married us either, if Paradine hadn't given her shoes to you to wear at the wedding."

Creed glanced at Edie's feet and noticed that she wasn't wearing any shoes.

Edie blushed and said, "Now you know that ain't so, Pa."

"It ain't? Then how come he hemmed and hawed around here until Paradine did give you the shoes to wear? Tell me that, will you, woman?"

"Don't pay him no mind, Mr. Creed," said Edie. "He's still angered at Brother Locke because he preached a sermon about children being born out of wedlock."

"Now, you didn't have to go and bring that up, did you, Miz Busybody? Get your ass inside the house, woman, and don't you come out again until I tell you to." Davis raised his hand as if he would strike Edie, and he reiterated the command, saying, "Now git!"

As casual as could be, Edie said, "I guess your rheumatiz is acting up on you again, Pa, and it's making you cranky. I'll get your jug for you." She went inside the house.

"Uppity gal!" grumped Davis. "She sure wasn't like that when Liza was living. Ain't that right, Scott?"

"I guess so, Pa," said Scott blandly.

Davis looked hard at his son and realized that he just might have said the wrong thing. Scott was Edie's son, not Liza's.

Unwilling to admit his mistake and apologize for it, Davis turned to Creed and said, "Come on and sit down, Slate, and tell us what happened with Brother Locke."

Creed sat down on the porch and related his misadventure with the parson. He finished the tale by saying, "I know I shouldn't have done it, but the man touched on a nerve that he had no right to touch on."

"Brother Locke can do that," said Scott.

"All them preachers do that," said Davis bitterly. "It ain't Brother Locke's exclusive ground. It's in their nature."

Edie had been listening just inside the door. She poked her head outside and said, "The Lord put men like Brother Locke here to keep the rest of us walking the straight and narrow, son. It's their job. Doing the Lord's work until we see Him ourselves and fess up for what we did or didn't do in this life. You understand, Scott. Brother Locke ain't a bad man or a bad preacher. He's only doing his job for the Lord, that's all."

"I just wish he'd do it elsewhere," said Davis.

"Amen," said Creed without thinking. Then, looking up at Edie's disappointed face, he added, "But I guess the Lord knew that when He had Jesus pick all those apostles to carry on for Him after He went up to Heaven. That's why we have preachers. Am I right, Mrs. Houchin?"

"Right as rain," said Edie, "but you were wrong to start up with Brother Locke like you did."

"Hush, woman!" snapped Davis. Then, looking at Creed, he said, "Edie's right, Slate. Brother Locke ain't likely to forget this too soon. Fact is, I'd bet he'll be going to the sheriff now to have him do something about it right away. If I was you, Slate, I'd go down to Glasgow Junction and stay there for a few days until Brother Locke has had a chance to cool off a spell."

"Pa's right, Mr. Creed," said Scott. "Brother Locke's sure to get the sheriff in on this, and then there will be trouble."

"Just go on down to Glasgow Junction or maybe up to Munfordsville for a few days," said Davis. "I'll try to smooth things out with the sheriff for you."

"I think I'll do just that," said Creed. "I've got to go down to Glasgow Junction and meet a train later on anyway. I might as well go now and stay there a few days."

"I'll send Scott down to tell you when it's safe to come back," said Davis.

"Well, before I go," said Creed, "I think you'll be glad to know that Mlle. Beaujeu has approved my plan for the racing meet and is coming here to watch the races herself."

"Is that her train you're planning to meet in Glasgow Junction?" asked Scott.

"Yes, it is. I don't expect her to arrive for several days yet. She'll be staying at the Mammoth Cave Hotel. Well, I'll be going now, Davis. I want to go up to the hotel and see Mr. Proctor and tell him the good news before I go on to Glasgow Junction."

"Good idea, Slate," said Davis. "Now you lay low like I said, and Scott will come and tell you when things are all right this way again."

Edie came out on the porch again to say farewell. Creed bade them good-bye, then the three Houchins watched him ride off.

"He sure stuck his foot in it this time, didn't he, Pa?" said Edie.

"He sure did, Ma. Brother Locke ain't one to give up easily. I know one thing for sure. I'm sure as hell glad he ain't preaching about me no more."

Edie knew exactly what her husband meant by that, and she worried all the more about Creed and the success of the proposed racing meet.

35

The news about the confrontation between Creed and Brother Locke raced across Edmondson County and overflowed into the surrounding counties. Of course, only one side of the story was being told, and Brother Locke was the one doing the telling. He started by haranguing Sheriff Mason Morris at the county courthouse.

"He drew his pistol and shot at me several times," said Locke. "The shots startled my horse, and she bolted and raced down the road, careening everywhere and endangering my life with every heartbeat. Not satisfied that he had nearly shot me to death and had scared my horse into trying to kill me, the fiend pursued me down the road. Once I was able to regain control of my rig, he came upon me and threatened to shoot me again."

Morris listened politely, then asked, "Where did all this happen, Brother Locke?"

"At the junction of the Brownsville road and the road to the Turnhole Bend Ferry."

"That would be Davis Houchin's place," said Morris. "That's a far piece from Elko, Brother Locke. What were you doing over there in the first place?"

"It's Monday, Sheriff," said Locke. "I was about the Lord's business as I usually am on Mondays."

"I see," said Morris. "Well, I'll get the constable for the district and ride out there and look for this Creed fellow."

"You can start by looking for him at Davis Houchin's place," said Locke.

"Why would I look there first?" asked Morris.

"Don't be the fool, Sheriff," said Locke. "Everybody in the county knows that this man Creed is friends with young Scott Houchin, Davis Houchin's oldest bastard. He might even have put this Creed fellow up to trying to kill me."

"Scott?" queried Morris.

"No, the father, Davis Houchin. The man still holds a grudge against me because I forced him to marry the mother of his three bastards. He said he'd get me someday."

"All right, Brother Locke," said Morris, "we'll ride out to Davis Houchin's and have a look around and ask those folks if they know what happened out there."

"I've already told you what happened out there, Sheriff," argued Locke. "I want you to find this man Creed and arrest him, and I want you to arrest Davis Houchin as well, because I'm sure he put this Creed up to it."

"I'm not arresting anybody without a warrant from the judge," said Morris, "and that's final."

"What in God's name is this country coming to when a man of the cloth is assaulted on the road and the law refuses to do anything about it?"

"I'm doing something about it, Brother Locke," said Morris. "I'm looking into your charges."

"I want arrests!" screamed Locke.

Morris glared at Locke and said, "Then you go see Judge Houchin and swear out a warrant and bring it back to me and I'll go arrest Davis Houchin and this man Creed."

"Judge Houchin is Davis Houchin's cousin," complained Locke. "He'll never sign a warrant for his cousin's arrest."

"You don't know that until you ask him," said Morris. "Either see the judge and get the warrant or leave me alone to do my job as I see fit to do it."

"Is that your final word, Sheriff?"

"It is."

"We'll just see about that!" snapped Locke, and he departed the sheriff's office in a huff.

Morris watched the minister storm out. He shook his head in disbelief that Locke could be that unreasonable, then he thought about what he should do next. "Ride out and see Davis Houchin," he said to himself. He stood to leave but stopped when his eye caught sight of the rack of shotguns and rifles mounted on the wall. "Better arm myself," he muttered. He took down a shotgun, made certain it was loaded, then went to his desk to retrieve a revolver. After checking the Colt's New Army .44 for powder, balls, and caps, he shoved it into a holster and strapped the leather holder to his belt. Still feeling insecure, he looked around the office as if it would be the last time he would set eyes on the place, then left to go about his business.

The sheriff and Constable Jethro Otter rode out to the Houchin farm that afternoon to talk to Davis and his family.

"He's full of it!" said Davis after Morris told him that Brother Locke had accused Creed of trying to kill him. "If Slate had wanted to kill that son of a bitch, he could have done it without giving it a second thought."

"Brother Locke claims you put Creed up to it," said Morris. "Is that true?"

"More of Locke's bullcrap, Sheriff," said Davis. "I don't need anybody else to fight my battles. Besides, if I'd wanted Locke dead, I'd have done it myself years ago when he was preaching about me and mine nearly every Sunday. Now, sir, I'll tell you what happened out here this morning. Locke was waiting for Slate out on the road. He insulted Slate, and Slate lost his temper and shot off his gun to scare Locke. Only he didn't scare the parson." He chuckled and added, "He scared the shit out of his horse, though."

"Brother Locke told me about that," said Morris. "He said Creed chased him and threatened him again."

"More bullcrap!" spat Davis. "Slate rode after him because Locke had lost control of his rig. He saved Locke's ass."

"Did you see this happen?" asked Morris.

Davis scratched his head and said, "Well, now, Sheriff, I ain't one to tell a lie, even if it means saving my own hide. I was right here in the house when we heard the shooting out to the road. I sent Scott out with the shotgun to see what the trouble was, and he came back in a few minutes with Slate. It was Slate who told us what happened between him and Locke, and if Slate says it happened that way, then that's how it happened. That boy don't lie neither, Sheriff."

"Well, I can believe that Brother Locke was out on the road laying for your friend Creed, Mr. Houchin," said Morris, "but that still don't give your friend the right to shoot at Brother Locke."

"He wasn't shooting at him, Sheriff," protested Scott.

"Hush up, boy!" snapped Davis. "I'll do the talking with the sheriff."

"What makes you think that, son?" asked Morris.

"Because he's a crack shot," said Scott.

"Have you seen him shoot?" asked Morris.

"No, but I know he's a crack shot," argued Scott.

"How do you know this, son, if you haven't seen him shoot before?" asked Morris.

"I heard about how he shot a fellow down in Texas," said Scott without thinking.

"So he shot a fellow down in Texas," said the sheriff. "That's interesting. And how do you know about this shooting down in Texas, son?"

"Scott, you've said enough," warned Davis.

"No, Mr. Houchin, he ain't," said Morris. "I want to hear more about this shooting down in Texas."

"It won't make no difference, Pa," said Scott. "It happened in Texas. It don't make no difference up here. Ain't that right, Sheriff?"

"That depends," said Morris, "on whether there's any circulars out on him. Where'd Creed shoot this fellow in Texas?"

"I don't rightly know that part," said Scott. "All I know is he was on a ship leaving port when these three fellows rode up on the pier and killed two of his friends, and Mr. Creed got his rifle and shot one of them for it while the ship was going out to sea."

"And who told this story to you?" asked Morris. "Creed?"

"No, another passenger and one of the ship's officers," said Scott a bit defiantly. "They saw him do it."

"I see," said Morris. "Well, Mr. Houchin, can you tell me where I might find Creed now?"

"I can," said Davis.

"But you won't," said the sheriff. "Is that how it is?"

"Something like that, Sheriff," said Davis.

"I see," said Morris, slightly exasperated. "Well, it's my guess that he's gone up to Mammoth Cave Hotel. I hear he's staging that horse race meet up there at the end of the month. I guess we'll ride up there and have a talk with Mr. Proctor, the manager. Thank you just the same, Mr. Houchin. And you, too, Scott. Your friend sounds like a real interesting fellow. I can't wait to meet him. Come on, Jethro."

36

Mr. Proctor was a bit more cooperative than the Houchins had been. Without hesitation, he told Sheriff Morris and Constable Otter exactly where they could find Creed. Morris thanked him and rode off toward Glasgow Junction.

"We ain't going down there, are we, Mase?" asked Otter as they rode along Mammoth Cave Ridge.

"Of course, we are," said Morris. "Mr. Proctor said Creed is in Glasgow Junction, and I intend to find out if he's telling me true or not."

"But that's across the county line, Mase," argued Otter nervously. "We ain't got no authority over there in Barren County."

"We don't need any," said Morris.

Otter's view fell on the Colt's strapped to Morris's hip. He said, "You ain't going to have it out with him, are you, Mase?"

"You worry too much, Jethro," said the sheriff. "Just keep you mouth shut and ride. It's getting dark, and I want to get there before too late." A moment later he added, "Your guns are loaded, ain't they, Jethro?"

"You are planning to have it out with him, ain't you?" whined Otter. "Damn! I knew it, I knew it! Damn, Mase! This fellow's from Texas. We can't be shooting it out with no Texan. You know how mean and nasty those Texans are. Don't you recollect that mean son of a bitch who was riding with Morgan when we was chasing that bastard all over the state?"

"Yes, Jethro," said Morris, not looking at Otter, but keeping his eyes on the road ahead of them, "I recall that fellow quite well. Who wouldn't? He rode that big Appaloosa and he had the coldest eyes of any man I ever saw in a fight."

"He murdered a lot of our boys," said Otter.

"It wasn't murder, Jethro. That was war. We were trying to kill him as much as he was trying to kill us, only he was better

183

at it than we were. I'm just glad he never had me in his sights or I probably wouldn't be here right now."

"Me, too," said Otter. "I'll never forget his face. Ugly cuss, he was."

"Hell, Jethro, you never got close enough to him to see his face plain like."

"And I suppose you did?"

"Yes, I did. Twice. Once was over to Breathitt County. We were riding along minding our own business when he jumped out of the brush with a pistol in each hand. Scared hell right out of us up in the front. We pulled up and started to draw our guns, but he started talking to us, and we stopped to listen. 'Hold it right there, Yanks!' he said. 'I'm from Texas, and I can shoot any one of you dead in the wink of an eye,' he said. To prove his point, he shot Captain Houchin's hat off his head. 'Now, I don't want to kill any of you unless I have to.' 'Then what do you want?' asked Captain Houchin. 'Time,' he said. 'You shot us up pretty bad the other day, Captain. We need time to care for our wounded. Now, I know you could shoot me dead and ride on by, but not before I kill six or eight of you first. And if you get past me, there's more like me waiting for you down the road, only they won't give you any warning. They'll just bushwhack you and be riding away before you know what hit you. Now that's how it is, Captain. You can either halt your men here and give us a day to care for our wounded, or you can try to ride by me and take your chances.' He raised his pistols at Captain Houchin, and his eyes became real cold like. Sent a shiver down my spine, I'll tell you. Then he said, 'What's it going to be, Captain?' Of course, you know we halted right then and there."

"Yeah, I remember that day," said Otter. "We needed that rest, didn't we?"

"We sure did. That damn Morgan was impossible to catch."

"He sure was," said Otter.

Both men fell into a reverie over their days in the war, and neither said another word until they reached Bell's Tavern in Glasgow Junction a half hour before sunset.

Bell's Tavern marked the halfway point on the turnpike between Louisville and Nashville. It was built before the turn of the century, and it symbolized the first bit of civilization in south central Kentucky. Until the Mammoth Cave Hotel was modernized and expanded and the new road to Mammoth Cave was built by Dr. Croghan in the 1840s, Bell's was the primary overnight stop for stagecoach passengers traveling along the turnpike, and it was the jumping-off place for visitors to the cave. With the construction of the Louisville & Nashville Railroad, Bell's lost even more of its prominence, as travelers no longer stayed overnight as often. Even so, it remained the only inn in that part of Barren County.

Creed had checked into Bell's just an hour before, and he was sitting at a table eating a supper of ham hocks, black-eyed peas, corn bread, and cold buttermilk. He was the only patron in the tavern when Morris and Otter came quietly through the front door. The first thing about them to catch Creed's eye was the tin badge pinned prominently on the lapel of Morris's coat. Then he saw the Colt's at the sheriff's side and the shotgun that Otter held in the crook of his left arm. Creed made a quick mental note that they were squinting, meaning their eyes were still adjusting to the dimmer light inside the saloon. He used that moment to casually switch his fork to his left hand and lower his right beneath the edge of the table to the butt of his Colt's.

Josiah Wilson, the innkeeper, was behind the bar when the sheriff and constable from Edmondson County entered his establishment. He saw their guns, and worry instantly coursed through him. "Evening, gentlemen," he said nervously.

The innkeeper's voice drew the attention of Morris and Otter. They still hadn't seen Creed sitting at the table to the side of the room. Morris moved toward the bar, while Otter remained in front of the door.

"Evening," said the sheriff as he stepped up to the bar. "I'm Sheriff Mason Morris from Edmondson County, and that fellow by the door is Constable Jethro Otter. We're down here from Mammoth Cave looking for a stranger in these parts. His name is Slate Creed. That name mean anything to you?"

Wilson's eyes shifted involuntarily toward Creed.

At the mention of his name, Creed cocked the revolver beneath his coat and simultaneously said, "I'm Slate Creed."

Morris stood still.

Otter put his thumb on the hammer of his shotgun and cocked it.

Creed drew his gun, took aim at Otter's face, and said, "Hold it right there, friend. I'm from Texas, and I can shoot you dead in the wink of an eye."

Otter froze.

Morris froze, too. He knew that voice and those words. Good Lord! he thought. I was just telling Jethro . . .

"Now I'm a peaceable man, Sheriff," said Creed, "and I don't wish to hurt anybody. But if you want to talk to me, I'd appreciate it if your constable would uncock his shotgun and put it down against the wall and walk away from it a piece."

"Do like he says, Jethro," said Morris.

"What?" queried Otter nervously.

"Put down your shotgun, Jethro, and walk away from it."

Otter said nothing more, but he did obey the sheriff, moving over to the bar beside Morris in full view of the muzzle of Creed's six-gun.

The sheriff turned slowly and looked Creed straight in the eyes. It is him! he thought. The Texan who halted Captain Houchin's company during the war. A cold sweat broke out all over Morris.

"Thank you, Sheriff," said Creed. "I really don't want to kill anybody, but I will if you force me into it."

Morris swallowed hard and said, "I don't want any killing either, friend."

"Well, so far we're seeing eye to eye," said Creed. "Now I suppose you want to talk to me about that little tiff I had with Brother Locke this morning."

"That's right," said Morris.

"I thought so," said Creed. He uncocked his Colt's and let his arm rest on the table. "Sheriff, Brother Locke brought on everything with that better-than-thou attitude of his. There's a few things I won't let any man call me, Sheriff, and one of them is a sinner. It's my belief that no man is free of sin, and that means no man has the right to judge another. When I made this point with Brother Locke, he started calling me all sorts of things, until I'd had my fill of him. That's when I shot my gun into the ground to shut him up. I admit that when I saw how it scared his horse, I got a little chuckle out of it and kept it up intentionally to really scare that poor horse of his into bolting, and that's exactly what happened. I shot off my gun three times, and Brother Locke's horse bolted. That's about all there was to it, Sheriff."

"I see," said Morris. "Brother Locke said you chased him. Is that true?"

Creed snorted a laugh, then said, "Sure, I chased him. He was holding on for dear life, and if I hadn't caught his mare and stopped her, he might have lost his grip and gotten thrown from the buggy and hurt real bad. Now how would that do me with the Lord to be the cause of one of his preachers getting hurt? Sure, I chased him, Sheriff, but it was to save his mangy hide, not hurt him."

Morris nodded and said, "That sounds too much like the truth not to be. I just wanted to get your side of things, Mr. Creed."

Creed put his gun away and kicked the other chair out from beneath the table. "I was in the middle of my supper when you came in, Sheriff. Care to join me? Your constable, too."

"Don't mind if I do," said Morris as he started toward the table.

Otter reached out, grabbed Morris by the arm, and whispered, "You ain't really going to eat with him, are you, Mase? Not after all the friends of ours he killed."

"In the first place, Jethro, the war's over. In the second, I ain't so sure he's the same fellow, and in the third place, I'm hungry. You'd be wise to think that way, too." He removed Otter's hand from his arm and joined Creed at the table.

37

Constable Jethro Otter chose not to eat at the same table with Creed, which was fine with Sheriff Morris. He explained, "You Texans scared the hell out of Jethro during the war, and he ain't forgot it yet."

Creed and Sheriff Morris enjoyed their meal together. They spoke of the war without bitterness, anger, or hatred, and they discussed the impending horse racing meet. The sheriff approved, saying it would be a good thing for the economy of the county, giving it an immediate boost and promoting Mammoth Cave, which would work positively on the county's economy in the future. Morris did warn Creed that Brother Locke was a thoroughly dangerous man, although not in the same manner as a man carrying a gun.

"The Bible is his weapon," said Morris. "He uses it to stir up folks, and when folks get stirred up, there's no telling what might happen."

"I know exactly what you mean," said Creed, recalling the events that he had witnessed the month before in Victoria, Texas.

"Of course, he ain't a bad person," said Morris. "Brother Locke is just a little overzealous at times, that's all. He's got his picture of how the Lord wants us to be, and there ain't no deviating him from that view, if you know what I mean."

"I know perfectly what you mean," said Creed, noting how Morris made the statement while he was looking at Otter.

Morris decided to stay the night at Bell's Tavern because it was well after dark by the time he finished his meal. This didn't sit well with Otter because he didn't have the price of a room. When Creed offered to pay for the accommodation, Otter told him that he didn't "want nothing from no Texas Reb." Morris gave Creed a look that said, "See what I mean?"

The next morning the sheriff and the constable headed home

to Brownsville, but not before Morris advised Creed to remain in Glasgow Junction for a while, at least until Brother Locke had cooled down a bit. Another confrontation between them would only add fuel to the fire that Brother Locke was already fanning real hard.

When the sheriff and the constable reached Elko near midday, Otter said he had business to tend to down to Pig, a little crossroads community southwest of Elko. Morris doubted this and said, "If you should run into Brother Locke while you're in this district, Jethro, I'd like it if you wouldn't say anything to him about our meeting with Mr. Creed. I'd rather discuss that with him myself, if you don't mind." Otter said he'd keep that in mind. They rode on until they reached the road to Pig, where Otter excused himself and went his own way.

Suspicious of Otter, Morris headed off down the road toward Davis Houchin's farm. As soon as he thought it was safe, he turned aside and worked his way back to Elko. Just as he thought, he found Otter's horse tied up outside Joppa Church. "Damn!" he swore aloud. He rode up to the hitching rail, dismounted, tied up his horse, and slipped quietly into the white frame building to discover Otter telling Brother Locke all about the night before.

"He's a killer," said Otter. "Scott Houchin said so, and he's one of them Texans that was riding with Morgan throughout the war. Mase recognized him but didn't do nothing about it. You should have seen them together, Brother Locke. Mase and a Reb! What's this world coming to?"

"I'll tell you what this world is coming to," said Morris, making his presence known.

"Mase!" exclaimed Otter.

"Yes, it's me, Jethro." Morris walked up to Locke and Otter, who were sitting in the first pew. "I thought I told you to stay away from Brother Locke, Jethro."

"Then it's true," said Locke, taking the offensive as always. "You have been conspiring against the Lord with this heathen Texan."

"No one is conspiring against the Lord, Brother Locke," said Morris, "and if I hear you say that to me one more time, I'll put you under arrest for interfering with a peace officer doing his duty. You got that?"

"Your duty is to uphold the law, Sheriff," said Locke.

"And that's exactly what I'm doing," said Morris. "I heard

your side of things, and I went all the way to Glasgow Junction to find Mr. Creed and hear his side of it."

"*Mister* Creed?" queried Locke. "When did this heathen suddenly earn so much respect, Sheriff Morris?"

"Since I had a chance to meet him and get to know him a bit," said Morris. "Unlike certain folks in these parts, I am not a man to judge another on the say-so of another man, if you get my meaning, Brother Locke."

"I understand you perfectly, Sheriff," said Locke. "You believe this Texas heathen and not me, a man of the cloth."

"You got that right," said Morris. "And that puts an end to it as far as I'm concerned." He looked at Otter and added, "As far as the law in this county is concerned. Ain't that right, Jethro?"

"If you say so, Mase," said Otter nervously.

"Good! Then we'll be going, won't we, Jethro?"

"Sure thing, Mase."

"Good-bye, Brother Locke," said Morris.

"This isn't the end of it, Sheriff," said Locke. "You may not lift a hand to do anything about this fellow Creed and his horse racing meet, but I—"

"You will not!" interjected Morris. "Mr. Creed has broken no laws by setting up that meet, and you, sir, will do nothing to interfere with Mr. Creed and the lawful enterprise that he and Mr. Proctor have begun. Do you understand me, Brother Locke?"

"Sheriff, this is a house of prayer," said Locke, ignoring the question. "You have entered it without invitation. I believe that makes you a trespasser here."

"Don't try to throw the law up to me, Brother Locke," said Morris angrily. "You have been warned. You will not interfere with Mr. Creed and Mr. Proctor, and that is final."

"There is the door, Sheriff," said Locke flatly, while pointing to the exit. "Get out."

Morris held his ground, glaring hard at Locke. He was on the verge of violence but managed to maintain control of himself, turning slowly away and starting for the door. "Come on, Jethro," he said over his shoulder.

Otter looked askance at Locke. The parson nodded his approval, and the constable followed Morris outside.

"You ain't angry with me, are you, Mase?" asked Otter as they mounted up.

"Now, what do you think, Jethro?"

Otter was too stupid to formulate an answer on his own, and he spent the entire ride back to Brownsville trying to find one.

38

By the end of the week, Brother Locke had rallied the clergy of Edmondson County to support his position against Creed and the horse racing meet. He prepared a scathing sermon that denounced the Texan, gambling, and horse racing, then made copies of it for all of the other ministers, who recited it verbatim that Sunday. By day's end, the populace of Edmondson was polarized into two factions: one supporting the preachers and one supporting the horse racing meet, although not necessarily gambling and not necessarily openly opposing Brother Locke and his cohorts.

Word of how matters were transpiring in Edmondson County was carried to Creed at Glasgow Junction by Scott Houchin, Sheriff Morris, and Mr. Proctor.

Scott told Creed how Pride was progressing with his training. "He gets faster every day," said Scott. And he related how his father's health was bad. "Ma says it's his rheumatiz acting up on him, but I know different. Pa's coughing a lot more than he ever has, and that ain't caused by the rheumatiz. There's something a lot worse wrong with Pa. I tried to get him to go to a doctor, but he won't have none of it. He says all he needs is his jug and Ma's medicine. She's giving him hickory and cherry bark syrup. It helps him some, I guess. Leastways, he says it does."

The sheriff told Creed how Brother Locke and several other ministers invaded his office on Monday morning and demanded that he put a stop to the horse racing meet at Mammoth Cave. When he refused to do anything about it, they threatened to take the matter to court, and he told them to go right ahead and do it. They did, but Judge Houchin told them that Mr. Proctor and Creed hadn't broken any laws that he knew about and that until they did there was nothing he could or would do to stop the meet.

In between visits by Morris, Proctor, and Scott, Creed filled the hours by brushing up on his Bible studies. He borrowed a copy from Josiah Wilson, telling the innkeeper that reading the Good Book helped him sleep better.

Mr. Proctor came down to Glasgow Junction to catch the train to Louisville. "I'm going up there to see the newspaper folks," said Proctor to Creed. "They'll put out the word throughout the state for us. Of course, I'll have to do some advertising, too." He winked at Creed and said, "It never hurts to grease a palm or two. A little gold can go a long way. All the way to Chicago, maybe, if the story rings right. I'll tell them to contact you down here to Bell's if they want more information or if anybody wants to enter a horse in the meet."

When Proctor returned later in the week, he reported that he had been given positive reactions by the press. News of sporting matters was always slow in the winter, being confined to the occasional game of professional billiards, which meant that the editors were more than happy that someone was doing something that would help them sell newspapers. Would they promote the event? Silly question!

"The Cincinnati papers are already carrying the story," said Proctor, "and that means the Chicago papers will soon follow and after them New York. This is the biggest sporting event in the country, Mr. Creed."

Proctor had no idea how right he was about that.

Sheriff Morris knew, though. He was the first to notice the daily increase in the number of strangers arriving and staying in Brownsville. By the end of the second week since Creed and Proctor had struck a deal on the horse racing meet, the Bob Hazelip Hotel was so full that Hazelip was renting floor space in the dining room to anyone with a blanket, and charging a little extra for those who needed one. And Hazelip wasn't the only businessman in the county to prosper from the sudden influx of money. John Harvey down to Chalybeate Springs owned a little store and barroom. Strangers were coming into the saloon and asking for lodging as well as his best liquor, and he was doing his best to accommodate them by renting them floor space, blankets, and straw pallets, and selling them all the mountain dew that they could consume. Outside the county, Josiah Wilson, the proprietor of Bell's Tavern, reaped his share, too, of the instant abundance in coin of the realm. Of course, it went without saying that the

Mammoth Cave Hotel was bursting at the seams with guests when the final week before the meet rolled around. Every room was booked in advance of the weekend races.

It wasn't the numbers of men and women that bothered Morris so much as it was the types of people who were coming into his county. At the Bob Hazelip Hotel in Brownsville and Harvey's Saloon in Chalybeate Springs, the customers appeared to be primarily gamblers, grifters, and girls whose morals were at the very least questionable. Up at Mammoth Cave, the guests were definitely of a higher social class but not always of a higher moral level.

When Josiah Wilson asked him to share his room at Bell's Tavern with another guest, Creed decided it was time for him to seek accommodations elsewhere. He had wished to stay in Glasgow Junction until Charlotte Beaujeu arrived from New Orleans, but since she had sent him word that she wouldn't be arriving until a few days before the races, he moved up to the Mammoth Cave Hotel. Of course, he knew this risked a confrontation with Brother Locke, but he didn't care about that any longer because now he had a plan to deal with the preacher. He returned the Bible to Wilson, thanked him, and moved on.

Since leading his brethren ministers to the county courthouse to demand some sort of action against Creed and the horse racing, and meeting with failure, Brother Locke had decided to lay low and wait for the right moment to press his cause again. Very quietly, he moved among his flock of followers, telling them to keep their distance from the outsiders who were pouring into their county like a plague of locusts. They would wait, he told them, until the time was right, and then, with the might of the Lord on their side, they would vanquish the sinners once and for all time.

39

Creed met Charlotte Beaujeu's train in Glasgow Junction, and much to his surprise, the lady was accompanied by her maid and Percy McGrath.

"Percy was in Memphis when I arrived there by steamboat," explained Charlotte. "He was through drumming up business for the meet, so we came here together. And, of course, I couldn't go anywhere without Meg."

Creed accepted her explanation without question, and the four of them took the stagecoach up to the Mammoth Cave Hotel. Meg and McGrath sat on one seat, although not as close together as Creed and Charlotte were on the other. Along the way, Creed reviewed the events of the past three weeks for them. In conclusion, he said, "Brother Locke is the only problem we have before us, but I'll deal with him if it becomes necessary."

"What about Pride?" asked Charlotte. "Is he faring well?"

"Scott has been working with him every day," said Creed. "He assures me that Pride is getting faster all the time. I don't think we have to worry about him losing his heat on Saturday."

"What about Sunday?" asked Charlotte.

"I think he can hold his own with the other heat winners," said Creed.

"How many entries do we have so far?" asked McGrath.

"As of this morning, one hundred twenty-two," said Creed. "That's ten races of eleven horses each and one of twelve. If we get ten more entries, we'll have twelve races with eleven horses in each one. I don't want more than twelve races. Anything over that will take too long to finish."

"The more the better, I say," said McGrath. "At fifty dollars a horse, we should have quite a purse for the winner."

"Let's not be greedy, Percy," scolded Charlotte gently. "We should be grateful for what we have, don't you agree, Slate?"

She leaned against him and squeezed his arm.

"Yes, we should be grateful," said Creed. "This is a good opportunity to help these folks around here. Especially the Houchins. They're good people, and this is their chance to make some decent money."

"What about my betting posts?" asked McGrath. "Where will I be able to set up shop?"

"Mr. Proctor has agreed to let you use the hotel dining hall," said Creed. "Bettors who are hotel guests can use the balcony doors to come inside and place their wagers, and those who aren't guests can use the veranda doors. You'll have use of the dining tables for the afternoon, but you have to clear out as soon as the last race of the day is over, so the hotel can feed its guests."

"I understand perfectly," said McGrath. "It wouldn't do to bite the hand that's feeding us." He laughed at his own joke, but Creed, Meg, and Charlotte saw nothing funny in his words. McGrath cleared his throat and said, "Well, I'll be certain that my boys are out of the way before supper."

"Just be sure they are," said Creed firmly.

Nearing the hotel, the stagecoach driver blew his horn to announce their arrival, and when the vehicle halted in front of the building, the passengers emerged to be welcomed by Mr. Proctor and a brass band playing "Dixie."

"You must be Mlle. Beaujeu," said Proctor, taking Charlotte's hand and helping her down from the coach.

"Yes, I am," said Charlotte.

"I am L. R. Proctor, the manager of this fine establishment. I welcome you to Mammoth Cave Hotel, Mlle. Beaujeu."

"Thank you, Mr. Proctor," said Charlotte. "Slate has told me much about you and this fine hotel of yours. I'm looking forward to my stay here."

"It will be my pleasure to serve you, mademoiselle," said Proctor. "It isn't often that we get someone of your obvious grace, charm, and beauty here at Mammoth Cave Hotel, mademoiselle." He turned and snapped his fingers at a line of porters who were waiting to take the luggage from the coach's roof and carry it into the hotel. "Right this way, mademoiselle. I've had our best room prepared for your stay."

"Thank you, Mr. Proctor," said Charlotte as she made her way toward the hotel lobby. "I trust that Slate's room is next door to mine and that there is a door adjoining our rooms."

A wave of nervousness swept over Proctor. He looked at Creed for help.

"I'm down the hall a ways," said Creed.

"I want you next door to me, Sugar," said Charlotte, looking at Creed. "Just in case I have a fright in the night and need someone to comfort me. After all, this is a strange place, and I am so far away from home." She turned her eyes on Proctor and added, "You can arrange to have Slate moved next door to me, can't you, Mr. Proctor?"

"Why, yes, certainly," said Proctor. "I'll see to it right away, mademoiselle."

"Good!" she said. "I'll also have to have the room on the other side of mine for my maid. You can arrange that, too, can't you, Mr. Proctor?"

"Yes, of course, mademoiselle. Moving them is no problem whatsoever."

"Then what is?" asked Charlotte, noting the worry in Proctor's voice.

"None of our rooms have doors adjoining them," explained Proctor, breaking out with a cold sweat.

"Then put them in," said Charlotte as if she were telling a waiter to put sour cream on her baked potato.

Proctor again looked askance at Creed, who said, "You heard the lady, Mr. Proctor. Put in the doors."

The hotel manager heaved a sigh, but he accepted the order.

They entered the lobby, and Proctor directed Charlotte toward her room, explaining that she had already been registered by Creed. McGrath still had to register, though; therefore, he left them for the moment. With an entourage of Creed, Meg, Proctor, and five porters carrying her bags behind them, Charlotte led a grand procession up the wide staircase to the second floor. At the top landing, they halted when confronted by a gentleman of obvious means.

"Is this your lady benefactor, Mr. Creed?" asked Potter Palmer as he allowed himself to drink in all of Charlotte with an appreciative scanning.

"Yes, Mr. Palmer," said Creed. "This is Mlle. Charlotte Beaujeu from New Orleans."

Palmer bowed from the waist, took Charlotte's proffered hand, kissed it, then straightened and said, "It is my distinct pleasure to meet you, mademoiselle."

"Charlotte," said Creed, "this gallant gentleman is Mr. Potter Palmer from Chicago."

"I am honored to meet you, M. Palmer," said Charlotte, affecting her best Creole manners. "Did you come all the way down here to Kentucky for the races or for the sights?"

"Ten minutes ago I would have said the races, mademoiselle," said Palmer, "but since your arrival, the scenery has begun to show a dramatic improvement."

"You flatter me too much, monsieur," said Charlotte, putting on her best ladylike smile, "but please don't stop."

McGrath came charging up the stairs, head bowed and concentrating on the steps, not looking up until he reached the landing. He saw Creed, then Charlotte, then Palmer—much to his fearful surprise. McGrath paled.

"Ah, Mr. McGrath," said Palmer, "how nice to see you again!" He turned to Charlotte and said, "I understand Mr. McGrath is associated with you, Mlle. Beaujeu."

"In a way, yes," said Charlotte.

"Has he told you how he cheated me at cards while we traveled together on the Mississippi?"

Creed might have expected this from Palmer, especially since the Texan was the one who told Palmer that McGrath and the boat captain had been in it together. He kept his eye on McGrath, almost hoping the slithering gambler would attempt something here and now, just so he could finish McGrath once and for all. Much to his chagrin, McGrath did nothing except paw the ear that Creed had shot when they were aboard the *Princess*.

McGrath glared at Creed, who was glaring back at him. He knew that Creed had told Palmer. This was betrayal. Creed would pay for it, thought McGrath.

Realizing that the moment was ripe for an explosion, Charlotte thought to diffuse the situation by saying, "Percy a cheat? Really, Mr. Palmer. I've known Percy for years and—"

Palmer raised his hand to interrupt her and said, "Please, mademoiselle, I am not angry with Mr. McGrath. The loss wasn't all that great, I assure you. Why, the show he and the captain of the boat put on was well worth the price of admission. Especially when Mr. Creed joined in the frolic. It was quite an excursion. You should have been there."

Charlotte frowned at McGrath and said, "Yes, maybe I should have been there."

"Charlotte, I can explain," stammered McGrath.

"Save it, McGrath," said Creed. "Mr. Palmer is too much of a gentleman to hold a grudge."

"That's right," said Palmer. "I've been taken before, and I'm sure I'll be taken again." He winked at Creed. "I can afford it." Then, turning to Charlotte, he said, "I'm off to a game right now, mademoiselle, but before I go, I would like to extend an invitation to you and Mr. Creed to join me for dinner this evening."

Intrigued by Palmer's cavalier attitude toward money, she said, "I wouldn't miss it, monsieur."

"Very good," said Palmer. "Until then." He bowed, then departed.

Proctor took them to Charlotte's room and excused himself immediately. The porters put down Charlotte's luggage and left.

"You told him, didn't you, Creed?" growled McGrath.

"Yes, I did," said Creed.

"Never mind, you two," snapped Charlotte. "Palmer has written off the incident. Therefore, you two can let it alone, too. Understand?"

"Of course, Charlotte," said McGrath quickly.

Creed said nothing.

"Good," said Charlotte, although she realized that Creed would never forget how McGrath had cheated and how he had set him up to be thrown off the boat. "Leave us now, Percy. I'm tired, and I want to rest before dining this evening. Slate, you can stay."

"No, I can't," said Creed. "I've still got business to attend to."

"Let it wait," said Charlotte.

"It can't wait," said Creed. "I'll see you later." He followed McGrath out of the room. In the hall, he said, "You stand to do well here, McGrath, as long as you do everything aboveboard. You don't have to cheat."

"Are you accusing me of cheating?" growled McGrath, reaching inside his coat for his gun.

Creed grabbed the gambler's arm with his left hand, then threw his body against McGrath, pressing him hard against the wall. Now nose to nose with his adversary, Creed said, "I'm not accusing you, McGrath. I'm warning you. I warned you in New Orleans that if you crossed me, I would kill you. That still stands." For emphasis, he drew his Colt's and put the muzzle up to McGrath's lips. "I'm from Texas, and I can shoot you dead in the wink of an eye. Understand, McGrath?"

The fear in McGrath's eyes said he did.

40

George Devol and Canada Bill Jones had arrived at the Mammoth Cave Hotel the day before. Creed saw them as soon as they stepped off the stage from Glasgow Junction and rushed up to greet them.

"We'd heard you were here," said Devol, shaking Creed's hand vigorously. "Glad to see you again, Creed."

"Same here," said Jones, offering his hand.

Devol and Jones wanted to know how Creed had gotten to Kentucky, and he related his adventure to them over cold drinks in the hotel's barroom. Then he got down to business.

"How did you two hear about the races?" asked Creed.

"McGrath," said Devol. "Percy's spreading the word all over that there's to be a horse racing meet here this weekend. We heard about it in St. Louis. Every gambler in the country must have heard about it by now. All the newspapers are carrying stories about it. You should see them. They're all talking about that horse the boy on the boat had. Kentucky's Pride they're calling him. They're saying he's the Pride of this county, and that the whole county owns him. Stuff like that. Newspaper stories like that are sure to bring in large crowds of spectators and bettors, too."

"That's what we'd hoped," said Creed. "But that's not what I'm worried about. It's McGrath. He left two weeks ago to spread the word in the gambling community, and I haven't heard anything about him or from him since then. Except what you fellows have told me. He left here in such a hurry. It was like he had an important meeting or something."

"He did," said Devol. "He had to meet with as many gamblers as he could and get the word out."

"That can only mean one thing," said Jones. "McGrath is planning something big here. I don't know what it could be, but he wouldn't be running around the country talking to other gamblers if he didn't have something big planned here."

"That's right," said Devol. "Percy McGrath isn't one to waste his strength on anything that doesn't have a good return in it for him."

"I was afraid of that," said Creed. "I've noticed that there's a lot of shady-looking fellows arriving in the county these past few days. And women, too. They sort of remind me of the buzzards back in Texas, circling over a dying cow."

"That sounds about right," said Jones. "All kinds of people come to these events, Creed, and that's what draws the sharpers. All kinds. Pickpockets, grifters, dicemen. You name them, and they'll be here."

"Pimps and whores, too," said Devol. "All trying to make a quick buck."

"That's to be expected, I guess," said Creed, "and I suppose that there's nothing I can do to stop them. But I can stop McGrath." He shifted his eyes back and forth between Jones and Devol. "With your help."

"How can we help?" asked Devol.

"Yes, what would you like us to do?" asked Jones.

"The two of you can move among these people without raising anybody's suspicions," said Creed. "Just start asking around about McGrath, and see if anybody knows what he might be up to."

That was the day before that both gamblers had agreed to do that much for Creed. Now he was headed downstairs to meet them in the saloon and tell them that McGrath had arrived. They were sitting at a corner table when he arrived.

"I trust Charlotte was her usual self," said Jones.

"She was," said Creed, "but so was McGrath."

"Yes, we saw him come in with you," said Devol. "It figures that he'd show up about now."

"Well, have you heard anything yet?" asked Creed.

"Not a thing," said Jones.

"Me neither," said Devol.

"Nothing?" queried Creed.

"Nothing," repeated Jones. "I know it's strange, but no one knows anything about what McGrath is up to. He's hired a few of the boys to handle some of the action for him, but that's the limit of it."

"He's not even picking up a percentage of anybody else's action," said Devol. "We aren't the only ones who are surprised by this, Creed. Everybody is astounded that McGrath isn't trying to rake in part of their trade. In fact, some of them even said that McGrath loaned them the price of a train ticket so they could get here."

"Why would he do that?" asked Creed. "From what I understand, McGrath isn't exactly the most generous fellow in your circles."

"That's right," said Jones. "Percy is real tight with his roll. I've never known him to help another bloke who might be down on his luck. Why the sudden change? I wonder."

"Yes, why the change?" queried Devol. "A leopard can't change his spots, and that goes for Percy McGrath, too. He's always been a polecat who can't change his stripes or his smell."

"Maybe he's going to play this one straight," suggested Jones. "With all this money floating around here, maybe he thinks there are enough marks to go around."

"Maybe so," said Devol. "Tell me, Creed. It's my understanding that you're allowing only Percy to set up betting posts in the hotel."

"That's right," said Creed. "He gets to use the dining hall to set up his posts. I thought I could keep a closer eye on him that way. The sheriff will be here to make sure there's no funny business with the money."

"Good thinking," said Devol. "Having the law looking over Percy's shoulder should help to keep him in line."

"Even so, he could fool the sheriff," said Jones, "if the sheriff doesn't know much about betting pools."

"That's right," said Devol. "It would do no good to have the sheriff watching Percy if the sheriff knows nothing about betting pools."

"Then we'll need someone who knows everything there is to know about gambling to watch McGrath," said Creed. "How about one of you?"

Devol and Jones exchanged questioning looks, then Devol said, "I think we'd rather be out with the crowd watching the races and covering our own action."

"That's right," said Jones.

"What if I paid you?" asked Creed.

Again, Devol and Jones looked at each other questioningly, but Jones was the one to say, "How much?"

"Not how much," said Devol, "but with what would you pay? Money or a different proposition?"

"I was thinking of money," said Creed. "What were you thinking of?"

"I was thinking of a piece of the action inside the dining hall," said Devol. "Let us set up our own post, and from there, we can keep an eye on Percy and make a few dollars at the same time."

Creed snickered and said, "A few dollars. You gamblers never quit, do you?"

Devol smiled and said, "Of course not."

"There's a growing expression in our profession that has to do with the gullibility of those transplanted Puritan farmers in Illinois," said Jones. "We used to say, 'Never give a mark an even break.' Now the boys are saying, 'Never give a sucker an even break.' Do you think men who say and believe such things would ever pass up an opportunity to make a few dollars wagering? Really, Creed!"

41

Creed and Charlotte sat on one side of the table. Palmer and Rosy, a red-haired lady of questionable repute who had accompanied the real estate magnate down to Kentucky from Chicago, sat on the other. Their table was separated from the others in the dining hall, having been placed in a corner for the privacy of these elite diners. The conversation was casual and lighthearted until it was interrupted by a voice out of the wilderness, crying, "Harlot! Jezebel! Shameless hussy!"

"What the hell is that?" queried Palmer angrily, startled by the shrieking.

Creed knew the voice and its owner. He turned to see Brother Locke, and a group of his followers that included Constable Jethro Otter, come storming through the dining hall toward his table. "Damn!" swore Creed. "He couldn't wait until later to do this?" He wadded up his napkin in disgust and threw it down on top of his plate of half-eaten steak, baked potato, and boiled carrots; then he slid away from the table.

Proctor and a gaggle of waiters rushed to intercept Locke and his people. The other diners ceased eating to follow the action with their eyes and ears.

The hotel manager and his employees surrounded the parson and his people. Proctor approached Locke. Otter stepped in front of Proctor, halting him in his tracks. The minister swept past them, stopped short of Creed's table, crooked a finger at Charlotte, and said, "You, madam! I am addressing you."

Creed came to his feet, opened his coat to let Locke see that he had his Colt's with him, then said in a tone almost as loud as Locke's but with more authority, "Brother Locke, I don't believe you know Mlle. Beaujeu well enough to be addressing her at all. In fact, I don't believe you have the right to call any woman in this establishment a harlot or anything similar to that misused epithet. Unless, of course, you have firsthand knowledge of her occupation."

That brought a roar of laughter from the crowd, although none of it came from Locke's people.

Like any good preacher, who knew that doing the Lord's work required a certain amount of theatrics, Locke waited until the audience was settled again before saying, "Hurl your insults and make your filthy jokes, if you will, Mr. Creed. They mean nothing to us. We are here in the name of Christ, and nothing can stay us from our duty to Him."

"And exactly what is your duty to the Lord?" asked Creed, making certain he was being heard plainly by every ear in the room.

"It is our duty to stop you from this debauchery," said Locke. "It is our duty to stop you from holding this horse racing meet. It is our duty to stop you from gambling on this horse racing meet of yours. It is our duty to stop you from ruining the lives of our people in this county. It is our duty to stop you from leading them down the path of wickedness, slovenliness, laziness, and sinfulness. It is our duty to—"

Creed couldn't listen to any more. He interrupted Locke, saying, "I think we've all figured out what you're getting at, Brother Locke. You're here to stop us from spending our money in your county. You're here to tell us to go home and quit paying for lodging here, quit paying for food here, quit paying for stagecoach rides, quit paying for tours through the caves. You're here trying to take the food out of the mouths of the babes of your friends and neighbors who are profiting quite handsomely from this horse racing meet that we're planning to hold here this Saturday and Sunday. Is that it, Brother Locke? You're here to keep your friends and neighbors from making a little money off us sinners, as you are so eager to call us. Is that it, Brother Locke?"

"Yes!" said Locke. "Yes, because they would be earning the wages of sin, and that, Mr. Creed, goes against the Word of the Lord." Locke held up his Bible for emphasis. "Ill-gotten gains are an abomination to the Lord, Mr. Creed."

"And you think the Lord considers horse racing to be sinful, Brother Locke?" asked Creed.

"Yes, He does," said Locke confidently.

"I see," said Creed. He turned and began to pace, drawing every eye in the place to him. He halted abruptly, spun on a heel, pointed a finger at Locke, and shouted, "I think you're wrong, Brother Locke. I think the Lord intended for His people to enjoy this life He has given them. I think He meant for us to be happy and have fun, Brother Locke, and horse racing is part of that happiness."

"Blasphemy!" screamed Locke, now pointing at Creed.

"Blasphemy, Brother Locke?" queried Creed. "God spent six days creating everything, and on the seventh day, He rested. How do you think He rested, Brother Locke? Do you think He curled up on a couch and took a snooze all day? Do you think He sat on a cloud up in Heaven and twiddled his thumbs all day long? Do you think He went to church and prayed to Himself, Brother Locke? Or do you think He said to Himself, 'I've worked for six days, now it's time I had some fun, now it's time I enjoyed the fruits of My labor. I made the earth and all those people down there. I think I'll take a look and see what they're all up to. Yes, that ought to be fun, watching My people.' "

"Yes, I believe that," said Brother Locke, surprising everyone in the hall with the single exception of Creed. "I believe He looks down on us on that seventh day, that day He commanded us to set aside to worship Him. The Sabbath Day, Mr. Creed! Yes, the Lord is looking down on us to see what we're doing on the Sabbath Day, His day. He wants to make sure we're all in church offering Him our prayers and worshiping Him. That's what he's doing on the seventh day, Mr. Creed."

"I believe you're right about that, Brother Locke," said Creed almost cordially, "but what about the week after God created everything, Brother Locke? Did He go back to work creating more worlds like ours? Or did He find a new job the week after He created everything down here?"

"How dare you question God?" roared Locke.

"I'm not questioning God, Brother Locke," Creed roared back. He squared himself toward Locke and put his fists on his hips, taking a position of challenge. "I'm questioning you. You came in here acting like you're the expert on God, so I'm asking you: What did God do the week after He created everything down here? Answer me that, Brother Locke. If you can."

Absolute silence. Not even breathing.

Locke wracked his mind seeking an answer to Creed's question. His hesitation, expanded by the quiet of the impromptu audience, seemed interminable. He was near to being catatonic when his hand sent a message to his brain.

"God went about giving us His Word!" shouted Locke triumphantly, holding his Bible high over his head for all to see. "That's what He did in the week after He created the world. He created His Word for us to live by."

"I see," said Creed. "That's a fair answer, Brother Locke, but are you telling me that God wrote the Bible in only six days? It seems to me that all those things that happened in the Bible took years to happen. Or did they happen in just six days like you just said, Brother Locke?"

"I didn't say He wrote the Bible in just six days," said Locke, suddenly on the defensive.

"No, you said He wrote it in the week after He created the world," said Creed, pressing his advantage. "Isn't that what you said, Brother Locke?"

"Yes, but I didn't mean that He wrote the whole thing in one week," said Locke.

"Then how long did it take Him?" countered Creed.

"Years, decades, centuries, of course," said Locke. "Everybody knows that."

"And He worked on the Bible every day during those years, decades, and centuries," said Creed. "Is that it, Brother Locke? God worked on the Bible every single day—except Sundays, of course. Is that right, Brother Locke?"

Locke had no taste for being on the defensive. It was his forte to attack, always attack. He figured it was high time he put Creed in his place.

"You seem to have all the answers here, Mr. Creed," said Locke with a smug smile. "You tell me if God worked on the Bible every day except Sundays for all those years."

Creed took note of Locke's ploy. He was ready for it.

"Brother Locke, I'm a simple man," said Creed as evenly and as softly as he could and still be heard by everyone. "A young man with lots of questions. I'm not a man of the cloth with a Bible in my hand. I'm just an ordinary man like most of the men in this room, and I depend on men like you, men of the cloth who are supposed to know the Bible and know God's ways, men like you, Brother Locke. I depend on you to answer my questions about God. That's why I go to church on Sundays, Brother Locke. The same as most of the folks in this room do. I go to hear men like you answer the questions I have about God. Of course, we're not in church right now, but I'm still depending on you, Brother Locke, to give me the answers to my questions about God. I'm depending on you because I don't have all the answers, and I expect you do have them because you're a man of God, Brother Locke. I suspect that's why most of your congregation come to hear your sermons on Sundays—because they depend on you to have the answers to their questions about God. Of course, I realize you're just a mortal man, the same as me, and you aren't exactly perfect, the same as me, and you just might not have all the answers to my questions about God, the same as me, and," he paused for effect, "I suspect you'd admit it, the same as me, if you didn't know all the answers. I would respect that, Brother Locke, and I would suspect that your congregation would respect you for admitting that you didn't have all the answers, that on some occasions a man has to go direct to God to get an answer to his question. Isn't that so, Brother Locke?"

Locke's eyebrows pinched together as he tried to sort out what Creed had just said. Still unsure of what Creed was getting at, the parson shook his head and said, "I'm not sure about that, Mr. Creed."

Creed feigned surprise and said, "You're not sure, Brother Locke? You? Do you mean to tell me that you've never told a member of your congregation to turn to God, to pray to God, to go and ask God for an answer to a question? Is that what you're saying, Brother Locke?"

"Of course not!" snapped Locke angrily. "I've told lots of my people to pray to God for answers to their questions."

"Good!" shouted Creed. "Now we're getting somewhere! So then you admit that you don't have all the answers, do you, Brother Locke?"

"No, of course not," said Locke. "Only a fool would say that he had all the answers to questions about God."

"We all know you're no fool, Brother Locke," said Creed. "No, sir. Not you. That's why you don't know if God worked on the Bible every single day. Is that right?"

"Yes, I suppose so," said Locke with all the conviction of a man whose pants have just fallen down on him, and who knows that the trapdoor of his long johns has no buttons.

Creed decided it was time for him to deliver the *coup de grace*. "That's all right, Brother Locke. I respect you for having the courage to admit that you don't know if God worked on the Bible every single day after He created the world in a week. In fact, Brother Locke, I admire you for your admission. Yes, sir, that is most admirable, sir." Creed paused for effect. "Even so, Brother Locke, I am troubled by something else you said earlier in this room." He waited for Locke to reply.

"What was that?" asked Locke.

"You insinuated that God didn't like horse racing, Brother Locke," said Creed. "In fact, you called horse racing an abomination before the Lord."

Locke was suddenly confident again. "No, sir, I did not say that horse racing was an abomination before the Lord. I said that the ill-gotten gains from horse racing were an abomination before the Lord."

Creed jumped quickly. "But horse racing itself is all right with the Lord. Am I right?"

"No, you are not right," said Locke powerfully. "Horse racing is an evil like gambling, and it is my duty to crush evil wherever it shows its head."

"Now, wait a minute, Brother Locke," said Creed. "I think I know what the Bible says about gambling, and if my memory serves me right, the only thing it says is that those Roman soldiers who crucified Jesus cast lots for His clothes. I don't believe it says anything in the Bible about gambling being a sin."

"Yes, it does!" shrieked Locke.

"Where?" countered Creed. "Show me, Brother Locke. Show me in the Bible where it says that gambling is a sin. Show me where, and I will cancel the horse racing meet right now. I will cancel it once and for all time. And if anybody else should try to carry on without me, I will stand at the starting line and shoot the first man to put a horse in the field. I will do that, Brother Locke, if you can show me in the Bible where it says that gambling is a sin."

Locke grinned broadly and said, "Come here, Mr. Creed, and I will show you." He thumbed through his Bible quickly, looking for the words that he was positive were printed there to support him. He had no success in the first passage he found. Nothing in the second. Nor the third. He began to worry about finding the Scripture about gambling. He flipped more pages. Still the wrong words. More pages turned. No success.

"It's all right, Brother Locke," said Creed. "I know that if you look long enough you'll find something that you'll interpret to mean that God is opposed to gambling, but instead of doing that, why don't we ask God Himself if He's really against gambling? Why don't we ask Him if He's against horse racing, too? What do you say to that, Brother Locke?"

The parson looked up at Creed, confusion all over his face. "What?" he asked. "Ask God what?"

"Why don't we pray to God, Brother Locke, and ask Him if He's against gambling and horse racing?"

"That's blasphemy!" snapped Locke. "Would you mock the Lord, Mr. Creed?"

"Never, Brother Locke," said Creed sincerely. "I just thought that you could lead us all in a prayer to God and ask Him for His guidance on this matter of gambling and horse racing."

"I've already done that," said Locke confidently.

"And what was God's reply, Brother Locke?"

Locke hesitated again, stammering, "His reply?"

"Yes, Brother Locke. What did God say to you about gambling and horse racing?"

"Well, He didn't say anything directly to me," said Locke.

"Then He gave you some sort of sign, right?"

"Well, no, not exactly."

"Then what exactly, Brother Locke?"

"Well, I suppose He hasn't answered me yet," admitted Locke.

Creed bowed his head for a second, then raised it again and said, "I was afraid of that. You see, Brother Locke, I asked God about gambling and horse racing, too, and I still haven't gotten an answer either. But something tells me that He's still going to answer us. I don't know how I know this, but I do. You can call it a feeling, a hunch, or anything you like. Maybe it came to me in a dream. I don't know. But I've got this idea that if God is against gambling and horse racing, at least our horse racing meet this Saturday and Sunday, He'll give us poor weather, meaning it will snow or rain heavily or it will be extremely cold. But if God is in favor of us having our meet, Saturday morning will be bright and shiny like a new penny and the air will be warm. That's what I think, Brother Locke. What do you think? Do you think the Lord will answer our prayers in this manner? I do. Don't you?"

"I don't know for sure," said Locke, suspicious of Creed.

"All right," said Creed, "what do you say we leave this matter in the hands of God? You can't argue with that, can you, Brother Locke? Putting our faith in God, I mean. That's what believing in God is all about, isn't it? Having faith in Him?"

"Yes, of course," said Locke firmly. "Faith is the cornerstone of Christianity."

"Good," said Creed. "Then you agree that we should leave this matter in God's hands. Good. So when Saturday morning comes God will answer us one way or the other. Either the sun will be shining and the day will be warm or it will be bitterly cold with lots of snow or pouring rain. Fair weather means God says it's all right for us to have the meet, and foul weather means He's against it."

Locke considered Creed's proposal for a moment, then said, "And will you continue to hold your meet if the weather is foul, Mr. Creed?" He was sure he had turned the tables on Creed.

"And go against the will of the Lord, Brother Locke?" queried Creed quite innocently. "Not this believer. If the weather is foul, then the horse racing meet is canceled. You have my word on it, Brother Locke."

Locke considered one more reply but never got the chance to say it.

"You have my word as well," said Proctor.

"Mine, too," said Charlotte.

"And mine," said Palmer, rising to emphasize his words.

"Mine, too," said several others, until every diner in the hall was giving his or her word that the meet would not be held if the weather was foul.

Locke looked around him, especially at the faces of his own followers. They all said the same thing. To refuse to accept the Lord's will would put him in a minority of one, and Brother Locke knew he was nothing alone.

"God's will be done," said Locke sternly. And he turned and marched out of the dining hall with his followers jubilantly parading behind him.

As soon as Locke and his people were gone, Rosy, Palmer's escort from Chicago, threw down a slug of whiskey and said, "Thank God! I thought they'd never leave."

And the house came down.

42

Word of Creed's challenge of Brother Locke accomplished one thing immediately: It spurred more betting. Not on the races but on the weather. The gamblers couldn't have been happier.

Brother Locke wasn't, though. He learned that some of his own congregation were making bets that the weather would be foul and that their parson would be vindicated by the Lord. Somehow, they had missed the point, and this, above all, perturbed the country minister, even more than Creed, the gamblers, and the horse racing meet.

Adding to Locke's chagrin was the weather. Thursday was warm and partly cloudy. Friday was warmer and sunnier. Even so, he refused to believe that the Lord would allow Saturday to be a nice day. He was greatly disappointed.

Never before in the history of Edmondson County did so many rise before the sun to await the new day. Every guest at Mammoth Cave Hotel was out of bed and down in the dining hall by first light. Mat, the cave guide, came into the room and announced that the sky was full of fading stars and that the temperature was a crisp thirty-four degrees. This brought a round of cheers from the throng. However, said Mat, a gentle breeze was coming from the north. The crowd became a little subdued at that point.

Parson Locke and a group of his followers were also up early that morning. They gathered at Joppa Church, then drove in a caravan up to Mammoth Cave Hotel, arriving on the grounds with first light. On Locke's signal, they left their conveyances and formed up on the hotel's front steps. They heard the cheer from the dining hall, and figuring what the reason was behind it, the minister led his flock in singing "Abide with Me."

Abide with me: fast falls the eventide;
The darkness deepens; Lord, with me abide;
When other helpers fail, and comforts fail;
Help of the helpless, O abide with me.

Hearing the gentle voices of Locke's people floating through the cool air, the guests inside the hotel fell silent to listen. A few verses into the song, Palmer's escort was heard to say, "What the hell is that?" But few people laughed, least of all Creed. He was disturbed over the way events were going. He had put himself and Locke in a corner where neither of them should have been in the first place. Although he hadn't wished it to be this way, he found himself at the forefront of those supporting the horse racing meet, and realizing his position, he thought to use this unasked-for power to help as many people as possible, including his adversary, Brother Locke.

Rising from his table and still holding his coffee cup, Creed walked slowly toward the hotel lobby. Curious about where he was going, Palmer followed him. Next came Charlotte and Meg, and in another breath, nearly everyone was moving toward the exit. "Where's everybody going?" asked Rosy before she got up and tagged along.

Creed opened the lobby door and stepped outside. He was only a few steps behind Locke, who was still conducting the song. He waited patiently as Locke and his people finished singing.

Palmer, Charlotte, and Meg joined Creed on the hotel's front veranda. Others crowded around them, but most of the guests stayed inside the lobby.

Locke brought the song to a close, then looked to the east to see the clear sunrise through his steamy breath. He was beginning to realize that the Lord was about to provide the horse racing meet with near perfect weather. He had started to express his dismay when he noticed that his church members were looking past him at the people behind him. He turned around and faced Creed.

"I suppose you've come out here to gloat over my defeat," said Locke, his voice filled with hollow bluff.

"No, Brother Locke," said Creed evenly. "I was attracted by the singing."

"Really, Mr. Creed?" asked Locke snidely.

"Yes."

"Then maybe we can sing you another hymn," said Locke angrily. He turned to his flock and started singing "A Mighty Fortress Is Our God." The congregation joined him.

> A mighty fortress is our God,
> A bulwark never failing;
> Our helper He, amid the flood
> Of mortal ills prevailing.
> For still our ancient foe
> Doth seek to work us woe;
> His craft and power are great;
> And armed with cruel hate,
> On earth is not his equal.

When they had finished, Locke spun around to face Creed again. "How does that one suit you, Mr. Creed?" he demanded.

"It suits me fine, Brother Locke," said Creed. "How does this one suit you?" And without another word, he began singing "Blest Be the Tie That Binds."

Quick to understand Creed's motive and purpose, Palmer lent his voice to the song, and in the next instant, several others behind them joined in.

> Blest be the tie that binds
> Our hearts in Christian love;
> The fellowship of kindred minds
> Is like to that above.

Locke didn't know what to think about this young man from Texas. Creed had fired his gun at him—well, maybe not at him, but in his presence and in a threatening manner anyway. Creed had committed blasphemy—well, was it really blasphemy to know and understand the Bible better than some ministers? Creed had used the Lord to discredit him—well, wasn't that what he was trying to do to Creed? The Texan had brought sin to his county—well, he brought a lot of prosperity with him, too, hard cash that folks around there needed in the worst way. Creed had killed other men—well, many of his own congregation had killed during the recent war; did that make them evil sinners? These questions and many more plagued Locke as he listened to Creed and Palmer and the others singing, and before he realized it, he turned to his flock and conducted them in singing the final verse and chorus with Creed and his people.

With the last stanza sung, Locke turned to face Creed one more time and saw that the Texan had extended his hand to him. "What's the meaning of this?" he asked quietly.

"How do the Beatitudes go, Brother Locke?" asked Creed. " 'Blessed are the poor . . . ' " Creed intentionally left the quote uncompleted.

Brother Locke finished it for him. " ' . . . for theirs shall be the kingdom of God. Blessed are those who mourn . . . ' "

" ' . . . for they shall be comforted,' " said Creed, finishing for Locke. " 'Blessed are the meek . . . ' " He hesitated, waiting for the parson to join him. Locke did, and together they quoted, " ' . . . for they shall inherit the earth. Blessed are those who hunger and thirst for righteousness, for they shall be satisfied. Blessed are the merciful, for they shall obtain mercy. Blessed are the pure of heart, for they shall see God. Blessed are the peacemakers, for they shall be called sons of God.' " And when they had finished, Creed repeated, "Blessed are the peacemakers."

Locke and Creed shook hands in friendship.

"Brother Creed," said Locke, looking at the rising sun, "it looks like it's going to be a beautiful day for horse racing."

43

The Davis Houchins were also up before the sun that Saturday morning. There was nothing unusual about that; they rose early every day. But this was a special day for them. This was the day that they hoped would mark the end of their days scratching a meager living out of the Kentucky hills and would begin an era of prosperity for them and their children, especially their children, because both Davis and Edie knew that his days on earth were drawing to a close.

After seeing to it that the younguns did their chores, Edie fed breakfast to her husband and their brood, all except Scott, who had spent the last few days up to Mammoth Cave Hotel getting Pride ready for the races. Then she got them ready for the wagon trip up to Mammoth Cave. Dressed in their Sunday meeting clothes, the children piled into the bed of the wagon, while their mother helped their father onto the seat. She put Davis's jug and a picnic basket in the back and warned the kids to stay out of the food, that was their dinner.

Davis reached for the reins, but his fingers just refused to hold them properly. "John Wesley!" he snapped over his shoulder. "You get up here."

"Yes, Pa," said John Wesley, not sure of what he had done to draw his father's wrath. He climbed over the girls and little brother Ben and stood behind the seat waiting for his parent's next harsh words. "Yes, Pa?"

"Get up here in the seat with me and your ma," said Davis. When the boy appeared to be confused, Davis added, "I want you to drive us up to the hotel, son."

John Wesley wasn't certain that he'd heard right. He'd better make sure. "Me, Pa?"

"Why, sure, son," said Davis. "You're old enough now. Come on now and get yourself up here. Daylight's wasting."

John Wesley took the reins and drove his family through the hollow to the main road. He halted the team there because several carriages and wagons were passing by, all headed in the direction of Elko. John Wesley rippled the leather lines over the team of mules, and the Houchin wagon fell in behind the line of vehicles.

"You think they're all going to the races, Pa?" asked John Wesley as he drove them up the hill to Joppa Ridge and Elko.

"Where else would so many folks be going on a Saturday?" replied Davis. He coughed and spit, then said, "Hand me my jug, Clarenda. I need to cut the dust a mite."

Several more wagons and carriages joined the caravan at Elko, and they all took the fork to Mammoth Cave.

"Never in all my born days have I seen so many folks on the road at one time," said Davis. He laughed and slapped his knee, then said, "This is going to be a helluva day, Ma."

"I think you're right, Pa," said Edie guardedly.

John Wesley maneuvered the wagon down into Bruce Hollow, keeping pace with everyone else on the road that morning. Then he maintained his place in line as every conveyance seemed to slow to a crawl to make its way up the switchback to its destination.

"Will you look at this, Ma?" said Davis, his eyes gleaming with an excitement that Edie hadn't seen in them for years. "There must be a thousand people here. Maybe two thousand."

Edie was speechless as she looked at all the surreys, coaches, buggies, wagons, carts, horses, mules, and people. The road was choking with them, and they weren't even up to the junction with Mammoth Cave Ridge Road yet.

"Where are they all coming from, Pa?" asked John Wesley, a bit of fright in his voice.

"From all over, son," said Davis. "I'll bet there's folks here all the way from Louisville and Nashville." He took a snort on his jug, then said, "This sure is going to be some day."

Their line of traffic melded with the line of vehicles on Mammoth Cave Ridge Road, slowing them even more. Then up ahead they saw a fellow in the middle of the road telling folks where to put their rigs and teams. When the Houchins got up to him, he pointed toward a clearing to the side of the road and said, "You can tie up over there and walk the rest of the way."

"Over there?" queried Davis. "But I got a horse running in a race this afternoon."

"So does everybody else, friend," said the stranger. "Now you put your wagon over there or you can turn around and go home."

"I tell you I've got a horse running in a race this afternoon," said Davis, "and that gives me the right to go up to the hotel and tie up."

The man flipped his coat lapel, revealing a deputy sheriff's badge. "I ain't telling you again, old-timer," he said. "Now tie up over there or get on out of here."

"And I'm telling you, smart ass," said Davis angrily, "that I've got a horse running in the races this afternoon and I'm going on up to the hotel with my whole family and you ain't going to stop us no how, no way." He reached for the whip, but Edie grabbed it before he could. "Give me that thing, Ma. I'm going to thrash this smart ass."

"You ain't going to do it, Davis Houchin," said Edie.

"Davis Houchin?" queried the man in the road. "You're Davis Houchin?"

"That's right, I am," growled Davis. "What of it?"

"Beg your pardon, Mr. Houchin," said the man, removing his hat and holding it with both hands in front of him. "I didn't know who you were, sir. You go on up to the hotel. You and your whole family there. Mr. Creed said to let you through. He's up to the hotel waiting for you."

"Creed, you say?"

"Yes, sir."

"Good man, Slate Creed," said Davis. "Go on, John Wesley. Drive us up to the hotel." He puffed up his chest and added, "We're expected."

Creed met the Houchins at the hotel's front steps. Porters circled the wagon and helped the children and Edie down from it. Not wishing to show his age and infirmity, Davis sucked up all his strength and climbed down on his own.

"Where do you want John Wesley to put the wagon?" asked Davis of Creed.

Creed smiled and said, "The porters will take care of it for you, Mr. Houchin. You and the family just come with me."

"Wait a second," said Davis. "Clarenda, fetch my jug along with us."

"And get the picnic basket, John Wesley," said Edie.

"That won't be necessary, Clarenda," said Creed. "The hotel has all the food and drink you'll need, Mrs. Houchin."

"I'm particular to my own brew, Slate," said Davis, trying to disguise his worry that he would have to pay for the food and his drinking and that he had no money for it.

"Maybe I should explain something here," said Creed. "You and your family are guests of the hotel, Davis."

"Guests of the hotel?" queried Edie.

"Yes, ma'am," said Creed. "If it wasn't for you and your horse, there wouldn't be any races here today, and the hotel wouldn't have all this business. So to show his appreciation, Mr. Proctor would like you to be his guests. There's a room for you and Davis and another room for Clarenda and the children. John Wesley, you can bunk in with Scott."

The boy looked at his mother for confirmation, and she said, "If Mr. Creed says you can bunk in with Scott, then I guess it must be all right."

"Yah-hoo!" yelled John Wesley.

"Settle down, boy!" snapped Davis. "Remember your place!"

"Yes, sir." But he was only calm on the outside. On the inside, he was as happy as if it were Christmas and he'd got a squirrel gun of his own.

"Come on," said Creed, "I'll show you to your rooms, then we'll go see Scott out at the stables. He'll be glad to see you, I know."

Creed had Proctor put the Houchins on the first floor because he knew Davis would have trouble negotiating the stairs and there was no sense in making him go upstairs more than was necessary. The only time that would be necessary was when Pride was running in a race—Davis would want the best seat in the house to see that.

After getting the Houchins settled in their rooms, Creed took them all to the stables to see Scott and Pride.

"How's the horse doing?" asked Davis.

"That's just like you, Pa," scolded Edie. "You ask about the animal before you ask about your own kin. How are you, son? You look a little pale. You eating all right?"

"I'm fine, Ma," said Scott. "I've been eating plenty up here. Mr. Creed sees to that."

"All right, enough of that now," said Davis. "How's Pride doing? Is he eating all right, too?"

"He's just fine, Pa," said Scott. "He's as fit as he'll ever be. He's ready to run right now."

Davis turned to Creed and asked, "What kind of race you got lined up for Pride?"

"We laid out a track on the east side of the hotel," said Creed. "It's a mile long. We're not exact on that mile, but we're real close."

"How many other horses has Pride got to beat to win the prize?" asked Davis.

"We have a hundred and twenty-nine horses entered in the meet," said Creed. "This afternoon, there will be eight races with twelve horses in each race, and we'll have three races with eleven horses in each race. That's eleven races in all. All of the horses that finish first, second, or third in today's races will get to race tomorrow in three heats that we'll run between one and two o'clock in the afternoon. The horses that finish first, second, and third in those heats will run the championship race at four o'clock."

"How come so long between the heats and the championship race?" asked Davis.

"That will give everybody a chance to cool down their horses," said Creed, "and it will give the gamblers a chance to make their pools."

"I see," said Davis. "What's the big prize worth?"

"The winners of today's races will get one hundred dollars each," said Creed. "The second place finishers today will get fifty dollars, and the third place finishers will get twenty-five. The same goes for the three heats tomorrow. But in the championship race the winner will receive two thousand dollars, the second place horse seven hundred fifty, and the third place horse two hundred fifty."

Davis shook his head and said, "That's twenty-two hundred that Pride can win. That don't seem like enough, but I guess it'll have to do." He laughed and said, "Hell, that's still three, four times as much as I make in a year farming and running the ferry."

"Don't go counting your chicks before their hatched, Pa,"

said Edie. "Pride ain't won anything yet."

"That's right, Pa," said Scott. "I've seen a lot of good horses here. Pride might not win anything."

"He won't win nothing if you two keep up that attitude," said Davis. "Just keep thinking like that, Scott, and you might as well get Pride and go home right now."

"Your father's right," said Creed. "You've got to believe in Pride. If you don't, he'll know it, and he won't run as fast as he could for you. If you're down, he'll be down. Do you understand, Scott?"

"Sure, I understand," said Scott.

"Which race is Pride in today?" asked Davis.

"I drew a two, Pa," said Scott.

"What does that mean?" asked Davis.

"It means he's in the second race, Davis," said Creed.

"Good," said Davis. "That way we won't have to be waiting around all afternoon wondering how Pride's going to do."

"Well, it's nearly time to eat," said Creed. "We have a special table set for your family, Davis."

"Special? What for?"

"It's for the children," explained Creed. "You and Mrs. Houchin will be sitting with me and Mlle. Beaujeu."

"Is that your French lady from New Orleans?" asked Davis with a twinkle in his eye that said he was having lascivious thoughts about Creed and Charlotte.

"Yes, sir," said Creed, tolerating Davis's insinuation.

"What about that fellow McGrath?" asked Davis. "Will he be eating with us, too?"

"No, sir," said Creed. "He'll be too busy with his gambling pools to eat this afternoon."

"Good," said Davis. "I didn't want nothing spoiling my appetite. I don't like him, you know. McGrath, I mean."

"Yes, sir, I know."

"You don't like him either, do you, Slate?"

"No, sir, I don't."

"Good," said Davis. He slapped Creed on the back and said, "Now why don't you show me where they serve that hotel whiskey? I'm starting to feel my rheumatiz pretty bad."

44

No one made an actual count, but it was estimated that close to five thousand people attended the Mammoth Cave Hotel Horse Racing Meet on its first day of races, as folks from several parts of the country managed to make it to Edmondson County in time for the first heat. The hotel's guests were primarily from big cities as far away as Chicago, St. Louis, New Orleans, Cincinnati, and Cleveland. Some gamblers who weren't staying at the hotel were said to have come all the way from New York and Philadelphia. Horse owners and breeders from Virginia, Missouri, Ohio, Indiana, Tennessee, and every part of Kentucky were also in attendance. The spectators ranged from the wealthy, such as Potter Palmer, to the poor, such as some of the local farmers and several drifters who were passing through the area.

Even with so many people in and about the hotel, the crowd was very well behaved. This was mostly due to Sheriff Morris, who wisely ordered every constable in the county to do his duty at the meet whether he approved of gambling or not. Besides the district lawmen, Morris deputized several dozen other men to help him police the event. He had over a hundred men wearing badges and enforcing the laws of Kentucky and Edmondson County that day. Not many dared to get out of line, and those few who did were quickly arrested and removed from the presence of law-abiding citizens.

"I'm greatly impressed, Slate," said Charlotte as they sat on the balcony outside their rooms waiting for the first race to be run. "I can't believe you did all this in such a short time. It's truly remarkable."

"I had a lot of help," said Creed. Then he looked at the Houchins, who were sitting on the other side of him, and said, "And I had a lot of inspiration, too."

223

The trumpeter from the hotel band sounded the call to post, and everyone stood to watch the horses for the first race approach the starting line, which was located just below Creed's spot on the balcony. Since the meet had been his idea, he was given the honor of being the starter. He moved to the railing, drew his Colt's, aimed it skyward, then waited for the horses to be lined up across the track behind the white chalk line. As soon as they were all close to it, he pulled the trigger and the race was on.

A huge hurrah went up from the crowd, then everyone settled back for a second breath before cheering for their favorite horse to win the opening heat. Those spectators who had taken up observation posts in the track infield ran to the far side of the course to watch the horses on the backstretch, and as soon as the racers sped past them, the same people hurried back to where they had started, because the starting line was also the finishing line. As the horses came around the last turn and entered the final stretch, every single witness to the event was on his or her feet, trying to scream home a winner, and when the lead horse crossed the finish line, the cheering ceased suddenly as winning bettors congratulated themselves and their fellow winners, and losing bettors fell silent or began complaining about their luck or the horse's poor showing or the jockey's ineptitude.

"Gosh, that was exciting!" said Edie Houchin as she returned to her seat.

"It was only the first race, Ma," said Davis. "Wait till the next one, when Scott will be riding Pride."

"That's right, Mrs. Houchin," said Charlotte. "We'll all be excited during the next race. Won't we, Slate?"

"No doubt about that," said Creed.

"I just hope Scott knows what he's doing," said Edie.

"Don't you worry about our boy, Ma," said Davis. "He can take care of himself."

"I've watched him work Pride these last few days, Mrs. Houchin," said Creed. "He's got real horse sense, Scott does. He knows how to make Pride run his best, and if I'm any judge of horseflesh, Pride won't let any horse get the best of him or Scott."

"I hope you're right," said Edie.

"He's right, Ma," said Davis. "Now hush up. The judge is going to announce the winner's name."

The head judge made the official announcement that the first race was won by a black stallion from Missouri named Bagatelle. The distant second and third place finishers were mares from up near Lexington. The judges paid off the winners, and preparations for the next race were begun.

Scott heard the call to post and started Pride toward the starting line along with the other eleven contestants in his heat. He had taken the time to accustom Pride to being around so many other horses at one time, but he hadn't prepared the horse for the presence of so many people and the noise they made. When Scott brought Pride onto the track, the stallion tried to bolt, but his master held him firmly, talking softly to Pride as he restrained the stallion with the reins.

"Never mind them now," said Scott, leaning forward and talking in the horse's ear. "They're just folks. You've seen people before. Now forget about them. We got us a race to run here. See them other horses? You got to beat them around this track. You know this track, Pride. We've been riding it four times a day since Tuesday. It's just a big circle, and all you have to do is run around it faster than those other horses. You can do that."

Scott stroked the horse's neck, and Pride seemed to calm down. Even so, the rider didn't relax his control of the animal. He knew that the stallion could bolt again at any second.

They moved up to the starting line.

"There's Scott on Pride!" shouted Clarenda from the balcony.

"Hey, Scott!" shouted John Wesley.

"Look at us up here, Scott!" shouted little Ben.

"Hush up, you brats!" shouted Davis at his children.

"Yes, hush," said Edie more evenly than her husband, "and sit back down."

They did as they were told.

Creed moved to the rail and drew his revolver. He waited until all the horses were close to the line. One jumped ahead and had to be turned around and brought back. As soon as it was, Creed pulled the trigger.

Once again the crowd gave out a roaring huzza as the horses sped off for the first turn. The Houchin children and their mother leaped to their feet and began cheering wildly for Scott and Pride. Charlotte stood up and took hold of Creed's arm, and

in tandem, as if being a few inches closer would give them
a much better view of the race, they pressed against the rail.
Only Davis remained seated until the horses came around the
final turn, then he rose to see Scott and Pride several lengths
ahead of the others as they entered the final stretch.

"Ride him, Scott!" shouted Davis.

"Come on, Scott!" shouted the Houchin children.

"Ride him, son!" shouted Edie.

Creed remembered his position and refrained from cheering.
He held tight to the rail, his knuckles turning white with
the strain.

Charlotte stood perfectly still, although she was breathing
heavily and her usually pallid skin was flushed with a rosiness
that suggested she was experiencing some sort of sensual pleasure
from watching the race. As Pride neared the finish line, her nails
dug into Creed's arm, and she sucked in a deep breath.

Creed felt a sharp pain in his arm and looked down to see
Charlotte's fingers digging into him. Then he glanced at her
face and saw the state she was in. He heard the air hissing into
her through her clenched teeth. In the next second, he knew—
from experience—that she would begin to shudder and let out
a low groan as her orgasm exploded from within her.

Charlotte saw Pride cross the finish line well ahead of the
pack, and her eyelids drooped over her now-blank eyes. Much to
Creed's surprise, she threw her arms around his waist, squeezed
him with incredible strength, and buried her face into his chest
to muffle the guttural sounds escaping her throat.

Sex being the benign contagion, Creed was instantly infected
with a desire for Charlotte. The fire flared in his loins, but before
he could give it a second thought, Charlotte went limp and started
to slip away from him. He grabbed her into his arms and held
her close.

The Houchins had been too busy jumping up and down,
yelling and screaming their joy over Scott's victory, to notice
Charlotte and Creed right away. One by one, they stopped their
celebrating to peer curiously at the couple. Davis envied Creed
and wished he could get his hands on that hot little Louisiana
gal. Edie wished her man were younger and in better physical
condition. Ben and Parizada turned their noses up at the adults
for hugging and kissing. John Wesley didn't know what to think.
And Clarenda was jealous of Charlotte. She didn't know why, but

she wished that she was the woman in Creed's arms, rubbing her body against his and making a fire.

Regaining control of herself, Charlotte glanced out of the corner of her eye to see the Houchins staring at them. Always a quick thinker on her feet, she took a deep breath, leaned back to look up at Creed's face, and said, "Slate, we won! I can't believe it! We won! Isn't it wonderful?"

Creed, realizing that they were center stage here, played along with her act. "Yes, we won! How about that, Davis?"

"Was there ever a doubt?" said Davis. "That's my boy on that horse!"

"Yes, I know," said Creed.

"Oh, will you look at me?" said Charlotte. "I'm so excited I forgot myself." She straightened up and adjusted her bonnet, even though it didn't need it. "I think I'd better go freshen up a bit before the next race. Please excuse me." Without waiting to be excused, she left.

Creed wanted to follow her, but he still had nine races to start. Damn! swore his hormones.

45

The remaining races came off as smoothly as the first two, although there wasn't as much interest by the locals after Pride had run. Creed started every race with his Colt's, having to reload it twice during the afternoon, it being his custom never to load all six chambers unless he was in the midst of a fight. When the day was finished, he put the gun back inside his waistband, not thinking anything about the fact that he only had four balls in it and that he might need that fifth shot before the night was over.

Creed took the Houchins to supper in the hotel dining hall, and they celebrated Scott's win that afternoon. Charlotte and Meg joined them late.

"Congratulations, Scott," said Charlotte. "That was a fine race you rode on Pride."

"Thank you, ma'am," said Scott, blushing.

"I hope you can repeat today's performance twice over tomorrow," said Charlotte.

"I hope I can, too," said Scott.

"Don't you worry none about Scott winning tomorrow, Miss Charlotte," said Davis. "He can do it. I know. Just you wait and see."

"I'm sure he can, Mr. Houchin," said Charlotte. She smiled and added, "This weather must agree with you, Mr. Houchin. Your color seems so much better this evening than it was this morning when you first arrived."

"I am feeling a darn sight better," said Davis. "Of course, winning a hundred dollars might have something to do with that."

"Fifty dollars, Mr. Houchin," said Charlotte. "Remember, half of Pride's winnings are mine."

"Yes, that's right," said Davis meekly. "I forgot." He frowned and looked down at his plate.

The rest of the family followed his example. They knew when they were being put in their place.

This didn't set well with Creed. "Could I have a word with you in private, Charlotte?" he said, taking her by the arm and practically lifting her from her chair.

"Why, of course, Slate," she said, rising awkwardly.

They stepped outside onto the veranda. The night was chilly, and Charlotte immediately felt uncomfortable in the crisp air. Not so Creed.

"What the hell are you doing, Charlotte?" he demanded.

"Whatever are you talking about, Sugar?"

"Did you have to remind the Houchins that they're beholden to you for Pride being in this meet?"

"Is that what I did?" she asked quite innocently.

"You know damn well that's what you did, Charlotte," said Creed. "Those are nice folks in there. They don't ask for much out of this world, and they're grateful for what little they've got. They may be poor, but they're still people who deserve to be treated with respect. And you had to go and remind them that you're rich and they aren't. What the hell's the matter with you, Charlotte? Do you like treating people like they're dirt?"

"Slate, I won't have you talking to me this way," said Charlotte. "I was only reminding him that we had a business arrangement. That's all."

"You didn't have to do it in front of his wife and children, did you?"

"All right, I'm sorry. Do you want me to go in there and tell the old man that I'm sorry that I embarrassed him in front of his family?"

"No, Charlotte, I don't. It's too late for that now."

"Then what do you want me to do?"

"I want you to go back in there and remember those people have feelings and that you have no right to walk on them."

"Is that all, Slate?"

"That's all." He turned and started down the veranda steps.

"Where are you going?" asked Charlotte.

"I need some time to myself," said Creed. "I'm going for a walk around the grounds."

"Let me get a wrap and I'll go with you."

"No. I said I needed some time to myself, and that means exactly what it sounds like, Charlotte. I want to be alone."

"All right, Slate. I'll leave you alone for now, but will I see you later in my room?"

"I don't know," said Creed. And with that, he was gone into the night.

Creed walked first around the racetrack. The infield was lit up by several campfires made by folks who didn't want to make the long drive home that night only to return on the morrow for the final races. The grounds south of the hotel were also glowing with campfires. As he moved along the track, Creed heard voices coming from this camp first, then the next. Everyone was reliving the excitement of the day. This was good, he thought. He'd brought some joy to a lot of people, and it made him feel good about himself. He sighed and headed around the hotel to the stables.

Four men sat around a fire just outside the corral. One of them sat with his back to the flames; he was using the light to read a book. The other three sat facing the fire and were talking. They fell silent when Creed approached them.

"Evening, boys," said Creed. He noted that they were all near his age, give or take a few years on one side or the other.

"Evening," said one.

"Cold out tonight," said Creed. "Mind if I warm myself at your fire?"

"No, go right ahead," said the same fellow.

"You boys from around here?" asked Creed, just trying to be friendly as he warmed his hands over the fire.

"No," said the same man.

The fellow who had been reading closed his book and turned around to see who had joined them. He peered hard at Creed and said, "Aren't you the starter?"

"Yes, I am," said Creed. "My name is Slate Creed."

"Alex James," said the reader. He came to his feet and offered to shake hands.

"Nice to meet you," said Creed, shaking hands with James.

"These ornery cusses are Jim White, George and Oll Shepherd," said James. "We came over here from Logan County to see the races you're putting on here."

Creed shook hands with each one of the men as they stood up, then said, "Seems I've heard a couple of your names before. White and Shepherd. Any of you ever ride with Morgan during the war?"

"We fought for the South," said James, "but none of us rode with Morgan that I know of. Leastways, not me. How about you boys? Any of you ride with Morgan at any time?"

"Not me," said White. "Of course, you might have heard my name before. It's fairly common."

"Well, I didn't want to say that," said Creed with an apologetic smile.

"I take it you rode with Morgan," said George Shepherd.

"That's right, I did."

"But I heard you were from Texas," said George. "Is that right?"

"I surely am a Texan," said Creed, "but after Shiloh, I fell in with Morgan's regiment."

"You were at Shiloh?" queried James. "I heard that was one hell of a fight. Is that so?"

"It was," said Creed, "from what little I saw of it. My outfit didn't get into it until the second day, and then we weren't more than a rearguard action."

"What brings you up to this country?" asked Shepherd.

"Same as you," said Creed. "The races."

"Ain't you the one behind all this with that gambler?" asked George. "What's his name?"

"McGrath," spat James. "Son of a bitch took my money today."

"I take it you didn't win today," said Creed.

"You got that right," said James.

"Don't pay no attention to him, Mr. Creed," said White. "He's just sore because he didn't win as much as he'd bragged he would while we was riding over here from Russellville."

"Russellville?" queried Creed. He stared at White for a second, then said, "Now I know where I heard your names before."

White and George Shepherd exchange glances, then reached for their guns. Creed drew first and had his cocked at White's nose before either of them could clear leather.

"Hold on, boys," said Creed. "I'm from Texas, and I can shoot you dead in the wink of an eye—if I have to. Just let those irons stay where they are and let's talk this out."

"I'd talk if I were you, Jim," said James casually as he sat down again. "Looks to me that he could kill you like he said. You better stay out of it, too, Oll. Looks like he could kill you, too, if he had a mind to."

Oll Shepherd sat down beside James and watched the scene unfold.

"All right, let's talk," said White, raising his hands.

Shepherd did the same.

"You two boys stole a couple of horses from around here a few years back," said Creed.

"I didn't steal them," said Shepherd.

"I know you didn't take them from the Houchins, George Shepherd," said Creed, "but you did, Jim White. You and another fellow who was killed that night."

"So what if I did steal a couple of horses?" said White defiantly. "What's it to you, Mr. Creed?"

Creed smiled and said, "Look, I'm not the law, and all that's in the past as far as I'm concerned. I was just trying to tell you where I'd heard your names before. I was told how you stole those horses on Christmas Eve a couple years ago. That's all. I don't care that you did it, because the owners got them back, thanks to you, George."

"Thanks to me?" queried Shepherd. "How's that?"

"You shot your mouth off to a grocer boy over in Russellville," said Creed. "You remember the grocer boy, don't you, George?"

"Sure, I do," said Shepherd. "What's he got to do with those horses Jim stole?"

"They were his horses," said Creed.

"Well, I'll be damned!" said Shepherd, shaking his head with disbelief.

"Do you know what's funnier than that, George?" asked Creed.

"No, what?"

"That colt you boys sold to the cattleman in St. Louis?"

"Yeah, what about him?" asked White.

"He was the winner of the second race today," said Creed.

"Well, I'll be damned again!" said Shepherd, shaking his head again.

"And the jockey was the grocer boy from Russellville," said Creed. "Now what do you think about that?"

"I think I'm going to bet on him tomorrow," said Shepherd. "What was his name? The horse, I mean."

"Pride," said Creed, replacing his Colt's. "Now if you boys will pardon me, I'll be moving along. I've had a long day, and it's not over yet."

"You ain't going to tell the law about us stealing those horses, are you, Mr. Creed?" asked White.

"I don't see any stolen horses around here," said Creed. "How about you, Mr. James?"

"Can't say that I do," said James. "It's been nice chatting with you, Mr. Creed."

Creed returned to the hotel to look for George Devol and Canada Bill Jones. He found them in their room.

"Have you been able to learn anything yet about McGrath's plans?" asked Creed.

"Nothing," said Devol.

"He's running as clean a pool game as I've ever seen," said Jones. "I'm not sure that I believe it myself, but that's what's happened so far, Creed."

"I know he's got to be up to something," said Creed.

"He's making a lot of dough in this deal," said Devol. "Maybe he doesn't want to muck it up by cheating."

"He cheated Potter Palmer on the *Princess*, didn't he?" said Creed. "What makes you think he's doing any different now?"

"We haven't caught him at anything," said Devol, "and neither have the laws. He's accounted for every penny he's taken in, and he's paid off every bet so far. Of course, the big betting won't come until tomorrow."

"Maybe that's it," said Creed. "Maybe he's waiting for the big betting tomorrow on the final race."

"Then what?" asked Jones. "Percy's no thief. He won't steal the money like a common highwayman."

"Maybe McGrath won't do it himself," said Creed, "but that's not to say that he hasn't hired somebody else to do it for him."

"What are you talking about?" asked Devol.

"Just suppose McGrath has accomplices like he did on the *Princess*," said Creed. "And suppose those accomplices steal the pool money tomorrow instead of McGrath, and they divide it with McGrath at some later time and place."

"But who would these accomplices be?" asked Jones.

"Yes, Creed," said Devol. "Who would they be?"

"They could be anybody who's handy with a gun," said Creed, and suddenly, a thought struck him.

46

When Creed and Brother Locke made their peace the day before, the clergyman was invited to hold his church services on the hotel grounds that Sunday. Realizing that he might never get another chance to preach to so many people and save so many souls all at one time, Locke jumped at the opportunity.

The second day of the horse racing meet dawned as beautifully as the one before. The air was soon filled with the smells of breakfast and the sounds of early morning chores. By mid-morning, the meals and the work were finished.

Brother Locke took his place on the balcony outside Creed's room, and his congregation went about the hotel grounds in pairs, inviting everyone to join them on the horse track to hear their minister speak in the name of the Lord. As folks began to gather beneath the upper veranda, Locke led them in singing some of the well-known hymns of the day. When he saw the last of his church members signal him that every one of them had done their duty and was present in the audience, the preacher began his sermon. He spoke of brotherly love, of forgiveness, and of every Christian's obligation to bring joy and happiness to the world. He closed by thanking everyone for coming to hear the Word, then he wished them good luck at the races.

After the church service, Creed met with Sheriff Morris in Proctor's office and told him about meeting up with Alex James, Jim White, George and Oll Shepherd the night before. Although he wasn't certain that they were the ones that might be in cahoots with McGrath, he cautioned the sheriff to watch out for them, or men like them, whenever they came near the dining hall.

"I know for a fact that White and George Shepherd were guerrillas during the war," said Creed. "That makes them thoroughly dangerous men, Sheriff. If they're here, there's no telling how many more like them are here."

234

"I know what you mean, Creed," said Morris. "I'll put extra men in the dining hall, and I'll stay so close to McGrath that he'll think I'm part of his hide."

"I don't think you'll have much to worry about until we get ready to run the championship race this afternoon," said Creed. "The gamblers will be closing down their pools a few minutes before the race is to begin, and everybody else will be watching the race. It's my guess that they'll strike then, steal the money, and make their escape while everybody is celebrating the winner of the race."

"My thoughts exactly," said Morris. "I'll be on special guard then."

"I wish I could be in the dining hall with you," said Creed, "but I've got to start the race."

"I know," said Morris. "I wouldn't mind having you and those Colt's of yours on my side for a change."

Creed's expression turned quizzical as he said, "What's that supposed to mean?"

Morris laughed, patted Creed on the shoulder, and said, "I'll tell you about it when this is all over."

Creed left the manager's office and went in search of Charlotte. He found her in her room, putting on her bonnet.

"I'll be ready for luncheon in a moment," she said when Creed entered the room.

"Don't hurry," said Creed. "I need to talk to you before we go down to eat."

"Oh? What about? Not the Houchins again. I was nice to them last night after you left."

"No, it's not that," said Creed. "It's McGrath."

"Percy? What about him? I've hardly seen him since we arrived here."

"I haven't seen much of him either," said Creed. "Not that I want to see him all that much, but I am worried that he's up to something here."

"He promised me he wouldn't do a thing to cheat a single bettor," said Charlotte.

"I'm not worried about him cheating," said Creed. "I've had some friends keeping an eye on him all the time, and they tell me that he hasn't done anything suspicious at all."

"Then what's troubling you, Sugar?"

"I think he's planning a robbery," said Creed.

"A robbery? Percy?" She burst into a laugh, but it seemed forced to Creed. "You must be joking, Slate. Percy McGrath is no thief."

"That's what everybody else tells me, Charlotte, and the more I hear it, the more convinced I am that he's planning to steal the pools this afternoon. There could be as much as ten or twelve thousand dollars in them for the final race, and that's not to mention how much profit he's taken in so far. Do you know how he did yesterday?"

"I believe we cleared about three thousand," said Charlotte, "but that was penny-ante stuff compared to what we'll take in today. Ten or twelve thousand? From the looks of this crowd, I'd say it should be more like twenty to twenty-five thousand."

"All the more reason for McGrath to steal it," said Creed. "If the prize is big enough, most people will risk anything to get it. Twenty to twenty-five thousand dollars should be enough loot for him to risk a robbery in front of everybody in the county."

"Just how do you think he's going to pull off this robbery?" asked Charlotte cautiously.

"I think he's hired some men to do it for him," said Creed.

Charlotte broke into forced laughter again and said, "That's absolutely preposterous, Slate. Where would he find men like that?"

"In just about any fair-sized town," said Creed. "There are thousands of men in this country who will do anything for money because they can't find decent work anywhere. I could probably line up twenty or thirty men within an hour who would ride with me and raid a Yankee supply wagon or something. It's not hard, Charlotte, to find honest men who are hungry enough to break the law for a little something to eat."

"All right, so it's possible that he could have hired some men to rob the pools for him. What do you expect me to do about it, Sugar?"

"I want you to go to him and tell him that we're wise to him and, if anybody tries to rob the pools, I will find him and shoot him dead in the wink of an eye."

Charlotte saw the chill of death in Creed's face and said, "I believe you would, Sugar." She swallowed hard and said, "All right, I'll tell him."

47

Charlotte sat down in her seat on the balcony. The first heat of the afternoon was soon to be run.

The Houchins sat down in their seats, still as fidgety as if they were all small children on Christmas morning waiting to open their presents.

Creed came out on the balcony, greeted the Houchins with a nod, then sat down. He leaned sideways toward Charlotte and whispered out of the corner of his mouth, "Did you tell him?"

"Yes, I did," said Charlotte in a low voice, while keeping her eyes trained on the track below them.

"And what did he say?"

Still refusing to look at Creed, Charlotte replied, "He swore that he hadn't hired anybody to rob the pools. In fact, he said that he was going to close down early and turn the money over to Sheriff Morris so he could come out on the balcony and watch the championship race."

"That only makes sense," said Creed. "If I was him and I'd hired a gang to rob the pools, I wouldn't want to be there either when they did it."

The band trumpeter blew the call to post.

"The horses are coming," said Clarenda excitedly as she leaned over the rail for a better look at the approaching racers.

"Can you see Scott yet?" asked Edie.

"Not yet, Ma," said Clarenda.

"Sit down, Clarenda!" snapped Davis. "You're blocking everybody's view."

Clarenda sat down.

Creed stood up. Because he wanted to be prepared for any kind of trouble that might come his way that day, he was carrying both of his revolvers. He drew one of them in preparation for starting the race.

Pride was behaving better today, making Scott's job easier. Rider and horse moved steadily toward the starting point with the other horses and jockeys. They came to the line and halted. Scott eased up on the reins as he anticipated the sound of Creed's starting shot. BANG! it came, and Scott kicked Pride into motion. The stallion leaped to the fore, then took the inside as they moved into the first turn.

The crowd let out its initial roar with the start of the race as it had eleven times the day before. But today the dissonance didn't die down and then build up again midway through the heat. Today, the cacophony of five thousand voices increased in a crescendo as the horses circled the track. When the final turn was made, a shrill, frantic cry rose up from the throng as the horses bore down on the finish line. Everyone tried to root home his favorite, but there could be but one winner. And his name was Pride. By one length.

The Houchins and Charlotte acted the same as they had the day before when Scott was racing. Davis and his family stood at the rail cheering as loudly as they could, while Charlotte held onto Creed's arm and took her pleasure as she watched her horse win the race.

"He won!" screamed Clarenda. "He won! He won!" She and John Wesley hugged and danced together, as did Ben and Parizada. Edie and Davis restrained their exuberance to a hug and laughter.

"That should raise your stud fees a mite, Davis," said Creed, slapping the old man on the back.

"I don't know about raising mine," said Davis with a mischievous grin, "but it ought to put Pride's in the neighborhood of a hundred dollars a leap."

"Oh, Pa!" said Edie, blushing at her husband's ribald joke and gently slapping him on the arm.

Creed could only laugh as he shared the family's joy. Their horse was in the championship race. Now to see who he would be running against.

Bagatelle, the black stallion from Missouri that had won the first heat the day before, won the second race with ease, being a full four lengths ahead at the finish. All ten of the other horses in his heat had run in the last four races the first day, when the track was pretty well chewed up. Running in the softer soil had worn them down a bit more than Bagatelle.

A two-year-old colt named Buttonhook and sired by the great Lexington won the third heat by a nose over two other sons of the champion Thoroughbred. Buttonhook and his half brothers, Eager and Dixie Boy, had finished one, two, and three in the third race the day before. Eager had finished first on Saturday, Dixie Boy had come in second, with Buttonhook a close third.

Davis figured Bagatelle and Lexington's trio of get were the horses that Pride would have to beat. The other qualifiers from Bagatelle's race and the two from Pride's heat had won slow races the day before, and for that reason, Davis thought them to be little competition. He sent John Wesley down to the stables to relay this information to Scott.

Creed accompanied John Wesley because he wanted to congratulate Scott on winning his heat and to make certain that John Wesley got his father's words to Scott straight. As soon as he was satisfied that John Wesley had it right, he said his piece to Scott and headed off toward Proctor's office to confer with Sheriff Morris.

"Those four boys you told me about came in here and made their bets with McGrath," said Morris. "All at the same time. I didn't hear everything that was said, but I think he told them they were being foolish to bet on Pride, and then one of them told him he was the fool. He just laughed at them then, and they walked away. Then McGrath wrote something on a piece of paper and took it over to one of his men. The man read the note, then nodded at McGrath. He came back to his place and sat down and started taking bets again. I tried to keep my eye on McGrath and the other fellow as well, but when things got real busy, I lost track of the other fellow and didn't see him leave the hall. When I asked about him, I was told he went to the outhouse. I sent a man to check, and that was where he went. He saw the gambler come out of the outhouse, but one of those boys from Russellville went in after him. My man searched him when he came out, but he didn't find any note on him."

"He probably used it to wipe himself," said Creed dryly.

Morris laughed and said, "That's what I figure, too, but I ain't about to have one of my boys climb down in that hole and look for the note."

Creed laughed and said, "No, I don't think you could force anyone at gunpoint to go looking for it. I know you'd have to shoot *me* in the foot first."

"Well, I guess that puts us back where we were in the first place," said Morris.

"No, I don't think so. I think McGrath took my warning seriously and called it off."

"Warning?"

"Yes, I sent him word that if anyone tried robbing the pools that I would shoot him dead in the wink of an eye."

Morris studied Creed and said, "I believe you would, too." He checked his watch for the time and said, "Three-thirty. I suppose you'd better get back upstairs."

Creed agreed and left.

48

This was it, the moment everyone had been eagerly awaiting, the championship race. The sun shone brightly in the sky, and there was no wind. The temperature outside Mammoth Cave was a very mild sixty degrees.

The trumpeter sounded the call to post, and the horses and jockeys started their parade to the starting line as their supporters cheered them and wished them well.

Creed stood to take his position as starter. He scanned the length of the balcony, looking for McGrath, and finally saw the gambler at the far end. Then he searched the crowd in the infield, hoping he would see Alex James and his three friends from Russellville. He was more than delighted to find them standing at the edge of the track, jostling each other and talking animatedly. These were not men bent on robbing anyone, thought Creed, and he relaxed for the first time in days.

Edie and Clarenda Houchin bowed their heads, folded their hands in front of their faces, and prayed to God to let Scott and Pride win the race. John Wesley, Ben, and little Parizada crossed their fingers, closed their eyes, and also prayed, although they weren't certain to whom they were praying. Davis Houchin took a big snort on his jug and muttered a wish for Scott and Pride to be successful.

Charlotte rose from her chair and stepped up beside Creed. She was already breathing heavily, and her color was becoming quite vivid. She took Creed's arm and held on as if her life depended on it.

Creed drew the Colt's that he had used to start the previous races of the day. The gun had two shots left in it. He waited for the horses to reach the starting line, and as soon as the last one was in place, he raised the pistol over his head and squeezed off a round.

The crowd roared its approval as all nine horses leaped ahead at the same time, trying to take the lead into the first turn. Pride and Bagatelle, being the only two horses to win their heats the day before as well as today, were positioned eighth and ninth, respectively, from the inside of the track. Beside them were two of Lexington's get, Eager and Buttonhook. Lexington's third son, Dixie Boy, had the second spot, and he was the first to break away from the pack and take a lead into the first turn.

As the racers moved into the backstretch, Dixie Boy was still in front by a length over Eager and Buttonhook. Pride and Bagatelle were side by side in fourth, and the other four horses were already losing ground and fading fast. By the time the final turn was reached, Eager had replaced Dixie Boy in the lead, and Pride was a clear-cut fourth on the tails of Buttonhook and Dixie Boy. Bagatelle had eased back a length behind Pride, and his jockey seemed content to remain there.

The crowd was delirious as the horses finished the last turn and entered the final stretch. Eager held the inside, and Buttonhook and Dixie Boy moved toward the outside, effectively blocking Pride's path. Bagatelle moved to the inside and tried to pass Pride, Dixie Boy, and Buttonhook.

"Give me room!" shouted Scott at the jockeys aboard Dixie Boy and Buttonhook. "Give me room!" He urged Pride to force his way between the two Thoroughbreds, and the jockeys did give Scott the space that he wanted. "Go, Pride!" shouted Scott.

The Houchin stallion burst ahead of Dixie Boy and Buttonhook to move up beside Eager. Bagatelle also moved ahead of Eager's half brothers but was still behind Pride and Eager with three hundred yards to go.

Scott moved Pride to the outside to ground that wasn't so torn up from the fourteen previous races. Eager moved with him, allowing Bagatelle to make his move for the lead. Dixie Boy and Buttonhook moved into the lanes vacated by Pride and Eager, and they started to gain on the leaders. Two hundred yards to go.

As Pride eased outside, he began to take the lead away from Eager. Bagatelle continued to press on the inside, and Dixie Boy and Buttonhook were side by side and only a half-length behind their half brother. One hundred yards to go.

Pride was the clear-cut leader by a full length over Bagatelle on the inside, a length and a half over Eager, and two lengths over Dixie Boy and Buttonhook. Fifty yards to go.

The sun was still shining brightly. It was a beautiful day, especially for late January in Kentucky. It was a day everyone who attended the Mammoth Cave Hotel Horse Racing Meet would remember forever. Davis Houchin's horse, Pride, ridden by Scott Houchin, looked like a sure winner with twenty-five yards to go to the finish line.

Suddenly, Pride and Eager broke stride. But not Bagatelle, Dixie Boy, or Buttonhook; they continued to race, all three passing the leaders. Pride stumbled but didn't fall until Eager bumped him from the rear. Both horses went down in a heap amid the screams and cries of the shocked spectators. Scott was thrown clear of Pride, but Eager's jockey fell beneath his mount.

Creed was the first person to realize what had just happened before their eyes. "My God!" he exclaimed. He wrenched away Charlotte's hand from his arm and climbed over the rail down to the lower veranda. He forced his way through the crowd that was now pouring from the porch onto the track. "Get back!" he yelled as loud as he could as he swam through the flood of bodies. "Get back!" He found his way to Scott.

Everything was in turmoil. People rushed forth to get a better look, but Sheriff Morris's deputies and the county constables headed them off. The last four horses in the race had to pull up to keep from running into the crowd. Bagatelle crossed the finish line a head in front of Buttonhook who was only a head in front of Dixie Boy.

"Get back!" screamed Creed. He knelt down beside Scott to check on the lad's condition. "Get back!"

Scott was breathing, but he was unconscious.

Creed lifted his head and heard the grind of broken bones. "Damn!" he swore aloud. He lowered Scott's head, thinking the boy had a broken neck.

"Out of my way!" shouted an unfamiliar voice. "Out of my way! Let me through!" A middle-aged gentleman knelt down beside Creed. "Out of my way, friend!"

"What's the use?" said Creed sadly. "His neck is broken."

"Are you a doctor?" asked the man.

"No."

"Well, I am. Dr. J. C. Gatewood, sir. I'll examine this boy now, if you don't mind."

Creed edged aside but didn't get up.

Dr. Gatewood checked Scott's eyes, then opened the victim's coat and shirt. "There! You see?" He pointed at a growing discoloration in the area of Scott's clavicle. "He's got a broken collarbone." He moved Scott's right arm, and the same crunching sound that Creed had heard before came forth. "Broken collarbone. Not neck."

Creed heaved a sigh of relief, ran his right hand over his scalp, knocking his hat off. He picked up the felt topper and held it in his hand as he watched Gatewood continue to examine Scott.

The youth was showing signs of coming around. He groaned, then his eyes fluttered open. "Oh, God!" cried Scott, reaching for his collarbone.

"Lay still, son," said Gatewood gently. "You've had a bad fall, but you'll be all right."

Scott scrambled to think, then he remembered. "Pride!" he rasped. "What happened to Pride?"

"He's right over there, Scott," said Creed.

Scott tried to move to look, but the pain in his shoulder stopped him. "Is he all right, Mr. Creed?"

"I don't know yet," said Creed. "He's up on his feet, but that's all I can tell from here."

"Do you hurt anywhere else besides your collarbone?" asked Dr. Gatewood.

"My head hurts a little," said Scott, "but that's all."

Gatewood felt around Scott's cranium and came across a lump just above the hairline. "You've got a knot growing there, son," he said, "but I don't think it's too much to worry about. You'll be all right. Now I'd better check on the other rider." He stood up and went to Eager's jockey.

Creed stayed with Scott. "What happened, Scott?" he asked.

"I don't know for sure, Mr. Creed," said Scott, wincing with pain. "We were almost to the finish line when the sunlight hit me in the eyes."

"Sunlight?" queried Creed.

"I guess that's what it was," said Scott. "A bright light suddenly hit me and Pride, and he pulled up on me."

"The other fellow is dying," said Dr. Gatewood to Creed when he returned to look at Scott again. "He's mumbling something about a light in his eyes." He knelt down to Scott. "But you'll be all right, son. Can you feel all your parts now?"

"Yes, sir," said Scott, wincing with each breath. "I don't seem to hurt anywhere else except my shoulder and my head. What about my horse? Is he all right?"

"I'll take a closer look at him," said Creed. He stood up and went over to Pride who was being held by Alex James. "How is he?" he asked James.

"I don't think he's broke anything," said James. "But the way he's favoring his right front leg, I'd say he's come up lame for sure. He won't be racing again, that's for sure."

Creed bent over and felt the stallion's fetlock. Pride didn't like the idea; he shied away. "Easy, boy," said Creed. "I'm not going to hurt you. Easy, Pride." The horse allowed Creed to touch him gently until the man felt the broken bone. "You're right," said Creed, lying, as he straightened up. "He's gone lame all right." He went back to tell Scott the bad news.

"How is he?" asked Scott.

Creed was a man of strong character and will, but he wasn't strong enough to tell an injured boy that his horse had a broken leg and would have to be destroyed. "I'm afraid he's pulled up lame, Scott," said Creed, refusing to look Scott straight in the eyes and keeping up the lie for the moment.

"He didn't break anything, did he?"

"Not that I can tell," said Creed, still lying. "I think he'll be all right in time." Then looking young Houchin in the eyes, he added, "But he won't be doing any more racing, Scott."

The lad sensed that Creed was lying, but he wanted to believe the Texan. He had to believe him for now. "I don't care about that," he said, "just as long as Pride's going to be all right."

Changing the subject, Creed asked, "Scott, what did you mean when you said the sunlight hit you in the eyes?"

"I don't know, Mr. Creed. It was this bright light coming from up ahead somewheres. It hit me and Pride, and that's when he pulled up on me."

A shadow fell over them.

"Is the boy all right?"

Creed looked up to see Brother Locke standing over them. When he heard the preacher's voice, Creed was certain that the minister's next words would be something to the effect that he had warned him that God didn't approve of gambling and horse racing and that the accident was God's punishment. He would head off the parson.

"I don't want to hear any of your sermons now, Brother Locke," said Creed.

"I haven't got any sermons for you, Mr. Creed," said Locke softly. His entire aspect spoke of the empathy that he was feeling for Creed and Scott. "The hand of God isn't in this, Mr. Creed. This is the work of the Devil."

49

Brother Locke had no idea how right he was. Creed did. The
Devil, you say? Yes, the Devil incarnate. Only Creed knew his
name was McGrath.

Creed stood and looked up at the sky. The sun was to the
southwest and below the tops of the trees. At least, it appeared to
be from where he was standing. Scanning the entire area around
him, he quickly noted that the sun was still shining on the upper
veranda of the hotel, especially at the far north end, the spot
where McGrath had been watching the races. He couldn't see
McGrath up there now.

Edie Houchin forced her way through the crowd to Creed.
"Is Scott all right?" she asked anxiously. She didn't wait for an
answer, going to her son and kneeling down beside him.

The Houchin children found their way through the throng to
be with their brother and mother.

"Is he all right, Ma?" asked Clarenda. She knelt down beside
Edie, and the others gathered around them.

Creed didn't stick around to listen to their conversation. He
headed for the hotel dining room to look for McGrath. At the
veranda steps, he met Davis Houchin.

"Scott's got a broken collarbone," said Creed, answering
the question on the old man's face. He pulled the Colt's
with one shot left in it from his waistband and handed it
butt-first to Davis. "Here. You'll need this for Pride, but
don't tell Scott just yet. I told him the horse had only gone
lame."

Davis looked down at the revolver in his hand. His eyes were
watering with pain and disbelief. He looked up at Creed again,
another question in his face. "Why?" he muttered.

Creed had no answer for him. He simply shook his head, then
went into the hotel.

If Pride had won the race, Creed would have had a tough time making his way through the bettors who had wagered on the local favorite. But he had no such difficulty. Bagatelle had won, and very few gamblers had bet on the Missouri stallion.

As he entered the dining hall, Creed saw McGrath at his table paying off the winners. Sheriff Morris was still there with the gambler, and Charlotte had come down to join them. Creed stalked toward the table, but Canada Bill Jones intercepted him.

"Before you go over there," said Jones, "I think you should know that McGrath had a shill place a bet for him. He put five thousand on Bagatelle to win."

Creed didn't quite understand at first, then it sank into his feverish brain what Jones was saying. "Thank you, Mr. Jones," he said softly. "Now, if you'll excuse me, I have business to attend to." He stepped past Jones to McGrath's table.

"Is the boy all right?" asked Charlotte.

"He's got a broken collarbone," said Creed without looking at her, "and he's got a nasty bump on his head. He'll be all right, though."

"What about Pride?" asked Charlotte.

"His leg is broken," said Creed, finally looking at her.

"That's too bad," said Charlotte. Her eyes were lowered, but there was anger in her face.

Creed opened his coat and drew the remaining Colt's. He cocked the hammer and took aim at McGrath.

"Stand back, Charlotte," said Creed evenly. "I'm going to shoot a snake."

The click of the Colt's gun hammer drew Charlotte's eyes to the Colt's. They widened with fright as she said, "Slate, what are you doing?"

"Creed, what's the meaning of this?" demanded McGrath, staring bug-eyed at the revolver's muzzle.

"Mr. Creed, what are you doing?" asked Sheriff Morris.

"He's got a gun!" shouted someone behind Creed.

Several people took cover, while others held their ground as they looked on.

"You fixed the race, McGrath," said Creed.

"No, I didn't," said the gambler.

"How could he fix the race?" asked Charlotte.

"Sheriff, Scott Houchin told me a light hit him and Pride in the eyes just before the horse pulled up. The other jockey who's dying right this minute said something of the same kind. He said it was like sunlight. You were in the Army, Sheriff. Did your outfit ever use mirrors to send signals?"

"Why, yes, we did," said Morris.

"Well, that's what McGrath did," said Creed. "He flashed sunlight off a mirror into the horse's eyes and caused him to pull up. That's how you fixed the race, McGrath. From the looks of things in here, not too many folks bet on Bagatelle to win, did they? No, almost everybody bet on Pride to win. You needed any other horse to win the race, and when Pride had it won, you flashed sunlight in his eyes and made him pull up lame. Isn't that it, McGrath?"

"You're crazy, Creed," said McGrath.

"Am I, McGrath? Sheriff, why don't you go round up those other jockeys and we'll ask them if they saw any light being flashed from the end of the balcony?"

"Good idea," said Morris. He looked around the room and saw the man that he wanted. "Jethro, go outside and get those other jockeys in here. Hurry up now."

Otter hurried outside.

"In the meantime, Sheriff," said Creed, "why don't you search McGrath and see if you can find a mirror or some other shiny object on him?"

"Another good idea," said Morris. "Get up, McGrath."

The gambler stood up slowly, saying, "So I made a little money because Bagatelle won and Pride didn't. So what?"

"A little money, McGrath?" queried Creed. "How much did you make off the bet your shill made for you?"

Charlotte spun and faced McGrath. "You had a shill place a bet for you, Percy?" she asked.

McGrath's accusing look said that she already knew the answer to her seemingly innocent and surprised question. "Shut up, you nigger bitch!" growled the gambler.

Morris began to search McGrath's coat pockets, but he made the mistake of placing himself between Creed and McGrath.

The gambler took advantage of the sheriff's error. He pushed Morris away from him toward Creed. As the sheriff stumbled backward toward the Texan, McGrath drew his Smith & Wesson .32 and fired at Creed, who stepped aside to avoid a collision.

It helped that the Texan did move. The ball missed him and hit a bystander instead. In the next instant, McGrath grabbed Charlotte with his free hand and pulled her in front of him as a shield. She screamed with fright.

Everyone else in the dining hall scattered, looking for cover from the gunfire.

Creed ducked down behind a table as McGrath fired at him again and missed again as the bullet nicked the corner of the table. The Texan wanted to shoot back but held his fire out of fear of hitting Charlotte. He tipped the table over in front of him and moved closer to it.

"Don't shoot me!" screamed Charlotte. "Don't shoot me!"

"Shut up, bitch!" shouted McGrath in her ear. "This is all your doing, anyway! You hear that, Creed? She planned this whole thing. She set up the deal with Captain Ritter." McGrath laughed. "Hell, she owns part of his boat." McGrath laughed again, then said, "But you couldn't take the hint, Creed. You had to come up here and get in the way again. You dumb ass."

"Don't listen to him, Slate," cried Charlotte. "He's lying. This is his doing."

"I told you to shut up, you bitch!" snapped McGrath. He jerked her against him, forcing the wind from her lungs.

"Let her go, McGrath!" shouted Creed. "Let her go and face me like a man!"

"Do I look crazy, Creed?" asked McGrath. "Face you in a fair fight? Never!" He started backing away, taking Charlotte with him. "Come on, bitch. We're getting out of here."

"Don't let him take me, Slate!" pleaded Charlotte breathlessly as McGrath forced her toward the exit to the lobby.

"McGrath, I'm ordering you to release that woman," said Morris, "in the name of the law."

"Save your breath, Sheriff!" said McGrath. He pulled Charlotte into the lobby with him. He saw Mat, the cave guide, and an idea struck him. "You, nigger! Come here."

"Me, sir?" queried Mat.

"Yes, you, nigger!" snapped McGrath, waving his gun at the guide. "Come here, and be quick about it."

Mat obeyed.

"Walk ahead of us," said McGrath.

"Ahead of you, sir?"

"That's right, you stupid nigger!" snapped McGrath. "Head for that door over there." The gambler pointed toward the door that led outside to the stables. He and Charlotte followed Mat through the door. "Get us some horses, nigger."

"Horses, sir?" queried Mat.

"Yes, for all three of us," said McGrath.

Creed followed McGrath at a distance. He went through the lobby and saw McGrath drag Charlotte outside. He edged his way over to the door and peeked out to see McGrath, Charlotte, and the cave guide heading toward the stable.

Some men saw McGrath forcing Charlotte to go with him, and they thought to stop him until he waved his gun at them and warned them to stand aside.

Mat brought horses for them. McGrath put the muzzle of his pistol up to Mat's nose and said, "I need to get away from here as fast as possible, nigger. I want you to lead me out of here."

"Yes, sir," said Mat, scared out of his wits.

"Get up on that horse, Charlotte," said McGrath. "You get on that one, nigger."

Mat obeyed instantly. Charlotte hesitated a second, then climbed into the saddle. As soon as she was atop the mare, she kicked it into motion and rode for the front of the hotel.

"Come here, you bitch!" shouted McGrath. He fired a shot at her but missed. "Don't you think about doing the same thing, nigger, or I won't miss you."

"Yes, sir," said Mat.

"Now let's ride."

"Yes, sir."

Mat led him toward the Green River and the ferry landing only a half mile away down the bluff trail.

Sheriff Morris had followed Creed to the door and had watched McGrath make his getaway. "He's heading toward the ferry," he said.

"What ferry?" asked Creed.

"It's about a half mile down the trail to the river," explained the sheriff. "It's not an easy trail."

Creed burst through the doorway and broke into a run for the stable. He quickly found Nimbus, put a bridle on the Appaloosa, then leaped onto the stallion's bare back.

Morris ran up to Creed, handed him a Henry repeater, and said, "Here, you might need this."

Creed took the weapon, said, "Thanks," then rode off after McGrath.

McGrath and Mat were starting down the first switchback to the ferry when Creed caught sight of them. He pulled up and took aim at the gambler. One squeeze of the trigger and McGrath toppled from the saddle. He was only wounded, hit in the meaty part of the upper arm.

"Son of a bitch!" swore McGrath as he scrambled to his feet holding his injured shoulder. He picked up his gun and jumped into some nearby bushes.

Creed dismounted and started after McGrath on foot.

McGrath had only two shots left in his pistol. He knew his only chance was to get across the river or to hide and bushwhack Creed when he got close enough. Looking down the trail toward the ferry, he felt the odds were against his reaching the landing ahead of a bullet from Creed's rifle. And should he get there safely, he wondered if he would survive the crossing, considering Creed had a rifle and was probably a fair shot. No, his best chance was to hide and bushwhack the Texan. The only question remaining was where he should hide. He scanned the area and saw the perfect place. Mammoth Cave.

50

Creed lost track of McGrath when the gambler jumped into the bushes. But Mat didn't.

Mat had come back up the trail to meet Creed. "I saw him head off for the cave," said the guide.

"The cave?" queried Creed.

"Yes, sir," said Mat. "He's gone into Mammoth Cave."

"Show me where the cave entrance is," said Creed.

As Creed followed Mat past the ruins of the saltpeter furnaces and the mounds of ash leftover from the days when the cave was mined for its mineral wealth, Sheriff Morris and several deputies and constables came riding and running up to join them.

"We heard shooting," said Morris. "Did you get him?"

"I winged him," said Creed. "He's afoot, and this man says he saw him heading into Mammoth Cave. I'm going in after him."

"We'll go with you," said Morris.

"I'd rather go alone," said Creed.

"I know you would," said Morris, "but this is my county and I'm the law here. We're going with you. Mat, get us some torches. We'll need enough for half the men."

"You won't be needing any torches, Mr. Morris," said Mat. "I left the place lit up from this morning's tour because I was going to take another tour down after the races."

"Good," said Morris. "Let's go."

"Sheriff, I'm asking you to let me go after him alone," said Creed. "I owe the bastard."

"Sorry, Creed, I can't do that," said Morris.

That wasn't what Creed wanted to hear. He drew his Colt's, cocked it, and took deliberate aim at Morris. The cold look of death was in his eyes. "I'm from Texas, Sheriff, and I can shoot you dead in the wink of an eye. Now I'll ask you just one more time to let me go after him alone."

Morris frowned. He felt positive that Creed wouldn't shoot him, but he didn't feel like taking any chances that he would. "All right," he said. "If you feel that strongly about it, go ahead and go after him alone. But first let me deputize you to make it all legal. We don't need to have any unnecessary trials around here if we can avoid them. Raise your right hand and take the oath."

Morris deputized Creed, then told his other deputies and the constables to sit tight until Creed had had a fair chance to get McGrath on his own.

Creed started for the cave entrance with Mat beside him. "I told you that I was going alone," said Creed.

"Yes, sir, I know," said Mat with a great smile, "but no one goes down in the cave without a guide. Mr. Creed, there's a thousand places in there that he could be hiding to bushwhack you. I know them all. Maybe I could go along and point them out to you."

"Not this time, Mat," said Creed.

"But, sir, you haven't been in the cave before," said Mat, "and that bad man you're after was on the tour the other day."

"He was?"

"Yes, sir."

"Even so, I have to go alone, Mat."

"If you say so, sir."

"I say so."

They parted company, and Creed stepped softly toward the entrance alone. A rush of cool air struck him as he entered the great cavern. He looked down and saw a trail of blood leading into the mouth of the cave. Descending ever so slowly some thirty feet down rather rude steps of stone, he came to the arch that began this netherworld.

Thinking to give McGrath a sporting chance to face him man-to-man, Creed called out, "McGrath, I know you're in the cave, and I'm coming to kill you. You can come out and meet me like a man, or I can hunt you down like the dirty bugger that you are. Which is it to be?"

When no reply came, Creed moved ahead. He passed the wooden pipes that had once conducted the water that fell from the ceiling of the cave, to the old saltpeter hoppers. With increasing stealth, he moved past the grave of the legendary giant whose skeletal remains had been unearthed by early niter diggers far within the cave, raising their fears and superstitions, which were only quieted when the owner of the cave had the giant buried again in this spot. Proceeding down the passageway, he came to a stone wall with a wooden door in it. The door was closed, and this made Creed think that McGrath could be just a few feet on the other side of it, waiting for him. With caution, he moved to the door, stood to one side of it, then lifted the latch slowly. In the next breath, he pushed the door wide open and waited to the side. When nothing happened, he decided to peek around the corner. Nothing there except the trail of blood leading down a long, narrow tunnel.

The passage led Creed to the great Rotunda of the Main Cave with its flat roof sixty feet above the irregular floor. Before the coming of Europeans, this cavern had been a cemetery for a people vanished long ago. More ruins of the saltpeter works were still in place here. Creed scanned the old plank vats and the small hills of nitrous earth, looking for McGrath but not seeing him. He did notice that the cave had two avenues leading from it, and McGrath's blood trail pointed to the left one. Hugging the wall and staying low, Creed moved across the Rotunda.

Once again in the passage of the Main Cave, Creed thought he heard something behind him. He crouched down and looked back to see Mat at the mouth of the tunnel leading back to the entrance. Damn! he thought. Can't that fellow take no for an answer? He decided to wait for the guide to catch up to him.

"I thought I told you to stay back," said Creed.

"Yes, sir, I know you did," said Mat, "but I forgot to tell you a few things about this cave."

"Such as?"

"Such as this room you just went through. I should have told you about the saltpeter works."

"But you didn't, and I made it through there."

"Yes, sir, I know," said Mat, "but you don't know about the Church up ahead."

"The Church?"

"Yes, sir. It's a room with a formation that looks like a pulpit in a church. A man with a gun could sit up there and shoot anybody walking below him."

Creed had to admit that he was at a real disadvantage here and that Mat would be handy to have around—at least, until he found McGrath. "All right," he said, "you can come along, but stay back a ways. I don't want your death on my conscience."

Mat smiled and said, "Yes, sir, Mr. Creed."

They moved down the passage until they came to the Kentucky Cliffs, a wall that resembled the cliffs along the Kentucky River. Mat tapped Creed on the shoulder and whispered, "The entrance to the Church is only twenty feet further on the left, Mr. Creed. If that man's blood says he went that way, go slow and look up as soon as you enter the room. The organ loft is right behind the pulpit. He could hide behind the pulpit or on it."

"Thanks, Mat," said Creed. "You stay back here until I find out whether he's in there or not."

"Yes, sir."

Creed moved ahead slower than before. His instincts said McGrath was near. He slipped into the short hall that led into the Church. He stopped at the entrance and scanned the room. Torches on either side of the hall cast eerie shadows everywhere in the Church. McGrath's blood was on the ground, little spots of it, and it pointed toward the pulpit. Looking up, Creed saw McGrath peering over the edge of the stone formation. He stepped back against the wall for protection.

The gambler saw Creed at the same time. He aimed his pistol at the Texan and fired. The bullet crashed into the rock beside Creed's head, exploding tiny chips of limestone into his face.

"Damn!" swore Creed, grabbing his left cheek. Blood seeped between his fingers. Out of anger, he stuck his gun into the Church and fired a shot at the top of the pulpit. The ball missed its intended victim.

McGrath caught a glimpse of Creed in the shadow and fired his last round, hitting nothing but the dirt floor of the cavern. He hadn't thought to bring along an extra cylinder for his .32, but he was hardly defenseless. All he needed to do was lure Creed close enough to him.

Creed backed into the passageway again. He took a handkerchief from an inside coat pocket and put it over the cuts in his face to stop the bleeding. The limestone slivers sticking in his cheek burned like hot coals. He thought of removing them then and there, but he knew that they could wait. Right now, he had to deal with McGrath.

The gambler had fired at him twice since entering the cave, and he had fired at him three times outside. That made five shots. Hadn't George Devol and Canada Bill Jones told him that McGrath carried a Smith & Wesson .32 pocket pistol? Yes, they had! And that meant the gun was empty. Empty, of course, unless McGrath carried an extra cylinder with him. That wasn't likely, but one could never know unless—

There was only one way to find out if McGrath was out of ammunition. Creed moved back toward the entrance to the Church. He made part of himself visible to McGrath, but the villain failed to fire. The son of a bitch is defenseless, thought Creed.

"I'm coming to get you, McGrath," said Creed. He stepped into the open. Nothing from the pulpit. He moved to one side to go around to the rear and come up behind McGrath. "I've got four shots left, McGrath, and they're all for you."

"I'm shot up bad, Creed," whined McGrath from atop the pulpit. "I need a doctor. I'm hurt bad."

"Don't worry about that, McGrath. In a minute, all you'll need is an undertaker."

"Don't kill me, Creed. I didn't mean for the horse to get hurt. I just wanted to scare him into pulling up and losing the race. That's all, I swear."

"I warned you, McGrath, that if you crossed me or Charlotte, I would kill you. I wasn't saying that just to hear myself talk. That horse has to die now because of you, and that's going to break Scott's heart. You had no right to hurt that boy like that, McGrath. Scott Houchin is my friend, and I can't let you get away with this, McGrath. You're a dirty bugger, and you deserve to die."

Creed began climbing the steps that led to the organ loft behind the pulpit. He had to mind his way and was forced to look away from McGrath's perch for a second. It was in that instant that the gambler raised up and threw his ivory-handled dirk at the Texan. Creed saw the movement in time to duck, but he wasn't able to avoid the blade completely as it penetrated his coat sleeve and stuck in the deltoid muscle of his left arm. Forgetting about McGrath for a moment, he grabbed the wounded limb with his gun hand without dropping the Colt's, bumped the knife's handle, and caused himself even more pain.

McGrath leaped from the pulpit, landing on Creed's good shoulder and slamming him against the wall. The two of them crumpled to the ground as Creed fired his revolver accidentally.

The ball ricocheted off the wall into the ceiling. McGrath tried to get his knife, but Creed pushed the much lighter man off him before he could touch the dirk. The Texan tried to get the villain in his sights, but McGrath rolled to the bottom of the steps, then into the passageway to the Main Cave. Creed took a moment to pull the knife from his arm. Just as he did, Mat came into the Church.

"Mr. Creed, are you all right?" asked the guide. Then he saw the knife in Creed's hand. "No, you're not, are you?"

Creed tossed the dirk down at Mat's feet and said, "You might need that if I don't catch up with that bastard." He stood up and asked, "Did you see which way he went?"

"He's going deeper in the cave," said Mat. When Creed started toward the exit, the guide became concerned and said, "Mr. Creed, don't you think you should get to a doctor now and let the sheriff and his men catch this bad man?"

"No, I have to do this myself," said Creed, and he went after McGrath again.

Leaving the Church, Creed ascended a large embankment of lixiviated earth thrown out by the miners more than fifty years ago, and here he saw how the print of wagon wheels and the tracks of oxen were still defined in the soil as if they had been made only yesterday. He continued on for a short distance and came upon the Second Hoppers, another set of ruins of the niter mining operations from the first two decades of the century. From the fresh trail of blood that McGrath was leaving, it was apparent that the gambler hadn't stopped to observe this historical place.

In looking to the left and some thirty feet above the old saltpeter works, Creed saw the mouth of a large cave, and from it, a balcony ran to another cave opposite it. This was Gothic Avenue. A set of steps led up to the opening on the right, but McGrath's blood continued to show on the Main Cave's floor, running straight ahead toward the Ballroom. From the distance between the red drops, Creed surmised that McGrath was running as fast as he could, and since McGrath had some knowledge of the cave, the Texan also figured that the wounded man knew exactly where he wanted to go.

McGrath's first destination was Wandering Willie's Spring, a beautifully fluted niche in the wall, caused by the continual attrition of water trickling down into a basin below. The gambler had stopped here to get a drink before moving on through the Standing Rocks to the Giant's Coffin, a huge rock that resembled a sarcophagus for a gargantuan being. This was a good hiding spot from which McGrath could leap out and attack Creed, but this wasn't the place that he had chosen to end this life and death struggle between them.

The Texan tracked McGrath around the Giant's Coffin to a narrow passage that led him to a circular room known as the Wooden Bowl, the vestibule to the Deserted Chambers, in which were the pits. Creed heard the thump of a body landing hard on the ground followed by the cry of a wounded animal. This had to be McGrath, he thought. Thinking the gambler wasn't too far ahead of him, Creed hurried to the Steps of Time, an almost perpendicular set of steps. He looked down and caught a glimpse of McGrath limping toward the Sidesaddle Pit. Quickly, he descended the dangerous stairs, then broke into a trot in order to catch up with the villain. Past the pit, the route divided. Creed stopped to look for a sign.

Sweat blurred his vision. He was breathing hard and his arm and cheek throbbed with pain. His own blood fell on the ground to mingle with McGrath's. Which way did the son of a bitch go? he asked himself. Before finding an answer in the dust, he heard Grandfather Hawk McConnell's voice telling him "Evil always takes the left path." Creed chose the trail to the left, only to find that it forked, and again he opted to veer to the left. He made the right choice.

McGrath was spent. His breath was gone; he could barely stand as he held on to the side rail of a bridge over an abyss that a small sign identified as the Bottomless Pit.

Creed couldn't help but appreciate the irony of the moment, and he thought to share it with McGrath. "You see that sign, McGrath?" he asked as he pointed with his left hand.

McGrath read the marker, then looked at Creed, panting. He said nothing.

"You're the Devil, McGrath," said Creed, "and I'm sending you back where you belong." He raised his Colt's to shoulder height, cocked the hammer, took careful aim, and fired.

The ball shattered McGrath's sternum, and the force of the slug striking him drove the gambler backward against the rail, breaking it. He dropped silently to his death.

51

It was dark when Mat led Creed out of Mammoth Cave. Sheriff Morris and his men were still waiting for them at the entrance.

"Did you get him, Creed?" asked Morris, rushing up to the Texan. Then, seeing the blood on Creed's coat, he said, "You're hurt. What happened?"

Creed said nothing, but Mat replied, "That bad man is lying at the bottom of the Bottomless Pit now. Mr. Creed shot him dead, and he fell off the bridge into the pit. I saw it all happen."

The lawmen gathered around Creed and Mat to hear the tale of Creed's pursuit of McGrath, and the guide was quite willing to oblige them with all the details.

Creed ignored pleas from Morris to tell the story. He forced his way through the deputies and constables to look for his horse as other folks from the hotel came to listen to Mat. He found Nimbus tied to a nearby tree and led him back to the stable. His face and shoulder had stopped bleeding, but they hurt, especially the knife wound. He hoped that Dr. Gatewood was still around to tend his injuries. He walked slowly to the hotel.

In the lobby, Creed was met by Proctor and several dozen others who had the same question: Did he get McGrath? He refused to answer any of them. Instead, he asked Proctor, "Where's Mlle. Beaujeu?"

"She's in my office," said Proctor.

"Good," said Creed. "Now go find Dr. Gatewood and tell him I am in need of his services."

Proctor took one look in Creed's eyes, saw the cold of death in them, then said, "Right away, Mr. Creed."

Creed opened the door to Proctor's office but didn't walk in just yet. He stood in the doorway and watched Charlotte as she sat at Proctor's desk counting money with the all the avarice

260

of a miserly banker. Finally, she realized that he was standing there looking at her.

"Slate!" she said, startled by his presence. Then, regaining her composure, she said, "Sugar, you're all right. I was so worried about you." Then she noticed his shoulder. "Oh, no, you're hurt." She rose to come to him.

"Don't bother, Charlotte," said Creed, entering the room and closing the door behind him. "Just stay there and keep counting your money. You earned it."

"But you're hurt, Slate," she protested. "You need a doctor. Let me get one for you."

"I've already sent for one. You just go on and count your money. That's all you really care about anyway."

"That's not true, Sugar. I love you, Slate."

"No, you don't. You love that money, and that's all you'll ever love. Well, you got your money. Are you happy now?"

"Slate, I don't like you like this," said Charlotte as she turned away from Creed.

"Stop it, Charlotte!" screamed the Texan.

Charlotte spun around. Her face was filled with fear.

"What was it McGrath called you, Charlotte? A bitch? A thieving, conniving, double-crossing, lying bitch is more like it." He moved closer to her, and she backed up toward the corner. "You cooked up this scheme, just like McGrath said you did. You used me and McGrath and Scott and his family and his horse. And all of us got hurt, Charlotte. Everybody except you. You're the only one who came out of this without a scratch. And on top of that, you made all that money. How much is there, Charlotte? Twenty thousand? Twenty-five?" When she didn't answer immediately, he shouted, "How much?"

"Twenty-seven thousand," she said meekly.

"Twenty-seven thousand dollars," repeated Creed slowly. "And how much of that was supposed to be McGrath's cut?"

"A tenth."

"A tenth. Twenty-seven hundred dollars. And how much were you planning to give me and the Houchins?"

"I was going to give you a thousand, and I was going to offer Mr. Houchin a thousand for Pride."

"And if he refused to sell, then what?"

"I would have given him a few hundred or so."

Creed slammed his hand down on the desk. "You're lying again, aren't you?" he shouted.

Charlotte was now too frightened to speak. She cowered in the corner.

"You dirty bitch!" snarled Creed. "McGrath said you planned this whole thing. Is that true?"

"Of course not, Slate."

"You're lying, Charlotte!" screamed Creed. "You planned to have Pride lose the race, didn't you? Pride had to lose so you could win all those bets that you knew would be made on him. Isn't that true, Charlotte?"

Very meekly, she said, "Yes."

Creed heaved an exasperated sigh, shook his head, and stared at Charlotte for a moment before saying, "You're worse than McGrath. He's dead, and you're not. But you should be." He drew his Colt's.

Charlotte's eyes bugged when she saw the revolver in his hand. "Don't kill me, Slate!" she shrieked. "Don't kill me, please, Slate! Please don't kill me!"

Creed raised the pistol to shoulder height and took aim at her eyes. He cocked the hammer and said, "Good-bye, Charlotte."

Charlotte screamed, "*No!*" and dropped to the floor in terror.

Creed fired the gun, intentionally at the spot where Charlotte's head had been a second before. As she continued to scream in horror, he cocked the hammer again and fired it into the wall a second time. Every chamber was now spent. He knew it, but he still wasn't satisfied. He put the muzzle to Charlotte's temple. She screamed louder. He cocked the hammer a third time. She screamed all the more. He pulled the trigger. CLICK! She let out one final scream.

Creed straightened up, put his Colt's back in his waistband, and waited for Charlotte's screaming to quiet down to a whimper before saying, "You're dead, Charlotte." He paused before adding, "You're dead, and you don't even know it."

With Charlotte still crouching in the corner sobbing, Creed counted out a thousand dollars for himself and twenty-seven hundred for the Houchins. "I'm sure McGrath would have wanted the Houchins to have his share, Charlotte." He pocketed the money and left without another word.

EPILOGUE

The next afternoon Creed was riding the Louisville & Nashville Railroad, heading south to Nashville. His left arm was in a sling, which made finding a comfortable sitting position difficult at best. He squirmed in his seat, making the letter from Texada that he had received that morning crinkle in his coat pocket. The sound made him think of her, and he wondered what he would write back to her once he reached the Tennessee capital.

Of course, Creed would tell her that he had given the money that he had taken from Charlotte Beaujeu's gambling winnings to the Houchins. It didn't make up for the loss of Pride, but it was something, better than nothing. Edie had thanked him on behalf of Davis, who was "feeling real poorly since he found out about Pride having a broke leg."

Then he would tell Texada that Scott had his right shoulder all trussed up and his arm in a sling when he last saw him. Young Houchin had returned the Colt's that Creed had given to Davis, thanking the Texan for the use of it. "Pride was mine," said Scott. "It was my job to end Pride's pain, not Pa's."

An image of Scott, tears flowing down his cheeks, shooting his horse, filled Creed's mind. It made him sad on the one hand but gratified on the other as he imagined Scott refusing to let his father do the loathsome chore for him. He was glad that he knew this proud, young Kentuckian.

Returning his thoughts to Texada, Creed felt that he would go on about how Dr. Gatewood had patched up his arm and how the physician had told him that he would be all right in a week or two. He would tell Texada not to worry about him, that he would be just fine, and that he was going to Nashville to look for Blackburn and the others now. She could write to him there.

He twisted in his seat again and felt the corner of Texada's letter dig into his chest. Heaving a sigh, he took it out and read it again.

My dearest darling Clete,

I hope this letter finds you in good health and good spirits. I miss you, my darling, and I love you always.

Granny made it through Christmas and the New Year, but she died on the second instant. I know we expected it to happen at any time, but I still cried like a baby. She was the only real parent that I ever knew, Clete. I will miss her terribly. Nearly everybody in LaVaca County came to her funeral. Malinda and Colonel Markham were there, too. She sends her love.

Harlan was the Detchen that you killed in Indianola. Everybody around here was sad to hear that Kent and Clark Reeves had been murdered, but we were just as glad to hear that you killed Harlan in return. Jim Kindred and Farley Detchen brought his body back here to Hallettsville for burial. They testified before a grand jury in Indianola that you shot Harlan in cold blood, and now you are wanted for murder down there. Of course, no charge was made against Kindred or Farley for murdering Kent and Clark because Kindred and Farley claimed that the brothers were resisting arrest and drew down on them first.

Kindred went to Markham and told him that you had gone to New Orleans on a boat, so Markham telegraphed the Army in New Orleans to arrest you when you landed there. I am glad you got away from them there. When Markham heard that you had escaped again, he threw a fit and sent Kindred to New Orleans to hunt for you. Malinda tells me that Markham got a letter from Kindred today saying that he was heading up the Mississippi to look for you because he had heard about a Texan who was running a horse racing meet up in Kentucky.

Please be on the lookout for Kindred, Clete. He is a Federal marshal now, and he can go anywhere to arrest you.

I hope you finish your business in Kentucky real soon, if you have not already, and that you will continue to pursue Blackburn and the others in Tennessee and that you find them and make them confess the truth about their crime so you can clear your name.

Jake says all the boys wish you were here because they are not sure what they should do with Double Star Ranch. It belongs to Jess Tate's brother Matt, if he is still alive. Of course, you know that already. Should they keep working it? Or should they leave it to the state to handle? They want to know.

Please write soon, my darling. I miss you and love you, and I wish you were here with me now. You are all I have now. I love you, my darling. May the good Lord keep you safe until the day when we can be together again.

Your ever loving,
Texada

Creed refolded the letter carefully and replaced it in his coat pocket. He looked wistfully out the window and saw the outskirts of Nashville ahead. He heaved a sigh and thought, Blackburn and the others: I've got to find them so I can go home once and for all.